Selections from

THE DECAMERON

Selections from

THE DECAMERON

Giovanni Boccaccio

WORDSWORTH CLASSICS

This edition published 1996 by
Wordsworth Editions Limited
Cumberland House, Crib Street
Ware, Hertfordshire SG12 9ET

ISBN 1 85326 618 3

Typeset by Antony Gray
Printed and bound in Great Britain by
Mackays of Chatham, Chatham, Kent

PUBLISHER'S NOTE

The full text of *The Decameron* consists of one hundred stories, told on ten successive days in the garden of a villa some way from Florence, where a number of young people have taken refuge from the Plague.

In the reckless atmosphere which arises when death is near and life uncertain, the company tell one another tales of every kind, but all of them underline the fact that love is the guiding force of the world in whatever form it takes.

Naturally, whenever young people talk about love, sex plays a major part in their stories. This selection includes those bawdy and scabrous tales that amused the company, and although they may seem tame by some of today's standards, *The Decameron* was considered to be an obscene book for centuries. Manuscripts and printed parts were burnt in Florence by Savonarola on his 'bonfire of the vanities' in 1497, it was placed on the *Index Librorum Prohibitorum* by Pope Paul IV in 1559, and as late as 1953 it was on the list of the British magazine *Newsagent Bookseller Stationer* of titles named for destruction, and on the blacklist of the National Organization of Decent Literature in the United States.

So fain I am of my own loveliness,
  I hope, nor think not e'er
The weight to feel of other amorousness.

When in the mirror I my face behold,
  That see I there which doth my mind content,
  Nor any present hap or memory old
  May me deprive of such sweet ravishment.
  Where else, then, should I find such blandishment
    Of sight and sense that e'er
  My heart should know another amorousness?

Nor need I fear lest the fair thing retreat,
  When fain I am my solace to renew;
  Rather, I know, 'twill me advance to meet,
  To pleasure me, and show so sweet a view
  That speech or thought of none its semblance true
    Paint or conceive may e'er,
  Unless he burn with ev'n such amorousness.

Thereon as more intent I gaze, the fire
  Waxeth within me hourly more and more,
  Myself I yield thereto, myself entire,
  And foretaste have of what it hath in store,
  And hope of greater joyance than before,
    Nay, such as ne'er
  None knew; for ne'er was felt such amorousness.

1

The fourth story of the first day, in which a monk lapses into a sin meriting the most severe punishment, justly censures the same fault in his abbot, and thus evades the penalty.

The silence which followed the conclusion of Filomena's tale [not included in this edition which is only a selection of the tales] was broken by Dioneo, who sat next her, and without waiting for the queen's word, for he knew that by the rule laid down at the commencement it was now his turn to speak, began on this wise: Loving ladies, if I have well understood the intention of you all, we are here to afford entertainment to one another by story-telling; wherefore, provided only nought is done that is repugnant to this end, I deem it lawful for each (and so said our queen a little while ago) to tell whatever story seems to him most likely to be amusing. Seeing, then, that we have heard how Abraham saved his soul by the good counsel of Jehannot de Chevigny, and Melchisedech by his own good sense safe-guarded his wealth against the stratagems of Saladin, I hope to escape your censure in narrating a brief story of a monk, who by his address delivered his body from imminent peril of most severe chastisement –

In the not very remote district of Lunigiana there flourished formerly a community of monks more numerous and holy than is there to be found today, among whom was a young brother whose vigour and lustihood neither the fasts nor the vigils availed to subdue. One afternoon, while the rest of the confraternity slept, our young monk took a stroll around the church, which lay in a very sequestered spot, and chanced to espy a young and very beautiful girl, a daughter, perhaps, of one of the husbandmen of those parts, going through the fields and gathering herbs as she went. No sooner had he seen her than he was sharply assailed by carnal concupiscence, insomuch that he made up to and accosted her; and (she harkening) little by little they came to an understanding, and unobserved by any entered his cell together. Now it so chanced that, while they fooled it within somewhat recklessly, he being overwrought with passion, the abbot awoke and passing slowly by the young monk's cell, heard the noise which they made within, and the better to distinguish the voices, came softly up to the door of the cell, and listening discovered that beyond all doubt there was a woman within. His first thought was to force the door open; but, changing his mind, he returned to his chamber and waited until the monk should come out.

Delightsome beyond measure though the monk found his intercourse with the girl, yet was he not altogether without anxiety. He had heard, as he thought, the sound of footsteps in the dormitory, and having applied his eye to a convenient aperture had had a good view of the abbot as he stood by the door listening. He was thus fully aware that the abbot might have detected the presence of a woman in the cell. Whereat he was exceedingly distressed, knowing that he had a severe punishment to expect; but he concealed his vexation from the girl while he busily cast about in his mind for some way of escape from his embarrassment. He thus hit on a novel stratagem which was exactly suited to his purpose. With the air of one who had had enough of the girl's company he said to her – 'I shall now leave you in order that I may arrange for your departure hence unobserved. Stay here quietly until I return.' So out he went, locking the door of the cell and withdrawing the key, which he carried straight to the abbot's chamber and handed to him, as was the custom when a monk was going out, saying with a composed air – 'Sir, I was not able this morning to bring in all the faggots which I had made ready, so with your leave I will go to the wood and bring them in.' The abbot, desiring to have better cognisance of the monk's offence, and not dreaming that the monk knew that he had been detected, was pleased with the turn matters had taken, and received the key gladly, at the same time giving the monk the desired leave. So the monk withdrew, and the abbot began to consider what course it were best for him to take, whether to assemble the brotherhood and open the door in their presence, that, being witnesses of the delinquency, they might have no cause to murmur against him when he proceeded to punish the delinquent, or whether it were not better first to learn from the girl's own lips how it had come about. And reflecting that she might be the wife or daughter of some man who would take it ill that she should be shamed by being exposed to the gaze of all the monks, he determined first of all to find out who she was, and then to make up his mind. So he went softly to the cell, opened the door, and, having entered, closed it behind him. The girl, seeing that her visitor was none other than the abbot, quite lost her presence of mind, and quaking with shame began to weep. Master abbot surveyed her from head to foot, and seeing that she was fresh and comely, fell a prey, old though he was, to fleshly cravings no less poignant and sudden than those which the young monk had experienced, and began thus to commune with himself – 'Alas! why take I not my pleasure when I may, seeing that I never need lack for occasions of trouble and vexation of spirit? Here is a fair wench, and no one in the world to know. If I can bring her to pleasure me, I know not why I should not do so. Who will know? No one will ever know; and sin that is hidden is half-forgiven; this chance may never come again; so, methinks, it were the part of wisdom to take the boon which God bestows.' So musing, with an altogether different purpose from that with which he had come, he drew near the girl, and softly bade her to be comforted, and besought her not to weep; and so little by little he came at last to show her what he would be at. The girl, being made neither of iron nor of adamant, was readily induced to gratify the abbot, who after bestowing upon her many an embrace and kiss, got upon the monk's bed, where, being sensible, perhaps, of the disparity between his reverend portliness and her tender youth, and fearing to injure her by his excessive weight, he refrained from lying upon her, but laid her upon him, and in that manner disported himself with her for a long time. The monk, who had only pretended to go to the wood, and had concealed himself in the dormitory, no sooner saw the abbot enter his cell than he was overjoyed to think that his plan would succeed; and when he saw that he had locked the door, he was well assured thereof. So he stole out of his hiding-place, and set his eye to an aperture through which he saw and heard all that the abbot did and said. At length the abbot, having had enough of dalliance with the girl, locked her in the cell and returned to his chamber. Catching sight of the monk soon afterwards, and supposing him to have returned from the wood, he determined to give him a sharp reprimand and have him imprisoned, that he might thus secure the prey for himself alone. He therefore caused him to be summoned, chid him very severely and with a stern countenance, and ordered him to be put in prison. The monk replied trippingly – 'Sir, I have not been so long in the order of St Benedict as to have every particular of the rule by heart; nor did you teach me before today in what posture it behoves the monk to have intercourse with women, but limited your instruction to such matters as fasts and vigils. As, however, you have now given me my lesson, I promise you, if you also pardon my offence, that I will never repeat it, but will always follow the example which you have set me.'

The abbot, who was a shrewd man, saw at once that the monk was not only more knowing than he, but had actually seen what he had done; nor, conscience-stricken himself, could he for shame mete out to the monk a measure which he himself merited. So pardon given, with an injunction to bury what had been seen in silence, they decently conveyed the young girl out of the monastery, whither, it is to be believed, they now and again caused her to return.

❧ 2 ❧

The fifth story of the first day, in which the Marchioness of Monferrato by a banquet of hens seasoned with wit checks the mad passion of the King of France.

The story told by Dioneo evoked at first some qualms of shame in the minds of the ladies, as was apparent by the modest blush that tinged their faces: then exchanging glances, and scarce able to refrain their mirth, they listened to it with half-suppressed smiles. On its conclusion they bestowed upon Dioneo a few words of gentle reprehension with intent to admonish him that such stories were not to be told among ladies. The queen then turned to Fiammetta, who was seated on the grass at her side, and bade her follow suit; and Fiammetta with a gay and gracious mien thus began: ❧ The line upon which our story-telling proceeds, to wit, to show the virtue that resides in apt and ready repartees, pleases me well; and as in affairs of love men and women are in diverse case, for to aspire to the love of a woman of higher lineage than his own is wisdom in man, whereas a woman's good sense is then most conspicuous when she knows how to preserve herself from becoming enamoured of a man her superior in rank, I am minded, fair my ladies, to show you by the story which I am now to tell, how by deed and word a gentlewoman both defended herself against attack, and weaned her suitor from his love –

The Marquis of Monferrato, a paladin of distinguished prowess, was gone overseas as standard-bearer of the Church in a general array of the Christian forces. Whose merits being canvassed at the court of Philippe le Borgne, on the eve of his departure from France on the same service, a knight observed that there was not under the stars a couple comparable to the Marquis and his lady; in that, while the Marquis was a paragon of the knightly virtues, his lady for beauty and honour was without a peer among all the other ladies of the world. These words made so deep an impression on the mind of the King of France that, though he had never seen the lady, he fell ardently in love with her, and, being to join the armada, resolved that his port of embarkation should be no other than Genoa, in order that, travelling thither by land, he might find a decent pretext for visiting the Marchioness, with whom in the absence of the Marquis he trusted to have the success which he desired; nor did he fail to put his design in execution. Having sent his main army on before, he took the road himself with a small company of gentlemen, and, as they approached the territory of the Marquis, he despatched a courier to the Marchioness, a day in advance, to let her know that he expected to breakfast with her the next morning. The lady, who knew her part and played it well, replied graciously that he would be indeed welcome, and that his presence would be the greatest of all favours. She then began to commune with herself what this might import, that so great a king should come to visit her in her husband's absence, nor was she so deluded as not to surmise that it was the fame of her beauty that drew him thither. Nevertheless she made ready to do him honour in a manner befitting her high degree, summoning to her presence such of the retainers as remained in the castle, and giving all needful directions with their advice, except that the order of the banquet and the choice of the dishes she reserved entirely to herself. Then, having caused all the hens that could be found in the countryside to be brought with all speed into the castle, she bade her cooks furnish forth the royal table with divers dishes made exclusively of such fare. The King arrived on the appointed day, and was received by the lady with great and ceremonious cheer. Fair and noble and gracious seemed she in the eyes of the King beyond all that he had conceived from the knight's words, so that he was lost in admiration and inwardly extolled her to the skies, his passion being the more inflamed in proportion as he found the lady surpass the idea which he had formed of her. A suite of rooms furnished with all the appointments befitting the reception of so great a king was placed at his disposal, and after a little rest, breakfast-time being come, he and the Marchioness took their places at the same table, while his suite were honourably entertained at other boards according to their several qualities. Many courses were served with no lack of excellent and rare wines, whereby the King was mightily pleased, as also by the extraordinary beauty of the Marchioness, on whom his eye from time to time rested. However, as course followed course, the King observed with some surprise, that, though the dishes were diverse, yet they were all but variations of one and the same fare, to wit, the pullet. Besides which he knew that the domain was one which could not but afford plenty of divers sorts of game, and by forewarning the lady of his approach, he had allowed time for hunting; yet, for all his surprise, he would not broach the question more directly with her than by a reference to her hens; so, turning to her with a smile, he said – 'Madam, do hens grow in this country without so much as a single cock?' The Marchioness, who perfectly apprehended the drift of the question, saw in it an opportunity, sent her by God, of evincing her virtuous resolution; so casting a haughty glance upon the King she answered thus – 'Sire, no; but the women, though they may differ somewhat from others in dress and rank, are yet of the same nature here as elsewhere.' The significance of the banquet of pullets was made manifest to the King by these words, as also the virtue which they veiled. He perceived that on a lady of such a temper words would be wasted, and that force was out of the question. Wherefore, yielding to the dictates of prudence and honour, he was now as prompt to quench, as he had been inconsiderate in conceiving, his unfortunate passion for the lady; and fearing her answers, he refrained from further jesting with her, and dismissing his hopes devoted himself to his breakfast, which done, he disarmed suspicion of the dishonourable purpose of his visit by an early departure, and thanking her for the honour she had conferred upon him, and commending her to God, took the road to Genoa.

3

The second story of the second day, in which Rinaldo d'Asti is robbed, arrives at Castel Guglielmo, and is entertained by a widow lady; his property is restored to him, and he returns home safe and sound.

The ladies and the young men, especially Filostrato, laughed inordinately at the foregoing narrative. Then Filostrato received the queen's command to take his turn and promptly thus began: Fair ladies, 'tis on my mind to tell you a story in which are mingled things sacred and passages of adverse fortune and love, which to hear will perchance be not unprofitable, more especially to travellers in love's treacherous lands; of whom if any fail to say St Julian's paternoster, it often happens that, though he may have a good bed, he is ill lodged –

Know, then, that in the time of the Marquis Azzo da Ferrara, a merchant, Rinaldo d'Asti by name, having disposed of certain affairs which had brought him to Bologna, set his face homeward, and having left Ferrara behind him was on his way to Verona, when he fell in with some men that looked like merchants, but were in truth robbers and men of evil life and condition, whose company he imprudently joined, riding and conversing with them. They, perceiving that he was a merchant, and judging that he must have money about him, plotted to rob him on the first opportunity; and to obviate suspicion they played the part of worthy and reputable men, their discourse of nought but what was seemly and honourable and honest, their demeanour at once as respectful and as cordial as they could make it; so that he deemed himself very lucky to have met with them, being otherwise alone save for a single mounted servant. Journeying thus they conversed, after the desultory manner of travellers, of divers matters until at last they fell to talking of the prayers which men address to God, and one of the robbers – there were three of them – said to Rinaldo – 'And you, gentle sir, what is your wonted prayer when you are on your travels?' Rinaldo answered – 'Why, to tell the truth, I am a man unskilled, unlearned in such matters, and few prayers have I at my command, being one that lives in the good old way and lets two soldi count for twenty-four deniers; nevertheless it has always been my custom in journeying to say of a morning, as I leave the inn, a paternoster and an avemaria for the souls of the father and mother of St Julian, after which I pray God and St Julian to provide me with a good inn for the night. And many a time in the course of my life have I met with great perils by the way, and evading them all have found comfortable quarters for the night: whereby my faith is assured, that St Julian, in whose honour I say my paternoster, has gotten me this favour of God; nor should I look for a prosperous journey and a safe arrival at night, if I had not said it in the morning.' Then said his interrogator – 'And did you say it this morning?' Whereto Rinaldo answered, 'Troth, did I,' which caused the other, who by this time knew what course matters would take, to say to himself – ' 'Twill prove to have been said in the nick of time; for if we do not miscarry, I take it thou wilt have but a sorry lodging.' Then turning to Rinaldo he said: – 'I also have travelled much, and never a prayer have I said, though I have heard them much commended by many; nor has it ever been my lot to find other than good quarters for the night; it may be that this very evening you will be able to determine which of us has the better lodging, you that have said the paternoster, or I that have not said it. True, however, it is that in its stead I am accustomed to say the "Dirupisti," or the "Intemerata," or the "De profundis," which, if what my grandmother used to say is to be believed, are of the greatest efficacy.' So, talking of divers matters, and ever on the look-out for time and place suited to their evil purpose, they continued their journey, until towards evening, some distance from Castel Guglielmo, as they were about to ford a stream, these three ruffians, profiting by the lateness of the hour, and the loneliness and straightness of the place, set upon Rinaldo and robbed him, and leaving him afoot and in his shirt, said by way of adieu – 'Go now, and see if thy St Julian will provide thee with good lodging tonight; our saint, we doubt not, will do as much by us;' and so crossing the stream, they went their way. Rinaldo's servant, coward that he was, did nothing to help his master when he saw him attacked, but turned his horse's head, and was off at a smart pace; nor did he draw rein until he was come to Castel Guglielmo; where, it being now evening, he put up at an inn and gave himself no further trouble. Rinaldo, left barefoot, and stripped to his shirt, while the night closed in very cold and snowy, was at his wits' end, and shivering so that his teeth chattered in his head, began to peer about, if haply he might find some shelter for the night, that so he might not perish with the cold; but, seeing none (for during a recent war the whole country had been wasted by fire), he set off for Castel Guglielmo, quickening his pace by reason of the cold. Whether his servant had taken refuge in Castel Guglielmo or elsewhere, he knew not, but he thought that, could he but enter the town, God would surely send him some succour. However, dark night overtook him while he was still about a mile from the castle; so that on his arrival he found the gates already locked and the bridges raised, and he could not pass in. Sick at heart, disconsolate and bewailing his evil fortune, he looked about for some place where he might ensconce himself, and at any rate find shelter from the snow. And by good luck he espied a house, built with a balcony a little above the castle-wall, under which balcony he purposed to shelter himself until daybreak. Arrived at the spot, he found beneath the balcony a postern, which, however, was locked; and having gathered some bits of straw that lay about, he placed them in front of the postern, and there in sad and sorrowful plight took up his quarters, with many a piteous appeal to St Julian, whom he reproached for not better rewarding the faith which he reposed in him. St Julian, however, had not abandoned him, and in due time provided him with a good lodging.

There was in the castle a widow lady of extraordinary beauty (none fairer) whom Marquis Azzo loved as his own life, and kept there for his pleasure. She lived in the very same house beneath the balcony of which Rinaldo had posted himself. Now it chanced that that very day the Marquis had come to Castel Guglielmo to pass the night with her, and had privily caused a bath to be made ready, and a supper suited to his rank, in the lady's own house. The arrangements were complete; and only the Marquis was stayed for, when a servant happened to present himself at the castle-gate, bringing tidings for the Marquis which obliged him suddenly to take horse. He therefore sent word to the lady that she must not wait for him, and forthwith took his departure. The lady, somewhat disconsolate, found nothing better to do than to get into the bath which had been intended for the Marquis, sup and go to bed: so into the bath she went. The bath was close to the postern on the other side of which hapless Rinaldo had ensconced himself, and thus the mournful and quavering music which Rinaldo made as he shuddered in the cold, and which seemed rather to proceed from a stork's beak than from the mouth of a human being, was audible to the lady in the bath. She therefore called her maid, and said to her – 'Go up and look out over the wall and down at the postern, and mark who is there, and what he is, and what he does there.' The maid obeyed, and, the night being fine, had no difficulty in making out Rinaldo as he sat there, barefoot, as I have said, and in his shirt, and trembling in every limb. So she called out to him, to know who he was. Rinaldo, who could scarcely articulate for shivering, told as briefly as he could who he was, and how and why he came to be there; which done, he began piteously to beseech her not, if she could avoid it, to leave him there all night to perish of cold. The maid went back to her mistress full of pity for Rinaldo, and told her all she had seen and heard. The lady felt no less pity for Rinaldo; and bethinking her that she had the key of the postern by which the Marquis sometimes entered when he paid her a secret visit, she said to the maid – 'Go, and let him in softly; here is this supper, and there will be none to eat it; and we can very well put him up for the night.' Cordially commending her mistress's humanity, the maid went and let Rinaldo in, and brought him to the lady, who, seeing that he was all but dead with cold, said to him – 'Quick, good man, get into that bath, which is still warm.' Gladly he did so, awaiting no second invitation, and was so much comforted by its warmth that he seemed to have passed from death to life. The lady provided him with a suit of clothes, which had been worn by her husband shortly before his death, and which, when he had them on, looked as if they had been made for him. So he recovered heart, and, while he awaited the lady's commands, gave thanks to God and St Julian for delivering him from a woeful night and conducting him, as it seemed, to comfortable quarters.

The lady meanwhile took a little rest, after which she had a roaring fire put in one of her large rooms, whither presently she came, and asked her maid how the good man did. The maid replied – 'Madam, he has put on the clothes, in which he shows to advantage, having a handsome person, and seeming to be a worthy man, and well-bred.' 'Go, call him then, 'said the lady, 'tell him to come hither to the fire, and we will sup; for I know that he has not supped.' Rinaldo, on entering the room and seeing the lady, took her to be of no small consequence. He therefore made her a low bow, and did his utmost to thank her worthily for the service she had rendered him. His words pleased her no less than his person, which accorded with what the maid had said: so she made him heartily welcome, installed him at his ease by her side before the fire, and questioned him of the adventure which had brought him thither. Rinaldo detailed all the circumstances, of which the lady had heard somewhat when Rinaldo's servant made his appearance at the castle. She therefore gave entire credence to what he said, and told him what she knew about his servant, and how he might easily find him on the morrow. She then bade her servants set the table, which done, Rinaldo and she washed their hands and sat down together to sup. Tall he was and comely of form and feature, debonair and gracious of mien and manner, and in his lusty prime. The lady had eyed him again and again to her no small satisfaction, and, her wantonness being already kindled for the Marquis, who was to have come to lie with her, she had let Rinaldo take the vacant place in her mind. So when supper was done, and they were risen from the table, she conferred with her maid, whether, after the cruel trick played upon her by the Marquis, it were not well to take the good gift which Fortune had sent her. The maid knowing the bent of her mistress's desire, left no word unsaid that might encourage her to follow it. Wherefore the lady, turning towards Rinaldo, who was standing where she had left him by the fire, began thus – 'So! Rinaldo, why still so pensive? Will nothing console you for the loss of a horse and a few clothes? Take heart, put a blithe face on it, you are at home; nay more, let me tell you that, seeing you in those clothes which my late husband used to wear, and taking you for him, I have felt, not once or twice, but perhaps a hundred times this evening, a longing to throw my arms round you and kiss you; and, in faith, I had so done, but that I feared it might displease you.' Rinaldo, hearing these words, and marking the flame which shot from the lady's eyes, and being no laggard, came forward with open arms, and confronted her and said – 'Madam, I am not unmindful that I must ever acknowledge that to you I owe my life, in regard of the peril whence you rescued me. If then there be any way in which I may pleasure you, churlish indeed were I not to devise it. So you may even embrace and kiss me to your heart's content, and I will embrace and kiss you with the best of good wills.' There needed no further parley. The lady, all aflame with amorous desire, forthwith threw herself into his arms, and straining him to her bosom with a thousand passionate embraces, gave and received a thousand kisses before they sought her chamber. There with all speed they went to bed, nor did day surprise them until again and again and in full measure they had satisfied their desire. With the first streaks of dawn they rose, for the lady was minded that none should surmise aught of the affair. So, having meanwhile habited Rinaldo and replenished his purse, she enjoined him to keep the secret, showed him the way to the castle, where he was to find his servant, and let him out by the same postern by which he had entered. When it was broad day the gates were opened, and Rinaldo, passing himself off as a traveller from distant parts, entered the castle, and found his servant. Having put on the spare suit which was in his valise, he was about to mount the servant's horse, when, as if by miracle, there were brought into the castle the three gentlemen of the road who had robbed him the evening before, having been taken a little while after for another offence. Upon their confession Rinaldo's horse was restored to him, as were also his clothes and money; so that he lost nothing except a pair of garters, of which the robbers knew not where they had bestowed them. Wherefore Rinaldo, giving thanks to God and St Julian, mounted his horse, and returned home safe and sound, and on the morrow the three robbers kicked heels in the wind.

4

The third story of the second day, in which three young men squander their substance and are reduced to poverty. Their nephew, returning home a desperate man, falls in with an abbot, in whom he discovers the daughter of the King of England. She marries him, and he retrieves the losses and re-establishes the fortune of his uncles.

The ladies marvelled to hear the adventures of Rinaldo d'Asti, praised his devotion, and gave thanks to God and St Julian for the succour lent him in his extreme need. Nor, though the verdict was hardly outspoken, was the lady deemed unwise to take the boon which God had sent her. So they tittered and talked of her night of delight, while Pampinea, being seated by Filostrato, and surmising that her turn would, as it did, come next, was lost in meditation on what she was to say. Roused from her reverie by the word of the queen, she put on a cheerful courage, and thus began: Noble ladies, discourse as we may of Fortune's handiwork, much still remains to be said if we but scan events aright, nor need we marvel thereat, if we but duly consider that all matters, which we foolishly call our own, are in her hands, and therefore subject, at her inscrutable will, to every variety of chance and change without any order therein by us discernible. Which is indeed signally manifest everywhere and all day long; yet, as 'tis our queen's will that we speak thereof, perhaps 'twill not be unprofitable to you, if, notwithstanding it has been the theme of some of the foregoing stories, I add to them another, which, I believe, should give you pleasure –

There was formerly in our city a knight, by name Messer Tedaldo, of the Lamberti, according to some, or, as others say, of the Agolanti family, perhaps for no better reason than that the occupation of his sons was similar to that which always was and is the occupation of the Agolanti. However, without professing to determine which of the two houses he belonged to, I say that he was in his day a very wealthy knight, and had three sons, the eldest being by name Lamberto, the second Tedaldo, and the third Agolante. Fine, spirited young men were they all, though the eldest was not yet eighteen years old when their father, Messer Tedaldo, died very rich leaving to them as his lawful heirs the whole of his property both movable and immovable. Finding themselves thus possessed of great wealth, both in money and in lands and chattels, they fell to spending without stint or restraint, indulging their every desire, maintaining a great establishment and a large and well-filled stable, besides dogs and hawks, keeping ever open house, scattering largesse, jousting, and, not content with these and the like pastimes proper to their condition, indulging every appetite natural to their youth. They had not long followed this course of life before the cash left them by their father was exhausted; and, their rents not sufficing to defray their expenditure, they began to sell and pledge their property, and disposing of it by degrees, one item today and another tomorrow, they hardly perceived that they were approaching the verge of ruin, until poverty opened the eyes which wealth had fast sealed. So one day Lamberto called his brothers to him, reminded them of the position of wealth and dignity which had been theirs and their father's before them, and showed them the poverty to which their extravagance had reduced them, and adjured them most earnestly that, before their destitution was yet further manifest, they should all three sell what little remained to them and depart thence; which accordingly they did. Without leave-taking, or any ceremony, they quitted Florence; nor did they rest until they had arrived in England and established themselves in a small house in London, where, by living with extreme parsimony and lending at exorbitant usances, they prospered so well that in the course of a few years they amassed a fortune; and so, one by one, they returned to Florence, purchased not a few of their former estates besides many others, and married. The management of their affairs in England where they continued their business of usurers, they left to a young nephew, Alessandro by name, while, heedless alike of the teaching of experience and of marital and parental duty, they all three launched out at Florence into more extravagant expenditure than before, and contracted debts on all hands and to large amounts. This expenditure they were enabled for some years to support by the remittances made by Alessandro, who, to his great profit, had lent money to the barons on the security of their castles and rents.

While the three brothers thus continued to spend freely, and, when short of money, to borrow it, never doubting of help from England, it so happened that, to the surprise of everybody, there broke out in England a war between the King and his son, by which the whole island was divided into two camps; whereby Alessandro lost all his mortgages of the baronial castles and every other source of income whatsoever. However, in the daily expectation that peace would be concluded between the King and his son, Alessandro, hoping that in that event all would be restored to him, principal and interest, tarried in the island; and the three brothers at Florence in no degree retrenched their extravagant expenditure, but went on borrowing from day to day. Several years thus passed; and, their hopes being frustrated, the three brothers not only lost credit, but, being pressed for payment by their creditors, were suddenly arrested, and, their property proving deficient, were kept in prison for the balance, while their wives and little children went into the country parts, or elsewhere, wretchedly equipped, and with no other prospect than to pass the rest of their days in destitution. Alessandro, meanwhile, seeing that the peace which he had for several years awaited in England, did not come, and deeming that he would hazard his life to no purpose by tarrying longer in the country, made up his mind to return to Italy. He travelled at first altogether alone; but it so chanced that he left Bruges at the same time with an abbot, habited in white, attended by a numerous retinue, and preceded by a goodly baggage-train. Behind the abbot rode two grey-beard knights, kinsmen of the King, in whom Alessandro recognised acquaintances, and, making himself known to them, was readily received into their company. As thus they journeyed together, Alessandro softly asked them who the monks were that rode in front with so great a train, and whither they were bound. 'The foremost rider,' replied one of the knights, 'is a young kinsman of ours, the newly-elected abbot of one of the greatest abbeys of England; and as he is not of legal age for such a dignity, we are going with him to Rome to obtain the Holy Father's dispensation and his confirmation in the office; but this is not a matter for common talk.' Now the new abbot, as lords are wont to do when they travel, was sometimes in front, sometimes in rear of his train; and thus it happened that, as he passed, he set eyes on Alessandro, who was still quite young, and very shapely and well-favoured, and as courteous, gracious and debonair as e'er another. The abbot was marvellously taken with him at first sight, having never seen aught that pleased him so much, called him to his side, addressed him graciously, and asked him who he was, whence he came, and whither he was bound. Alessandro frankly told all about himself, and having thus answered the abbot's questions, placed himself at his service as far as his small ability might extend. The abbot was struck by his easy flow of apt speech, and observing his bearing more closely, he made up his mind that, albeit his occupation was base, he was nevertheless of gentle blood, which added no little to his interest in him; and being moved to compassion by his misfortunes, he gave him friendly consolation, bidding him be of good hope, that if he lived a worthy life, God would yet set him in a place no less or even more exalted than that whence Fortune had cast him down, and prayed him to be of his company as far as Tuscany, as both were going the same way. Alessandro thanked him for his words of comfort, and professed himself ready to obey his every command.

So fared on the abbot, his mind full of new ideas begotten by the sight of Alessandro, until some days later they came to a town which was none too well provided with inns; and, as the abbot must needs put up there, Alessandro, who was well acquainted with one of the innkeepers, arranged that the abbot should alight at his house, and procured him the least discomfortable quarters which it could afford. He thus became for the nonce the abbot's seneschal, and being very expert for such office, managed excellently, quartering the retinue in divers parts of the town. So the abbot supped, and, the night being far spent, all went to bed except Alessandro, who then asked the host where he might find quarters for the night. 'In good sooth, I know not,' replied the host; 'thou seest that every place is occupied, and that I and my household must lie on the benches. However, in the abbot's chamber there are some corn-sacks. I can show thee the way thither, and lay a bit of a bed upon them, and there, an it like thee, thou mayst pass the night very well.' 'How sayst thou?' said Alessandro; 'in the abbot's chamber, which thou knowest is small, so that there was not room for any of the monks to sleep there? Had I understood this when the curtains were drawn, I would have quartered his monks on the corn-sacks, and slept myself where the monks sleep.' ''Tis even so, however,' replied the host, 'and thou canst, if thou wilt, find excellent quarters there: the abbot sleeps, the curtains are close drawn; I will go in softly and lay a small bed there, on which thou canst sleep.' Alessandro, satisfied that it might be managed without disturbing the abbot, accepted the offer, and made his arrangements for passing the night as quietly as he could.

The abbot was not asleep; his mind being far too overwrought by certain newly-awakened desires. He had heard what had passed between Alessandro and the host, he had marked the place where Alessandro had lain down, and in the great gladness of his heart had begun thus to commune with himself – 'God has sent me the opportunity of gratifying my desire; if I let it pass, perchance it will be long before another such opportunity occurs.' So, being minded by no means to let it slip, when all was quiet in the inn, he softly called Alessandro, and bade him lie down by his side. Alessandro made many excuses, but ended by undressing and obeying; whereupon the abbot laid a hand on Alessandro's breast, and began to caress him just as amorous girls do their lovers; whereat Alessandro marvelled greatly, doubting the abbot was prompted to such caresses by a shameful love. Which the abbot speedily divined, or else surmised from some movement on Alessandro's part, and, laughing, threw off a chemise which she had upon her, and taking Alessandro's hand, laid it on her bosom, saying – 'Alessandro, dismiss thy foolish thought, feel here, and learn what I conceal.' Alessandro obeyed, laying a hand upon the abbot's bosom, where he encountered two little teats, round, firm and delicate, as they had been of ivory; whereby he at once knew that 'twas a woman, and without awaiting further encouragement forthwith embraced her, and would have kissed her, when she said: – 'Before thou art more familiar with me hearken to what I have to say to thee. As thou mayst perceive, I am no man, but a woman. Virgin I left my home, and was going to the Pope to obtain his sanction for my marriage, when, as Fortune willed, whether for thy gain or my loss, no sooner had I seen thee the other day, than I burned for thee with such a flame of love as never yet had lady for any man. Wherefore I am minded to have thee for my husband rather than any other; so, if thou wilt not have me to wife, depart at once, and return to thine own place.' Albeit he knew not who she was, Alessandro by the retinue which attended her conjectured that she must be noble and wealthy, and he saw that she was very fair; so it was not long before he answered that, if such were her pleasure, it was very much to his liking. Whereupon she sat up, set a ring on his finger, and espoused him before a tiny picture of our Lord; after which they embraced, and to their no small mutual satisfaction solaced themselves for the rest of the night. At daybreak Alessandro rose, and by preconcert with the lady, left the chamber as he had entered it, so that none knew where he had passed the night: then, blithe at heart beyond measure, he rejoined the abbot and his train, and so, resuming their journey, they after many days arrived at

Rome. They had not been there more than a few days, when the abbot, attended by the two knights and Alessandro, waited on the Pope, whom, after making the due obeisance, he thus addressed – 'Holy Father, as you must know better than any other, whoso intends to lead a true and honourable life ought, as far as may be, to shun all occasion of error; for which cause I, having a mind to live honourably, did, the better to accomplish my purpose, assume the habit in which you see me, and depart by stealth from the court of my father, the King of England, who was minded to marry me, young as you see me to be, to the aged King of Scotland; and, carrying with me not a little of his treasure, set my face hitherward that your Holiness might bestow me in marriage. Nor was it the age of the King of Scotland that moved me to flee so much as fear lest the frailty of my youth should, were I married to him, betray me to commit some breach of divine law, and sully the honour of my father's royal blood. And as in this frame of mind I journeyed, God, who knows best what is meet for everyone, did, as I believe, of His mercy show me him whom He is pleased to appoint me for my husband, even this young man' (pointing to Alessandro) 'whom you see by my side, who for nobility of nature and bearing is a match for any great lady, though the strain of his blood, perhaps, be not of royal purity. Him, therefore, have I chosen, him will I have, and no other, no matter what my father or anyone else may think. And albeit the main purpose with which I started is fulfilled, yet I have thought good to continue my journey, that I may visit the holy and venerable places which abound in this city, and your Holiness, and that so in your presence, and by consequence in the presence of others, I may renew my marriage-vow with Alessandro, whereof God alone was witness. Wherefore I humbly pray you that God's will and mine may be also yours, and that you pronounce your benison thereon, that therewith, having the more firm assurance of the favour of Him, whose vicar you are, we may both live together, and, when the time comes, die to God's glory and yours.'

Alessandro was filled with wonder and secret delight, when he heard that his wife was the daughter of the King of England; but greater still was the wonder of the two knights, and such their wrath that, had they been anywhere else than in the Pope's presence, they would not have spared to affront Alessandro, and perhaps the lady too. The Pope, on his part, found matter enough for wonder as well in the lady's habit as in her choice; but, knowing that he could not refuse, he consented to grant her request.

He therefore began by smoothing the ruffled tempers of the knights, and having reconciled them with the lady and Alessandro, proceeded to put matters in train for the marriage. When the day appointed was come, he gave a great reception, at which were assembled all the cardinals and many other great lords to whom he presented the lady royally robed, and looking so fair and so gracious that she won, as she deserved, the praise of all, and likewise Alessandro, splendidly arrayed, and bearing himself not a whit like the young usurer but rather as one of royal blood, for which cause he received due honour from the knights. There, before the Pope himself, the marriage-vows were solemnly renewed; and afterwards the marriage, which was accompanied by every circumstance that could add grace and splendour to the ceremony, received the sanction of his benediction. Alessandro and the lady on leaving Rome saw fit to visit Florence, whither fame had already wafted the news, so that they were received by the citizens with every token of honour. The lady set the three brothers at liberty, paying all their creditors, and reinstated them and their wives in their several properties. So, leaving gracious memories behind them, Alessandro and his lady, accompanied by Agolante, quitted Florence, and arriving at Paris were honourably received by the King. The two knights went before them to England, and by their influence induced the King to restore the lady to his favour, and receive her and his son-in-law with every circumstance of joy and honour. Alessandro he soon afterwards knighted with unwonted ceremony, and bestowed on him the earldom of Cornwall. And such was the Earl's consequence and influence at court that he restored peace between father and son, thereby conferring a great boon on the island and gaining the love and esteem of all the people. Agolante, whom he knighted, recovered all the outstanding debts in full, and returned to Florence immensely rich. The Earl passed the rest of his days with his lady in great renown. Indeed there are those who say, that with the help of his father-in-law he effected by his policy and valour the conquest of Scotland, and was crowned king of that country.

5

The sixth story of the second day, in which Madam Beritola loses two sons, is found with two kids on an island, goes thence to Lunigiana, where one of her sons takes service with her master, and lies with his daughter, for which he is put in prison. Sicily rebels against King Charles, the son is recognised by the mother, marries the master's daughter, and, his brother being discovered, is reinstated in great honour.

The ladies and the young men alike had many a hearty laugh over the previous narrative, which ended, Emilia, at the queen's command, thus began: Grave and grievous are the vicissitudes with which Fortune makes us acquainted, and as discourse of such matter serves to awaken our minds, which are so readily lulled to sleep by her flatteries, I deem it worthy of attentive hearing by all, whether they enjoy her favour or endure her frown, in that it ministers counsel to the one sort and consolation to the other. Wherefore, albeit great matters have preceded it, I mean to tell you a story, not less true than touching, of adventures whereof the issue was indeed felicitous, but the antecedent bitterness so long drawn out that scarce can I believe that it was ever sweetened by ensuing happiness –

Dearest ladies, you must know that after the death of the Emperor Frederic II the crown of Sicily passed to Manfred; whose favour was enjoyed in the highest degree by a gentleman of Naples, Arrighetto Capece by name, who had to wife Madonna Beritola Caracciola, a fair and gracious lady, likewise a Neapolitan. Now when Manfred was conquered and slain by King Charles I at Benevento, and the whole realm transferred its allegiance to the conqueror, Arrighetto, who was then governor of Sicily, no sooner received the tidings than he prepared for instant flight, knowing that little reliance was to be placed on the fleeting faith of the Sicilians, and not being minded to become a subject of his master's enemy. But the Sicilians having intelligence of his plans, he and many other friends and servants of King Manfred were surprised, taken prisoner and delivered over to King Charles, to whom the whole island was soon afterwards surrendered. In this signal reversal of the wonted course of things Madam Beritola, knowing not what was become of Arrighetto, and from the past ever auguring future evil, lest she should suffer foul dishonour, abandoned all that she possessed, and with a son of, perhaps, eight years, Giusfredi by name, being also pregnant, fled in a boat to Lipari, where she gave birth to another male child, whom she named Outcast. Then with her sons and a hired nurse she took ship for Naples, intending there to rejoin her family. Events, however, fell out otherwise than she expected; for by stress of weather the ship was carried out of her course to the desert island of Ponza,* where they put in to a little bay until such time as they might safely continue their voyage. Madam Beritola landed with the rest on the island, and, leaving them all, sought out a lonely and secluded spot, and there abandoned herself to melancholy brooding on the loss of her dear Arrighetto. While thus she spent her days in solitary preoccupation with her grief it chanced that a galley of corsairs swooped down upon the island, and, before either the mariners or any other folk were aware of their peril, made an easy capture of them all and sailed away; so that, when Madam Beritola, her wailing for that day ended, returned, as was her wont, to the shore to solace herself with the sight of her sons, she found none there. At first she was lost in wonder, then with a sudden suspicion of the truth she bent her eyes seaward, and there saw the galley still at no great distance, towing the ship in her wake. Thus apprehending beyond all manner of doubt that she had lost her sons as well as her husband, and that, alone, desolate and destitute, she might not hope that any of her lost ones would ever be restored to her, she fell down on the shore in a swoon with the names of her husband and sons upon her lips. None was there to administer cold water or aught else that might recall her truant powers; her animal spirits might even wander whithersoever they would at their sweet will: strength, however, did at last return to her poor exhausted frame, and therewith tears and lamentations, as, plaintively repeating her sons' names, she roamed in quest of them from cavern to cavern. Long time she sought them thus; but when she saw that her labour was in vain,

* The largest, now inhabited, of a group of islets in the Gulf of Gaeta.

and that night was closing in, hope, she knew not why, began to return, and with it some degree of anxiety on her own account. Wherefore she left the shore and returned to the cavern where she had been wont to indulge her plaintive mood. She passed the night in no small fear and indescribable anguish; the new day came, and, as she had not supped, she was fain after tierce to appease her hunger, as best she could, by a breakfast of herbs: this done, she wept and began to ruminate on her future way of life. While thus engaged, she observed a she-goat come by and go into an adjacent cavern, and after a while come forth again and go into the wood: thus roused from her reverie she got up, went into the cavern from which the she-goat had issued, and there saw two kids, which might have been born that very day, and seemed to her the sweetest and the most delicious things in the world: and, having, by reason of her recent delivery, milk still within her, she took them up tenderly, and set them to her breast. They, nothing loath, sucked at her teats as if she had been their own dam; and thenceforth made no distinction between her and the dam. Which caused the lady to feel that she had found company in the desert; and so, living on herbs and water, weeping as often as she bethought her of her husband and sons and her past life, she disposed herself to live and die there, and became no less familiar with the she-goat than with her young.

The gentle lady thus leading the life of a wild creature, it chanced that after some months stress of weather brought a Pisan ship to the very same bay in which she had landed. The ship lay there for several days, having on board a gentleman, Currado de' Malespini by name (of the same family as the Marquis), who with his noble and most devout lady was returning home from a pilgrimage, having visited all the holy places in the realm of Apulia. To beguile the tedium of the sojourn Currado with his lady, some servants and his dogs, set forth one day upon a tour through the island. As they neared the place where Madam Beritola dwelt, Currado's dogs on view of the two kids, which, now of a fair size, were grazing, gave chase. The kids, pursued by the dogs, made straight for Madam Beritola's cavern. She, seeing what was toward, started to her feet, caught up a stick, and drove the dogs back. Currado and his lady coming up after the dogs, gazed on Madam Beritola, now tanned and lean and hairy, with wonder, which she more than reciprocated. At her request Currado called off the dogs; and then he and his lady besought her again and again to say who she was and what she did there. So she told them all about herself, her rank, her misfortunes, and the savage life which she was minded to lead. Currado, who had known Arrighetto Capece very well, was moved to tears by compassion, and exhausted all his eloquence to induce her to change her mind, offering to escort her home, or to take her to live with him in honourable estate as his sister until God should vouchsafe her kindlier fortune. The lady declining all his offers, Currado left her with his wife, whom he bade see that food was brought thither, and let Madam Beritola, who was all in rags, have one of her own dresses to wear, and do all that she could to persuade her to go with them. So the gentle lady stayed with Madam Beritola, and after condoling with her at large on her misfortunes, had food and clothing brought to her, and with the greatest difficulty in the world prevailed upon her to eat and dress herself. At last, after much beseeching, she induced her to depart from her oft-declared intention never to go where she might meet any that knew her, and accompany them to Lunigiana, taking with her the two kids and the dam, which latter had in the meantime returned, and to the gentle lady's great surprise had greeted Madam Beritola with the utmost affection. So with the return of fair weather Madam Beritola, taking with her the dam and the two kids, embarked with Currado and his lady on their ship, being called by them – for her true name was not to be known of all – Cavriuola;* and the wind holding fair, they speedily reached the mouth of the Magra,† and landing hied them to Currado's castle; where Madam Beritola abode with Currado's lady in the quality of her maid serving her well and faithfully, wearing widow's weeds and feeding and tending her kids with assiduous and loving care.

The corsairs, who, not espying Madam Beritola, had left her at Ponza when they took the ship on which she had come thither, had made a course to Genoa, taking with them all the other folk. On their arrival the owners of the galley shared the booty, and so it happened that as part thereof Madam Beritola's nurse and her two boys fell to the lot of one Messer Guasparrino d'Oria, who sent all three to his house, being minded to keep them there as domestic slaves. The nurse, beside herself with grief at the loss of her mistress and the woeful plight in which she found herself and her two charges, shed many a bitter tear. But, seeing that they were unavailing, and that she and the boys were slaves together, she, having, for all her low estate, her share of wit and good sense, made it her first care to comfort them; then, regardful of the condition to which they were reduced, she bethought her, that, if the lads were recognised, 'twould very likely be injurious to them. So, still hoping that sometime or another Fortune would change her mood, and they be able, if living, to regain their lost estate, she resolved

* i.e. she-goat. † Between Liguria and Tuscany.

to let none know who they were, until she saw a fitting occasion; and accordingly, whenever she was questioned thereof by any, she gave them out as her own children. The name of the elder she changed from Giusfredi to Giannotto di Procida; the name of the younger she did not think it worth while to change. She spared no pains to make Giusfredi understand the reason why she had changed his name, and the risk which he might run if he were recognised. This she impressed upon him not once only but many times; and the boy, who was apt to learn, followed the instructions of the wise nurse with perfect exactitude.

So the two boys, ill clad and worse shod, continued with the nurse in Messer Guasparrino's house for two years, patiently performing all kinds of menial offices. But Giannotto, being now sixteen years old, and of a spirit that consorted ill with servitude, brooked not the baseness of his lot, and dismissed himself from Messer Guasparrino's service by getting aboard a galley bound for Alexandria, and travelled far and wide, and fared never the better. In the course of his wanderings he learned that his father, whom he had supposed to be dead, was still living, but kept in prison under watch and ward by King Charles. He was grown a tall handsome young man, when, perhaps three or four years after he had given Messer Guasparrino the slip, weary of roaming and all but despairing of his fortune, he came to Lunigiana, and by chance took service with Currado Malespini, who found him handy, and was well-pleased with him. His mother, who was in attendance on Currado's lady, he seldom saw, and never recognised her, nor she him; so much had time changed both from their former aspect since they last met. While Giannotto was thus in the service of Currado, it fell out by the death of Niccolo da Grignano that his widow, Spina, Currado's daughter, returned to her father's house. Very fair she was and loveable, her age not more than sixteen years, and so it was that she saw Giannotto with favour, and he her, and both fell ardently in love with one another. Their passion was early gratified; but several months elapsed before any detected its existence. Wherefore, growing overbold, they began to dispense with the precautions which such an affair demanded. So one day, as they walked with others through a wood, where the trees grew fair and close, the girl and Giannotto left the rest of the company some distance behind, and, thinking that they were well in advance, found a fair pleasance girt in with trees and carpeted with abundance of grass and flowers, and fell to solacing themselves after the manner of lovers. Long time they thus dallied, though such was their delight that all too brief it seemed to them, and so it befell that they were surprised first by the girl's mother and then by Currado. Pained beyond measure by what he had seen, Currado, without assigning any cause, had them both arrested by three of his servants and taken in chains to one of his castles; where in a frenzy of passionate wrath he left them, resolved to put them to an ignominious death. The girl's mother was also very angry, and deemed her daughter's fall deserving of the most rigorous chastisement, but, when by one of Currado's chance words she divined the doom which he destined for the guilty pair, she could not reconcile herself to it, and hasted to intercede with her angry husband, beseeching him to refrain the impetuous wrath which would hurry him in his old age to murder his daughter and imbrue his hands in the blood of his servant, and vent it in some other way, as by close confinement and duress, whereby the culprits should be brought to repent them of their fault in tears. Thus, and with much more to the like effect, the devout lady urged her suit, and at length prevailed upon her husband to abandon his murderous design. Wherefore, he commanded that the pair should be confined in separate prisons, and closely guarded, and kept short of food and in sore discomfort, until further order; which was accordingly done; and the life which the captives led, their endless tears, their fasts of inordinate duration, may be readily imagined.

Giannotto and Spina had languished in this sorry plight for full a year, entirely ignored by Currado, when in concert with Messer Gian di Procida, King Peter of Arragon raised a rebellion* in the island of Sicily, and wrested it from King Charles, whereat Currado, being a Ghibelline, was overjoyed. Hearing the tidings from one of his warders, Giannotto heaved a great sigh, and said – 'Alas, fourteen years have I been a wanderer upon the face of the earth, looking for no other than this very event; and now, that my hopes of happiness may be for ever frustrated, it has come to pass only to find me in prison, whence I may never think to issue alive.' 'How?' said the warder; 'what signify to thee these doings of these mighty monarchs? What part hadst thou in Sicily?' Giannotto answered – ' 'Tis as if my heart were breaking when I bethink me of my father and what part he had in Sicily. I was but a little lad when I fled the island, but yet I remember him as its governor in the time of King Manfred.' 'And who then was thy father?' demanded the warder. 'His name,' rejoined Giannotto, 'I need no longer scruple to disclose, seeing that I find myself in the very strait

* The Sicilian Vespers, Easter, 1282.

which I hoped to avoid by concealing it. He was and still is, if he live, Arrighetto Capece; and my name is not Giannotto but Giusfredi; and I doubt not but, were I once free, and back in Sicily, I might yet hold a very honourable position in the island.'

The worthy man asked no more questions, but, as soon as he found opportunity, told what he had learned to Currado; who, albeit he made light of it in the warder's presence, repaired to Madam Beritola, and asked her in a pleasant manner, whether she had had by Arrighetto a son named Giusfredi. The lady answered, in tears, that, if the elder of her two sons were living, such would be his name, and his age twenty-two years. This inclined Currado to think that Giannotto and Giusfredi were indeed one and the same; and it occurred to him, that, if so it were, he might at once show himself most merciful and blot out his daughter's shame and his own by giving her to him in marriage; wherefore he sent for Giannotto privily, and questioned him in detail touching his past life. And finding by indubitable evidence that he was indeed Giusfredi, son of Arrighetto Capece, he said to him – 'Giannotto, thou knowest the wrong which thou hast done me in the person of my daughter, what and how great it is, seeing that I used thee well and kindly, and thou shouldst therefore, like a good servant, have shown thyself jealous of my honour, and zealous in my interest; and many there are who, hadst thou treated them as thou hast treated me, would have caused thee to die an ignominious death; which my clemency would not brook. But now, as it is even so as thou sayst, and thou art of gentle blood by both thy parents, I am minded to put an end to thy sufferings as soon as thou wilt, releasing thee from the captivity in which thou languishest, and setting thee in a happy place, and reinstating at once thy honour and my own. Thy intimacy with Spina – albeit shameful to both – was yet prompted by love. Spina, as thou knowest, is a widow, and her dower is ample and secure. What her breeding is, and her father's and her mother's, thou knowest: of thy present condition I say nought. Wherefore, when thou wilt, I am consenting, that, having been with dishonour thy friend, she become with honour thy wife, and that, so long as it seem good to thee, thou tarry here with her and me as my son.'

Captivity had wasted Giannotto's flesh, but had in no degree impaired the generosity of spirit which he derived from his ancestry, or the whole-hearted love which he bore his lady. So, albeit he ardently desired that which Currado offered, and knew that he was in Currado's power, yet, even as his magnanimity prompted, so, unswervingly, he made answer – 'Currado, neither ambition nor cupidity nor aught else did ever beguile me to any treacherous machination against either thy person or thy property. Thy daughter I loved, and love and shall ever love, because I deem her worthy of my love; and, if I dealt with her after a fashion which to the mechanic mind seems hardly honourable, I did but commit that fault which is ever congenial to youth, which can never be eradicated so long as youth continues, and which, if the aged would but remember that they were once young and would measure the delinquencies of others by their own and their own by those of others, would not be deemed so grave as thou and many others depict it; and what I did, I did as a friend, not as an enemy. That which thou offerest I have ever desired, and should long ago have sought, had I supposed that thou wouldst grant it, and 'twill be the more grateful to me in proportion to the depth of my despair. But if thy intent be not such as thy words import, feed me not with vain hopes, but send me back to prison, there to suffer whatever thou mayst be pleased to inflict; nor doubt that even as I love Spina, so for love of her shall I ever love thee, though thou do thy worst, and still hold thee in reverent regard.'

Currado marvelled to hear him thus speak, and being assured of his magnanimity and the fervour of his love, held him the more dear; wherefore he rose, embraced and kissed him, and without further delay bade privily bring thither Spina, who left her prison wasted and wan and weak, and so changed that she seemed almost another woman than of yore, even as Giannotto was scarce his former self. Then and there in Currado's presence they plighted their troth according to our custom of espousals; and some days afterwards Currado, having in the meantime provided all things meet for their convenience and solace, yet so as that none should surmise what had happened, deemed it now time to gladden their mothers with the news. So he sent for his lady and Cavriuola, and thus, addressing first Cavriuola, he spoke – 'What would you say, madam, were I to restore you your elder son as the husband of one of my daughters?' Cavriuola answered – 'I should say, that, were it possible for you to strengthen the bond which attaches me to you, then assuredly you had so done, in that you restored to me that which I cherish more tenderly than myself, and in such a guise as in some measure to renew within me the hope which I had lost: more I could not say.' And so, weeping, she was silent. Then, turning to his lady, Currado said – 'And thou, madam, what wouldst thou think if I were to present thee with such a son-in-law?' 'A son-in-law,' she answered, 'that was not of gentle blood, but a mere churl, so he pleased you, would well content me.' 'So!' returned Currado; 'I hope within a few days to gladden the hearts of both of you.'

He waited only until the two young folk had recovered their wonted mien, and were clad in a manner befitting their rank. Then, addressing Giusfredi, he said – 'Would it not add to thy joy to see thy mother here?' 'I dare not hope,' returned Giusfredi, 'that she has survived calamities and sufferings such as hers; but were it so, great indeed would be my joy, and none the less that by her counsel I might be aided to the recovery (in great measure) of my lost heritage in Sicily.' Whereupon Currado caused both the ladies to come thither, and presented to them the bride. The gladness with which they both greeted her was a wonder to behold, and no less great was their wonder at the benign inspiration that had prompted Currado to unite her in wedlock with Giannotto, whom Currado's words caused Madam Beritola to survey with some attention. A hidden spring of memory was thus touched; she recognised in the man the lineaments of her boy, and awaiting no further evidence she ran with open arms and threw herself upon his neck. No word did she utter, for very excess of maternal tenderness and joy; but, every avenue of sense closed, she fell as if bereft of life within her son's embrace. Giannotto, who had often seen her in the castle and never recognised her, marvelled not a little, but nevertheless it at once flashed upon him that 'twas his mother, and blaming himself for his past inadvertence he took her in his arms and wept and tenderly kissed her. With gentle solicitude Currado's lady and Spina came to her aid, and restored her suspended animation with cold water and other remedies. She then with many tender and endearing words kissed him a thousand times or more, which tokens of her love he received with a look of reverential acknowledgement. Thrice, nay a fourth time were these glad and gracious greetings exchanged, and joyful indeed were they that witnessed them, and hearkened while mother and son compared their past adventures. Then Currado, who had already announced his new alliance to his friends, and received their felicitations, proceeded to give order for the celebration of the event with all becoming gaiety and splendour. As he did so, Giusfredi said to him – 'Currado, you have long given my mother honourable entertainment, and on me you have conferred many boons; wherefore, that you may fill up the measure of your kindness, 'tis now my prayer that you be pleased to gladden my mother and my marriage feast and me with the presence of my brother, now in servitude in the house of Messer Guasparrino d'Oria, who, as I have already told you, made prize of both him and me; and that then you send someone to Sicily, who shall make himself thoroughly acquainted with the circumstances and condition of the country, and find out how it has fared with my father Arrighetto, whether he be alive or dead, and if alive, in what circumstances, and being thus fully informed, return to us with the tidings.' Currado assented, and forthwith sent most trusty agents both to Genoa and to Sicily. So in due time an envoy arrived at Genoa, and made instant suit to Guasparrino on Currado's part for the surrender of Outcast and the nurse, setting forth in detail all that had passed between Currado and Giusfredi and his mother. Whereat Messer Guasparrino was mightily astonished, and said – 'Of a surety there is nought that, being able, I would not do to pleasure Currado; and true it is that I have had in my house for these fourteen years the boy whom thou dost now demand of me, and his mother, and gladly will I surrender them; but tell Currado from me to beware of excessive credulity, and to put no faith in the idle tales of Giannotto, or Giusfredi, as thou sayst he calls himself, who is by no means so guileless as he supposes.'

Then, having provided for the honourable entertainment of the worthy envoy, he sent privily for the nurse, and cautiously sounded her as to the affair. The nurse had heard of the revolt of Sicily, and had learned that Arrighetto was still alive. She therefore banished fear, and told Messer Guasparrino the whole story, and explained to him the reasons why she had acted as she had done. Finding that what she said accorded very well with what he had learned from Currado's envoy, he inclined to credit the story, and most astutely probing the matter in divers ways, and always finding fresh grounds for confidence, he reproached himself for the sorry manner in which he had treated the boy, and by way of amends gave him one of his own daughters, a beautiful girl of eleven years, to wife with a dowry suited to Arrighetto's rank, and celebrated their nuptials with great festivity. He then brought the boy and girl, Currado's envoy, and the nurse in a well-armed galliot to Lerici, being there met by Currado, who had a castle not far off, where great preparations had been made for their entertainment: and thither accordingly he went with his whole company. What cheer the mother had of her son, the brothers of one another, and all the three of the faithful nurse; what cheer Messer Guasparrino and his daughter had of all, and all of them, and what cheer all had of Currado and his lady and their sons and their friends, words may not describe; wherefore, my ladies, I leave it to your imagination. And that their joy might be full, God, who, when He gives, gives most abundantly, added the glad tidings that Arrighetto Capece was alive and prosperous. For, when in the best of spirits the ladies and gentlemen had sat them down to feast, and they were yet at the first course, the envoy from Sicily arrived, and among other matters reported that, no sooner had the insurrection broken out in the island than the people hied them in hot haste to the prison where Arrighetto was kept in confinement by King Charles, and despatching the guards, brought him forth, and knowing him to be a capital enemy to King Charles made him their captain, and under his command fell upon and massacred the French. Whereby he had won the highest place in the favour of King Peter, who had granted him restitution of all his estates and honours, so that he was now both prosperous and mighty. The envoy added that Arrighetto had received him with every token of honour, had manifested the utmost delight on hearing of his lady and son, of whom no tidings had reached him since his arrest, and had sent, to bring them home, a brigantine with some gentlemen aboard, whose arrival might hourly be expected.

The envoy, and the good news which he brought, were heartily welcome; and presently Currado, with some of his friends, encountered the gentlemen who came for Madam Beritola and Giusfredi, and saluting them cordially invited them to his feast, which was not yet half done. Joy unheard-of was depicted on the faces of the lady, of Giusfredi, and of all the rest as they greeted them; nor did they on their part take their places at the table before, as best they might, they had conveyed to Currado and his lady Arrighetto's greetings and grateful acknowledgements of the honour which they had conferred upon his lady and his son, and had placed Arrighetto, to the uttermost of his power, entirely at their service. Then, turning to Messer Guasparrino, of whose kindness Arrighetto surmised nothing, they said that they were very sure that, when he learned the boon which Outcast had received at his hands, he would pay him the like and an even greater tribute of gratitude. This speech ended, they feasted most joyously with the brides and bridegrooms. So passed the day, the first of many which Currado devoted to honouring his son-in-law and his other intimates, both kinsfolk and friends. The time of festivity ended, Madam Beritola and Giusfredi and the rest felt that they must leave: so, taking Spina with them, they parted, not without many tears, from Currado and his lady and Guasparrino, and went aboard the brigantine, which, wafted by a prosperous wind, soon brought them to Sicily. At Palermo they were met by Arrighetto, who received them all, ladies and sons alike, with such cheer as it were vain to attempt to describe. There it is believed that they all lived long and happily and in amity with God, being not unmindful of the blessings which He had conferred upon them.

❧ 6 ❧

The seventh story of the second day, in which the Soldan of Babylon sends one of his daughters overseas, designing to marry her to the King of Algarve. By divers adventures she comes in the space of four years into the hands of nine men in divers places. At last she is restored to her father, whom she quits again in the guise of a virgin, and, as was at first intended, is married to the King of Algarve.

Had Emilia's story but lasted a little longer, the young ladies would perhaps have been moved to tears, so great was the sympathy which they felt for Madam Beritola in her various fortunes. But now that it was ended, the Queen bade Pamfilo follow suit; and he, than whom none was more obedient, thus began: ❧ Hardly, gracious ladies, is it given to us to know that which makes for our good; insomuch that, as has been observable in a multitude of instances, many, deeming that the acquisition of great riches would ensure them an easy and tranquil existence, have not only besought them of God in prayer, but have sought them with such ardour that they have spared no pains and shrunk from no danger in the quest, and have attained their end only to lose, at the hands of someone covetous of their vast inheritance, a life with which before the days of their prosperity they were well content. Others, whose course, perilous with a thousand battles, stained with the blood of their brothers and their friends, has raised them from base to regal estate, have found in place of the felicity they expected an infinity of cares and fears, and have proved by experience that a chalice may be poisoned, though it be of gold, and set on the table of a king. Many have most ardently desired beauty and strength and other advantages of person, and have only been taught their error by the death or dolorous life which these very advantages entailed upon them. And so, not to instance each particular human desire, I say, in sum, that there is none of them that men may indulge in full confidence as exempt from the chances and changes of fortune; wherefore, if we would act rightly, we ought to school ourselves to take and be content with that which He gives us, who alone knows and can afford us that of which we have need. But, divers as are the aberrations of desire to which men are prone, so, gracious ladies, there is one to which you are especially liable, in that you are unduly solicitous of beauty, insomuch that, not content with the charms which nature has allotted you, you endeavour to enhance them with wondrous ingenuity of art; wherefore I am minded to make you acquainted with the coil of misadventures in which her beauty involved a fair Saracen, who in the course of, perhaps, four years was wedded nine several times –

There was of yore a Soldan of Babylon,* by name of Beminedab, who in his day had cause enough to be well content with his luck. Many children male and female had he, and among them a daughter, Alatiel by name, who by common consent of all that saw her was the most beautiful woman then to be found in the world. Now the Soldan, having been signally aided by the King of Algarve† in inflicting a great defeat upon a host of Arabs that had attacked him, had at his instance and by way of special favour given Alatiel to the King to wife; wherefore, with an honourable escort of gentlemen and ladies most nobly and richly equipped, he placed her aboard a well-armed, well-furnished ship, and, commending her to God, sped her on her journey. The mariners, as soon as the weather was favourable, hoisted sail, and for some days after their departure from Alexandria had a prosperous voyage; but when they had passed Sardinia, and were beginning to think that they were nearing their journey's end, they were caught one day between divers cross winds, each blowing with extreme fury, whereby the ship laboured so sorely that not only the lady but the seamen from time to time gave themselves up for lost. But still, most manfully and skilfully they struggled might and main with the tempest, which, ever waxing rather than waning, buffeted them for two days with immense unintermittent surges; and being not far from the island

* i.e. according to medieval usage, Egypt.

† i.e. Garbo, the coast of Africa opposite Andalusia and Granada.

of Majorca, as the third night began to close in, wrapped in clouds and mist and thick darkness, so that they saw neither the sky nor aught else, nor by any nautical skill might conjecture where they were, they felt the ship's timbers part. Wherefore, seeing no way to save the ship, each thought only how best to save himself, and, a boat being thrown out, the masters first, and then the men, one by one, though the first-comers sought with knives in their hands to bar the passage of the rest, all, rather than remain in the leaky ship, crowded into it, and there found the death which they hoped to escape. For the boat, being in such stress of weather and with such a burden quite unmanageable, went under, and all aboard her perished; whereas the ship, leaky though she was, and all but full of water, yet, driven by the fury of the tempest, was hurled with prodigious velocity upon the shore of the island of Majorca, and struck it with such force as to embed herself in the sand, perhaps a stone's throw from *terra firma*, where she remained all night beaten and washed by the sea, but no more to be moved by the utmost violence of the gale. None had remained aboard her but the lady and her women, whom the malice of the elements and their fears had brought to the verge of death. When it was broad day and the storm was somewhat abated, the lady, half-dead, raised her head, and in faltering accents began to call first one and then another of her servants. She called in vain, however; for those whom she called were too far off to hear. Great indeed was her wonder and fear to find herself thus without sight of human face or sound of other voice than her own; but, struggling to her feet as best she might, she looked about her, and saw the ladies that were of her escort, and the other women, all prostrate on the deck; so, after calling them one by one, she began at length to touch them, and finding few that showed sign of life, for indeed, between grievous sea-sickness and fear, they had little life left, she grew more terrified than before. However, being in sore need of counsel, all alone as she was, and without knowledge or means of learning where she was, she at last induced such as had life in them to get upon their feet, with whom, as none knew where the men were gone, and the ship was now full of water and visibly breaking up, she abandoned herself to piteous lamentations.

It was already noon before they descried anyone on the shore or elsewhere to whom they could make appeal for help; but shortly after noon it so chanced that a gentleman, Pericone da Visalgo by name, being on his return from one of his estates, passed that way with some mounted servants. Catching sight of the ship, he apprehended the circumstances at a glance, and bade one of his servants try to get aboard her, and let him know the result. The servant with some difficulty succeeded in boarding the vessel, and found the gentle lady with her few companions ensconced under shelter of the prow, and shrinking timidly from observation. At the first sight of him they wept, and again and again implored him to have pity on them; but finding that he did not understand them, nor they him, they sought by gestures to make him apprehend their forlorn condition.

With these tidings the servant, after making such survey of the ship as he could, returned to Pericone, who forthwith caused the ladies, and all articles of value which were in the ship and could be removed, to be brought off her, and took them with him to one of his castles. The ladies' powers were soon in a measure restored by food and rest, and by the honour which was paid to Alatiel, and Alatiel alone by all the rest, as well as by the richness of her dress, Pericone perceived that she must be some great lady. Nor, though she was still pale, and her person bore evident marks of the sea's rough usage, did he fail to note that it was cast in a mould of extraordinary beauty. Wherefore his mind was soon made up that, if she lacked a husband, he would take her to wife, and that, if he could not have her to wife, then he would make her his mistress. So this ardent lover, who was a man of powerful frame and haughty mien, devoted himself for several days to the service of the lady with excellent effect, for the lady completely recovered her strength and spirits, so that her beauty far exceeded Pericone's most sanguine conjectures. Great therefore beyond measure was his sorrow that he understood not her speech, nor she his, so that neither could know who the other was; but being inordinately enamoured of her beauty, he sought by such mute blandishments as he could devise to declare his love, and bring her of her own accord to gratify his desire. All in vain, however; she repulsed his advances point blank; whereby his passion only grew the stronger. So some days passed; and the lady perceiving Pericone's constancy, and bethinking her that sooner or later she must yield either to force or to love, and gratify his passion, and judging by what she observed of the customs of the people that she was amongst Christians, and in a part where, were she able to speak their language, she would gain little by making herself known, determined with a lofty courage to stand firm and immovable in this extremity of her misfortunes. Wherefore she bade the three women, who were all that were left to her, on no account to let any know who they were, unless they were so circumstanced that they might safely count on assistance in effecting their escape: she also exhorted them most earnestly to preserve their chastity, averring that she was firmly resolved that none but her husband should enjoy her. The women heartily assented, and promised that her injunctions should be obeyed to the utmost of their power.

Day by day Pericone's passion waxed more ardent, being fomented by the proximity and contrariety of its object. Wherefore seeing that blandishment availed nothing, he was minded to have recourse to wiles and stratagems, and in the last resort to force. The lady, debarred by her law from the use of wine, found it, perhaps, on that account all the more palatable; which Pericone observing determined to enlist Bacchus in the service of Venus. So, ignoring her coyness, he provided one evening a supper which was ordered with all possible pomp and beauty, and graced by the presence of the lady. No lack was there of incentives to hilarity; and Pericone directed the servant who waited on Alatiel to ply her with divers sorts of blended wines; which command the man faithfully executed. She, suspecting nothing, and seduced by the delicious flavour of the liquor, drank somewhat more freely than was seemly, and forgetting her past woes, became frolicsome, and incited by some women who trod some measures in the Majorcan style, she showed the company how they footed it in Alexandria. This novel demeanour was by no means lost on Pericone, who saw in it a good omen of his speedy success; so, with profuse relays of food and wine he prolonged the supper far into the night.

When the guests were at length gone, he attended the lady alone to her chamber, where, the heat of the wine overpowering the cold counsels of modesty, she made no more account of Pericone's presence than if he had been one of her women, and forthwith undressed and went to bed. Pericone was not slow to follow her, and as soon as the light was out lay down by her side, and taking her in his arms, without the least demur on her part, began to solace himself with her after the manner of lovers; which experience – she knew not till then with what horn men butt – caused her to repent that she had not yielded to his blandishments; nor did she thereafter wait to be invited to such nights of delight, but many a time declared her readiness, not by words, for she had none to convey her meaning, but by gestures.

But this great felicity which she now shared with Pericone was not to last: for not content with making her, instead of the consort of a king, the mistress of a castellan, Fortune had now in store for her a harsher experience, though of an amorous character. Pericone had a brother, twenty-five years of age, fair and fresh as a rose, his name Marato. On sight of Alatiel Marato had been mightily taken with her; he inferred from her bearing that he stood high in her good graces; he believed that nothing stood between him and the gratification of his passion but the jealous vigilance with which Pericone guarded her. So musing, he hit upon a ruthless expedient, which had effect in action as hasty as heinous.

It so chanced that there then lay in the port of the city a ship commanded by two Genoese, bound with a cargo of merchandise for Klarenza in the Morea: her sails were already hoist; and she tarried only for a favourable breeze. Marato approached the masters and arranged with them to take himself and the lady aboard on the following night. This done he concerted further action with some of his most trusty friends, who readily lent him their aid to carry his design into execution. So on the following evening towards nightfall, the conspirators stole unobserved into Pericone's house, which was entirely unguarded, and there hid themselves, as pre-arranged. Then, as the night wore on, Marato showed them where Pericone and the lady slept, and they entered the room, and slew Pericone. The lady thus rudely roused wept; but silencing her by menaces of death they carried her off with the best part of Pericone's treasure, and hied them unobserved to the coast, where Marato parted from his companions, and forthwith took the lady aboard the ship. The wind was now fair and fresh, the mariners spread the canvas, and the vessel sped on her course.

This new misadventure, following so hard upon the former, caused the lady no small chagrin; but Marato, with the aid of the good St Crescent-in-hand that God has given us, found means to afford her such consolation that she was already grown so familiar with him as entirely to forget Pericone, when Fortune, not content with her former caprices, added a new dispensation of woe; for what with the beauty of her person, which, as we have often said, was extraordinary, and the exquisite charm of her manners, the two young men who commanded the ship fell so desperately in love with her that they thought of nothing but how they might best serve and please her, so only that Marato should not discover the reason of their assiduous attentions. And neither being ignorant of the other's love, they held secret counsel together, and resolved to make conquest of the lady on joint account: as if love admitted of being held in partnership like merchandise or money. Which design being thwarted by the jealousy with which Alatiel was guarded by Marato, they chose a day and hour when the ship was speeding amain under canvas and Marato was on the poop looking out over the sea and quite off his guard; and going stealthily up behind him, they suddenly laid hands on him, and threw him into the sea, and were already more than a mile on their course before any perceived that Marato was overboard. Which when the lady learned, and knew that he was irretrievably lost, she relapsed into her former plaintive mood. But the twain were forthwith by her side with soft speeches and profuse promises, which, however ill she understood them, were not altogether inapt to allay a grief which had in it more of concern for her own hapless self than of sorrow for her lost lover. So, in course of time, the lady beginning visibly to recover heart, they began privily to debate which of them should first take her to bed with him; and neither being willing to give way to the other, and no compromise being discoverable, high words passed between them, and the dispute grew so hot, that they both waxed very wroth, drew their knives, and rushed madly at one another, and before they could be parted by their men, several stabs had been given and received on either side, whereby the one fell dead on the spot, and the other was severely wounded in divers parts of the body. The lady was much disconcerted to find herself thus alone with none to afford her either succour or counsel, and was mightily afraid lest the wrath of the kinsfolk and friends of the twain should vent itself upon her. From this mortal peril she was, however, delivered by the intercessions of the wounded man and their speedy arrival at Klarenza.

As there she tarried at the same inn with her wounded lover, the fame of her great beauty was speedily bruited abroad, and reached the ears of the Prince of the Morea, who was then staying there. The Prince was curious to see her, and having so done, pronounced her even more beautiful than rumour had reported her; nay, he fell in love with her in such a degree that he could think of nought else; and having heard in what guise she had come thither, he deemed that he might have her. While he was casting about how to compass his end, the kinsfolk of the wounded man, being apprised of the fact, forthwith sent her to him to the boundless delight as well of the lady, who saw therein her deliverance from a great peril, as of the Prince. The royal bearing, which enhanced the lady's charms, did not escape the Prince, who, being unable to discover her true rank, set her down as at any rate of noble lineage; wherefore he loved her as much again as before, and showed her no small honour, treating her not as his mistress but as his wife. So the lady, contrasting her present happy estate with her past woes, was comforted; and, as her gaiety revived, her beauty waxed in such a degree that all the Morea talked of it and of little else: insomuch that the Prince's friend and kinsman, the young, handsome and gallant Duke of Athens, was smitten with a desire to see her, and taking occasion to pay the Prince a visit, as he was now and again wont to do, came to Klarenza with a goodly company of honourable gentlemen. The Prince received him with all distinction and made him heartily welcome, but did not at first show him the lady. By and by, however, their conversation began to turn upon her and her charms, and the Duke asked if she were really so marvellous a creature as folk said. The Prince replied – 'Nay, but even more so; and thereof thou shalt have better assurance than my words, to wit, the witness of thine own eyes.' So, without delay, for the Duke was now all impatience, they waited on the lady, who was prepared for their visit, and received them very courteously and graciously. They seated her between them, and being debarred from the pleasure of conversing with her, for of their speech she understood little or nothing, they both, and especially the Duke, who was scarce able to believe that she was of mortal mould, gazed upon her in mute admiration; whereby the Duke, cheating himself with the idea that he was but gratifying his curiosity, drank with his eyes, unawares, deep draughts of the poisoned chalice of love, and, to his own lamentable hurt, fell a prey to a most ardent passion. His first thought, when they had left her and he had time for reflection, was that the Prince was the luckiest man in the world to have a creature so fair to solace him; and swayed by his passion, his mind soon inclined to divers other and less honourable meditations, whereof the issue was that, come what might, he would despoil the Prince of his felicity, and, if possible, make it his own. This resolution was no sooner taken than, being of a hasty temperament, he cast to the winds all considerations of honour and justice, and studied only how to compass his end by craft. So one day, as the first step towards the accomplishment of his evil purpose, he arranged with the Prince's most trusted chamberlain, one Ciuriaci, that his horses and all his other personal effects should, with the utmost secrecy, be got ready against a possible sudden departure: and then at nightfall, attended by a single comrade (both carrying arms), he was privily admitted by Ciuriaci into the Prince's chamber. It was a hot night, and the Prince had risen without disturbing the lady, and was standing bare to the skin at an open window fronting the sea, to enjoy a light breeze that blew thence. So, by preconcert with his comrade, the Duke stole up to the window, and in a trice ran the Prince through the body, and caught him up, and threw him out of the window. The palace was close by the sea, but at a considerable altitude above it, and the window through which the Prince's body was thrown looked over some houses, which, being sapped by the sea, had become ruinous, and were rarely or never visited by a soul; whereby, as the

Duke had foreseen, the fall of the Prince's body passed, as indeed it could not but pass, unobserved. Thereupon the Duke's accomplice whipped out a halter, which he had brought with him for the purpose, and, making as if he were but in play, threw it round Ciuriaci's neck, drew it so tight that he could not utter a sound, and then, with the Duke's aid, strangled him, and sent him after his master. All this was accomplished, as the Duke knew full well, without awakening any in the palace, not even the lady, whom he now approached with a light, and holding it over the bed gently uncovered her person, as she lay fast asleep, and surveyed her from head to foot to his no small satisfaction; for fair as she had seemed to him dressed, he found her unadorned charms incomparably greater. As he gazed, his passion waxed beyond measure, and, reckless of his recent crime, and of the blood which still stained his hands, he got forthwith into the bed; and she, being too sound asleep to distinguish between him and the Prince, suffered him to lie with her.

But, boundless as was his delight, it brooked no long continuance; so, rising, he called to him some of his comrades, by whom he had the lady secured in such manner that she could utter no sound, and borne out of the palace by the same secret door by which he had gained entrance; he then set her on horseback and in dead silence put his troop in motion, taking the road to Athens. He did not, however, venture to take the lady to Athens, where she would have encountered his Duchess – for he was married – but lodged her in a very beautiful villa which he had hard by the city overlooking the sea, where, most forlorn of ladies, she lived secluded, but with no lack of meet and respectful service.

On the following morning the Prince's courtiers awaited his rising until noon, but perceiving no sign of it, opened the doors, which had not been secured, and entered his bedroom. Finding it vacant, they supposed that the Prince was gone off privily somewhere to have a few days of unbroken delight with his fair lady; and so they gave themselves no further trouble. But the next day it so chanced that an idiot, roaming about the ruins where lay the corpses of the Prince and Ciuriaci, drew the latter out by the halter and went off dragging it after him. The corpse was soon recognised by not a few, who, at first struck dumb with amazement, soon recovered sense enough to cajole the idiot into retracing his steps and showing them the spot where he had found it; and having thus, to the immeasurable grief of all the citizens, discovered the Prince's body, they buried it with all honour. Needless to say that no pains were spared to trace the perpetrators of so heinous a crime, and that the absence and evidently furtive departure of the

Duke of Athens caused him to be suspected both of the murder and of the abduction of the lady. So the citizens were instant with one accord that the Prince's brother, whom they chose as his successor, should exact the debt of vengeance; and he, having satisfied himself by further investigation that their suspicion was well founded, summoned to his aid his kinsfolk, friends and divers vassals, and speedily gathered a large, powerful and well-equipped army, with intent to make war upon the Duke of Athens. The Duke, being informed of his movements, made ready likewise to defend himself with all his power; nor had he any lack of allies, among whom the Emperor of Constantinople sent his son, Constantine, and his nephew, Manuel, with a great and goodly force. The two young men were honourably received by the Duke, and still more so by the Duchess, who was Constantine's sister.

Day by day war grew more imminent; and at last the Duchess took occasion to call Constantine and Manuel into her private chamber, and with many tears told them the whole story at large, explaining the *casus belli*, dilating on the indignity which she suffered at the hands of the Duke, if, as was believed, he really kept a mistress in secret, and beseeching them in most piteous accents to do the best they could to devise some expedient whereby the Duke's honour might be cleared, and her own peace of mind assured. The young men knew exactly how matters stood; and so, without wearying the Duchess with many questions, they did their best to console her, and succeeded in raising her hopes. Before taking their leave they learned from her where the lady was whose marvellous beauty they had heard lauded so often; and being eager to see her, they besought the Duke to afford them an opportunity. Forgetful of what a like complaisance had cost the Prince, he consented, and next morning brought them to the villa where the lady lived, and with her and a few of his boon companions regaled them with a lordly breakfast, which was served in a most lovely garden. Constantine had no sooner seated himself and surveyed the lady, than he was lost in admiration, inwardly affirming that he had never seen so beautiful a creature, and that for such a prize the Duke, or any other man, might well be pardoned treachery or any other crime: he scanned her again and again, and ever with more and more admiration; whereby it fared with him even as it had fared with the Duke. He went away hotly in love with her, and dismissing all thought of the war, cast about for some method by which, without betraying his passion to any, he might devise some means of wresting the lady from the Duke.

As he thus burned and brooded, the Prince drew dangerously near the Duke's dominions; wherefore order was given for an advance, and the Duke, with Constantine and the rest, marshalled his forces and led them forth from Athens to bar the Prince's passage of the frontier at certain points. Some days thus passed, during which Constantine, whose mind and soul were entirely absorbed by his passion for the lady, bethought him that as the Duke was no longer in her neighbourhood, he might readily compass his end. He therefore feigned to be seriously unwell, and, having by this pretext obtained the Duke's leave, he ceded his command to Manuel, and returned to his sister at Athens. He had not been there many days before the Duchess recurred to the dishonour which the Duke did her by keeping the lady; whereupon he said that of that, if she approved, he would certainly relieve her by seeing that the lady was removed from the villa to some distant place. The Duchess, supposing that Constantine was prompted not by jealousy of the Duke but by jealousy for her honour, gave her hearty consent to his plan, provided he so contrived that the Duke should never know that she had been privy to it; on which point Constantine gave her ample assurance. So, being authorised by the Duchess to act as he might deem best, he secretly equipped a light bark and manned her with some of his men, to whom he confided his plan, bidding them lie to off the garden of the lady's villa; and so, having sent the bark forward, he hied him with other of his men to the villa. He gained ready admission of the servants, and was made heartily welcome by the lady, who, at his desire, attended by some of her servants, walked with him and some of his comrades in the garden. By and by, feigning that he had a message for her from the Duke, he drew her aside towards a gate that led down to the sea, and which one of his confederates had already opened. A concerted signal brought the bark alongside, and to seize the lady and set her aboard the bark was but the work of an instant. Her retinue hung back as they heard Constantine menace with death whoso but stirred or spoke, and suffered him, protesting that what he did was done not to wrong the Duke but solely to vindicate his sister's honour, to embark with his men. The lady wept, of course, but Constantine was at her side, the rowers gave way, and the bark, speeding like a thing of life over the waves, made Egina shortly after dawn. There Constantine and the lady landed, she still lamenting her fatal beauty, and took a little rest and pleasure. Then, re-embarking, they continued their voyage, and in the course of a few days reached Chios, which Constantine, fearing paternal censure, and that he might be deprived of his fair booty, deemed a safe place of sojourn. So, after some days of repose the lady ceased to bewail her harsh destiny, and suffering Constantine to console her as his predecessors had done, began once more to enjoy the good gifts which Fortune sent her.

Now while they thus dallied, Osbech, King of the Turks, who was perennially at war with the Emperor, came by chance to Smyrna; and there learning that Constantine was wantoning in careless ease at Chios with a lady of whom he had made prize, he made a descent by night upon the island with an armed flotilla. Landing his men in dead silence, he made captives of not a few of the Chians whom he surprised in their beds; others, who took the alarm and rushed to arms, he slew; and having wasted the whole island with fire, he shipped the booty and the prisoners, and sailed back to Smyrna. As there he overhauled the booty, he lit upon the fair lady, and knew her for the same that had been taken in bed and fast asleep with Constantine: whereat, being a young man, he was delighted beyond measure, and made her his wife out of hand with all due form and ceremony. And so for several months he enjoyed her.

Now there had been for some time and still was a treaty pending between the Emperor and Basano, King of Cappadocia, whereby Basano with his forces was to fall on Osbech on one side while the Emperor attacked him on the other. Some demands made by Basano, which the Emperor deemed unreasonable, had so far retarded the conclusion of the treaty; but no sooner had the Emperor learned the fate of his son than, distraught with grief, he forthwith conceded the King of Cappadocia's demands, and was instant with him to fall at once upon Osbech while he made ready to attack him on the other side. Getting wind of the Emperor's design, Osbech collected his forces, and, lest he should be caught and crushed between the convergent armies of two most mighty potentates, advanced against the King of Cappadocia. The fair lady he left at Smyrna in the care of a faithful dependant and friend, and after a while joined battle with the King of Cappadocia, in which battle he was slain, and his army defeated and dispersed. Wherefore Basano with his victorious host advanced, carrying everything before him, upon Smyrna, and receiving everywhere the submission due to a conqueror.

Meanwhile Osbech's dependant, by name Antioco, who had charge of the fair lady, was so smitten with her charms that, albeit he was somewhat advanced in years, he broke faith with his friend and lord, and allowed himself to become enamoured of her. He had the advantage of knowing her language, which counted for much with one who for some years had been, as it were, compelled to live the life of a deaf mute, finding none whom she could understand or by whom she might be understood; and goaded by passion, he in the course of a few days established such a degree of intimacy with her that in no long time it passed from friendship into love, so that their lord, far away amid the clash of arms and the tumult of the battle, was forgotten, and marvellous pleasure had they of one another between the sheets.

However, news came at last of Osbech's defeat and death, and the victorious and unchecked advance of Basano, whose advent they were by no means minded to await. Wherefore, taking with them the best part of the treasure that Osbech had left there, they hied them with all possible secrecy to Rhodes. There they had not long abode before Antioco fell ill of a mortal disease. He had then with him a Cypriot merchant, an intimate and very dear friend, to whom, as he felt his end approach, he resolved to leave all that he possessed, including his dear lady. So, when he felt death imminent, he called them to him and said – ''Tis now quite evident to me that my life is fast ebbing away; and sorely do I regret it, for never had I so much pleasure of life as now. Well content indeed I am in one respect, in that, as die I must, I at least die in the arms of the two persons whom I love more than any other in the world, to wit, in thine arms, dearest friend, and those of this lady, whom, since I have known her, I have loved more than myself. But yet 'tis grievous to me to know that I must leave her here in a strange land with none to afford her either protection or counsel; and but that I leave her with thee, who, I doubt not, wilt have for my sake no less care of her than thou wouldst have had of me, 'twould grieve me still more; wherefore with all my heart and soul I pray thee, that, if I die, thou take her with all else that belongs to me into thy charge, and so acquit thyself of thy trust as thou mayst deem conducive to the peace of my soul. And of thee, dearest lady, I entreat one favour, that I be not forgotten of thee, after my death, so that there whither I go it may still be my boast to be beloved here of the most beautiful lady that nature ever formed. Let me but die with these two hopes assured, and without doubt I shall depart in peace.'

Both the merchant and the lady wept to hear him thus speak, and, when he had done, comforted him, and promised faithfully, in the event of his death, to do even as he besought them. He died almost immediately afterwards, and was honourably buried by them. A few days sufficed the merchant to wind up all his affairs in Rhodes; and being minded to return to Cyprus aboard a Catalan boat that was there, he asked the fair lady what she purposed to do if he went back to Cyprus. The lady answered, that, if it were agreeable to him, she would gladly accompany him, hoping that for love of Antioco he would treat and regard her as his sister. The merchant replied that it would afford him all the pleasure in the world; and, to protect her from insult until their arrival in Cyprus, he gave her out as his wife, and, suiting action to word, slept with her on the boat in an alcove in a little cabin in the poop. Whereby that happened which on neither side was intended when they left Rhodes, to wit, that the darkness and the comfort and the warmth of the bed, forces of no mean efficacy, did so prevail with them that dead Antioco was forgotten alike as lover and as friend, and by a common impulse they began to wanton together, insomuch that before they were arrived at Baffa, where the Cypriot resided, they were indeed man and wife. At Baffa the lady tarried with the merchant a good while, during which it so befell that a gentleman, Antigono by name, a man of ripe age and riper wisdom but no great wealth, being one that had had vast and various experience of affairs in the service of the King of Cyprus but had found fortune adverse to him, came to Baffa on business; and passing one day by the house where the fair lady was then living by herself, for the Cypriot merchant was gone to Armenia with some of his wares, he chanced to catch sight of the lady at one of the windows, and, being struck by her extraordinary beauty, regarded her attentively, and began to have some vague recollection of having seen her before, but could by no means remember where. The fair lady, however, so long the sport of Fortune, but now nearing the term of her woes, no sooner saw Antigono than she remembered to have seen him in her father's service, and in no mean capacity, at Alexandria. Wherefore she forthwith sent for him, hoping that by his counsel she might elude her merchant and be reinstated in her true character and dignity of princess. When he presented himself, she asked him with some embarrassment whether he were, as she took him to be, Antigono of Famagosta. He answered in the affirmative, adding – 'And of you, madam, I have a sort of recollection, though I cannot say where I have seen you; wherefore, so it irk you not, bring, I pray you, yourself to my remembrance.' Satisfied that it was Antigono himself, the lady in a flood of tears threw herself upon him to his no small amazement, and embraced his neck: then, after a little while, she asked him whether he had never seen her in Alexandria. The question awakened Antigono's memory; he at once recognised Alatiel, the Soldan's daughter, whom he had thought to have been drowned at sea, and would have paid her due homage; but she would not suffer it, and bade him be seated with her for a while. Being seated, he respectfully asked her, how, and when and whence she had come thither, seeing that all Egypt believed for certain that she had been drowned at sea some years before. 'And would that so it had been,' said the lady, 'rather than I should have led the life that I have led; and so doubtless will my father say, if he shall ever come to know of it.' And so saying, she burst into such a flood of tears that 'twas a wonder to see. Wherefore Antigono said to her – 'Nay but, madam, be not distressed before the occasion arises. I pray you, tell me the story of your adventures, and what has been the tenor of your life; perchance 'twill prove to be no such matter but, God helping us, we may set it all straight.' 'Antigono,' said the fair lady, 'when I saw thee, 'twas as if I saw my father, and 'twas the tender love I bear him that prompted me to make myself known to thee, though I might have kept my secret; and few indeed there are whom to have met would have afforded me such pleasure as this which I have in meeting and recognising thee before all others; wherefore I will now make known to thee as to a father that which in my evil fortune I have ever kept close. If, when thou hast heard my story, thou seest any means whereby I may be reinstated in my former honour, I pray thee use it. If not, disclose to none that thou hast seen me or heard aught of me.'

Then, weeping between every word, she told him her whole story from the day of the shipwreck at Majorca to that hour. Antigono wept in sympathy, and then said – 'Madam, as throughout this train of misfortunes you have happily escaped recognition, I undertake to restore you to your father in such sort that you shall be dearer to him than ever before, and be afterwards married to the King of Algarve.' 'How?' she asked. Whereupon he explained to her in detail how he meant to proceed; and, lest delay should give occasion to another to interfere, he went back at once to Famagosta, and having obtained audience of the King, thus he spoke – 'Sire, so please you, you have it in your power at little cost to yourself to do a thing which will at once redound most signally to your honour and confer a great boon on me, who have grown poor in your service.' 'How?' asked the King. Then said Antigono – 'At Baffa is of late arrived a fair damsel, daughter of the Soldan, long thought to be drowned, who to preserve her chastity has suffered long and severe hardship. She is now reduced to poverty, and is desirous of returning to her father. If you should be pleased to send her back to him under my escort, your honour and my interest would be served in high and equal measure; nor do I think that such a service would ever be forgotten by the Soldan.'

With true royal generosity the King forthwith signified his approval, and had Alatiel brought under honourable escort to Famagosta, where, attended by his Queen, he received her with every circumstance of festal pomp and courtly magnificence. Schooled by Antigono, she gave the King and Queen such a version of her adventures as satisfied their enquiries in every particular. So, after a few days, the King sent her back to the Soldan under escort of Antigono, attended by a goodly company of honourable men and women; and of the cheer which the Soldan made her, and not her only but Antigono and all his company, it boots not to ask. When she was somewhat rested, the Soldan enquired how it was that she was yet alive, and where she had been so long without letting him know how it fared with her. Whereupon the lady, who had got Antigono's lesson by heart, answered thus – 'My father, 'twas perhaps the twentieth night after my departure from you when our ship parted her timbers in a terrible storm and went ashore nigh a place called Aguamorta, away there in the West: what was the fate of the men that were aboard our ship I know not, nor knew I ever; I remember only, that, when day came, and I returned, as it were, from death to life, the wreck, having been sighted, was boarded by folk from all the countryside, intent on plunder; and I and two of my women were taken ashore, where the women were forthwith parted from me by the young men, nor did I ever learn their fate. Now hear my own. Struggling might and main, I was seized by two young men, who dragged me, weeping bitterly, by the hair of the head, towards a great forest; but, on sight of four men who were then passing that way on horseback, they forthwith loosed me and took to flight. Whereupon the four men, who struck me as persons of great authority, ran up to me; and much they questioned me, and much I said to them; but neither did they understand me, nor I them. So, after long time conferring together, they set me on one of their horses and brought me to a house, where dwelt a community of ladies, religious according to their law; and what the men may have said I know not, but there I was kindly received and ever honourably treated by all; and with them I did afterwards most reverentially pay my devotions to St Crescent-in-Hollow, who is held in great honour by the women of that country. When I had been some time with them, and had learned something of their language, they asked me who and whence I was: whereto I, knowing that I was in a convent, and fearing to be cast out as a foe to their law if I told the truth, answered that I was the daughter of a great gentleman of Cyprus, who had intended to marry me to a gentleman of Crete; but that on the voyage we had been driven out of our course and wrecked at Aguamorta. And so I continued, as occasion required, observing their usages with much assiduity, lest worse should befall me; but being one day asked by their superior, whom they call abbess, whether I was minded to go back to Cyprus, I answered that there was nought that I desired so much. However, so solicitous for my honour was the abbess, that there was none going to Cyprus to whom she would entrust me, until, two months or so ago, there arrived some worthy men from France, of whom one was a kinsman of the abbess, with their wives. They were on their way to visit the sepulchre where He whom they hold to be God was buried after He had suffered death at the hands of the Jews; and the abbess, learning their destination, prayed them to take charge of me, and restore me to my father in Cyprus. With what cheer, with what honour, these gentlemen and their wives entertained me, 'twere long to tell. But, in brief, we embarked, and in the course of a few days arrived at Baffa, where it was so ordered by the providence of God, who perchance took pity on me, that in the very hour of our disembarkation I, not knowing a soul and being at a loss how to answer the gentlemen, who would fain have discharged the trust laid upon them by the reverend abbess and restored me to my father, fell in, on the shore, with Antigono, whom I forthwith called, and in our language, that I might be understood neither of the gentlemen nor of their wives, bade him acknowledge me as his daughter. He understood my case at once, made much of me, and to the utmost of his slender power honourably requited the gentlemen. He then brought me to the King of Cyprus, who accorded me welcome there and conduct hither so honourable as words of mine can never describe. If aught remains to tell, you may best learn it from the lips of Antigono, who has often heard my story.'

Then Antigono, addressing the Soldan, said – 'Sire, what she has told you accords with what she has often told me, and with what I have learned from the gentlemen and ladies who accompanied her. One thing, however, she has omitted, because, I suppose, it hardly becomes her to tell it; to wit, all that the gentlemen and ladies, who accompanied her, said of the virtuous and gracious and noble life which she led with the devout ladies, and of the tears and wailings of both the ladies and the gentlemen, when they parted with her to me. But were I to essay to repeat all that they said to me, the day that now is, and the night that is to follow, were all too short: suffice it to say so much as this, that by what I gathered from their words and have been able to see for myself, you may make it your boast that among all the daughters of all your peers that wear the crown none can be matched with yours for virtue and true worth.'

By all which the Soldan was so overjoyed that 'twas a wonder to see. Again and again he made supplication to God, that of His grace power might be vouchsafed him adequately to recompense all who had done honour to his daughter, and most especially the King of Cyprus, for the honourable escort under which he had sent her thither; for Antigono he provided a magnificent reward, and some days later gave him his *congé* to return to Cyprus, at the same time by a special messenger conveying to the King his grateful acknowledgements of the manner in which he had treated his daughter. Then, being minded that his first intent, to wit, that his daughter should be the bride of the King of Algarve, should not be frustrated, he wrote to the King telling him all, and adding that, if he were still minded to have her, he might send for her. The King was overjoyed by these tidings, and having sent for her with great pomp, gave her on her arrival a hearty welcome. So she, who had lain with eight men in all, perhaps ten thousand times, was bedded with him as a virgin, and made him believe that a virgin she was, and lived long and happily with him as his queen: wherefore 'twas said – 'Mouth, for kisses, was never the worse: like as the moon reneweth her course.'

❧ 7 ❧

The tenth story of the second day, in which Paganino da Monaco carries off the wife of Messer Ricciardo di Chinzica, who, having learned where she is, goes to Paganino and in a friendly manner asks him to restore her. He consents, provided she be willing. She refuses to go back with her husband. Messer Ricciardo dies, and she marries Peganino.

Their queen's story [not included here] elicited hearty commendation from all the honourable company, and most especially from Dioneo, with whom it now rested to conclude the day's narration. Again and again he renewed his eulogy of the queen's story; and then began on this wise: ❧ Fair ladies, there is that in the queen's story which has caused me to change my purpose, and substitute another story for that which I had meant to tell: I refer to the insensate folly of Bernabò (well though it was with him in the end) and of all others, who delude themselves, as he seemed to do, with the vain imagination that, while they go about the world, taking their pleasure now of this, now of the other woman, their wives left at home suffer not their hands to stray from their girdles; as if we, who are born of them and bred among them, could be ignorant of the bent of their desires. Wherefore, by my story I purpose at one and the same time to show you how great is the folly of all such, and how much greater is the folly of those who, deeming themselves mightier than nature, think by sophistical arguments to bring that to pass which is beyond their power, and strive might and main to conform others to their own pattern, however little the nature of the latter may brook such treatment –

Know then that there was in Pisa a judge, better endowed with mental than with physical vigour, by name Messer Ricciardo di Chinzica, who, being minded to take a wife, and thinking, perhaps, to satisfy her by the same resources which served him for his studies, was to be suited with none that had not both youth and beauty, qualities which he would rather have eschewed, if he had known how to give himself as good counsel as he gave to others. However, being very rich, he had his desire. Messer Lotto Gualandi gave him in marriage one of his daughters, Bartolomea by name, a maid as fair and fit for amorous dalliance as any in Pisa, though few maids be there that do not show as spotted lizards. The judge brought her home with all pomp and ceremony, and had a brave and lordly wedding; but in the essay which he made the very first night to serve her so as to consummate the marriage he made a false move, and drew the game much to his own disadvantage; for next morning his lean, withered and scarce animate frame was only to be re-quickened by draughts of vernaccia,* artificial restoratives and the like remedies. So, taking a more sober estimate of his powers than he had been wont, the worthy judge began to give his wife lessons from a calendar, which might have served as a horn-book, and perhaps had been put together at Ravenna:† inasmuch as, according to his showing, there was not a day in the year but was sacred, not to one saint only, but to many; in honour of whom for divers reasons it behoved men and women to abstain from carnal intercourse; whereto he added fast-days, Ember-days, vigils of Apostles and other saints, Friday, Saturday, Sunday, the whole of Lent, certain phases of the moon, and many other exceptions, arguing perchance, that the practice of men with women abed should have its times of vacation no less than the administration of the law. In this method, which caused the lady grievous dumps, he long persisted, hardly touching her once a month, and observing her closely lest another should give her to know working-days, as he had taught her holidays.

Now it so befell that, one hot season, Messer Ricciardo thought he would like to visit a very beautiful estate which he had near Monte Nero, there to take the air and recreate himself for some days, and thither accordingly he went with his fair lady. While there, to amuse her, he arranged for a day's fishing; and so, he in one boat with the fishermen, and she in another with other ladies, they put out to watch

* A strong white wine.

† The saying went, that owing to the multitude of churches at Ravenna every day was there a saint's day.

the sport, which they found so delightsome that almost before they knew where they were they were some miles out to sea. And while they were thus engrossed with the sport, a galliot of Paganino da Mare, a very famous corsair of those days, hove in sight and bore down upon the boats, and, for all the speed they made, came up with that in which were the ladies; and on sight of the fair lady Paganino, regardless of all else, bore her off to his galliot before the very eyes of Messer Ricciardo, who was by this time ashore, and forthwith was gone. The chagrin of the judge, who was jealous of the very air, may readily be imagined. But 'twas to no purpose that, both at Pisa and elsewhere, he moaned and groaned over the wickedness of the corsairs, for he knew neither by whom his wife had been abducted, nor whither she had been taken. Paganino, meanwhile, deemed himself lucky to have got so beautiful a prize; and being unmarried, he was minded never to part with her, and addressed himself by soft words to soothe the sorrow which kept her in a flood of tears. Finding words of little avail, he at night passed – the more readily that the calendar had slipped from his girdle, and all feasts and holidays from his mind – to acts of love, and on this wise administered consolation so effective that before they were come to Monaco she had completely forgotten the judge and his canons, and had begun to live with Paganino as merrily as might be. So he brought her to Monaco, where, besides the daily and nightly solace which he gave her, he honourably treated her as his wife.

Not long afterwards Messer Ricciardo coming to know where his wife was, and being most ardently desirous to have her back, and thinking none but he would understand exactly what to do in the circumstances, determined to go and fetch her himself, being prepared to spend any sum of money that might be demanded by way of ransom. So he took ship, and being come to Monaco, he both saw her and was seen by her; which news she communicated to Paganino in the evening, and told him how she was minded to behave. Next morning Messer Ricciardo, encountering Paganino, made up to him; and soon assumed a very familiar and friendly air, while Paganino pretended not to know him, being on his guard to see what he would be at. So Messer Ricciardo, as soon as he deemed the time ripe, as best and most delicately he was able, disclosed to Paganino the business on which he had come, praying him to take whatever in the way of ransom he chose and restore him the lady. Paganino replied cheerily – 'Right glad I am to see you here, Sir; and briefly thus I answer you – True it is that I have here a young woman; whether she be your wife or another man's, I know not, for you are none of my acquaintance, nor is she, except for the short time that she has been with me. If, as you say, you are her husband, why, as you seem to me to be a pleasant gentleman, I will even take you to her, and I doubt not she will know you well; if she says that it is even as you say, and is minded to go with you, you shall give me just what you like by way of ransom, so pleasant have I found you; otherwise 'twill be churlish in you to think of taking her from me, who am a young man, and as fit to keep a woman as another, and moreover never knew any woman so agreeable.' 'My wife,' said Ricciardo, 'she is beyond all manner of doubt, as thou shalt see; for so soon as thou bringest me to her, she will throw her arms about my neck; wherefore as thou art minded, even so be it; I ask no more.' 'Go we then,' said Paganino; and forthwith they went into the house, and Paganino sent for the lady while they waited in one of the halls. By and by she entered from one of the adjoining rooms all trim and tricked out, and advanced to the place where Paganino and Messer Ricciardo were standing, but never a word did she vouchsafe to her husband, any more than if he had been some stranger whom Paganino had brought into the house. Whereat the judge was mightily amazed, having expected to be greeted by her with the heartiest of cheer, and began to ruminate thus – Perhaps I am so changed by the melancholy and prolonged heartache, to which I have been a prey since I lost her, that she does not recognise me. Wherefore he said – 'Madam, cause enough have I to rue it that I took thee a-fishing, for never yet was known such grief as has been mine since I lost thee; and now it seems as if thou dost not recognise me, so scant of courtesy is thy greeting. Seest thou not that I am thy Messer Ricciardo, come hither prepared to pay whatever this gentleman, in whose house we are, may demand, that I may have thee back and take thee away with me: and he is so good as to surrender thee on my own terms?' The lady turned to him with a slight smile, and said – 'Is it to me you speak, Sir? Bethink you that you may have mistaken me for another, for I, for my part, do not remember ever to have seen you.' 'Nay,' said Messer Ricciardo, 'but bethink thee what thou sayst; scan me closely; and if thou wilt but search thy memory, thou wilt find that I am thy Ricciardo di Chinzica.' 'Your pardon, Sir,' answered the lady, ' 'tis not, perhaps, as seemly for me as you imagine to gaze long upon you; but I have gazed long enough to know that I never saw you before.' Messer Ricciardo supposed that she so spoke for fear of Paganino, in whose presence she durst not acknowledge that she knew him: so, after a while, he craved as a favour of Paganino that he might speak with her in a room alone. Which request Paganino granted, so only that he did not kiss her against her will. He then bade the lady go with Messer Ricciardo into a room apart, and hear what he had to say, and give him such answer as she deemed meet. So the lady and Messer Ricciardo went together into a room alone, and sat down, and Messer Ricciardo began on this wise – 'Ah! dear heart of me, sweet soul of me, hope of me, dost not recognise thy Ricciardo that loves thee better than himself? how comes it thus to pass? am I then so changed? Ah! goodly eye of me, do but look on me a little.' Whereat the lady burst into a laugh, and interrupting him, said – 'Rest assured that my memory is not so short but that I know you for what you are, my husband, Messer Ricciardo di Chinzica; but far enough you showed yourself to be, while I was with you, from knowing me for what I was, young, lusty, lively; which, had you been the wise man you would fain be reputed, you would not have ignored, nor by consequence that which, besides food and clothing, it behoves men to give young ladies, albeit for shame they demand it not; which in what sort you gave, you know. You should not have taken a wife if she was to be less to you than the study of the law, albeit 'twas never as a judge that I regarded you, but rather as a bellman of dedicaton festivals and saints' days, so well you knew them all, and fasts and vigils. And I tell you that, had you imposed the observance of as many saints' days on the labourers that till your lands as on yourself who had but my little plot to till, you would never have harvested a single grain of corn. God in His mercy, having regard unto my youth, has caused me to fall in with this gentleman, with whom I am much closeted in this room, where nought is known of feasts, such feasts, I mean, as you, more devoted to the service of God than to the service of ladies, were wont to observe in such profusion; nor was this threshold ever crossed by Saturday or Friday or vigil or Ember-days or Lent, that is so long; rather here we are at work day and night, threshing the wool, and well I know how featly it went when the matin bell last sounded. Wherefore with him I mean to stay, and to work while I am young, and postpone the observance of feasts and times of indulgence and fasts until I am old: so get you hence, and good luck go with you, but depart with what speed you may, and observe as many feasts as you like, so I be not with you.

The pain with which Messer Ricciardo followed this outburst was more than he could bear, and when she had done, he exclaimed – 'Ah! sweet soul of me, what words are these that thou utterest? Hast thou no care for thy parents' honour and thine own? Wilt thou remain here to be this man's harlot, and to live in mortal sin, rather than live with me at Pisa as my wife? Why, when he is tired of thee, he will cast thee out to thy most grievous dishonour. I will ever cherish thee, and ever, will I nill I, thou wilt be the mistress of my house. Wouldst thou, to gratify this unbridled and unseemly passion, part at once with thy honour and with me, who love thee more dearly than my very life? Ah! cherished hope of me, say not so again: make up thy mind to come with me. As I now know thy bent, I will henceforth constrain myself to pleasure thee: wherefore, sweet my treasure, think better of it, and come with me, who have never known a happy hour since thou wert reft from me.' The lady answered – 'I expect not, nor is it possible, that another should be more tender of my honour than I am myself. Were my parents so, when they gave me to you? I trow not; nor mean I to be more tender of their honour now than they were then of mine. And if now I live in mortar sin, I will ever abide there until it be pestle sin:* concern yourself no further on my account. Moreover, let me tell you that, whereas at Pisa 'twas as if I were your harlot, seeing that the planets in conjunction according to astronomical table and geometric square intervened between you and me, here with Paganino I deem myself a wife, for he holds me in his arms all night long and hugs and bites me, and how he serves me, God be my witness. Ah! but you say you will constrain yourself to serve me: to what end? to do it on the third essay, and raise it by stroke of bâton? I doubt not you are become a perfect knight since last I saw you. Begone, and constrain yourself to live; for here, methinks, your tenure is but precarious, so hectic and wasted is your appearance. Nay more; I tell you this, that, should Paganino desert me (which he does not seem disposed to do so long as I am willing to stay with him), never will I return to your house, where for one while I stayed to my most grievous loss and prejudice, but will seek my commodity elsewhere than with one from whose whole body I could not wring a single cupful of sap. So, again, I tell you that here is neither feast nor vigil; wherefore here I mean to abide; and you, get you gone in God's name with what speed you may, lest I raise the cry that you threaten to violate me.'

Messer Ricciardo felt himself hard bested, but he could not but recognise that, worn out as he was, he had been foolish to take a young wife; so sad and woebegone he quitted the room, and, after expending on Paganino a wealth of words which signified nothing, he at last gave up his bootless enterprise, and leaving the lady to her own devices, returned to Pisa; where for very grief he lapsed into such utter imbecility that, when he was met by any with greeting or question in the street, he made no other answer than 'the evil hole brooks no

* A poor *jeu de mots*, mortar being substituted for mortal.

holiday,' and soon afterwards died. Which when Paganino learned, being well assured of the love the lady bore him, he made her his lawful wife; and so, keeping neither feast nor vigil nor Lent, they worked as hard as their legs permitted, and had a good time. Wherefore, dear my ladies, I am of opinion that Messer Bernabò in his altercation with Ambrogiuolo rode the goat downhill.*

This story provoked so much laughter that the jaws of everyone in the company ached; and all the ladies by common consent acknowledged that Dioneo was right, and pronounced Bernabò a blockhead. But when the story was ended and the laughter had subsided, the queen, observing that the hour was now late, and that with the completion of the day's storytelling the end of her sovereignty was come, followed the example of her predecessor, and took off her wreath and set it on Neifile's brow, saying with gladsome mien, 'Now, dear gossip, thine be the sovereignty of this little people;' and so she resumed her seat. Neifile coloured somewhat to receive such honour, showing of aspect even as the fresh-blown rose of April or May in the radiance of the dawn, her eyes rather downcast and glowing with love's fire like the morning-star. But when the respectful murmur by which the rest of the company gave blithe token of the favour in which they held their queen was hushed, and her courage revived, she raised herself somewhat more in her seat than she was wont, and thus spoke – 'As so it is that I am your queen, I purpose not to depart from the usage observed by my predecessors, whose rule has commanded not only your obedience but your approbation. I will therefore in few words explain to you the course which, if it commend itself to your wisdom, we will follow. Tomorrow, you know, is Friday, and the next day Saturday, days which most folk find somewhat wearisome by reason of the viands which are then customary, to say nothing of the reverence in which Friday is meet to be held, seeing that 'twas on that day that He who died for us bore His passion; wherefore 'twould be in my judgement both right and very seemly if, in honour of God, we then bade story-telling give place to prayer. On Saturday ladies are wont to wash the head, and rid their persons of whatever of dust or other soiling they may have gathered by the labours of the past week; not a few, likewise, are wont to practise abstinence for devotion to the Virgin Mother of the Son of God, and to honour the approaching Sunday by an entire surcease from work. Wherefore, as we cannot then

* i.e. argued preposterously, the goat being the last animal to carry a rider comfortably downhill.

completely carry out our plan of life, we shall, I think, do well to intermit our story-telling on that day also. We shall then have been here four days; and lest we should be surprised by new-comers, I deem it expedient that we shift our quarters, and I have already taken thought for our next place of sojourn. Where, being arrived on Sunday, we will assemble after our sleep; and whereas today our discourse has had an ample field to range in, I propose, both because you will thereby have more time for thought, and it will be best to set some limits to the licence of our story-telling, that of the many diversities of Fortune's handiwork we make one our theme, whereof I have also made choice, to wit, the luck of such as have painfully acquired some much-coveted thing, or having lost, have recovered it. Wherein let each meditate some matter which to tell may be profitable or at least delectable to the company, saving always Dioneo's privilege.'

All applauded the queen's speech and plan, to which, therefore, it was decided to give effect. Thereupon the queen called her seneschal, told him where to place the tables that evening, and then explained to him all that he had to do during the time of her sovereignty. This done, she rose with her train, and gave leave to all to take their pleasure as to each might seem best. So the ladies and the men hied them away to a little garden, where they diverted themselves a while; then supper-time being come, they supped with all gay and festal cheer. When they were risen from the table, Emilia, at the queen's command, led the dance, while Pampinea, the other ladies responding, sang the ensuing song.

Shall any lady sing, if I not sing,
I to whom Love did full contentment bring?

Come hither, Love, thou cause of all my joy,
Of all my hope, and all its sequel blest,
And with me tune the lay,
No more to sighs and bitter past annoy,
That now but serve to lend thy bliss more zest;
But to that fire's clear ray,
Wherewith enwrapped I blithely live and gay,
Thee as my God for ever worshipping.

'Twas thou, O Love, didst set before mine eyes,
When first thy fire my soul did penetrate,
A youth to be my fere,
So fair so fit for deeds of high emprise,

That ne'er another shall be found more great,
Nay, nor, I ween, his peer:
Such flame he kindled that my heart's full cheer
I now pour out in chant with thee, my King.

And that wherein I most delight is this,
That as I love him, so he loveth me:
So thank thee, Love, I must.
For whatsoe'er this world can yield of bliss
Is mine, and in the next at peace to be
I hope through that full trust
I place in him. And thou, O God, that dost
It see, wilt grant of joy thy plenishing.

Some other songs and dances followed, to the accompaniment of divers sorts of music; after which, the queen deeming it time to go to rest, all, following in the wake of the torches, sought their several chambers. The next two days they devoted to the duties to which the queen had adverted, looking forward to the Sunday with eager expectancy.

8

The first story of the third day, in which Masetto da Lamporecchio feigns to be dumb, and obtains a gardener's place at a convent of women, who with one accord make haste to lie with him.

Fairest ladies, not a few there are both of men and of women who are so foolish as blindly to believe that, so soon as a young woman has been veiled in white and cowled in black, she ceases to be a woman, and is no more subject to the cravings proper to her sex, than if, in assuming the garb and profession of a nun, she had put on the nature of a stone: and if, perchance, they hear of aught that is counter to this their faith, they are no less vehement in their censure than if some most heinous and unnatural crime had been committed; neither bethinking them of themselves, whom unrestricted liberty avails not to satisfy, nor making due allowance for the powerful forces of idleness and solitude. And likewise not a few there are that blindly believe that, what with the hoe and the spade and coarse fare and hardship, the carnal propensities are utterly eradicated from the tillers of the soil, and therewith all nimbleness of wit and understanding. But how gross is the error of such as so suppose, I, on whom the queen has laid her commands, am minded, without deviating from the theme prescribed by her, to make manifest to you by a little story –

In this very countryside of ours there was and yet is a convent of women of great repute for sanctity – name it I will not, lest I should in some measure diminish its repute – the nuns being at the time of which I speak but nine in number, including the abbess, and all young women. Their very beautiful garden was in charge of a foolish fellow, who, not being content with his wage, squared accounts with their steward and hied him back to Lamporecchio whence he came. Among others who welcomed him home was a young husbandman, Masetto by name, a stout and hardy fellow, and handsome for a contadino, who asked him where he had been so long. Nuto, as our good friend was called, told him. Masetto then asked how he had been employed at the convent, and Nuto answered – 'I kept their large and beautiful garden in good trim, and, besides, I sometimes went to the wood to fetch the faggots, I drew water, and did some other trifling services; but the ladies gave so little wage that it scarce kept me in shoes. And moreover they are all young, and I think they are one and all possessed of the devil, for 'tis impossible to do anything to their mind; indeed, when I would be at work in the kitchen-garden, "put this here," would say one, "put that here," would say another, and a third would snatch the hoe from my hand, and say, "that is not as it should be"; and so they would worry me until I would give up working and go out of the garden; so that, what with this thing and that, I was minded to stay there no more, and so I am come hither. The steward asked me before I left to send him anyone whom on my return I might find fit for the work, and I promised; but God bless his loins, I shall be at no pains to find out and send him anyone.'

As Nuto thus ran on, Masetto was seized by such a desire to be with these nuns that he had quite pined, as he gathered from what Nuto said that his desire must be gratified. And as that could not be, if he said nothing to Nuto, he remarked – 'Ah! 'twas well done of thee to come hither. A man to live with women! he might as well live with so many devils: six times out of seven they know not themselves what they want.' There the conversation ended; but Masetto began to cast about how he should proceed to get permission to live with them. He knew that he was quite competent for the services of which Nuto spoke, and had therefore no fear of failing on that score; but he doubted he should not be received, because he was too young and well-favoured. So, after much pondering, he fell into the following train of thought – The place is a long way off, and no one there knows me; if I make believe that I am dumb, doubtless I shall be admitted. Whereupon he made his mind up, laid a hatchet across his shoulder, and saying not a word to any of his destination, set forth, intending to present himself at the convent in the character of a destitute man. Arrived there, he had no sooner entered than he chanced to encounter the steward in the courtyard, and making signs to him as dumb folk do, he let him know that of his charity he craved something to eat, and that, if need were, he would split firewood. The steward promptly gave him to eat, and then set before him some logs which Nuto had not been able to split, all which Masetto, who was very strong, split in a very short time. The steward, having occasion to go to the wood, took him with him, and there set him at work on the lopping; which done he placed the ass in front of him, and by signs made him understand that he was to take the loppings back to the convent. This he did so well that the steward kept him for some days to do one or two odd jobs. Whereby it so befell that one day the abbess saw him, and asked the steward who he was. 'Madam,' replied the steward, ' 'tis a poor deaf mute that came here a day or two ago craving alms, so I have treated him kindly, and have let him make himself useful in many ways. If he knew how to do the work of the kitchen-garden and would stay with us, I doubt we should be well served; for we have need of him, and he is strong, and would be able for whatever he might turn his hand to; besides which you would have no cause to be apprehensive lest he should be cracking his jokes with your young women.' 'As I trust in God,' said the abbess, 'thou sayst sooth; find out if he can do the garden work, and if he can, do all thou canst to keep him with us; give him a pair of shoes, an old hood, and speak him well, make much of him, and let him be well fed.' All which the steward promised to do.

Masetto, meanwhile, was close at hand, making as if he were sweeping the courtyard, and heard all that passed between the abbess and the steward, whereat he gleefully communed with himself on this wise – Put me once within there, and you will see that I will do the work of the kitchen-garden as it never was done before. So the steward set him to work in the kitchen-garden, and finding that he knew his business excellently well, made signs to him to know whether he would stay, and he made answer by signs that he was ready to do whatever the steward wished. The steward then signified that he was engaged, told him to take charge of the kitchen-garden, and showed him what he had to do there. Then, having other matters to attend to, he went away, and left him there. Now, as Masetto worked there day by day, the nuns began to tease him, and make him their butt (as it commonly happens that folk serve the dumb) and used bad language to him, the worst they could think of, supposing that he could not understand them: all which passed scarce heeded by the abbess, who perhaps deemed him as destitute of virility as of speech. Now it so befell that after a hard day's work he was taking a little rest, when two young nuns, who were walking in the garden, approached the spot where he lay, and stopped to look at him, while he pretended to be asleep. And so the bolder of the two said to the other – 'If I thought thou wouldst keep the secret, I would tell thee what I have sometimes meditated, and which thou perhaps mightest also find agreeable.' The other replied – 'Speak thy mind freely and be sure that I will never tell a soul.' Whereupon the bold one began – 'I know not if thou hast ever considered how close we are kept here, and that within these precincts dare never enter any man, unless it be the old steward or this mute: and I have often heard from ladies that have come hither, that all the other sweets that the world has to offer signify not a jot in comparison of the pleasure that a woman has in connection with a man. Whereof I have more than once been minded to make experiment with this mute, no other man being available. Nor, indeed, could one find any man in the whole world so meet therefore; seeing that he could not blab if he would; thou seest that he is but a dull clownish lad, whose size has increased out of all proportion to his sense; wherefore I would fain hear what thou hast to say to it.' 'Alas!' said the other, 'what is 't thou sayst? Knowest thou not that we have vowed our virginity to God?' 'Oh,' rejoined the first, 'think but how many vows are made to Him all day long, and never a one performed: and so, for our vow, let Him find another or others to perform it.' 'But,' said her companion, 'suppose that we conceived, how then?' 'Nay but,' protested the first, 'thou goest about to imagine evil before it befalls thee: time enough to think of that when it comes to pass; there will be a thousand ways to prevent its ever being known, so only we do not publish it ourselves.' Thus reassured, the other was now the more eager of the two to test the quality of the male human animal. 'Well then,' she said, 'how shall we go about it?' and was answered – 'Thou seest 'tis past noon; I make no doubt but all the sisters are asleep, except ourselves; search we through the kitchen-garden, to see if there be any there, and if there be none, we have but to take him by the hand and lead him hither to the hut where he takes shelter from the rain; and then one shall mount guard while the other has him with her inside. He is such a simpleton that he will do just whatever we bid him.' No word of this conversation escaped Masetto, who, being disposed to obey, hoped for nothing so much as that one of them should take him by the hand. They, meanwhile, looked carefully all about them, and satisfied themselves that they were secure from observation: then she that had broached the subject came close up to Masetto, and shook him; whereupon he started to his feet. So she took him by the hand with a blandishing air, to which he replied with some clownish grins. And then she led him into the hut, where he needed no pressing to do what she desired of him. Which done, she changed places with the other, as loyal comradeship required; and Masetto, still keeping up the pretence of simplicity, did their pleasure. Wherefore before they left, each must needs make another assay of the mute's powers of riding; and afterwards, talking the matter over many times, they agreed that it was in truth not less but even more delightful than they had been given to understand; and so, as they found convenient opportunity, they continued to go and disport themselves with the mute.

Now it so chanced that one of their gossips, looking out of the window of her cell, saw what they did, and imparted it to two others. The three held counsel together whether they should not denounce the offenders to the abbess, but soon changed their mind, and came to an understanding with them, whereby they became partners in Masetto. And in course of time by divers chances the remaining three nuns also entered the partnership. Last of all the abbess, still witting nought of these doings, happened one very hot day, as she walked by herself through the garden, to find Masetto, who now rode so much by night that he could stand very little fatigue by day, stretched at full length asleep under the shade of an almond tree, his person quite exposed in front by reason that the wind had disarranged his clothes. Which the lady observing, and knowing that she was alone, fell a prey to the same appetite to which her nuns had yielded: she aroused Masetto, and took him with her to her chamber, where, for some days, though the nuns loudly complained that the gardener no longer came to work in the kitchen-garden, she kept him, tasting and re-tasting the sweetness of that indulgence which she was wont to be the first to censure in others. And when at last she had sent him back from her chamber to his room, she must needs send for him again and again, and made such exorbitant demands upon him, that Masetto, not being able to satisfy so many women, bethought him that his part of mute, should he persist in it, might entail disastrous consequences. So one night, when he was with the abbess, he cut the tongue-string, and thus broke silence – 'Madam, I have understood that a cock may very well serve ten hens, but that ten men are sorely tasked to satisfy a single woman; and here am I expected to serve nine, a burden quite beyond my power to bear; nay, by what I have already undergone I am now so reduced that my strength is quite spent; wherefore either bid me Godspeed, or find some means to make matters tolerable.' Wonder-struck to hear the supposed mute thus speak, the lady exclaimed – 'What means this? I took thee to be dumb.' 'And in sooth, Madam, so was I,' said Masetto, 'not indeed from my birth, but through an illness which took from me the power of speech, which only this very night have I recovered; and so I praise God with all my heart.' The lady believed him; and asked him what he meant by saying that he had nine to serve. Masetto told her how things stood; whereby she perceived that of all her nuns there was not any but was much wiser than she; and lest, if Masetto were sent away, he should give the convent a bad name, she discreetly determined to arrange matters with the nuns in such sort that he might remain there. So, the steward having died within the last few days, she assembled all the nuns; and their and her own past errors being fully avowed, they by common consent, and with Masetto's concurrence, resolved that the neighbours should be given to understand that by their prayers and the merits of their patron saint, Masetto, long mute, had recovered the power of speech; after which they made him steward, and so ordered matters among themselves that he was able to endure the burden of their service. In the course of which, though he procreated not a few little monastics, yet 'twas all managed so discreetly that no breath of scandal stirred, until after the abbess's death, by which time Masetto was advanced in years and minded to return home with the wealth that he had gotten; which he was suffered to do as soon as he made his desire known. And so Masetto, who had left Lamporecchio with a hatchet on his shoulder, returned thither in his old age rich and a father, having by the wisdom with which he employed his youth, spared himself the pains and expense of rearing children, and averring that such was the measure that Christ meted out to the man that set horns on his cap.

❧ 9 ❧

The second story of the third day, in which a groom lies with the wife of King Agilulf, who learns the fact, keeps his own counsel, finds out the groom and shears him. The shorn shears all his fellows, and so comes safe out of the scrape.

Filostrato's story, which the ladies had received now with blushes now with laughter, being ended, the queen bade Pampinea follow suit. Which behest Pampinea smilingly obeyed, and thus began: ❧ Some there are whose indiscretion is such that they must needs evince that they are fully cognisant of that which it were best they should not know, and censuring the covert misdeeds of others, augment beyond measure the disgrace which they would fain diminish. The truth whereof, fair ladies, I mean to show you in the contrary case, wherein appears the astuteness of one that held, perhaps, an even lower place than would have been Masetto's in the esteem of a doughty king –

Agilulf, King of the Lombards, who like his predecessors made the city of Pavia in Lombardy the seat of his government, took to wife Theodelinde, the widow of Authari, likewise King of the Lombards, a lady very fair, wise and virtuous, but who was unfortunate in her lover. For while the Lombards prospered in peace under the wise and firm rule of King Agilulf, it so befell that one of the Queen's grooms, a man born to very low estate, but in native worth far above his mean office, and moreover not a whit less tall and goodly of person than the King, became inordinately enamoured of her. And as, for all his base condition, he had sense enough to recognise that his love was in the last degree presumptuous, he disclosed it to none, nay, he did not even venture to tell her the tale by the mute eloquence of his eyes. And albeit he lived without hope that he should ever be able to win her favour, yet he inwardly gloried that he had fixed his affections in so high a place; and being all aflame with passion, he showed himself zealous beyond any of his comrades to do whatever he thought was likely to please the Queen. Whereby it came about that when the Queen had to take horse, she would mount the palfrey that he groomed rather than any other; and when she did so, he deemed himself most highly favoured, and never quitted her stirrup, esteeming himself happy if he might but touch her clothes. But as 'tis frequently observed that love waxes as hope wanes, so was it with this poor groom, insomuch that the burden of this great hidden passion, alleviated by no hope, was most grievous to bear, and from time to time, not being able to shake it off, he purposed to die. And meditating on the mode, he was minded that it should be of a kind to make it manifest that he died for the love which he had borne and bore to the Queen, and also to afford him an opportunity of trying his fortune whether his desire might in whole or in part be gratified. He had no thought of speaking to the Queen, nor yet of declaring his love to her by letter, for he knew that 'twould be vain either to speak or to write; but he resolved to try to devise some means whereby he might lie with the Queen; which end might in no other way be compassed than by contriving to get access to her in her bedroom; which could only be by passing himself off as the King, who, as he knew, did not always lie with her. Wherefore, that he might observe the carriage and dress of the King as he passed to her room, he contrived to conceal himself for several nights in a great hall of the King's palace which separated the King's room from that of the Queen: and on one of these nights he saw the King issue from his room, wrapped in a great mantle, with a lighted torch in one hand and a wand in the other, and cross the hall, and, saying nothing, tap the door of the Queen's room with the wand once or twice; whereupon the door was at once opened and the torch taken from his hand. Having observed the King thus go and return, and being bent on doing likewise, he found means to come by a mantle like that which he had seen the King wear, and also a torch and a wand: he then took a warm bath, and having thoroughly cleansed himself, that the smell of the foul straw might not offend the lady, or discover to her the deceit, he in this guise concealed himself as he was wont in the great hall. He waited only until all were asleep, and then, deeming the time come to accomplish his purpose, or by his presumption clear a way to the death which he coveted, he struck a light with the flint and steel which he had brought with him; and having kindled his torch and wrapped himself close in his mantle, he went to the door of the Queen's room and tapped on it twice with his wand. The door was opened by a very drowsy chambermaid, who took the torch and put it out of sight; whereupon without a word he passed within the curtain, laid aside the mantle, and got into the bed where the Queen lay asleep. Then, taking her in his arms and straining her to him with ardour, making as if he were moody, because he knew that, when the King was in such a frame, he would never hear aught, in such wise, without word said either on his part or on hers, he had more than once carnal cognisance of the Queen. Loath indeed was he to leave her, but fearing lest by too long tarrying his achieved delight might be converted into woe, he rose, resumed the mantle and the light, and leaving the room without a word returned with all speed to his bed. He was hardly there when the King got up and entered the Queen's room; whereat she wondered not a little; but, reassured by the gladsome greeting which he gave her as he got into bed, she said – 'My lord, what a surprise is this tonight! 'Twas but now you left me after an unwonted measure of enjoyment, and do you not return so soon? consider what you do.' From these words the King at once inferred that the Queen had been deceived by someone that had counterfeited his person and carriage; but at the same time bethinking himself that, as neither the Queen nor any other had detected the cheat, 'twas best to leave her in ignorance, he wisely kept silence. Which many a fool would not have done, but would have said – 'Nay, 'twas not I that was here. Who was it that was here? How came it to pass? Who came hither?' Whereby in the sequel he might have caused the lady needless chagrin, and given her occasion to desire another such experience as she had had; and so have brought disgrace upon himself by uttering that from which, unuttered, no shame could have resulted. Wherefore betraying little either by his mien or by his words of the disquietude which he felt, the King replied – 'Madam, seem I such to you that you cannot suppose that I should have been with you once, and returned to you immediately afterwards?' 'Nay, not so, my lord,' returned the lady, 'but none the less I pray you to look to your health.' Then said the King – 'And I am minded to take your advice; wherefore, without giving you further trouble I will leave you.' So, angered and incensed beyond measure by the trick which he saw had been played upon him, he resumed his mantle and quitted the room with the intention of privily detecting the offender, deeming that he must belong to the palace, and that, whoever he might be, he could not have quitted it. So taking with him a small lantern which showed only a glimmer of light, he went into the dormitory which was over the palace-stables and was of great length, insomuch that well-nigh all the men-servants slept there in divers beds, and arguing that, by whomsoever that of which the Queen spoke was done, his heart and pulse could not after such a strain as yet have ceased to throb, he began cautiously with one of the head-grooms, and so went from bed to bed feeling at the heart of each man to see if it was thumping. All were asleep, save only he that had been with the Queen, who, seeing the King come, and guessing what he sought to discover, began to be mightily afraid, insomuch that to the agitation which his late exertion had communicated to his heart, terror now added one yet more violent; nor did he doubt that, should the King perceive it, he would kill him. Divers alternatives of action thronged his mind; but at last, observing that the King was unarmed, he resolved to make as if he were asleep and wait to see what the King would do. So, having tried many and found none that he deemed the culprit, the King came at last to the culprit himself, and marking the thumping of his heart, said to himself – This is he. But being minded to afford no clue to his ulterior purpose, he did no more than with a pair of scissors which he had brought with him shear away on one side of the man's head a portion of his locks, which, as was then the fashion, he wore very long, that by this token he might recognise him on the morrow; and having so done, he departed and returned to his room. The groom, who was fully sensible of what the King had done and being a shrewd fellow understood very well to what end he was so marked, got up without a moment's delay; and having found a pair of scissors – for, as it chanced, there were several pairs there belonging to the stables for use in grooming the horses – he went quietly through the dormitory and in like manner sheared the locks of each of the sleepers just above the ear; which done without disturbing any, he went back to bed.

On the morrow, as soon as the King was risen, and before the gates of the palace were opened, he summoned all his menservants to his presence, and, as they stood bareheaded before him, scanned them closely to see whether the one whom he had sheared was there; and observing with surprise that the more part of them were all sheared in the same manner, said to himself – Of a surety this fellow, whom I go about to detect, evinces, for all his base condition, a high degree of sense. Then, recognising that he could not compass his end without causing a rumour, and not being minded to brave so great a dishonour in order to be avenged upon so petty an offender, he was content by a single word of admonition to show him that his offence had not escaped notice. Wherefore turning to them all, he said – 'He that did it, let him do it no more, and get you hence in God's peace.' Another would have put them to the strappado, the question, the torture, and thereby have brought to light that which one should rather be sedulous to cloak; and having so brought it to light, would, however complete the retribution which he exacted, have not lessened but vastly augmented his disgrace, and sullied the fair fame of his lady. Those who heard the King's parting admonition wondered, and made much question with one another what the King might have meant to convey by it: but 'twas understood by none but him to whom it referred: who was discreet enough never to reveal the secret as long as the King lived, or again to stake his life on such a venture.

☙ 10 ❧

The third story of the third day, in which under cloak of confession and a most spotless conscience, a lady, enamoured of a young man, induces a booby friar unwittingly to provide a means to the entire gratification of her passion.

When Pampinea had done, and several of the company had commended the hardihood and wariness of the groom, as also the wisdom of the King, the queen, turning to Filomena, bade her follow suit: wherefore with manner debonair Filomena thus began: ❧ The story which I shall tell you is of a trick which was actually played by a fair lady upon a booby religious, and which every layman should find the more diverting that these religious, being, for the most part, great blockheads and men of odd manners and habits, do nevertheless credit themselves with more ability and knowledge in all kinds than fall to the lot of the rest of the world; whereas, in truth, they are far inferior, and so, not being able, like others, to provide their own sustenance, are prompted by sheer baseness to fly thither for refuge where they may find provender, like pigs. Which story, sweet my ladies, I shall tell you, not merely that thereby I may continue the sequence in obedience to the queen's behest, but also to the end that I may let you see that even the religious, in whom we in our boundless credulity repose exorbitant faith, may be, and sometimes are, made – not to say by men – even by some of us women the sport of their sly wit –

In our city, where wiles do more abound than either love or faith, there dwelt, not many years ago, a gentlewoman richly endowed (none more so) by nature with physical charms, as also with gracious manners, high spirit and fine discernment. Her name I know, but will not disclose it, nor yet that of any other who figures in this story, because there yet live those who might take offence thereat, though after all it might well be passed off with a laugh. High-born and married to an artificer of woollen fabrics, she could not rid her mind of the disdain with which, by reason of his occupation, she regarded her husband; for no man, however wealthy, if he were of low condition seemed to her worthy to have a gentlewoman to wife; and seeing that for all his wealth he was fit for nothing better than to devise a blend, set up a warp, or higgle about yarn with a spinster, she determined to dispense with his embraces, save so far as she might find it impossible to refuse them; and to find her satisfaction elsewhere with one that seemed to her more meet to afford it than her artificer of woollens. In this frame of mind she became enamoured of a man well worthy of her love and not yet past middle age, insomuch that if she saw him not in the day she must needs pass an unquiet night. The gallant, meanwhile, remained fancy-free for he knew nought of the lady's case; and she, being apprehensive of possible perils to ensue, was far too circumspect to make it known to him either by writing or by word of mouth of any of her female friends. Then she learned that he had much to do with a religious, a simple, clownish fellow, but nevertheless, as being a man of most holy life, reputed by almost everybody a most worthy friar, and decided that she could not find a better intermediary between herself and her lover than this same friar. So, having matured her plan, she hied her at a convenient time to the convent where the friar abode, and sent for him, saying that if he so pleased, she would be confessed by him. The friar, who saw at a glance that she was a gentlewoman, gladly heard her confession; which done, she said – 'My father, I have yet a matter to confide to you in which I must crave your aid and counsel. Who my kinsfolk and husband are, I wot you know, for I have myself told you. My husband loves me more dearly than his life, and being very wealthy, he can well and does forthwith afford me whatever I desire. Wherefore, as he loves me, even so I love him more dearly than myself; nor was there ever yet wicked woman that deserved the fire so richly as should I, were I guilty – I speak not of acts, but of so much as a single thought of crossing his will or tarnishing his honour. Now a man there is – his name, indeed, I know not, but he seems to me to be a gentleman, and, if I mistake not, he is much with you – a fine man and tall, his garb dun and very decent, who, the bent of my mind being, belike, quite unknown to him, would seem to have laid siege to me, insomuch that I cannot show myself at door or casement, or quit the house, but forthwith he presents himself before me; indeed I find it passing strange that he is not here now; whereat I am sorely troubled, because when men so act unmerited reproach will often thereby be cast upon honest women. At times I have been minded to inform my brothers of the matter; but then I have bethought me that men sometimes frame messages in such a way as to evoke untoward answers, whence follow high words; and so they proceed to rash acts: wherefore, to obviate trouble and scandal, I have kept silence, and by preference have made you my confidant both because you are the gentleman's friend and because it befits your office to censure such behaviour not only in friends but in strangers. And so I beseech you for the love of our only Lord God to make him sensible of his fault, and pray him to offend no more in such sort. Other ladies there are in plenty, who may, perchance, be disposed to welcome such advances, and be flattered to attract his fond and assiduous regard, which to me, who am in no wise inclined to encourage it, is but a most grievous molestation.'

Having thus spoken, the lady bowed her head as if she were ready to weep. The holy friar was at no loss to apprehend who it was of whom she spoke; he commended her virtuous frame, firmly believing that what she said was true, and promised to take such action that she should not again suffer the like annoyance: nor, knowing that she was very wealthy, did he omit to extol works of charity and almsgiving, at the same time opening to her his own needs. 'I make my suit to you,' said she, 'for the love of God; and if your friend should deny what I have told you, tell him roundly that 'twas from me you had it, and that I made complaint to you thereof.' So, her confession ended and penance imposed, bethinking her of the hints which the friar had dropped touching almsgiving, she slipped into his hand as many coins as it would hold, praying him to say masses for the souls of her dead. She then rose and went home.

Not long afterwards the gallant paid one of his wonted visits to the holy friar. They conversed for a while of divers topics, and then the friar took him aside and very courteously reproved him for so haunting and pursuing the lady with his gaze, as from what she had given him to understand, he supposed was his wont. The gallant, who had never regarded her with any attention, and very rarely passed her house, was amazed, and was about to clear himself, when the friar closed his mouth, saying – 'Now away with this pretence of amazement, and waste not words in denial, for 'twill not avail thee. I have it not from the neighbours; she herself, bitterly complaining of thy conduct, told it me. I say not how ill this levity beseems thee; but of her I tell thee so much as this, that, if I ever knew woman averse to such idle philandering, she is so; and therefore for thy honour's sake, and that she be no more vexed, I pray thee refrain therefrom, and let her be in peace.' The gallant, having rather more insight than the holy friar, was not slow to penetrate the lady's finesse; he therefore made as if he were rather shame-stricken, promised to go no further with the matter, and hied him straight from the friar to the lady's house, where she was always posted at a little casement to see if he were passing by. As she saw him come she showed him so gay and gracious a mien that he could no longer harbour any doubt that he had put the true construction upon what he had heard from the friar; and thenceforth, to his own satisfaction and the immense delight and solace of the lady, he omitted not daily to pass that way, being careful to make it appear as if he came upon other business. 'Twas thus not long before the lady understood that she met with no less favour in his eyes than he in hers; and being desirous to add fuel to his flame, and to assure him of the love she bore him, as soon as time and occasion served, she returned to the holy friar, and having sat herself down at his feet in the church, fell a-weeping. The friar asked her in a soothing tone what her new trouble might be. Whereto the lady answered – 'My father, 'tis still that accursed friend of thine, of whom I made complaint to you some days ago, and who would now seem to have been born for my most grievous torment, and to cause me to do that by reason whereof I shall never be glad again, nor venture to place myself at your feet.' 'How?' said the friar; 'has he not forborne to annoy thee?' 'Not he, indeed,' said the lady; 'on the contrary, 'tis my belief that since I complained to you of him he has, as if in despite, being offended belike that I did so, passed my house seven times for once that he did so before. Nay, would to God he were content to pass and fix me with his eyes; but he is waxed so bold and unabashed that only yesterday he sent a woman to me at home with his compliments and cajoleries, and, as if I had not purses and girdles enough, he sent me a purse and a girdle; whereat I was, as I still am, so wroth, that, had not conscience first, and then regard for you, weighed with me, I had flown into a frenzy of rage. However, I restrained myself, and resolved neither to do nor to say aught without first letting you know it. Nor only so; but, lest the woman who brought the purse and girdle, and to whom I at first returned them, shortly bidding her begone and take them back to the sender, should keep them and tell him that I had accepted them, as I believe they sometimes do, I recalled her and had them back, albeit 'twas in no friendly spirit that I received them from her hand; and I have brought them to you, that you may return them to him and tell him that I stand in no need of such gifts from him, because, thanks be to God and my husband, I have purses and girdles enough to smother him in. And if after this he leave me not alone I pray you as my father to hold me excused if, come what may, I tell it to my husband and brothers; for much liefer had I that he suffer indignity, if so it must be, than that my fair fame should be sullied on his account: that holds good, friar.' Weeping bitterly as she thus ended, she drew from under her robe a purse of very fine and ornate workmanship and a dainty and costly little girdle, and threw them into the lap of the friar, who, fully believing what she said, manifested the utmost indignation as he took them, and said – 'Daughter, that by these advances thou shouldst be moved to anger, I deem neither strange nor censurable; but I am instant with thee to follow my advice in the matter. I chid him some days ago, and ill has he kept the promise that he made me; for which cause and this last feat of his I will surely make his ears so tingle that he will give thee no more trouble; wherefore, for God's sake, let not thyself be so overcome by wrath as to tell it to any of thy kinsfolk; which might bring upon him a retribution greater than he deserves. Nor fear lest thereby thy fair fame should suffer; for I shall ever be thy most sure witness before God and men that thou art innocent.' The lady made a show of being somewhat comforted: then after a pause – for well she knew the greed of him and his likes – she said – 'Of late, Sir, by night, the spirits of divers of my kinsfolk have appeared to me in my sleep, and methinks they are in most grievous torment; alms, alms, they crave, nought else, especially my mother, who seems to be in so woeful and abject a plight that 'tis pitiful to see. Methinks 'tis a most grievous torment to her to see the tribulation which this enemy of God has brought upon me. I would therefore have you say for their souls the forty masses of St Gregory and some of your prayers, that God may deliver them from this purging fire.' So saying she slipped a florin into the hand of the holy friar, who took it gleefully, and having with edifying words and many examples fortified her in her devotion, gave her his benediction, and suffered her to depart.

The lady gone, the friar, who had still no idea of the trick that had been played upon him, sent for his friend; who was no sooner come than he gathered from the friar's troubled air that he had news of the lady, and waited to hear what he would say. The friar repeated what he had said before, and then broke out into violent and heated objurgation on the score of the lady's latest imputation. The gallant, who did not as yet apprehend the friar's drift, gave but a very faint denial to the charge of sending the purse and girdle, in order that he might not discredit the lady with the friar, if, perchance, she had given him the purse and girdle. Whereupon the friar exclaimed with great heat – 'How canst thou deny it, thou wicked man? Why, here they are; she brought them to me in tears with her own hand. Look at them, and say if thou knowest them not.' The gallant now feigned to be much ashamed, and said – 'Why, yes, indeed, I do know them; I confess that I did wrong; and I swear to you that, now I know her character, you shall never hear word more of this matter.' Many words followed; and then the blockheadly friar gave the purse and girdle to his friend, after which he read him a long lecture, besought him to meddle no more with such matters, and on his promising obedience dismissed him.

Elated beyond measure by the assurance which he now had of the lady's love, and the beautiful present, the gallant, on leaving the friar, hied him straight to a spot whence he stealthily gave the lady to see that he had both her gifts: whereat the lady was well content, the more so as her intrigue seemed ever to prosper more and more. She waited now only for her husband's departure from home to crown her enterprise with success. Nor was it long before occasion required that her husband should go to Genoa. The very morning that he took horse and rode away she hied her to the holy friar, and after many a lamentation she said to him betwixt her sobs – 'My father, now at last I tell you out and out that I can bear my suffering no longer. I promised you some days ago to do nought in this matter without first letting you know it: I am now come to crave release from that promise; and that you may believe that my lamentations and complaints are not groundless, I will tell you how this friend of yours, who should rather be called a devil let loose from hell, treated me only this very morning, a little before matins. As ill-luck would have it he learned, I know not how, that yesterday morning my husband went to Genoa, and so this morning at the said hour he came into my garden and got up by a tree to the window of my bedroom which looks out over the garden, and had already opened the casement and was about to enter the room, when I suddenly awoke, and got up and uttered a cry, and should have continued to cry out had not he, who was still outside, implored my mercy for God's sake and yours, telling me who he was. So, for love of you I was silent, and naked as I was born, ran and shut the window in his face, and he – bad luck to him – made off, I suppose, for I saw him no more. Consider now if such behaviour be seemly and tolerable: I for my part am minded to put up with no more of it; indeed I have endured too much already for love of you.'

Wroth beyond measure was the friar, as he heard her thus speak, nor knew he what to say, except that he several times asked her if she were quite certain that it was no other than he. 'Holy name of God!' replied the lady, 'as if I did not yet know him from another! He it was, I tell you; and do you give no credence to his denial.' 'Daughter,' said then the friar, 'there is here nought else to say but that this is a monstrous presumption and a most heinous offence; and thou didst well to send him away as thou didst. But seeing that God has preserved thee from shame, I would implore thee that, as thou hast twice followed my advice, thou do so likewise on this occasion and making no complaint to any of thy kinsfolk, leave it to me to try if I can control this devil that has slipped his chain, whom I supposed to be a saint; and if I succeed in weaning him from this insensate folly, well and good; and if I fail, thenceforth I give thee leave, with my blessing, to do whatsoever may commend itself to thy own judgement.' 'Lo now,' answered the lady, 'once again I will not vex or disobey you; but be sure that you so order matters that he refrain from further annoyance, as I give you my word that never will I have recourse to you again touching this matter.' Then, without another word, and with a troubled air, she took leave of him. Scarcely was she out of the church when the gallant came up. The friar called him, took him aside, and gave him the affront in such sort as 'twas never before given to any man, reviling him as a disloyal and perjured traitor. The gallant, who by his two previous lessons had been taught how to value the friar's censures, listened attentively, and sought to draw him out by ambiguous answers. 'Wherefore this wrath, Sir?' he began. 'Have I crucified Christ?' 'Ay, mark the fellow's effrontery!' retorted the friar: 'list to what he says! He talks, forsooth, as if 'twere a year or so since, and his villainies and lewdnesses were clean gone from his memory for lapse of time. Between matins and now hast thou forgotten this morning's outrage? Where wast thou this morning shortly before daybreak?' 'Where was I?' rejoined the gallant; 'that know not I. 'Tis indeed betimes that the news has reached you.' 'True indeed it is,' said the friar, 'that the news has reached me: I suppose that, because the husband was not there, thou never doubtedst that thou wouldst forthwith be received by the lady with open arms. Ah! the gay gallant! the honourable gentleman! he is now turned prowler by night, and breaks into gardens, and climbs trees! Dost thou think by sheer importunity to vanquish the virtue of this lady, that thou climbedst her windows at night by the trees? She dislikes thee of all things in the world, and yet thou must still persist. Well indeed hast thou laid my admonitions to heart, to say nothing of the many proofs which she has given thee of her disdain! But I have yet a word for thee:

hitherto, not that she bears thee any love, but that she has yielded to my urgent prayers, she has kept silence as to thy misdeeds: she will do so no more: I have given her leave to act as she may think fit if thou givest her any further annoyance. And what wilt thou do if she informs her brothers?' The gallant, now fully apprised of what it imported him to know, was profuse in promises, whereby as best he might he reassured the friar, and so left him. The very next night, as soon as the matin hour was come, he entered the garden, climbed up the tree, found the window open, entered the chamber, and in a trice was in the embrace of his fair lady. Anxiously had she expected him, and blithely did she now greet him, saying – 'All thanks to master friar that he so well taught thee the way hither.' Then, with many a jest and laugh at the simplicity of the asinine friar, and many a flout at distaff-fuls and combs and cards, they solaced themselves with one another to their no small delight. Nor did they omit so to arrange matters that they were well able to dispense with master friar, and yet pass many another night together with no less satisfaction: to which goal I pray that I, and all other Christian souls that are so minded, may be speedily guided of God in His holy mercy.

☙ 11 ❧

The fourth story of the third day, in which Dom Felice instructs Fra Puccio how to attain blessedness by doing a penance. Fra Puccio does the penance, and meanwhile Dom Felice has a good time with Fra Puccio's wife.

When Filomena, having concluded her story, was silent, and Dioneo had added a few honeyed phrases in praise of the lady's wit and Filomena's closing prayer, the queen glanced with a smile to Pamfilo, and said – 'Now, Pamfilo, give us some pleasant trifle to speed our delight.' 'That gladly will I,' returned forthwith Pamfilo, and then: ❧ Madam, he began, not a few there are that while they use their best endeavours to get themselves places in Paradise, do, by inadvertence, send others thither: as did not long ago betide a fair neighbour of ours, as you shall hear –

Hard by San Pancrazio there used to live, as I have heard tell, a worthy man and wealthy, Puccio di Rinieri by name, who in later life, under an overpowering sense of religion, became a tertiary of the order of St Francis, and was thus known as Fra Puccio. In which spiritual life he was the better able to persevere that his household consisted but of a wife and a maid, and having no need to occupy himself with any craft, he spent no small part of his time at church; where, being a simple soul and slow of wit, he said his paternosters, heard sermons, assisted at the mass, never missed lauds (*i.e.* when chanted by the seculars), fasted and mortified his flesh; nay – so 'twas whispered – he was of the Flagellants. His wife, Monna Isabetta by name, a woman of from twenty-eight to thirty summers, still young for her age, lusty, comely and plump as a casolan* apple, had not

* Perhaps from Casoli, near Naples.

unfrequently, by reason of her husband's devoutness, if not also of his age, more than she cared for of abstinence; and when she was sleepy, or, maybe, riggish, he would repeat to her the life of Christ, and the sermons of Fra Nastagio, or the lament of the Magdalen, or the like. Now, while such was the tenor of her life, there returned from Paris a young monk, by name Dom Felice, of the convent of San Pancrazio, a well-favoured man and keen-witted, and profoundly learned, with whom Fra Puccio became very intimate; and as there was no question which he could put to him but Dom Felice could answer it, and moreover he made great show of holiness, for well he knew Fra Puccio's bent, Fra Puccio took to bringing him home and entertaining him at breakfast and supper, as occasion served; and for love of her husband the lady also grew familiar with Dom Felice, and was zealous to do him honour. So the monk, being a constant visitor at Fra Puccio's house, and seeing the lady so lusty and plump, surmised that of which she must have most lack, and made up his mind to afford, if he could, at once relief to Fra Puccio and contentment to the lady. So cautiously, now and again, he cast an admiring glance in her direction with such effect that he kindled in her the same desire with which he burned, and marking his success, took the first opportunity to declare his passion to her. He found her fully disposed to gratify it; but how this might be he was at a loss to discover, for she would not trust herself with him in any place whatever except her own house, and there it could not be, because Fra Puccio never travelled; whereby the monk was greatly dejected. Long he pondered the matter, and at length thought of an expedient, whereby he might be with the lady in her own house without incurring suspicion, notwithstanding that Fra Puccio was there. So, being with Fra Puccio one day, he said to him – 'Reasons many have I to know, Fra Puccio, that all thy desire is to become a saint; but it seems to me that thou farest by a circuitous route, whereas there is one very direct, which the Pope and the greater prelates that are about him know and use, but will have it remain a secret, because otherwise the clergy, who for the most part live by alms, and could not then expect alms or aught else from the laity, would be speedily ruined. However, as thou art my friend, and hast shown me much honour, I would teach thee that way, if I were assured that thou wouldst follow it without letting another soul in the world hear of it.' Fra Puccio was now all agog to hear more of the matter, and began most earnestly entreating Dom Felice to teach him the way, swearing that without Dom Felice's leave none should ever hear of it from him, and averring that, if he found it practicable, he would certainly follow it. 'I am satisfied with thy promises,' said the monk, 'and I will show thee the way. Know then that the holy doctors hold that whoso would achieve blessedness must do the penance of which I shall tell thee; but see thou take me judiciously. I do not say that after the penance thou wilt not be a sinner, as thou art; but the effect will be that the sins which thou hast committed up to the very hour of the penance will all be purged away and thereby remitted to thee, and the sins which thou shalt commit thereafter will not be written against thee to thy damnation, but will be quit by holy water, like venial sins. First of all then the penitent must with great exactitude confess his sins when he comes to begin the penance. Then follows a period of fasting and very strict abstinence which must last for forty days, during which time he is to touch no woman whomsoever, not even his wife. Moreover, thou must have in thy house some place whence thou mayst see the sky by night, whither thou must resort at compline; and there thou must have a beam, very broad, and placed in such a way, that, standing, thou canst rest thy nether part upon it, and so, not raising thy feet from the ground, thou must extend thy arms, so as to make a sort of crucifix, and if thou wouldst have pegs to rest them on thou mayst; and on this manner, thy gaze fixed on the sky, and never moving a jot, thou must stand until matins. And wert thou lettered, it were proper for thee to say meanwhile certain prayers that I would give thee; but as thou art not so, thou must say three hundred paternosters and as many avemarias in honour of the Trinity; and thus contemplating the sky, be ever mindful that God was the creator of the heaven and the earth, and being set even as Christ was upon the cross meditate on His passion. Then, when the matin-bell sounds, thou mayst, if thou please, go to bed – but see that thou undress not – and sleep; but in the morning thou must go to church, and hear at least three masses, and say fifty paternosters and as many avemarias; after which thou mayst with a pure heart do aught that thou hast to do, and breakfast; but at vespers thou must be again at church, and say there certain prayers, which I shall give thee in writing and which are indispensable, and after compline thou must repeat thy former exercise. Do this, and I, who have done it before thee, have good hope that even before thou shalt have reached the end of the penance, thou wilt, if thou shalt do it in a devout spirit, have already a marvellous foretaste of the eternal blessedness.' 'This,' said Fra Puccio, 'is neither a very severe nor a very long penance, and can be very easily managed: wherefore in God's name I will begin on Sunday.' And so he took his leave of Dom Felice, and went home, and, by Dom Felice's permission, informed his wife of every particular of his intended penance.

The lady understood very well what the monk meant by enjoining him not to stir from his post until matins; and deeming it an excellent device, she said that she was well content that he should do this or aught else that he thought good for his soul; and to the end that his penance might be blest of God, she would herself fast with him, though she would go no further. So they did as they had agreed: when Sunday came Fra Puccio began his penance, and master monk, by understanding with the lady, came most evenings at the hour when he was secure from discovery to sup with her, always bringing with him abundance both of meat and of drink, and after slept with her till the matin hour when he got up and left her and Fra Puccio went to bed. The place which Fra Puccio had chosen for his penance was close to the room in which the lady slept, and only separated from it by the thinnest of partitions; so that, the monk and the lady disporting themselves with one another without stint or restraint, Fra Puccio thought he felt the floor of the house shake a little, and pausing at his hundredth paternoster, but without leaving his post, called out to the lady to know what she was about. The lady, who dearly loved a jest, and was just then riding the horse of St Benedict or St John Gualbert, answered – 'I'faith, husband. I am as restless as may be.' 'Restless,' said Fra Puccio, 'how so? What means this restlessness?' Whereto with a hearty laugh, for which she doubtless had good occasion, the bonny lady replied – 'What means it? How should you ask such a question? Why, I have heard you say a thousand times – "Who fasting goes to bed, uneasy lies his head." ' Fra Puccio, supposing that her wakefulness and restlessness abed was due to want of food, said in good faith – 'Wife, I told thee I would have thee not fast; but as thou hast chosen to fast, think not of it, but think how thou mayst compose thyself to sleep; thou tossest about the bed in such sort that the shaking is felt here.' 'That need cause thee no alarm,' rejoined the lady. 'I know what I am about; I will manage as well as I can, and do thou likewise.' So Fra Puccio said no more to her, but resumed his paternosters; and thenceforth every night while Fra Puccio's penance lasted, the lady and master monk, having had a bed made up for them in another part of the house, did there wanton it most gamesomely, the monk departing and the lady going back to her bed at one and the same time, being shortly before Fra Puccio's return from his nightly vigil. The friar thus persisting in his penance while the lady took her fill of pleasure with the monk, she would from time to time say jestingly to him – 'Thou layest a penance upon Fra Puccio whereby we are rewarded with Paradise.' So well indeed did she relish the dainties with which the monk regaled her, the more so by contrast with the abstemious life to which her husband had long accustomed her, that, when Fra Puccio's penance was done she found means to enjoy them elsewhere and ordered her indulgence with such discretion as to ensure its long continuance. Whereby (that my story may end as it began) it came to pass that Fra Puccio, hoping by his penance to win a place for himself in Paradise, did in fact translate thither the monk who had shown him the way, and the wife who lived with him in great dearth of that of which the monk in his charity gave her superabundant largesse.

❧ 12 ❧

The fifth story of the third day, in which Zima gives a palfrey to Messer Francesco Vergellesi, who in return suffers him to speak with his wife. She keeping silence, he answers in her stead, and the sequel is in accordance with his answer.

When Pamfilo had brought the story of Fra Puccio to a close amid the laughter of the ladies, the queen debonairly bade Elisa follow suit; and she, whose manner had in it a slight touch of severity which betokened not despite but was habitual to her, thus began: ❧ Many there are that, being very knowing, think that others are quite the reverse; and so, many a time, thinking to beguile others, are themselves beguiled; wherefore I deem it the height of folly for anyone wantonly to challenge another to a contest of wit. But, as, perchance, all may not be of the same opinion, I am minded, without deviating from the prescribed order, to acquaint you with that which thereby befell a certain knight of Pistoia –

Know then that at Pistoia there lived a knight, Messer Francesco by name, of the Vergellesi family, a man of much wealth and good parts, being both wise and clever, but withal niggardly beyond measure. Which Messer Francesco, having to go to Milan in the capacity of podestà, had provided himself with all that was meet for the honourable support of such a dignity save only a palfrey handsome enough for him; and not being able to come by any such he felt himself at a loss. Now there was then in Pistoia a young man, Ricciardo by name, of low origin but great wealth, who went always so trim and fine and foppish of person, that folk had bestowed upon him the name of

Zima,* by which he was generally known. Zima had long and to no purpose burned and yearned for love of Messer Francesco's very fair and no less virtuous wife. His passion was matter of common notoriety; and so it befell that someone told Messer Francesco that he had but to ask Zima, who was the possessor of one of the handsomest palfreys in Tuscany, which on that account he greatly prized, and he would not hesitate to give him the horse for the love which he bore his wife. So our niggardly knight sent for Zima, and offered to buy the horse of him, hoping thereby to get him from Zima as a gift. Zima heard the knight gladly, and thus made answer – 'Sell you my horse, Sir, I would not, though you gave me all that you have in the world; but I shall be happy to give him to you, when you will, on this condition, that before he pass into your hands I may by your leave and in your presence say a few words to your wife so privately that I may be heard by her alone.' Thinking at once to gratify his cupidity and to outwit Zima, the knight answered that he was content that it should be even as Zima wished. Then, leaving him in the hall of the palace he went to his lady's chamber and told her the easy terms on which he might acquire the palfrey, bidding her give Zima his audience, but on no account to vouchsafe him a word of reply. This the lady found by no means to her mind, but, as she must needs obey her husband's commands, she promised compliance, and followed him into the hall to hear what Zima might have to say. Zima then renewed his contract with the knight in due form; whereupon, the lady being seated in a part of the hall where she was quite by herself, he sat down by her side and thus began – 'Noble lady, I have too much respect for your understanding to doubt that you have long been well aware of the extremity of passion whereto I have been brought by your beauty, which certainly exceeds that of any other lady that I have ever seen, to say nothing of your exquisite manners and incomparable virtues, which might well serve to captivate every soaring spirit that is in the world; wherefore there need no words of mine to assure you that I love you with a love greater and more ardent than any that man yet bore to woman, and so without doubt I shall do, as long as my woeful life shall hold this frame together; nay, longer yet, for if love there be in the next world as in this, I shall love you evermore. And so you may make your mind secure that there is nothing that is yours, be it precious or be it common, which you may count as in such and so sure a sort your own as me, for

* From the Low Latin *aczima*, explained by Du Cange as *tonture de draps*, the process of dressing cloth so as to give it an even nap.

all that I am and have. And that thereof you may not lack evidence of infallible cogency, I tell you that I should deem myself more highly favoured if I might at your command do somewhat to pleasure you, than if at my command the whole world were forthwith to yield me obedience. And as 'tis even in such sort that I am yours, 'tis not unworthily that I make bold to offer my petitions to Your Highness, as being to me the sole, exclusive source of all peace, of all bliss, of all health. Wherefore, as your most lowly vassal, I pray you, dear my bliss, my soul's one hope wherein she nourishes herself in love's devouring flame, that in your great benignity you deign so far to mitigate the harshness which in the past you have shown towards me, yours though I am, that, consoled by your compassion, I may say that as 'twas by your beauty that I was smitten with love, so 'tis to your pity that I owe my life which, if in your haughtiness you lend not ear unto my prayers, will assuredly fail, so that I shall die and, it may be, 'twill be said that you slew me. 'Twould not redound to your honour that I died for love of you; but let that pass; I cannot but think, however, that you would sometimes feel a touch of remorse, and would grieve that 'twas your doing, and that now and again, relenting, you would say to yourself – "Ah! how wrong it was of me that I had not pity on my Zima;" by which too late repentance you would but enhance your grief. Wherefore, that this come not to pass, repent you while it is in your power to give me ease, and show pity on me before I die, seeing that with you it rests to make me either the gladdest or the saddest man that lives. My trust is in your generosity, that 'twill not brook that a love so great and of such a sort as mine should receive death for reward, and that by a gladsome and gracious answer you will repair my shattered spirits, which are all a-tremble in your presence for very fear.' When he had done he heaved several very deep sighs and a few tears started from his eyes while he awaited the lady's answer.

Long time he had wooed her with his eyes, had tilted in her honour, had greeted her rising with music; and against these and all like modes of attack she had been proof; but the heartfelt words of her most ardent lover were not without their effect, and she now began to understand what she had never till then understood, to wit, what love really means. So, albeit she obeyed her lord's behest and kept silence, yet she could not but betray by a slight sigh that which, if she might have given Zima his answer, she would readily have avowed. After waiting a while, Zima found it strange that no answer was forthcoming; and he then began to perceive the trick which the knight had played him. However, he kept his eyes fixed on the lady, and observing that her eyes glowed now and again as they met his, and noting the partially suppressed sighs which escaped her, he gathered a little hope which gave him courage to try a novel plan of attack. So, while the lady listened, he began to make answer for her to himself on this wise – 'Zima mine, true indeed it is that long since I discerned that thou didst love me with a love exceeding great and whole-hearted, whereof I have now yet ampler assurance by thine own words, and well content I am therewith, as indeed I ought to be. And however harsh and cruel I may have seemed to thee, I would by no means have thee believe that I have been such at heart as I have seemed in aspect; rather, be assured that I have ever loved thee and held thee dear above all other men; the mien which I have worn was but prescribed by fear of another and solicitude for my fair fame. But a time will soon come when I shall be able to give thee plain proof of my love, and to accord the love which thou hast borne and dost bear me its due reward. Wherefore be comforted and of good hope; for Messer Francesco is to go in a few days' time to Milan as podestà, as thou well knowest, seeing that for love of me thou hast given him thy fine palfrey; and I vow to thee upon my faith, upon the true love which I bear thee, that without fail, within a few days thereafter thou shalt be with me, and we will give our love complete and gladsome consummation. And that I may have no more occasion to speak to thee of this matter, be it understood between us that henceforth when thou shalt observe two towels disposed at the window of my room which overlooks the garden, thou shalt come to me after nightfall of that same day by the garden door (and look well to it that thou be not seen), and thou shalt find me waiting for thee, and we will have our fill of mutual cheer and solace all night long.'

Having thus answered for the lady, Zima resumed his own person and thus replied to the lady – 'Dearest madam, your boon response so overpowers my every faculty that scarce can I frame words to render you due thanks; and, were I able to utter all I feel, time, however long, would fail me fully to thank you as I would fain and as I ought: wherefore I must even leave it to your sage judgement to divine that which I yearn in vain to put in words. Let this one word suffice, that as you bid me, so I shall not fail to do; and then having, perchance, firmer assurance of the great boon which you have granted me, I will do my best endeavour to thank you in terms the amplest that I may command. For the present there is no more to say; and so, dearest my lady, I commend you to God; and may He grant you your heart's content of joy and bliss.' To all which the lady returned never a word: wherefore Zima rose and turned to rejoin the knight who, seeing him on his feet, came towards him, and said with a laugh – 'How sayst thou? Have I faithfully kept my promise to thee?' 'Not so, Sir,' replied Zima; 'for by thy word I was to have spoken with thy wife, and by thy deed I have spoken to a statue of marble.' Which remark was much relished by the knight, who, well as he had thought of his wife, thought now even better of her, and said – 'So thy palfrey, that was, is now mine out and out.' ' 'Tis even so, Sir,' replied Zima; 'but had I thought to have gotten such fruit as I have from this favour of yours, I would not have craved it, but would have let you have the palfrey as a free gift: and would to God I had done so, for, as it is, you have bought the palfrey and I have not sold him.' This drew a laugh from the knight who within a few days thereafter mounted the palfrey which he had got, and took the road for Milan, there to enter on his podestate. The lady, now mistress of herself, bethought her of Zima's words and the love which he bore her, and for which he had parted with his palfrey; and observing that he frequently passed her house, said to herself – 'What am I about? Why throw I my youth away? My husband is gone to Milan, and will not return for six months, and when can he ever restore them to me? When I am old! And besides, shall I ever find another such lover as Zima? I am quite by myself. There is none to fear. I know not why I take not my good time while I may: I shall not always have the like opportunity as at present: no one will ever know; and if it should get known, 'tis better to do and repent than to forbear and repent.' Of which meditations the issue was that one day she set two towels in the window overlooking the garden, according to Zima's word; and Zima having marked them with much exultation, stole at nightfall alone to the door of the lady's garden, and finding it open, crossed to another door that led into the house where he found the lady awaiting him. On sight of him she rose to meet him, and gave him the heartiest of welcomes. A hundred thousand times he embraced and kissed her, as he followed her upstairs: then without delay they hied them to bed, and knew love's furthest bourne. And so far was the first time from being in this case the last that while the knight was at Milan, and indeed after his return, there were seasons not a few at which Zima resorted thither to the immense delight of both parties.

❧ 13 ☙

The sixth story of the third day, in which Ricciardo Minutolo loves the wife of Filippello Fighinolfi, and knowing her to be jealous, makes her believe that his own wife is to meet Filippello at a bagnio on the ensuing day; whereby she is induced to go thither, where, thinking to have been with her husband, she discovers that she has tarried with Ricciardo.

When Elisa had quite done, the queen, after some commendation of Zima's sagacity, bade Fiammetta follow with a story. Whereto Fiammetta, all smiles, responded – 'Madam, with all my heart;' and thus began: ☙ Richly though our city abounds, as in all things else, so also in instances to suit every topic, yet I am minded to journey some distance thence, and, like Elisa, to tell you something of what goes on in other parts of the world: wherefore pass we to Naples, where you shall hear how one of these sanctified that show themselves so shy of love was by the subtlety of her lover brought to taste of the fruit before she had known the flowers of love; whereby at one and the same time you may derive from the past counsel of prudence for the future, and present delectation –

In the very ancient city of Naples, which for loveliness has not its superior or perhaps its equal in Italy, there once lived a young man, renowned alike for noble blood and the splendour of his vast wealth, his name Ricciardo Minutolo. He was mated with a very fair and loving wife; but nevertheless he became enamoured of a lady who in the general opinion vastly surpassed in beauty every other lady in Naples. Catella – such was the lady's name – was married to a young man, likewise of gentle blood, Filippello Fighinolfi by name, whom she, most virtuous of ladies, loved and held dear above all else in the world. Being thus enamoured of Catella, Ricciardo Minutolo left none of those means untried whereby a lady's favour and love are wont to be gained, but for all that he made no way towards the attainment of his heart's desire: whereby he fell into a sort of despair, and witless and powerless to loose himself from his love, found life scarce tolerable, and yet knew not how to die. While in this frame he languished, it befell one day that some ladies that were of kin to him counselled him earnestly to be quit of such a love, whereby he could but fret himself to no purpose, seeing that Catella cared for nought in the world save Filippello, and lived in such a state of jealousy on his account that never a bird flew but she feared lest it should snatch him from her. So soon as Ricciardo heard of Catella's jealousy, he forthwith began to ponder how he might make it subserve his end. He feigned to have given up his love for Catella as hopeless, and to have transferred it to another lady, in whose honour he accordingly began to tilt and joust and do all that he had been wont to do in honour of Catella. Nor was it long before well-nigh all the Neapolitans, including Catella herself, began to think that he had forgotten Catella, and was to the last degree enamoured of the other lady. In this course he persisted, until the opinion was so firmly rooted in the minds of all that even Catella laid aside a certain reserve which she had used towards him while she deemed him her lover, and, coming and going, greeted him in friendly, neighbourly fashion like the rest. Now it so befell that during the hot season, when according to the custom of the Neapolitans many companies of ladies and gentlemen went down to the sea-coast to recreate themselves and breakfast and sup, Ricciardo, knowing that Catella was gone thither with her company, went likewise with his, but making as if he were not minded to stay there, he received several invitations from the ladies of Catella's company before he accepted any. When the ladies received him they all with one accord, including Catella, began to rally him on his new love, and he furnished them with more matter for talk by feigning a most ardent passion. At length most of the ladies being gone off one hither, another thither, as they do in such places, leaving Catella and a few others with Ricciardo, he tossed at Catella a light allusion to a certain love of her husband Filippello which threw her at once into such a fit of jealousy that she inwardly burned with a vehement desire to know what Ricciardo meant. For a while she kept her own counsel; then, brooking no more suspense, she adjured Ricciardo by the love he bore the lady whom most he loved, to expound to her what he had said touching Filippello. He answered –

'You have adjured me by her to whom I dare not deny aught that you may ask of me; my riddle therefore I will presently read you, provided you promise me that neither to him nor to anyone else will you impart aught of what I shall relate to you, until you shall have ocular evidence of its truth; which, so you desire it, I will teach you how you may obtain.' The lady accepted his terms, which rather confirmed her belief in his veracity, and swore that she would not tell a soul. They then drew a little apart, that they might not be overheard by the rest, and Ricciardo thus began – 'Madam, did I love you, as I once did, I should not dare to tell you aught that I thought might cause you pain; but now that that love is past I shall have the less hesitation in telling you the truth. Whether Filippello ever resented the love which I bore you, or deemed that it was returned by you, I know not: whether it were so or no, he certainly never showed any such feeling to me; but so it is that now, having waited, perhaps, until, as he supposes, I am less likely to be on my guard, he shows a disposition to serve me as I doubt he suspects that I served him; that is to say, he would fain have his pleasure of my wife, whom for some time past he has, as I discover, plied with messages through most secret channels. She has told me all, and has answered him according to my instructions: but only this morning, just before I came hither, I found a woman in close parley with her in the house, whose true character and purpose I forthwith divined; so I called my wife and asked what the woman wanted. Whereto she answered – " 'Tis this persecution by Filippello which thou hast brought upon me by the encouraging answers that thou wouldst have me give him: he now tells me that he is most earnestly desirous to know my intentions, and that, should I be so minded, he would contrive that I should have secret access to a bagnio in this city, and he is most urgent and instant that I should consent. And hadst thou not, wherefore I know not, bidden me keep the affair afoot I would have dismissed him in such a sort that my movements would have been exempt from his prying observation for ever." Upon this I saw that the affair was going too far; I determined to have no more of it, and to let you know it that you may understand how he requites your whole-hearted faith, which brought me of late to the verge of death. And that you may not suppose that these are but empty words and idle tales, but may be able, should you so desire, to verify them by sight and touch, I caused my wife to tell the woman who still waited her answer that she would be at the bagnio tomorrow during the siesta: with which answer the woman went away well content. Now you do not, I suppose, imagine that I would send her thither; but if I were in your place, he should find me there instead of her whom he thinks to find there; and when I had been some little time with him, I would give him to understand with whom he had been, and he should have of me such honour as he deserved. Whereby, I doubt not, he would be put to such shame as would at one and the same time avenge both the wrong which he has done to you and that which he plots against me.'

Catella, as is the wont of the jealous, hearkened to Ricciardo's words without so much as giving a thought to the speaker or his wiles, inclined at once to credit his story, and began to twist certain antecedent matters into accord with it; then suddenly kindling with wrath she answered that to the bagnio she would certainly go; 'twould cause her no great inconvenience, and if he should come, she would so shame him that he should never again set eyes on woman but his ears would tingle. Satisfied by what he heard that his stratagem was well conceived and success sure, Ricciardo added much in corroboration of his story, and having thus confirmed her belief in it, besought her to keep it always close, whereto she pledged her faith.

Next morning Ricciardo hied him to the good woman that kept the bagnio to which he had directed Catella, told her the enterprise which he had in hand, and prayed her to aid him therein so far as she might be able. The good woman, who was much beholden to him, assured him that she would gladly do so, and concerted with him all that was to be said and done. She had in the bagnio a room which was very dark, being without any window to admit the light. This room, by Ricciardo's direction, she set in order, and made up a bed there as well as she could, into which bed Ricciardo got, as soon as he had breakfasted, and there awaited Catella's coming.

Now Catella, still giving more credence to Ricciardo's story than it merited, had gone home in the evening in a most resentful mood, and Filippello, returning home the same evening with a mind greatly preoccupied, was scarce as familiar with her as he was wont to be. Which she marking, grew yet more suspicious than before and said to herself – 'Doubtless he is thinking of the lady of whom he expects to take his pleasure tomorrow, as most assuredly he shall not;' and so, musing and meditating what she should say to him after their encounter at the bagnio, she spent the best part of the night. But – to shorten my story – upon the stroke of noon Catella, taking with her a single attendant but otherwise adhering to her original intention, hied her to the bagnio which Ricciardo had indicated; and finding the good woman there, asked her whether Filippello had been there that day. Primed by Ricciardo, the good woman asked her whether she were the lady that was to come to speak with him; to which she answered in the affirmative. 'Go to him, then,' said the good woman. And so Catella, in quest of that which she would gladly not have found, was shown to the chamber where Ricciardo was, and having entered without uncovering her head, closed the door behind her. Overjoyed to see her, Ricciardo sprang out of bed, took her in his arms, and said caressingly – 'Welcome, my soul.' Catella, dissembling, for she was minded at first to counterfeit another woman, returned his embrace, kissed him, and lavished endearments upon him; saying the while not a word lest her speech should betray her. The darkness of the room, which was profound, was equally welcome to both; nor were they there long enough for their eyes to recover power. Ricciardo helped Catella on to the bed, where, with no word said on either side in a voice that might be recognised, they lay a long while, much more to the solace and satisfaction of the one than of the other party. Then Catella, deeming it high time to vent her harboured resentment, burst forth in a blaze of wrath on this wise – 'Alas! how wretched is the lot of women, how misplaced of not a few the love they bear their husbands! Ah, woe is me! for eight years have I loved thee more dearly than my life; and now I find that thou, base miscreant that thou art, dost nought but burn and languish for love of another woman! Here thou hast been – with whom, thinkest thou? Even with her whom thou hast too long deluded with thy false blandishments, making pretence to love her while thou art enamoured of another. 'Tis I, Catella, not the wife of Ricciardo, false traitor that thou art; list if thou knowest my voice; 'tis I indeed! Ah! would we were but in the light! – it seems to me a thousand years till then – that I might shame thee as thou deservest, vile, pestilent dog that thou art! Alas! woe is me! such love as I have borne so many years – to whom? To this faithless dog, that, thinking to have a strange woman in his embrace, has in the brief while that I have been with him here lavished upon me more caresses and endearments than during all the forepast time that I have been his! A lively spark indeed art thou today, renegade dog, that showest thyself so limp and enervate and impotent at home! But, God be praised, thou hast tilled thine own plot, and not another's, as thou didst believe. No wonder that last night thou heldest aloof from me; thou wast thinking of scattering thy seed elsewhere, and wast minded to show thyself a lusty knight when thou shouldst join battle. But praise be to God and my sagacity, the water has nevertheless taken its proper course. Where is thy answer, culprit? Hast thou nought to say? Have my words struck thee dumb? God's faith! I know not why I forbear to pluck thine eyes out with my fingers! Thou thoughtest to perpetrate this treason with no small secrecy; but, by God, one is as knowing as another; thy plot has failed; I had better hounds on thy trail than thou didst think for.' Ricciardo, inwardly delighted by her words, made no answer but embraced and kissed her more than ever and overwhelmed her with his endearments. So she continued her reproaches, saying – 'Ay, thou thinkest to cajole me with thy feigned caresses, wearisome dog that thou art, and so to pacify and mollify me; but thou art mistaken. I shall never be mollified, until I have covered thee with infamy in the presence of all our kinsfolk and friends and neighbours. Am I not, miscreant, as fair as the wife of Ricciardo Minutolo? Am I not as good a lady as she? Why dost not answer, vile dog? Wherein has she the advantage of me? Away with thee! touch me not; thou hast done feats of arms more than enough for today. Well I know that, now that thou knowest who I am, thou wilt wreak thy will on me by force: but by God's grace I will yet disappoint thee. I know not why I forbear to send for Ricciardo, who loved me more than himself and yet was never able to boast that he had a single glance from me; nor know I why 'twere wrong to do so. Thou thoughtest to have his wife here, and 'tis no fault of thine that thou hadst her not: so, if I had him, thou couldst not justly blame me.'

Enough had now been said: the lady's mortification was extreme; and as she ended Ricciardo bethought him that if he suffered her, thus deluded, to depart, much evil might ensue. He therefore resolved to make himself known, and disabuse her of her error. So, taking her in his arms, and clipping her so close that she could not get loose, he said – 'Sweet my soul, be not wroth: that which, while artlessly I loved I might not have, Love has taught me to compass by guile: know that I am thy Ricciardo.'

At these words and the voice, which she recognised, Catella started, and would have sprung out of the bed; which being impossible she essayed a cry; but Ricciardo laid a hand upon her mouth and closed it, saying – 'Madam, that which is done can never be undone, though you should cry out for the rest of your days, and should you in such or any other wise publish this matter to any, two consequences will ensue. In the first place (and this is a point which touches you very nearly) your honour and fair fame will be blasted; for however you may say that I lured you hither by guile, I shall deny it and affirm, on the contrary, that I induced you to come hither by promises of money and gifts, and that 'tis but because you are vexed that what I gave you did not altogether come up to your expectations that you make such a cry and clamour; and you know that folk are more prone to believe evil than good, and therefore I am no less likely to be believed than you. The further consequence will be mortal enmity between your husband and me, and the event were as like to be that I killed him as that he killed me: which if I did, you would never more know joy or peace. Wherefore, heart of my body, do not at one and the same time bring dishonour upon yourself and set your husband and me at strife and in jeopardy of our lives. You are not the first nor will you be the last to be beguiled; nor have I beguiled you to rob you of aught, but for excess of love that I bear and shall ever bear you, being your most lowly vassal. And though it is now a great while that I, and what I have and can and am worth, are yours, yet I am minded that so it shall be henceforth more than ever before. Your discretion in other matters is not unknown to me, and I doubt not 'twill be equally manifest in this.'

Ricciardo's admonitions were received by Catella with many a bitter tear; but though she was very wroth and very sad at heart, yet Ricciardo's true words so far commanded the assent of her reason that she acknowledged that 'twas possible they might be verified by the event. Wherefore she made answer – 'Ricciardo, I know not how God will grant me patience to bear the villainy and knavery which thou hast practised upon me; and though in this place, to which simplicity and excess of jealousy guided my steps, I raise no cry, rest assured that I shall never be happy until in one way or another I know myself avenged of that which thou hast done to me. Wherefore unhand me, let me go: thou hast had thy desire of me and hast tormented me to thy heart's content: tis time to release me; let me go, I pray thee.' But Ricciardo, seeing that she was still much ruffled in spirit, was resolved not to let her go until he had made his peace with her. So he addressed himself to soothe her; and by dint of most dulcet phrases and entreaties and adjurations he did at last prevail with her to give him her pardon; nay, by joint consent they tarried there a great while to the exceeding great delight of both. Indeed the lady, finding her lover's kisses smack much better than those of her husband, converted her asperity into sweetness, and from that day forth cherished a most tender love for Ricciardo; whereof, using all circumspection, they many a time had solace. God grant us solace of ours.

❧ 14 ❧

The seventh story of the third day, in which Tedaldo, being in disfavour with his lady, departs from Florence. He returns thither after a while in the guise of a pilgrim, has speech of his lady, and makes her sensible of her fault. Her husband, convicted of slaying him, he delivers from peril of death, reconciles him with his brothers, and thereafter discreetly enjoys his lady.

So ceased Fiammetta; and, when all had bestowed on her their meed of praise, the queen – to lose no time – forthwith bade Emilia resume the narration. So thus Emilia began: ❧ I am minded to return to our city, whence my two last predecessors saw fit to depart, and to show you how one of our citizens recovered the lady he had lost –

Know then that there was in Florence a young noble, his name Tedaldo Elisei, who being beyond measure enamoured of a lady called Monna Ermellina, wife of one Aldobrandino Palermini, and by reason of his admirable qualities richly deserving to have his desire, found Fortune nevertheless adverse, as she is wont to be to the prosperous. Inasmuch as, for some reason or another, the lady, having shown herself gracious towards Tedaldo for a while, completely altered her mien, and not only showed him no further favour, but would not so much as receive a message from him or suffer him to see her face; whereby he fell a prey to a grievous and distressful melancholy; but so well had he concealed his love that the cause of his melancholy was surmised by none. He tried hard in divers ways to recover the love which he deemed himself to have lost for no fault of his, and finding all his efforts unavailing, he resolved to bid the world adieu, that he might not afford her who was the cause of his distress the satisfaction of seeing him languish. So he got together as much money as he might, and secretly, no word said to friend or kinsman except only a familiar gossip, who knew all, he took his departure for Ancona. Arrived there, he assumed the name of Filippo Santodeccio, and having forgathered with a rich merchant, entered his service. The merchant took him with him to Cyprus aboard one of his ships, and was so well pleased with his bearing and behaviour that he not only gave him a handsome salary but made him in a sort his companion, and entrusted him with the management of no small part of his affairs: wherein he proved himself so apt and assiduous, that in the course of a few years he was himself established in credit and wealth and great repute as a merchant. Seven years thus passed, during which, albeit his thoughts frequently reverted to his cruel mistress, and sorely love smote him, and much he yearned to see her again, yet such was his firmness that he came off conqueror, until one day in Cyprus it so befell that there was sung in his hearing a song that he had himself composed, and of which the theme was the mutual love that was between his lady and him, and the delight that he had of her; which as he heard, he found it incredible that she should have forgotten him, and burned with such a desire to see her once more, that, being able to hold out no longer, he made up his mind to return to Florence. So, having set all his affairs in order, he betook him, attended only by a single servant, to Ancona; whence he sent all his effects, as they arrived, forward to Florence, consigning them to a friend of his Ancontan partner, and followed with his servant in the disguise of a pilgrim returned from the Holy Sepulchre. Arrived at Florence, he put up at a little hostelry kept by two brothers hard by his lady's house, whither he forthwith hied him, hoping that, perchance, he might have sight of her from the street; but, finding all barred and bolted, doors, windows and all else, he doubted much, she must be dead, or have removed thence. So, with a very heavy heart, he returned to the house of the two brothers, and to his great surprise found his own four brothers standing in front of it, all in black. He knew that he was so changed from his former semblance, both in dress and in person, that he might not readily be recognised, and he had therefore no hesitation in going up to a shoemaker and asking him why these men were all dressed in black. The shoemaker answered – ''Tis because 'tis not fifteen days since a brother of theirs, Tedaldo by name, that had been long abroad, was slain; and I understand that they have proved in court that one Aldobrandino Palermini, who is under arrest, did the deed, because Tedaldo, who loved his wife, was come back to Florence incognito to forgather with her.' Tedaldo found it passing strange that there should be anyone so like him as to be mistaken for him, and deplored Aldobrandino's evil plight. He had learned, however, that the lady was alive and well. So, as 'twas now night, he hied him, much perplexed in mind, into the inn, and supped with his servant. The bedroom assigned him was almost at the top of the house, and the bed was none of the best. Thoughts many and disquieting haunted his mind, and his supper had been but light. Whereby it befell that midnight came and went, and Tedaldo was still awake. As thus he watched, he heard shortly after midnight, a noise as of persons descending from the roof into the house, and then through the chinks of the door of his room he caught the flicker of an ascending light. Wherefore he stole softly to the door, and peeping through a chink to make out what was afoot, he saw a very fine young woman bearing a light, and three men making towards her, being evidently those that had descended from the roof. The men exchanged friendly greetings with the young woman, and then one said to her – 'Now, God be praised, we may make our minds easy, for we are well assured that judgement for the death of Tedaldo Elisei is gotten by his brothers against Aldobrandino Palermini, and he has confessed, and the sentence is already drawn up; but still it behoves us to hold our peace for, should it ever get abroad that we were guilty, we shall stand in the like jeopardy as Aldobrandino.' So saying, they took leave of the woman, who seemed much cheered, and went to bed. What he had heard set Tedaldo musing on the number and variety of the errors to which men are liable: as, first, how his brothers had mourned and interred a stranger in his stead, and then charged an innocent man upon false suspicion, and by false witness brought him into imminent peril of death: from which he passed to ponder the blind severity of laws and magistrates, who from misguided zeal to elicit the truth not unfrequently become ruthless, and, adjudging that which is false, forfeit the title which they claim of ministers of God and justice, and do but execute the mandates of iniquity and the Evil One. And so he came at last to consider the possibility of saving Aldobrandino, and formed a plan for the purpose. Accordingly, on the morrow, when he was risen, he left his servant at the inn, and hied him alone, at what he deemed a convenient time, to his lady's house, where, finding, by chance, the door open, he entered, and saw his lady sitting, all tears and lamentations, in a little parlour on the ground-floor. Whereat he all but wept for sympathy; and drawing near her, he said – 'Madam, be not troubled in spirit: your peace is nigh you.' Whereupon the lady raised her head, and said between her sobs – 'Good man, what dost thou, a pilgrim, if I mistake not, from distant parts, know either of my peace or of my affliction?' 'Madam,' returned the pilgrim, 'I am of Constantinople, and am but now come hither, at God's behest, that I may give you laughter for tears, and deliver your husband from death.' 'But,' said the lady, 'if thou art of Constantinople, and but now arrived, how is 't that thou knowest either who my husband is, or who I am?' Whereupon the pilgrim gave her the whole narrative, from the very beginning, of Aldobrandino's sufferings; he also told her, who she was, how long she had been married, and much besides that was known to him of her affairs: whereat the lady was lost in wonder, and, taking him to be a prophet, threw herself on her knees at his feet, and besought him for God's sake, if he were come to save Aldobrandino, to lose no time, for the matter brooked no delay. Thus adjured, the pilgrim assumed an air of great sanctity, as he said – 'Arise, Madam, weep not, but hearken diligently to what I shall say to you, and look to it that you impart it to none. I have it by revelation of God that the tribulation wherein you stand is come upon you in requital of a sin which you did once commit, of which God is minded that this suffering be a partial purgation, and that you make reparation in full, if you would not find yourself in a far more grievous plight.' 'Sir,' replied the lady, 'many sins have I committed, nor know I how among them all to single out that whereof, more than another, God requires reparation at my hands: wherefore, if you know it, tell it me, and what by way of reparation I may do, that will I do.' 'Madam,' returned the pilgrim, 'well wot I what it is, nor shall I question you thereof for my better instruction, but that the rehearsal may give you increase of remorse therefore. But pass we now to fact. Tell me, mind you ever to have had a lover?' Whereat the lady heaved a deep sigh; then, marvelling not a little, for she had thought 'twas known to none, albeit on the day when the man was slain, who was afterwards buried as Tedaldo, there had been some buzz about it, occasioned by some indiscreet words dropped by Tedaldo's gossip and confidant, she made answer – 'I see that there is nought that men keep secret but God reveals it to you; wherefore I shall not endeavour to hide my secrets from you. True it is that in my youth I was beyond measure enamoured of the unfortunate young man whose death is imputed to my husband; whom I mourned with grief unfeigned, for, albeit I showed myself harsh and cruel towards him before his departure, yet neither thereby, nor by his long absence, nor yet by his calamitous death was my heart estranged from him.' Then said the pilgrim – ' 'Twas not the unfortunate young man now dead that you did love, but Tedaldo Elisei. But let that pass; now tell me: wherefore lost he your good graces? Did he ever offend you?' 'Nay verily,' answered the lady, 'he never offended me at all. My harshness was prompted by an accursed friar, to whom I once confessed, and who, when I told him of the love I bore Tedaldo, and my intimacy with him, made my ears so tingle and sing that I still shudder to think of it, warning me that, if I gave it not up, I should fall into the jaws of the Devil in the abyss of hell, and be cast into the avenging fire. Whereby I was so terrified that I quite made my mind up to discontinue my intimacy with him, and, to seal the matter, I would thenceforth have none of his letters or messages; and so, I suppose, he went away in despair, though I doubt not, had he persevered a while longer, I should not have seen him wasting away like snow in sunshine without relenting of my harsh resolve; for in sooth there was nothing in the world I would so gladly have done.' Then said the pilgrim – 'Madam, 'tis this sin, and this only, that has brought upon you your present tribulation. I know positively that Tedaldo did never put force upon you: 'twas of your own free will, and because he pleased you, that you became enamoured of him: your constant visitor, your intimate friend he became, because you yourself would have it so; and in the course of your intimacy you showed him such favour by word and deed that, if he loved you first, you multiplied his love full a thousandfold. And if so it was, and well I know it was so, what justification had you for thus harshly severing yourself from him? You should have considered the whole matter before the die was cast, and not have entered upon it, if you deemed you might have cause to repent of it as a sin. As soon as he became yours, you became his. Had he not been yours, you might have acted as you had thought fit, at your own unfettered discretion; but, as you were his, 'twas robbery, 'twas conduct most disgraceful, to sever yourself from him against his will. Now you must know that I am a friar; and therefore all the ways of friars are familiar to me; nor does it misbecome me, as it might another, to speak for your behoof somewhat freely of them; as I am minded to do that you may have better understanding of them in the future than you would seem to have had in the past. Time was when the friars were most holy and worthy men, but those who today take the name and claim the reputation of friars have nought of the friar save only the habit: nay, they have not even that: for, whereas their founders ordained that their habits should be strait, of a sorry sort, and of coarse stuff, apt symbols of a soul that in arraying the body in so mean a garb did despite to all things temporal, our modern friars will have them full, and double, and resplendent, and of the finest stuff, and of a fashion goodly and pontifical, wherein without shame they flaunt it like peacocks in the church, in the piazza, even as do the laity in their robes. And as the fisherman casts his net into the stream with intent to take many fish at one throw: so 'tis the main solicitude and study, art and craft of these friars to embrace and entangle within the ample folds of their vast swelling skirts beguines, widows and other foolish women, ay, and men likewise in great number. Wherefore, to speak with more exactitude, the friars of today have nought of the habit of the friar save only the colour thereof. And whereas the friars of old time sought to win men to their salvation, those of today seek to win their women and their wealth; wherefore they have made it and make it their sole concern by declamation and imagery to strike terror into the souls of fools, and to make believe that sins are purged by alms and masses; to the end that they, base wretches that have fled to friarage not to practice holiness but to escape hardship, may receive from this man bread, from that man wine, and from the other man a donation for masses for the souls of his dead. True indeed it is that sins are purged by almsgiving and prayer; but, did they who give the alms know, did they but understand to whom they give them, they would be more apt to keep them to themselves, or throw them to so many pigs. And, knowing that the fewer be they that share great riches, the greater their ease, 'tis the study of each how best by declamation and intimidation to oust others from that whereof he would fain be the sole owner. They censure lust in men, that, they turning therefrom, the sole use of their women may remain to the censors: they condemn usury and unlawful gains, that, being entrusted with the restitution thereof, they may be able to enlarge their habits, and to purchase bishoprics and other great preferments with the very money which they have made believe must bring its possessor to perdition. And when they are taxed with these and many other discreditable practices, they deem that there is no censure, however grave, of which they may not be quit by their glib formula – "Follow our precepts, not our practice:" as if 'twere possible that the sheep should be of a more austere and rigid virtue than the shepherds. And how many of these, whom they put off with this formula, understand it not in the way in which they enunciate it, not a few of them know. The friars of today would have you follow their precepts, that is to say, they would have you fill their purses with coin, confide to them your secrets, practise continence, be long-suffering, forgive those that trespass against you, keep yourselves from evil speaking; all which things are good, seemly, holy. But to what end? To the end that they may be able to do that which, if the laity do it, they will not be able to do. Who knows not that idleness cannot subsist without money? Spend thy money on thy pleasures, and the friar will not be able to live in sloth in his order. Go after women, and there will be no place for the friar. Be not long suffering, pardon not the wrong-doer, and the friar will not dare to cross thy threshold to corrupt thy family. But wherefore pursue I the topic through every detail? They accuse themselves as often as they so excuse themselves in the hearing of all that have understanding. Why seclude they not themselves, if they misdoubt their power to lead continent and holy lives? Or if they must needs not live as recluses, why follow they not that other holy text of the Gospel – Christ began to do and to teach?* Let them practise first, and school us with their precepts afterwards. A thousand such have I seen in my day, admirers, lovers, philanderers, not of ladies of the world alone, but of nuns; ay, and they too such as made the most noise in the pulpits. Is it such as they that we are to follow? He that does so, pleases himself; but God knows if he do wisely. But assume that herein we must allow that your censor, the friar, spoke truth, to wit, that none may break the marriage-vow without very grave sin. What then? to rob a man, to slay him, to make of him an exile and a wanderer on the face of the earth, are not these yet greater sins? None will deny that so they are. A woman that indulges herself in the intimate use with a man commits but a sin of nature; but if she rob him, or slay him, or drive him out into exile, her sin proceeds from depravity of spirit. That you did rob Tedaldo, I have already shown you, in that, having of your own free will become his, you tore yourself from him. I now go further and say that, so far as in you lay, you slew him, seeing that, showing yourself ever more and more cruel, you did your utmost to drive him to take his own life; and in the law's intent he that is the cause that wrong is done is as culpable as he that does it. Nor is it deniable that you were the cause that for seven years he has been an exile and a wanderer upon the face of the earth. Wherefore upon each of the said three articles you are found guilty of a greater crime than you committed by your intimacy with him. But consider we the matter more closely: perchance Tedaldo merited such treatment: nay, but assuredly 'twas not so. You have yourself so confessed: besides which I know that he loves you more dearly than himself. He would laud, he would extol, he would magnify you above all other ladies so as never was heard the like,

* These words are not from any of the Gospels, but from the first verse of the Acts of the Apostles. Boccaccio doubtless used 'Evangelio' in a large sense for the whole of the New Testament.

wheresoever 'twas seemly for him to speak of you, and it might be done without exciting suspicion. All his bliss, all his honour, all his liberty he avowed was entirely in your disposal. Was he not of noble birth? And for beauty might he not compare with the rest of his townsfolk? Did he not excel in all the exercises and accomplishments proper to youth? Was he not beloved, held dear, well seen of all men? You will not deny it. How then could you at the behest of a paltry friar, silly, brutish and envious, bring yourself to deal with him in any harsh sort? I cannot estimate the error of those ladies who look askance on men and hold them cheap; whereas, bethinking them of what they are themselves, and what and how great is the nobility with which God has endowed man above all the other animals, they ought rather to glory in the love which men give them, and hold them most dear, and with all zeal study to please them, that so their love may never fail. In what sort you did so, instigated by the chatter of a friar, some broth-guzzling, pastry-gorging knave without a doubt, you know; and peradventure his purpose was but to instal himself in the place whence he sought to oust another. This then is the sin which the Divine justice, which, ever operative, suffers no perturbation of its even balance, or arrest of judgement, has decreed not to leave unpunished: wherefore, as without due cause you devised how you might despoil Tedaldo of yourself, so without due cause your husband has been placed and is in jeopardy of his life on Tedaldo's account, and to your sore affliction. Wherefrom if you would be delivered, there is that which you must promise, ay, and (much more) which you must perform: to wit, that, should it ever betide that Tedaldo return hither from his long exile, you will restore to him your favour, your love, your tender regard, your intimacy, and reinstate him in the position which he held before you foolishly hearkened to the halfwitted friar.'

Thus ended the pilgrim; and the lady, who had followed him with the closest attention, deeming all that he advanced very sound, and doubting not that her tribulation was, as he said, in requital of her sin, spoke thus – 'Friend of God, well I wot that the matters which you discourse are true, and, thanks to your delineation, I now in great measure know what manner of men are the friars, whom I have hitherto regarded as all alike holy; nor doubt I that great was my fault in the course which I pursued towards Tedaldo; and gladly, were it in my power, would I make reparation in the manner which you have indicated. But how is this feasible? Tedaldo can never return to us. He is dead. Wherefore I know not why I must needs give you a promise which cannot be performed.' 'Madam,' returned the pilgrim, ' 'tis revealed to me by God that Tedaldo is by no means dead, but alive and well and happy, so only he enjoyed your favour.' 'Nay, but,' said the lady, 'speak advisedly; I saw his body done to death by more than one knife-wound; I folded it in these arms, and drenched the dead face with many a tear; whereby, perchance, I gave occasion for the bruit that has been made to my disadvantage.' 'Say what you may, Madam,' rejoined the pilgrim, 'I assure you that Tedaldo lives, and if you will but give the promise, then, for its fulfilment, I have good hope that you will soon see him.' Whereupon: 'I give the promise,' said the lady, 'and right gladly will I make it good; nor is there aught that might happen that would yield me such delight as to see my husband free and scatheless, and Tedaldo alive.' Tedaldo now deemed it wise to make himself known, and establish the lady in a more sure hope of her husband's safety. Wherefore he said – 'Madam, to set your mind at ease in regard of your husband, I must first impart to you a secret, which be mindful to disclose to none so long as you live.' Then – for such was the confidence which the lady reposed in the pilgrim's apparent sanctity that they were by themselves in a place remote from observation – Tedaldo drew forth a ring which he had guarded with the most jealous care, since it had been given him by the lady on the last night when they were together, and said, as he showed it to her – 'Madam, know you this?' The lady recognised it forthwith, and answered – 'I do, Sir; I gave it long ago to Tedaldo.' Then the pilgrim, rising and throwing off his sclavine* and hat, said with the Florentine accent – 'And know you me?' The lady, recognising forthwith the form and semblance of Tedaldo, was struck dumb with wonder and fear as of a corpse that is seen to go about as if alive, and was much rather disposed to turn and flee from Tedaldo returned from the tomb than to come forward and welcome Tedaldo arrived from Cyprus. But when Tedaldo said to her – 'Fear not, Madam, your Tedaldo am I, alive and well, nor was I ever dead, whatever you and my brothers may think,' the lady, partly awed, partly reassured by his voice, regarded him with rather more attention, and inwardly affirming that 'twas in very truth Tedaldo, threw herself upon his neck, and wept, and kissed him, saying – 'Sweet my Tedaldo, welcome home.' 'Madam,' replied Tedaldo after he had kissed and embraced her, 'time serves not now for greetings more intimate. 'Tis for me to be up and doing, that Aldobrandino may be restored to you safe and sound; touching which matter you will, I trust,

* *Schiavina*, Low Lat. *sclavina*, the long coarse frock worn, among others, by palmers.

before tomorrow at even hear tidings that will gladden your heart; indeed I expect to have good news tonight, and, if so, will come and tell it you, when I shall be less straitened than I am at present.' He then resumed his sclavine and hat, and having kissed the lady again, and bade her be of good cheer, took his leave, and hied him to the prison, where Aldobrandino lay more occupied with apprehension of imminent death than hope of deliverance to come. As ministrant of consolation, he gained ready admittance of the warders, and, seating himself by Aldobrandino's side, he said – 'Aldobrandino, in me thou seest a friend sent thee by God, who is touched with pity of thee by reason of thy innocence; wherefore, if in reverent submission to Him thou wilt grant me a slight favour that I shall ask of thee, without fail, before tomorrow at even, thou shalt, in lieu of the doom of death that thou awaitest, hear thy acquittal pronounced.' 'Worthy man,' replied Aldobrandino, 'I know thee not, nor mind I ever to have seen thee; wherefore, as thou showest thyself solicitous for my safety, my friend indeed thou must needs be, even as thou sayst. And in sooth the crime, for which they say I ought to be doomed to death, I never committed, though others enough I have committed, which perchance have brought me to this extremity. However, if so be that God has now pity on me, this I tell thee in reverent submission to Him, that, whereas 'tis but a little thing that thou cravest of me, there is nought, however great, but I would not only promise but gladly do it; wherefore, even ask what thou wilt, and, if so be that I escape, I will without fail keep my word to the letter.' 'Nay,' returned the pilgrim, 'I ask but this of thee, that thou pardon Tedaldo's four brothers, that in the belief that thou wast guilty of their brother's death they brought thee to this strait, and, so they ask thy forgiveness, account them as thy brothers and friends.' 'How sweet,' replied Aldobrandino, 'is the savour, how ardent the desire, of vengeance, none knows but he that is wronged; but yet, so God may take thought for my deliverance, I will gladly pardon, nay, I do now pardon them, and if I go hence alive and free, I will thenceforth have them in such regard as shall content thee.' Satisfied with this answer, the pilgrim, without further parley, heartily exhorted Aldobrandino to be of good cheer; assuring him that, before the next day was done, he should be certified beyond all manner of doubt of his deliverance; and so he left him.

On quitting the prison the pilgrim hied him forthwith to the signory, and being closeted with a knight that was in charge, thus spoke – 'My lord, 'tis the duty of all, and most especially of those who hold your place, zealously to bestir themselves that the truth be brought to light, in order as well that those bear not the penalty who have not committed the crime, as that the guilty be punished. And that this may come to pass to your honour and the undoing of the delinquent, I am come hither to you. You wot that you have dealt rigorously with Aldobrandino Palermini, and have found, as you think, that 'twas he that slew Tedaldo Elisei, and you are about to condemn him; wherein you are most certainly in error, as I doubt not before midnight to prove to you, delivering the murderers into your hands.' The worthy knight, who was not without pity for Aldobrandino, readily gave ear to the pilgrim's words. He conversed at large with him, and availing himself of his guidance, made an easy capture of the two brothers that kept the inn and their servant in their first sleep. He was about to put them to the torture to elicit the true state of the case, when, their courage failing, they confessed without the least reserve, severally at first, and then jointly, that 'twas they that had slain Tedaldo Elisei, not knowing who he was. Asked for why, they answered that 'twas because he had sorely harassed the wife of one of them, and would have constrained her to do his pleasure, while they were out of doors. Whereof the pilgrim was no sooner apprised, than by leave of the knight he withdrew, and hied him privily to the house of Madonna Ermellina, whom (the rest of the household being gone to bed) he found awaiting him alone, and equally anxious for good news of her husband and a complete reconciliation with her Tedaldo. On entering, he blithely exclaimed: – 'Rejoice, dearest my lady, for thou mayst rest assured that tomorrow thou shalt have thy Aldobrandino back here safe and sound;' and to confirm her faith in his words, he told her all that he had done. Greater joy was never woman's than hers of two such glad surprises; to wit, to have Tedaldo with her alive again, whom she had wailed for verily dead, and to know Aldobrandino, whom she had thought in no long time to wail for dead, now out of jeopardy. Wherefore, when she had affectionately embraced and kissed her Tedaldo, they hied them to bed together, and with hearty goodwill made gracious and gladsome consummation of their peace by interchange of sweet solace.

With the approach of day Tedaldo rose, and having first apprised the lady of his purpose and enjoined her, as before, to keep it most secret, resumed his pilgrim's habit, and sallied forth of her house, to be ready, as occasion should serve, to act in Aldobrandino's interest. As soon as 'twas day, the signory, deeming themselves amply conversant with the affair, set Aldobrandino at large; and a few days later they caused the malefactors to be beheaded in the place where they had done the murder.

Great was Aldobrandino's joy to find himself free, nor less great was that of his lady and all his friends and kinsfolk; and as 'twas through the pilgrim that it had come about, they brought him to their house, there to reside as long as he cared to tarry in the city; nor could they do him honour and cheer enough, and most of all the lady, who knew her man. But after a while, seeing that his brothers were not only become a common laughing-stock by reason of Aldobrandino's acquittal, but had armed themselves for very fear, he felt that their reconciliation with him brooked no delay, and accordingly craved of him performance of his promise. Aldobrandino replied handsomely that it should be had at once. The pilgrim then bade him arrange for the following day a grand banquet, at which he and his kinsfolk and their ladies were to entertain the four brothers and their ladies, adding that he would himself go forthwith as Aldobrandino's envoy, and bid them welcome to his peace and banquet. All which being approved by Aldobrandino, the pilgrim hied him with all speed to the four brothers, whom by ample, apt and unanswerable argument he readily induced to reinstate themselves in Aldobrandino's friendship by suing for his forgiveness: which done, he bade them and their ladies to breakfast with Aldobrandino on the morrow, and they, being assured of his good faith, were consenting to come. So, on the morrow, at the breakfast hour, Tedaldo's four brothers, still wearing their black, came with certain of their friends to Aldobrandino's house, where he awaited them; and, in presence of the company that had been bidden to meet them, laid down their arms, and made surrender to Aldobrandino, asking his pardon of that which they had done against him. Aldobrandino received them compassionately, wept, kissed each on the mouth, and let few words suffice to remit each offence. After them came their sisters and their wives, all habited sadly, and were graciously received by Madonna Ermellina and the other ladies. The guests, men and women alike, found all things ordered at the banquet with magnificence, nor aught unmeet for commendation save the restraint which the yet recent grief, betokened by the sombre garb of Tedaldo's kinsfolk, laid upon speech (wherein some had found matter to except against the banquet and the pilgrim for devising it, as he well knew), but, as he had premeditated, in due time, he stood up, the others being occupied with their dessert, and spoke thus – 'Nothing is wanting to complete the gaiety of this banquet except the presence of Tedaldo; whom, as you have been long time with him and have not known him, I will point out to you.' So, having divested himself of his sclavine and whatever else in his garb denoted the pilgrim, he remained habited in a tunic of green taffeta, in which guise, so great was the wonder with which all regarded him that, though they recognised him, 'twas long before any dared to believe that 'twas actually Tedaldo. Marking their surprise, Tedaldo told them not a little about themselves, their family connections, their recent history, and his own adventures. Whereat his brothers and the rest of the men, all weeping for joy, hastened to embrace him, followed by the women, as well those that were not, as those that were, of kin to him, save only Madonna Ermellina. Which Aldobrandino observing, said – 'What is this, Ermellina? How comes it that, unlike the other ladies, thou alone dost Tedaldo no cheer?' 'Cheer,' replied the lady in the hearing of all, 'would I gladly do him such as no other woman has done or could do, seeing that I am more beholden to him than any other woman, in that to him I owe it that I have thee with me again; 'tis but the words spoken to my disadvantage, while we mourned him that we deemed Tedaldo, that give me pause.' 'Now out upon thee,' said Aldobrandino, 'thinkest thou that I heed the yelping of these curs? His zeal for my deliverance has abundantly disproved it, besides which I never believed it. Quick, get thee up, and go and embrace him.' The lady, who desired nothing better, was in this not slow to obey her husband; she rose forthwith, and embraced Tedaldo as the other ladies had done, and did him gladsome cheer. Tedaldo's brothers and all the company, men and women alike, heartily approved Aldobrandino's handsomeness; and so whatever of despite the rumour had engendered in the minds of any was done away. And, now that all had done him cheer, Tedaldo with his own hands rent his brothers' suits of black upon their backs, as also the sad-hued garments which his sisters and sisters-in-law wore, and bade bring other apparel. Which when they had donned, there was no lack of singing, dancing and other sorts of merry-making; whereby the banquet, for all its subdued beginning, had a sonorous close. Then, just as they were, in the blithest of spirits, they hied them all to Tedaldo's house, where in the evening they supped; and in this manner they held festival for several days.

'Twas some time before the Florentines ceased to look on Tedaldo as a portent, as if he were risen from the dead; and a shadow of doubt whether he were really Tedaldo or no continued to lurk in the minds of not a few, including even his brothers: they had no assured belief; and in that frame had perchance long continued, but for a casual occurrence that showed them who the murdered man was. It so befell that one day some men-at-arms from Lunigiana passed by their house, and seeing Tedaldo accosted him, saying – 'Good-morrow to thee, Faziuolo.' To whom Tedaldo, in the presence of his brothers, answered – 'You take me for another.' Whereat they were abashed, and asked his pardon, saying – 'Sooth to tell, you are liker than we ever knew any man like to another to a comrade of ours, Faziuolo da Pontremoli by name, who came hither a fortnight ago, or perhaps a little more, since when we have not been able to learn what became of him. Most true it is that your dress surprised us, because he, like ourselves, was a soldier.' Whereupon Tedaldo's eldest brother came forward, and asked how their comrade had been accoutred. They told him, and 'twas found to have been exactly as they said: by which and other evidence 'twas established that 'twas Faziuolo that had been murdered, and not Tedaldo; of whom thenceforth no suspicion lurked in the minds of his brothers or anyone else.

So, then, Tedaldo returned home very rich, and remained constant in his love; nor did the lady again treat him harshly; but, using discretion, they long had mutual solace of their love. God grant us solace of ours.

❧ 15 ❧

The eighth story of the third day, in which Ferondo, having taken a certain powder, is interred for dead; is disinterred by the abbot, who enjoys his wife; is put in prison and taught to believe that he is in purgatory; is then resuscitated, and rears as his own a boy begotten by the abbot upon his wife.

Ended Emilia's long story, which to none was the less pleasing for its length, but was deemed of all the ladies brief in regard of the number and variety of the events therein recounted, a gesture of the queen sufficed to convey her behest to Lauretta, and cause her thus to begin: ❧ Dearest ladies, I have it in mind to tell you a true story, which wears far more of the aspect of a lie than of that which it really was: 'tis brought to my recollection by that which we have heard of one being bewailed and buried in lieu of another. My story then is of one that, living, was buried for dead, and after believed with many others that he came out of the tomb not as one that had not died but as one risen from the dead; whereby he was venerated as a saint who ought rather to have been condemned as a criminal –

Know then that there was and still is in Tuscany an abbey, situated, as we see not a few, in a somewhat solitary spot, wherein the office of abbot was held by a monk, who in all other matters ordered his life with great sanctity, save only in the commerce with women, and therein knew so well how to cloak his indulgence, that scarce any there were that so much as suspected – not to say detected it – so holy and just was he reputed in all matters. Now the abbot consorted much with a very wealthy contadino, Ferondo by name, a man coarse and gross beyond measure, whose friendship the abbot only cared for because of the opportunities which it afforded of deriving amusement from his simplicity; and during their intercourse the abbot discovered that Ferondo had a most beautiful wife; of whom he became so hotly enamoured that he could think of nought else either by day or by night. But learning that, however simple and inept in all other matters, Ferondo showed excellent good sense in cherishing and watching over this wife of his, he almost despaired. However, being very astute, he prevailed so far with Ferondo, that he would sometimes bring his wife with him to take a little recreation in the abbey-garden, where he discoursed to them with all lowliness of the blessedness of life eternal, and the most pious works of many men and women of times past, insomuch that the lady conceived a desire to confess to him, and craved and had Ferondo's leave therefore. So, to the abbot's boundless delight, the lady came and seated herself at his feet to make her confession, whereto she prefixed the following exordium – 'If God, Sir, had given me a husband, or had not permitted me to have one, perchance 'twould be easy for me, under your guidance, to enter the way, of which you have spoken, that leads to life eternal. But, considering what manner of man Ferondo is, and his stupidity, I may call myself a widow while yet I am married in that, so long as he lives, I may have no other husband; and he, fool that he is, is without the least cause so inordinately jealous of me that 'tis not possible but that my life with him be one of perpetual tribulation and woe. Wherefore, before I address myself to make further confession, I in all humility beseech you to be pleased to give me some counsel of this matter, for here or nowhere is to be found the source of the amelioration of my life, and if it be not found, neither confession nor any other good work will be of any avail.' The abbot was overjoyed to hear her thus speak, deeming that Fortune had opened a way to the fulfilment of his heart's desire. Wherefore he said – 'My daughter, I doubt not that 'tis a great affliction to a lady, fair and delicate as you are, to have a fool for a husband, and still more so that he should be jealous: and as your husband is both the one and the other, I readily credit what you say of your tribulation. But, to come to the point, I see no resource or remedy in this case, save this only, that Ferondo be cured of his jealousy. The medicine that shall cure him I know very well how to devise, but it behoves you to keep secret what I am about to tell you.' 'Doubt not of it, my father,' said the lady; 'for I had rather suffer death than tell aught that you forbade me to tell. But the medicine, how is it to be devised?' 'If we would have him cured,' replied the abbot, 'it can only be by his going to purgatory.' 'And how may that be?' returned the lady; 'can he go thither while he yet lives?' 'He must die,' answered the abbot; 'and so he will go thither; and when he has suffered pain enough to be cured of his jealousy, we have certain prayers with which we will supplicate God to restore him to life, and He will do so.' 'Then,' said the lady; 'am I to remain a widow?' 'Yes,' replied the abbot, 'for a certain time, during which you must be very careful not to let yourself be married to another, because 'twould offend God, and when Ferondo was restored to life, you would have to go back to him, and he would be more jealous than ever.' 'Be it so then,' said the lady; 'if he be but cured of his jealousy, and so I be not doomed to pass the rest of my days in prison, I shall be content: do as you think best.' 'And so will I,' said the abbot; 'but what reward shall I have for such a service?' 'My father,' said the lady, 'what you please; so only it be in my power. But what may the like of me do that may be acceptable to a man such as you?' 'Madam,' replied the abbot, ' 'tis in your power to do no less for me than I am about to do for you: as that which I am minded to do will ensure your comfort and consolation, so there is that which you may do which will be the deliverance and salvation of my life.' 'If so it be,' said the lady, 'I shall not be found wanting.' 'In that case,' said the abbot, 'you will give me your love, and gratify my passion for you, with which I am all afire and wasting away.' Whereto the lady, all consternation, replied – 'Alas! my father, what is this you crave? I took you for a holy man; now does it beseem holy men to make such overtures to ladies that come to them for counsel?' 'Marvel not, fair my soul,' returned the abbot; 'hereby is my holiness in no wise diminished, for holiness resides in the soul, and this which I ask of you is but a sin of the flesh. But, however it may be, such is the might of your bewitching beauty, that love constrains me thus to act. And, let me tell you, good cause have you to vaunt you of your beauty more than other women, in that it delights the saints, who are used to contemplate celestial beauties; whereto I may add that, albeit I am an abbot, yet I am a man even as others, and, as you see, not yet old. Nor need this matter seem formidable to you, but rather to be anticipated with pleasure, for, while Ferondo is in purgatory, I shall be your nightly companion, and will give you such solace as he should have given you; nor will it ever be discovered by any, for all think of me even as you did a while ago, or even more so. Reject not the grace that God accords you; for 'tis in your power to have, and, if you are wise and follow my advice, you shall have that which women not a few desire in vain to have. And moreover I have jewels fair and rare, which I am minded shall be yours and none other's. Wherefore, sweet my hope, deny me not due reward of the service which I gladly render you.'

The lady, her eyes still downcast, knew not how to deny him, and yet scrupled to gratify him: wherefore the abbot, seeing that she had hearkened and hesitated to answer, deemed that she was already half won, and following up what he had said with much more to the like effect, did not rest until he had persuaded her that she would do well to comply: and so with some confusion she told him that she was ready to obey his every behest; but it might not be until Ferondo was in purgatory. The abbot, well content, replied – 'And we will send him thither forthwith: do but arrange that he come hither to stay with me tomorrow or the day after.' Which said, he slipped a most beautiful ring on her finger, and dismissed her. Pleased with the gift, and expecting more to come, the lady rejoined her attendants, with whom she forthwith fell a-talking marvellous things of the abbot's sanctity, and so went home with them.

Some few days after, Ferondo being come to the abbey, the abbot no sooner saw him than he resolved to send him to purgatory. So he selected from among his drugs a powder of marvellous virtue, which he had gotten in the Levant from a great prince, who averred that 'twas wont to be used by the Old Man of the Mountain, when he would send anyone to or bring him from his paradise, and that, without doing the recipient any harm, 'twould induce in him, according to the quantity of the dose, a sleep of such duration and quality that, while the efficacy of the powder lasted, none would deem him to be alive.* Whereof he took enough to cause a three days' sleep, and gave it to Ferondo in his cell in a beaker that had still some wine in it, so that he drank it unwittingly: after which he took Ferondo to the cloister, and there with some of his monks fell to making merry with him and his ineptitudes. In no long time, however, the powder so wrought, that Ferondo was seized in the head with a fit of somnolence so sudden and violent that he slept as he stood, and sleeping fell to the ground. The abbot put on an agitated air, caused him to be untrussed, sent for cold water, and had it sprinkled on his face, and applied such other remedies as if he would fain call back life and sense banished by vapours of the stomach, or some other intrusive force; but, as, for all that he and his monks did, Ferondo did not revive, they, after feeling his pulse and finding there no sign of life, one and all pronounced him certainly dead. Wherefore they sent word to his wife and kinsfolk, who came forthwith, and mourned a while; after which Ferondo in his clothes was by the abbot's

* By the Old Man of the Mountain is meant the head of the confraternity of hashish-eaters (Assassins), whose chief stronghold was at Alamut in Persia (1090–1256).

order laid in a tomb. The lady went home, saying that nothing should ever part her from a little son that she had borne Ferondo; and so she occupied herself with the care of her son and Ferondo's estate. At night the abbot rose noiselessly, and with the help of a Bolognese monk, in whom he reposed much trust, and who was that very day arrived from Bologna, got Ferondo out of the tomb, and bore him to a vault, which admitted no light, having been made to serve as a prison for delinquent monks; and having stripped him of his clothes, and habited him as a monk, they laid him on a truss of straw, and left him there until he should revive. Expecting which event, and instructed by the abbot how he was then to act, the Bolognese monk (none else knowing aught of what was afoot) kept watch by the tomb.

The day after, the abbot with some of his monks paid a pastoral visit to the lady's house, where he found her in mourning weeds and sad at heart; and, after administering a little consolation, he gently asked her to redeem her promise. Free as she now felt herself, and hampered neither by Ferondo nor by any other, the lady, who had noticed another beautiful ring on the abbot's finger, promised immediate compliance, and arranged with the abbot that he should visit her the very next night. So, at nightfall, the abbot donned Ferondo's clothes, and, attended by his monk, paid his visit, and lay with her until matins to his immense delight and solace, and so returned to the abbey; and many visits he paid her on the same errand; whereby some that met him, coming or going that way, supposed that 'twas Ferondo perambulating those parts by way of penance; and fables not a few passed from mouth to mouth of the foolish rustics, and sometimes reached the ears of the lady, who was at no loss to account for them.

As for Ferondo, when he revived, 'twas only to find himself he knew not where, while the Bolognese monk entered the tomb, gibbering horribly, and armed with a rod, wherewith, having laid hold of Ferondo, he gave him a severe thrashing. Blubbering and bellowing for pain, Ferondo could only ejaculate – 'Where am I?' 'In purgatory,' replied the monk. 'How?' returned Ferondo, 'am I dead then?' and the monk assuring him that 'twas even so, he fell a bewailing his own and his lady's and his son's fate, after the most ridiculous fashion in the world. The monk brought him somewhat to eat and drink. Of which when Ferondo caught sight, 'Oh!' said he, 'dead folk eat then, do they?' 'They do,' replied the monk; 'and this, which I bring thee, is what the lady that was thy wife sent this morning to the church by way of alms for masses for thy soul; and God is minded that it be assigned to thee.' 'Now God grant her a happy year,' said Ferondo; 'dearly I loved her while I yet lived, and would hold her all night long in my arms, and cease not to kiss her, ay, and would do yet more to her, when I was so minded.' Whereupon he fell to eating and drinking with great avidity, and finding the wine not much to his taste, he said – 'Now God do her a mischief! Why gave she not the priest of the wine that is in the cask by the wall?' When he had done eating, the monk laid hold of him again, and gave him another sound thrashing with the rod. Ferondo bellowed mightily, and then cried out: – 'Alas! why servest thou me so?' 'God,' answered the monk, 'has decreed that thou be so served twice a day.' 'For why?' said Ferondo. 'Because,' returned the monk, 'thou wast jealous, notwithstanding thou hadst to wife a woman that has not her peer in thy countryside.' 'Alas,' said Ferondo, 'she was indeed all that thou sayst, ay, and the sweetest creature too – no comfit so honeyed – but I knew not that God took it amiss that a man should be jealous, or I had not been so.' 'Of that,' replied the monk, 'thou shouldst have bethought thee while thou wast there, and have amended thy ways; and should it fall to thy lot ever to return thither, be sure that thou so lay to heart the lesson that I now give thee, that thou be no more jealous.' 'Oh!' said Ferondo; 'dead folk sometimes return to earth, do they?' 'They do,' replied the monk; 'if God so will.' 'Oh!' said Ferondo; 'if I ever return, I will be the best husband in the world; never will I beat her or scold her, save for the wine that she has sent me this morning, and also for sending me never a candle, so that I have had perforce to eat in the dark.' 'Nay,' said the monk, 'she sent them, but they were burned at the masses.' 'Oh!' said Ferondo, 'I doubt not you say true; and, of a surety, if I ever return, I will let her do just as she likes. But tell me, who art thou that entreatest me thus?' 'Late of Sardinia I,' answered the monk, 'dead too; and, for that I gave my lord much countenance in his jealousy, doomed by God for my proper penance to entreat thee thus with food and drink and thrashings, until such time as He may ordain otherwise touching thee and me.' 'And are we two the only folk here?' enquired Ferondo. 'Nay, there are thousands beside,' answered the monk; 'but thou canst neither see nor hear them, nor they thee.' 'And how far,' said Ferondo, 'may we be from our country?' 'Oh! ho!' returned the monk, 'why, 'tis some miles clean out of shit-range.' 'I'faith,' said Ferondo, 'that is far indeed: methinks we must be out of the world.'

In such a course, alternately beaten, fed and amused with idle tales, was Ferondo kept for ten months, while the abbot to his great felicity, paid many a visit to the fair lady, and had the jolliest time in the world with her. But, as misfortunes will happen, the lady conceived, which fact, as soon as she was aware of it, she imparted to the abbot; whereupon both agreed that Ferondo must without delay be brought back from purgatory to earth and her, and be given to understand that she was with child of him. So the very next night the abbot went to the prison, and in a disguised voice pronounced Ferondo's name, and said to him – 'Ferondo, be of good cheer, for God is minded that thou return to earth; and on thy return thou shalt have a son by thy lady, and thou shalt call him Benedetto; because 'tis in answer to the prayers of thy holy abbot and thy lady, and for love of St Benedict, that God accords thee this grace.' Whereafter Ferondo was overjoyed, and said – 'It likes me well. God give a good year to Master Lord God, and the abbot, and St Benedict, and my cheese-powdered, honey-sweet wife.' Then, in the wine that he sent him, the abbot administered enough of the powder to cause him to sleep for four hours; and so, with the aid of the monk, having first habited him in his proper clothes, he privily conveyed him back to the tomb in which he had been buried. On the morrow at daybreak Ferondo revived, and perceiving through a chink in the tomb a glimmer of light, to which he had been a stranger for full ten months, he knew that he was alive, and began to bellow – 'Let me out, let me out:' then, setting his head to the lid of the tomb, he heaved amain; whereby the lid, being insecure, started; and he was already thrusting it aside, when the monks, matins being now ended, ran to the spot and recognised Ferondo's voice, and saw him issue from the tomb; by which unwonted event they were all so affrighted that they took to flight, and hied them to the abbot: who, rising as if from prayer, said – 'Sons, be not afraid; take the cross and the holy water, and follow me, and let us see what sign of His might God will vouchsafe us.' And so he led the way to the tomb; beside which they found Ferondo standing, deathly pale by reason of his long estrangement from the light. On sight of the abbot he ran and threw himself at his feet, saying – 'My father, it has been revealed to me that 'tis to your prayers and those of St Benedict and my lady that I owe my release from purgatorial pain, and restoration to life; wherefore 'tis my prayer that God give you a good year and good calends, today and all days.' 'Laud we the power of God!' said the abbot. 'Go then, son, as God has restored thee to earth, comfort thy wife, who, since thou didst depart this life, has been ever in tears, and mayst thou live henceforth in the love and service of God.' 'Sir,' answered Ferondo, ' 'tis well said; and, for the doing, trust me that, as soon as I find her, I shall kiss her, such is the love I bear her.' So saying, he went his way; and the abbot, left alone with his monks, made as if he marvelled greatly at the affair, and caused devoutly chant the

Miserere. So Ferondo returned to his hamlet, where all that saw him fleeing, as folk are wont to flee from spectacles of horror, he called them back, asseverating that he was risen from the tomb. His wife at first was no less timorous: but, as folk began to take heart of grace, perceiving that he was alive, they plied him with many questions, all which he answered as one that had returned with ripe experience, and gave them tidings of the souls of their kinsfolk, and told of his own invention the prettiest fables of the purgatorial state, and in full folkmoot recounted the revelation vouchsafed him by the mouth of Ragnolo Braghiello* before his resuscitation.

Thus was Ferondo reinstated in his property and reunited to his wife, who, being pregnant, as he thought, by himself, chanced by the time of her delivery to countenance the vulgar error that the woman must bear the infant in the womb for exactly nine months, and gave birth to a male child, who was named Benedetto Ferondi. Ferondo's return from purgatory, and the report he brought thence, immeasurably enhanced the fame of the abbot's holiness. So Ferondo, cured of his jealousy by the thrashings which he had gotten for it, verified the abbot's prediction, and never offended the lady again in that sort. Wherefore she lived with him, as before, in all outward seemliness; albeit she failed not, as occasion served, to forgather with the holy abbot, who had so well and sedulously served her in her especial need.

* Derisively for Agnolo Gabriello (the *h* having merely the effect of preserving the hardness of the *g* before *i*), i.e. Angel Gabriel.

⁓ 16 ⁓

The ninth story of the third day, in which Gillette of Narbonne cures the King of France of a fistula, craves for spouse Bertrand de Roussillon, who marries her against his will, and hies him in despite to Florence, where, as he courts a young woman, Gillette lies with him in her stead, and has two sons by him; for which cause he afterwards takes her into favour and treats her as his wife.

Lauretta's story being ended, and the queen being minded not to break her engagement with Dioneo, 'twas now her turn to speak. Wherefore without awaiting the call of her subjects, thus with mien most gracious she began: ⁓ Now that we have heard Lauretta's story, who shall tell any to compare with it for beauty? Lucky indeed was it that she was not the first; for few that followed would have pleased; and so, I misdoubt me, 'twill fare ill with those that remain to complete the day's narration. However, for what it may be worth, I will tell you a story which seems to me germane to our theme –

Know, then, that in the realm of France there was a gentleman, Isnard, Comte de Roussillon, by name, who, being in ill-health, kept ever in attendance on him a physician, one Master Gerard of Narbonne. The said Count had an only son named Bertrand, a very fine and winsome little lad; with whom were brought up other children of his own age, among them the said physician's little daughter Gillette; who with a love boundless and ardent out of all keeping with her tender years became enamoured of this Bertrand. And so, when the Count died, and his son, being left a ward of the King, must needs go to Paris, the girl remained beside herself with grief, and, her father dying soon after, would gladly have gone to Paris to see Bertrand, might she but have found a fair excuse; but no decent pretext could she come by, being left a great and sole heiress and very closely guarded. So being come of marriageable age, still cherishing Bertrand's memory, she rejected not a few suitors, to whom her kinsfolk would fain have married her, without assigning any reason.

Now her passion waxing ever more ardent for Bertrand, as she learned that he was grown a most goodly gallant, tidings reached her that the King of France, in consequence of a tumour which he had had in the breast and which had been ill tended, was now troubled with a fistula, which occasioned him extreme distress and suffering; nor had he as yet come by a physician that was able, though many had essayed, to cure him, but had rather grown worse under their hands; wherefore in despair he was minded no more to have recourse to any for counsel or aid. Whereat the damsel was overjoyed, deeming not only that she might find therein lawful occasion to go to Paris, but, that, if the disease was what she took it to be, it might well betide that she should be wedded to Bertrand. So – for not a little knowledge had she gotten from her father – she prepared a powder from certain herbs serviceable in the treatment of the supposed disease, and straightway took horse, and hied her to Paris. Arrived there she made it her first concern to have sight of Bertrand; and then, having obtained access to the King, she besought him of his grace to show her his disease. The King knew not how to refuse so young, fair and winsome a damsel, and let her see the place. Whereupon, no longer doubting that she should cure him, she said – 'Sire, so please you, I hope in God to cure you of this malady within eight days without causing you the least distress or discomfort.' The King inwardly scoffed at her words, saying to himself – 'How should a damsel have come by a knowledge and skill that the greatest physicians in the world do not possess?' He therefore graciously acknowledged her good intention, and answered that he had resolved no more to follow advice of physician. 'Sire,' said the damsel, 'you disdain my art, because I am young and a woman; but I bid you bear in mind that I rely not on my own skill, but on the help of God, and the skill of Master Gerard of Narbonne, my father, and a famous physician in his day.' Whereupon the King said to himself – 'Perchance she is sent me by God; why put I not her skill to the proof, seeing that she says that she can cure me in a short time, and cause me no distress?' And being minded to make the experiment, he said – 'Damsel, and if, having caused me to cancel my resolve, you should fail to cure me, what are you content should ensue?' 'Sire,' answered the damsel, 'set a guard upon me; and if within eight days I cure you not, have me burned; but if I cure you, what shall be my reward?' 'You seem,' said the King, 'to be yet unmarried; if you shall effect the cure, we will marry you well and in high place.' 'Sire,' returned the damsel, 'well content indeed am I that you should marry me, so it be to such a husband as I shall ask of you, save that I may not ask any of your sons or any other member of the royal house.' Whereto the King forthwith consented, and the damsel, thereupon applying her treatment, restored him to health before the period assigned. Wherefore, as soon as the King knew that he was cured – 'Damsel,' said he, 'well have you won your husband.' She answered – 'In that case, Sire, I have won Bertrand de Roussillon, of whom, while yet a child, I was enamoured, and whom I have ever since most ardently loved.' To give her Bertrand seemed to the King no small matter; but, having pledged his word, he would not break it: so he sent for Bertrand, and said to him – 'Bertrand, you are now come to man's estate, and fully equipped to enter on it; 'tis therefore our will that you go back and assume the governance of your county, and that you take with you a damsel, whom we have given you to wife.' 'And who is the damsel, Sire?' said Bertrand. 'She it is,' answered the King, 'that has restored us to health by her physic.' Now Bertrand, knowing Gillette, and that her lineage was not such as matched his nobility, albeit, seeing her, he had found her very fair, was overcome with disdain, and answered – 'So, Sire, you would fain give me a she-doctor to wife. Now God forbid that I should ever marry any such woman.' 'Then,' said the King, 'you would have us fail of the faith which we pledged to the damsel, who asked you in marriage by way of reward for our restoration to health.' 'Sire,' said Bertrand, 'you may take from me all that I possess, and give me as your man to whomsoever you may be minded; but rest assured that I shall never be satisfied with such a match.' 'Nay, but you will,' replied the King; 'for the damsel is fair and discreet, and loves you well; wherefore we anticipate that you will live far more happily with her than with a dame of much higher lineage.' Bertrand was silent; and the King made great preparations for the celebration of the nuptials. The appointed day came, and Bertrand, albeit reluctantly, nevertheless complied, and in the presence of the King was wedded to the damsel, who loved him more dearly than herself. Which done, Bertrand, who had already taken his resolution, said that he was minded to go down to his county, there to consummate the marriage; and so, having craved and had leave of absence of the King, he took horse, but instead of returning to his county he hied him to Tuscany; where, finding the Florentines at war with the Siennese, he determined to take service with the Florentines, and being made heartily and honourably welcome, was appointed to the command of part of their forces, at a liberal stipend, and so remained in their service for a long while. Distressed by this turn of fortune, and hoping by her wise management to bring Bertrand back to his county, the bride hied her to Roussillon, where she was received by all the tenants as their liege lady. She found that during the long absence of the lord, everything had fallen into decay and disorder; which, being a capable woman, she rectified with great and sedulous care, to the great joy of the tenants, who held her in great esteem and love, and severely censured the Count, that he was not satisfied with her. When the lady had duly ordered all things in the county, she despatched two knights to the Count with the intelligence, praying him, that, if 'twas on her account that he came not home, he would so inform her; in which case she would gratify him by departing. To whom with all harshness he replied – 'She may even please herself in the matter. For my part I will go home and live with her, when she has this ring on her finger and a son gotten of me upon her arm.' The ring was one which he greatly prized, and never removed from his finger, by reason of a virtue which he had been given to understand that it possessed. The knights appreciated the harshness of a condition which contained two articles, both of which were all but impossible; and, seeing that by no words of theirs could they alter his resolve, they returned to the lady, and delivered his message. Sorely distressed, the lady after long pondering determined to try how and where the two conditions might be satisfied, that so her husband might be hers again. Having formed her plan, she assembled certain of the more considerable and notable men of the county, to whom she gave a consecutive and most touching narrative of all that she had done for love of the Count, with the result; concluding by saying that she was not minded to tarry there to the Count's perpetual exile, but to pass the rest of her days in pilgrimages and pious works for the good of her soul: wherefore she prayed them to undertake the defence and governance of the county, and to inform the Count that she had made entire and absolute cession of it to him, and was gone away with the intention of never more returning to Roussillon. As she spoke, tears not a few coursed down the cheeks of the honest men, and again and again they besought her to change her mind, and stay. All in vain, however; she commended them to God, and, accompanied only by one of her male cousins and a chambermaid (all three habited as pilgrims and amply provided with money and precious jewels), she took the road, nor tarried until she was arrived at Florence. There she lodged in a little inn kept by a good woman that was a widow, bearing herself lowly as a poor pilgrim, and eagerly expectant of news of her lord.

Now it so befell that the very next day she saw Bertrand pass in front of the inn on horseback at the head of his company; and though she knew him very well, nevertheless she asked the good woman of the inn who he was. The hostess replied – ' 'Tis a foreign gentleman – Count Bertrand they call him – a very pleasant gentleman, and courteous, and much beloved in this city; and he is in the last degree enamoured of one of our neighbours here, who is a gentlewoman, but in poor circumstances. A very virtuous damsel she is too, and, being as yet unmarried by reason of her poverty, she lives with her mother, who is an excellent and most discreet lady, but for whom, perchance, she would before now have yielded and gratified the Count's desire.' No word of this was lost on the lady; she pondered and meditated every detail with the closest attention, and having laid it all to heart, took her resolution: she ascertained the names and abode of the lady and her daughter that the Count loved, and hied her one day privily, wearing her pilgrim's weeds, to their house, where she found the lady and her daughter in very evident poverty, and after greeting them, told the lady that, if it were agreeable to her, she would speak with her. The gentlewoman rose and signified her willingness to listen to what she had to say; so they went into a room by themselves and sat down, and then the Countess began thus – 'Madam, methinks you are, as I am, under Fortune's frown; but perchance you have it in your power, if you are so minded, to afford solace to both of us.' The lady answered that, so she might honourably find it, solace indeed was what she craved most of all things in the world. Whereupon the Countess continued – 'I must first be assured of your faith, wherein if I confide and am deceived, the interests of both of us will suffer.' 'Have no fear,' said the gentlewoman, 'speak your whole mind without reserve, for you will find that there is no deceit in me.' So the Countess told who she was, and the whole course of her love affair, from its commencement to that hour, on such wise that the gentlewoman, believing her story the more readily that she had already heard it in part from others, was touched with compassion for her. The narrative of her woes complete, the Countess added – 'Now that you have heard my misfortunes, you know the two conditions that I must fulfil, if I would come by my husband; nor know I any other person than you, that may enable me to fulfil them; but so you may, if this which I hear is true, to wit, that my husband is in the last degree enamoured of your daughter.' 'Madam,' replied the gentlewoman, 'I know not if the Count loves my daughter, but true it is that he makes great show of loving her; but how may this enable me to do aught for you in the matter that you have at heart?' 'The how, madam,' returned the Countess, 'I will shortly explain to you; but you shall first hear what I intend shall ensue, if you serve me. Your daughter, I see, is fair and of marriageable age, and, by what I have learned and may well understand, 'tis because you have not the wherewith to marry her that you keep her at home. Now, in recompense of the service that you shall do me, I mean to provide her forthwith from my own moneys with such a dowry as you yourself shall deem adequate for her marriage.' The lady was too needy not to be gratified by the proposal; but, nevertheless, with the true spirit of the gentlewoman, she answered – 'Nay but, madam, tell me that which I may do for you, and if it shall be such as I may honourably do, gladly will I do it, and then you shall do as you may be minded.' Said then the Countess – 'I require of you, that through someone in whom you trust you send word to the Count, my husband, that your daughter is ready to yield herself entirely to his will, so she may be sure that he loves her even as he professes; whereof she will never be convinced, until he send her the ring which he wears on his finger, and which, she understands, he prizes so much: which, being sent, you shall give to me, and shall then send him word that your daughter is ready to do his pleasure, and, having brought him hither secretly, you shall contrive that I lie by his side instead of your daughter. Perchance, by God's grace I shall conceive, and so, having his ring on my finger, and a son gotten of him on my arm, shall have him for my own again, and live with him even as a wife should live with her husband, and owe it all to you.'

The lady felt that 'twas not a little that the Countess craved of her, for she feared lest it should bring reproach upon her daughter: but she reflected that to aid the good lady to recover her husband was an honourable enterprise, and that in undertaking it she would be subserving a like end; and so, trusting in the good and virtuous disposition of the Countess, she not only promised to do as she was required, but in no long time, proceeding with caution and secrecy, as she had been bidden, she both had the ring from the Count, loath though he was to part with it, and cunningly contrived that the Countess should lie with him in place of her daughter. In which first commingling, so ardently sought by the Count, it so pleased God that the lady was gotten, as in due time her delivery made manifest, with two sons. Nor once only, but many times did the lady gratify the Countess with the embraces of her husband, using such secrecy that no word thereof ever got wind, the Count all the while supposing that he lay, not with his wife, but with her that he loved, and being wont to give her, as he left her in the morning, some fair and rare jewel, which she jealously guarded.

When she perceived that she was with child, the Countess, being minded no more to burden the lady with such service, said to her – 'Madam, thanks be to God and to you, I now have that which I desired, and therefore 'tis time that I make you grateful requital, and take my leave of you.' The lady answered that she was glad if the Countess had gotten aught that gave her joy; but that 'twas not as hoping to have reward thereof that she had done her part, but simply because she deemed it meet and her duty so to do. 'Well said, madam,' returned the Countess, 'and in like manner that which you shall ask of me I shall not give you by way of reward, but because I deem it meet and my duty to give it.' Whereupon the lady, yielding to necessity, and abashed beyond measure, asked of her a hundred pounds wherewith to marry her daughter. The Countess, marking her embarrassment, and the modesty of her request, gave her five hundred pounds besides jewels fair and rare, worth, perhaps, no less; and having thus much more than contented her, and received her superabundant thanks, she took leave of her and returned to the inn. The lady, to render purposeless further visits or messages on Bertrand's part, withdrew with her daughter to the house of her kinsfolk in the country; nor was it long before Bertrand, on the urgent entreaty of his vassals and intelligence of the departure of his wife, quitted Florence and returned home. Greatly elated by this intelligence, the Countess tarried awhile in Florence, and was there delivered of two sons as like as possible to their father, whom she nurtured with sedulous care. But by and by she saw fit to take the road, and being come, unrecognised by any, to Montpellier, rested there a few days; and being on the alert for news of the Count and where he was, she learned that on All Saints' day he was to hold a great reception of ladies and gentlemen at Roussillon. Whither, retaining her now wonted pilgrim's weeds, she hied her, and finding that the ladies and gentlemen were all gathered in the Count's palace and on the point of going to table, she tarried not to change her dress, but went up into the hall, bearing her little ones in her arms, and threading her way through the throng to the place where she saw the Count stand, she threw herself at his feet, and sobbing, said to him – 'My lord, thy hapless bride am I, who to ensure thy homecoming and dwelling in peace have long time been a wanderer, and now demand of thee observance of the condition whereof word was brought me by the two knights whom I sent to thee. Lo in my arms not one son only but twain, gotten of thee, and on my finger thy ring. 'Tis time, then, that I be received of thee as thy wife according to thy word.' Whereat the Count was all dumbfounded, recognising the ring and his own lineaments in the children, so like were they to him; but saying to himself nevertheless – 'How can it have come about?' So the Countess, while the Count and all that were present marvelled exceedingly, told what had happened, and the manner of it, in precise detail. Wherefore the Count, perceiving that she spoke truth, and having regard to her perseverance and address and her two fine boys, and the wishes of all his vassals and the ladies, who with one accord besought him to own and honour her thenceforth as his lawful bride, laid aside his harsh obduracy, and raised the Countess to her feet, and embraced and kissed her, and acknowledged her for his lawful wife, and the children for his own. Then, having caused her to be rearrayed in garments befitting her rank, he, to the boundless delight of as many as were there, and of all other his vassals, gave up that day and some that followed to feasting and merrymaking; and did ever thenceforth honour, love and most tenderly cherish her as his bride and wife.

17

The first story of the fourth day, in which Tancred, Prince of Salerno, slays his daughter's lover, and sends her his heart in a golden cup: she pours upon it a poisonous distillation, which she drinks and dies.

A direful theme has our king allotted us for today's discourse; seeing that, whereas we are here met for our common delectation, needs must we now tell of others' tears whereby whether telling or hearing, we cannot but be moved to pity. Perchance 'twas to temper in some degree the gaiety of the past days that he so ordained, but whatever may have been his intent his will must be to me immutable law; wherefore I will narrate to you a matter that befell piteously, nay woefully, and so as you may well weep thereat –

Tancred, Prince of Salerno, a lord most humane and kind of heart, but that in his old age he imbrued his hands in the blood of a lover, had in the whole course of his life but one daughter; and had he not had her, he had been more fortunate.

Never was daughter more tenderly beloved of father than she of the Prince, who, for that cause not knowing how to part with her, kept her unmarried for many a year after she had come of marriageable age: then at last he gave her to a son of the Duke of Capua, with whom she had lived but a short while when he died and she returned to her father. Most lovely was she of form and feature (never woman more so), and young and light of heart, and more knowing, perchance, than beseemed a woman. Dwelling thus with her loving father as a great lady, in no small luxury, nor failing to see that the Prince, for the great love he bore her, was at no pains to provide her with another husband, and deeming it unseemly on her part to ask one of him, she cast about how she might come by a gallant to be her secret lover. And seeing at her father's court not a few men, both gentle and simple, that resorted thither, as we know men use to frequent courts, and closely scanning their mien and manners, she preferred before all others the Prince's page, Guiscardo by name, a man of very humble origin, but pre-eminent for native worth and noble bearing; of whom, seeing him frequently, she became hotly enamoured, hourly extolling his qualities more and more highly. The young man, who for all his youth by no means lacked shrewdness, read her heart, and gave her his own on such wise that his love for her engrossed his mind to the exclusion of almost everything else. While thus they burned in secret for one another, the lady, desiring of all things a meeting with Guiscardo, but being shy of making any her confidant, hit upon a novel expedient to concert the affair with him. She wrote him a letter containing her commands for the ensuing day, and thrust it into a cane in the space between two of the knots, which cane she gave to Guiscardo, saying – 'Thou canst let thy servant have it for a bellows to blow thy fire up to night.' Guiscardo took it, and feeling sure that 'twas not unadvisedly that she made him such a present, accompanied with such words, hied him straight home, where, carefully examining the cane, he observed that it was cleft, and, opening it, found the letter; which he had no sooner read, and learned what he was to do, than, pleased as ne'er another, he fell to devising how to set all in order that he might not fail to meet the lady on the following day, after the manner she had prescribed.

Now hard by the Prince's palace was a grotto, hewn in days of old in the solid rock, and now long disused, so that an artificial orifice, by which it received a little light, was all but choked with brambles and plants that grew about and overspread it. From one of the ground-floor rooms of the palace, which room was part of the lady's suite, a secret stair led to the grotto, though the entrance was barred by a very strong door. This stair, having been from time immemorial disused, had passed out of mind so completely that there was scarce any that remembered that it was there: but Love, whose eyes nothing, however secret, may escape, had brought it to the mind of the enamoured lady. For many a day, using all secrecy, that none should discover her, she had wrought with her tools, until she had succeeded in opening the door; which done, she had gone down into the grotto alone, and having observed the orifice, had by her letter apprised Guiscardo of its apparent height above the floor of the grotto, and bidden him contrive some means of descending thereby. Eager to carry the affair through, Guiscardo lost no time in rigging up a ladder of ropes, whereby he might ascend and descend; and having put on a suit of leather to protect him from the brambles, he hied him the following night (keeping the affair close from all) to the orifice, made the ladder fast by one of its ends to a massive trunk that was rooted in its mouth, climbed down the ladder and awaited the lady. On the morrow, making as if she would fain sleep, the lady dismissed her damsels, and locked herself into her room: she then opened the door of the grotto, hied her down, and met Guiscardo, to their marvellous mutual satisfaction. The lovers then repaired to her room, where in exceeding great joy they spent no small part of the day. Nor were they neglectful of the precautions needful to prevent discovery of their amour; but in due time Guiscardo returned to the grotto; whereupon the lady locked the door and rejoined her damsels. At nightfall Guiscardo reascended his ladder, and, issuing forth of the orifice, hied him home; nor, knowing now the way, did he fail to revisit the grotto many a time thereafter.

But Fortune, noting with envious eye a happiness of such degree and duration, gave to events a dolorous turn, whereby the joy of the two lovers was converted into bitter lamentation. 'Twas Tancred's custom to come from time to time quite alone to his daughter's room, and tarry talking with her a while. Whereby it so befell that he came down there one day after breakfast, while Ghismonda – such was the lady's name – was in her garden with her damsels; so that none saw or heard him enter; nor would he call his daughter, for he was minded that she should not forgo her pleasure. But, finding the windows closed and the bed-curtains drawn down, he seated himself on a divan that stood at one of the corners of the bed, rested his head on the bed, drew the curtain over him, and thus, hidden as if of set purpose, fell asleep. As he slept Ghismonda, who, as it happened, had caused Guiscardo to come that day, left her damsels in the garden, softly entered the room, and having locked herself in, unwitting that there was another in the room, opened the door to Guiscardo, who was in waiting. Straightway they got them to bed, as was their wont; and, while they there solaced and disported them together, it so befell that Tancred awoke, and heard and saw what they did: whereat he was troubled beyond measure, and at first was minded to upbraid them; but on second thoughts he deemed it best to hold his peace, and avoid discovery, if so he might with greater stealth and less dishonour carry out the design which was already in his mind. The two lovers continued long together, as they were wont, all unwitting of Tancred; but at length they saw fit to get out of bed, when Guiscardo went back to the grotto, and the lady hied her forth of the room. Whereupon Tancred, old though he was, got out at one of the windows, clambered down into the garden, and, seen by none, returned sorely troubled to his room. By his command two men took Guiscardo early that same night, as he issued forth of the orifice accoutred in his suit of leather, and brought him privily to Tancred; who, as he saw him, all but wept, and said – 'Guiscardo, my kindness to thee is ill requited by the outrage and dishonour which thou hast done me in the person of my daughter, as today I have seen with my own eyes.' To whom Guiscardo could answer nought but – 'Love is more potent than either you or I.' Tancred then gave order to keep him privily under watch and ward in a room within the palace; and so 'twas done. Next day, while Ghismonda wotted nought of these matters, Tancred, after pondering divers novel expedients, hied him after breakfast, according to his wont, to his daughter's room, where, having called her to him and locked himself in with her, he began, not without tears, to speak on this wise – 'Ghismonda, conceiving that I knew thy virtue and honour, never, though it had been reported to me, would I have credited, had I not seen with my own eyes, that thou wouldst so much as in idea, not to say fact, have ever yielded thyself to any man but thy husband: wherefore, for the brief residue of life that my age has in store for me, the memory of thy fall will ever be grievous to me. And would to God, as thou must needs demean thyself to such dishonour, thou hadst taken a man that matched thy nobility; but of all the men that frequent my court, thou must needs choose Guiscardo, a young man of the lowest condition, a fellow whom we brought up in charity from his tender years; for whose sake thou hast plunged me into the abyss of mental tribulation, insomuch that I know not what course to take in regard of thee. As to Guiscardo, whom I caused to be arrested last night as he issued from the orifice, and keep in durance, my course is already taken, but how I am to deal with thee, God knows, I know not. I am distraught between the love which I have ever borne thee, love such as no father ever bore to daughter, and the most just indignation evoked in me by thy signal folly; my love prompts me to pardon thee, my indignation bids me harden my heart against thee, though I do violence to my nature. But before I decide upon my course, I would fain hear what thou hast to say to this.' So saying, he bent his head, and wept as bitterly as any child that had been soundly thrashed.

Her father's words, and the tidings they conveyed that not only was her secret passion discovered, but Guiscardo taken, caused Ghismonda immeasurable grief, which she was again and again on the point of evincing, as most women do, by cries and tears; but her high spirit triumphed over this weakness; by a prodigious effort she composed her countenance, and taking it for granted that her Guiscardo was no more, she inwardly devoted herself to death rather than a single prayer for herself should escape her lips. Wherefore, not as a woman stricken with grief or chidden for a fault, but unconcerned and unabashed, with tearless eyes, and frank and utterly dauntless mien, thus answered she her father – 'Tancred, your accusation I shall not deny, neither will I cry you mercy, for nought should I gain by denial, nor aught would I gain by supplication: nay more; there is nought I will do to conciliate thy humanity and love; my only care is to confess the truth, to defend my honour by words of sound reason, and then by deeds most resolute to give effect to the promptings of my high soul. True it is that I have loved and love Guiscardo, and during the brief while I have yet to live shall love him, nor after death, so there be then love, shall I cease to love him; but that I love him, is not imputable to my womanly frailty so much as to the little zeal thou showedst for my bestowal in marriage, and to Guiscardo's own worth. It should not have escaped thee, Tancred, creature of flesh and blood as thou art, that thy daughter was also a creature of flesh and blood, and not of stone or iron; it was, and is, thy duty to bear in mind (old though thou art) the nature and the might of the laws to which youth is subject; and, though thou hast spent part of thy best years in martial exercises, thou shouldst nevertheless have not been ignorant how potent is the influence even upon the aged – to say nothing of the young – of ease and luxury. And not only am I, as being thy daughter, a creature of flesh and blood, but my life is not so far spent but that I am still young, and thus doubly fraught with fleshly appetite, the vehemence whereof is marvellously enhanced by reason that, having been married, I have known the pleasure that ensues upon the satisfaction of such desire. Which forces being powerless to withstand, I did but act as was natural in a young woman, when I gave way to them, and yielded myself to love. Nor in sooth did I fail to the utmost of my power so to order the indulgence of my natural propensity that my sin should bring shame neither upon thee nor upon me. To which end Love in his pity, and Fortune in a friendly mood, found and discovered to me a secret way, whereby, none witting, I attained my desire: this, from whomsoever thou hast learned it, howsoever thou comest to know it, I deny not. 'Twas not at random, as many women do, that I loved Guiscardo; but by deliberate choice I preferred him before all other men, and of determinate forethought I lured him to my love, whereof, through his and my discretion and constancy, I have long had enjoyment. Wherein 'twould seem that thou, following rather the opinion of the vulgar than the dictates of truth, find cause to chide me more severely than in my sinful love, for, as if thou wouldst not have been vexed, had my choice fallen on a nobleman, thou complainest that I have forgathered with a man of low condition; and dost not see that therein thou censurest not my fault but that of Fortune, which not seldom raises the unworthy to high place and leaves the worthiest in low estate. But leave we this: consider a little the principles of things: thou seest that in regard of our flesh we are all moulded of the same substance, and that all souls are endowed by one and the same Creator with equal faculties, equal powers, equal virtues. 'Twas merit that made the first distinction between us, born as we were, nay, as we are, all equal, and those whose merits were and were approved in act the greatest were called noble, and the rest were not so denoted. Which law, albeit overlaid by the contrary usage of after times, is not yet abrogated, nor so impaired but that it is still traceable in nature and good manners; for which cause whoso with merit acts, does plainly show himself a gentleman; and if any denote him otherwise, the default is his own and not his whom he so denotes. Pass in review all thy nobles, weigh their merits, their manners and bearing, and then compare Guiscardo's qualities with theirs: if thou wilt judge without prejudice, thou wilt pronounce him noble in the highest degree, and thy nobles one and all churls. As to Guiscardo's merits and worth I did but trust the verdict which thou thyself didst utter in words, and which mine own eyes confirmed. Of whom had he such commendation as of thee for all those excellences whereby a good man and true merits commendation? And in sooth thou didst him but justice; for, unless mine eyes have played me false, there was nought for which thou didst commend him but I had seen him practise it, and that more admirably than words of thine might express; and had I been at all deceived in this matter, 'twould have been by thee. Wilt thou say then that I have forgathered with a man of low condition? If so, thou wilt not say true. Didst thou say with a poor man, the impeachment might be allowed, to thy shame, that thou so ill hast known how to requite a good man and true that is thy servant; but poverty, though it take away all else, deprives no man of nobility. Many kings, many great princes, were once poor, and many a ditcher or herdsman has been and is very wealthy. As for thy last doubt, to wit, how thou shouldst deal with me, banish it utterly from thy thoughts. If in thy extreme old age thou art minded to manifest a harshness unwonted in thy youth, wreak thy harshness on me, resolved as I am to cry thee no mercy, prime cause as I am that this sin, if sin it be, has been committed; for of this I warrant thee, that as thou mayst have done or shalt do to Guiscardo, if to me thou do not the like, I with my own hands will do it. Now get thee gone to shed thy tears with the women, and when thy melting mood is over, ruthlessly destroy Guiscardo and me, if such thou deem our merited doom, by one and the same blow.'

The loftiness of his daughter's spirit was not unknown to the Prince; but still he did not credit her with a resolve quite as firmly fixed as her words implied, to carry their purport into effect. So, parting from her without the least intention of using harshness towards her in her own person, he determined to quench the heat of her love by wreaking his vengeance on her lover, and bade the two men that had charge of Guiscardo to strangle him noiselessly that same night, take the heart out of the body, and send it to him. The men did his bidding: and on the morrow the Prince had a large and beautiful cup of gold brought to him, and having put Guiscardo's heart therein, sent it by the hand of one of his most trusted servants to his daughter, charging the servant to say, as he gave it to her – 'Thy father sends thee this to give thee joy of that which thou lovest best, even as thou hast given him joy of that which he loved best.'

Now when her father had left her, Ghismonda, wavering not a jot in her stern resolve, had sent for poisonous herbs and roots, and therefrom had distilled a water, to have it ready for use, if that which she apprehended should come to pass. And when the servant appeared with the Prince's present and message, she took the cup unblenchingly, and having lifted the lid, and seen the heart, and apprehended the meaning of the words, and that the heart was beyond a doubt Guiscardo's, she raised her head, and looking straight at the servant, said – 'A tomb less honourable than of gold had ill befitted heart such as this: herein has my father done wisely.' Which said, she raised it to her lips, and kissed it, saying – 'In all things and at all times, even to this last hour of my life, have I found my father most tender in his love, but now more so than ever before; wherefore I now render him the last thanks which will ever be due from me to him for this goodly present.' So she spoke, and straining the cup to her, bowed her head over it, and gazing at the heart, said – 'Ah! sojourn most sweet of all my joys, accursed be he by whose ruthless act I see thee with the bodily eye: 'twas enough that to the mind's eye thou wert hourly present. Thou hast run thy course; thou hast closed the span that Fortune allotted thee; thou hast reached the goal of all; thou hast left behind thee the woes and weariness of the world; and thy enemy has himself granted thee a tomb accordant with thy deserts. No circumstance was wanting duly to celebrate thy obsequies, save the tears of her whom, while thou livedst, thou didst so dearly love; which that thou shouldst not lack, my remorseless father was prompted of God to send thee to me, and, albeit my resolve was fixed to die with eyes unmoistened and front all unperturbed by fear, yet will I accord thee my tears; which done, my care shall be forthwith by thy means to join my soul to that most precious soul which thou didst once enshrine. And is there other company than hers, in which with more of joy and peace I might fare to the abodes unknown? She is yet here within, I doubt not, contemplating the abodes of her and my delights, and – for sure I am that she loves me – awaiting my soul that loves her before all else.'

Having thus spoken, she bowed herself low over the cup; and, while no womanish cry escaped her, 'twas as if a fountain of water were unloosed within her head, so wondrous a flood of tears gushed from her eyes, while times without number she kissed the dead heart. Her damsels that stood around her knew not whose the heart might be or what her words might mean, but melting in sympathy, they all wept, and compassionately, as vainly, enquired the cause of her lamentation, and in many other ways sought to comfort her to the best of their understanding and power. When she had wept her fill, she raised her head, and dried her eyes. Then – 'O heart,' said she, 'much cherished heart, discharged is my every duty towards thee; nought now remains for me to do but to come and unite my soul with thine.' So saying, she sent for the vase that held the water which the day before she had distilled, and emptied it into the cup where lay the heart bathed in her tears; then, nowise afraid, she set her mouth to the cup, and drained it dry, and so with the cup in her hand she got her upon her bed, and having there disposed her person in guise as seemly as she might, laid her dead lover's heart upon her own, and silently awaited death. Meanwhile the damsels, seeing and hearing what passed, but knowing not what the water was that she had drunk, had sent word of each particular to Tancred; who, apprehensive of that which came to pass, came down with all haste to his daughter's room, where he arrived just as she got her upon her bed, and, now too late, addressed himself to comfort her with soft words, and seeing in what plight she was, burst into a flood of bitter tears. To whom the lady – 'Reserve thy tears, Tancred, till Fortune send thee a fate less longed for than this: waste them not on me who care not for them. Whoever yet saw any but thee bewail the consummation of his desire? But, if of the love thou once didst bear me any spark still lives in thee, be it thy parting grace to me, that, as thou brookedst not that I should live with Guiscardo in privacy and seclusion, so wherever thou mayst have caused Guiscardo's body to be cast, mine may be united with it in the common view of all.' The Prince replied not for excess of grief; and the lady, feeling that her end was come, strained the dead heart to her bosom, saying – 'Fare ye well; I take my leave of you;' and with eyelids drooped and every sense vanished departed this life of woe. Such was the lamentable end of the loves of Guiscardo and Ghismonda; whom Tancred, tardily repentant of his harshness, mourned not a little, as did also all the folk of Salerno, and had honourably interred side by side in the same tomb.

18

The second story of the fourth day, in which Fra Alberto gives a lady to understand that she is beloved of the Angel Gabriel, in whose shape he lies with her sundry times; afterward, for fear of her kinsmen, he flings himself forth of her house, and finds shelter in the house of a poor man, who on the morrow leads him in the guise of a wild man into the piazza, where, being recognised, he is apprehended by his brethren and imprisoned.

More than once had Fiammetta's story brought tears to the eyes of her fair companions; but now that it was ended the king said with an austere air – 'I should esteem my life but a paltry price to pay for half the delight that Ghismonda had with Guiscardo: whereat no lady of you all should marvel, seeing that each hour that I live I die a thousand deaths; nor is there so much as a particle of compensating joy allotted me. But a truce to my own concerns: I ordain that Pampinea do next ensue our direful argument, wherewith the tenor of my life in part accords, and if she follow in Fiammetta's footsteps I doubt not I shall presently feel some drops of dew distil upon my fire.' Pampinea received the king's command in a spirit more accordant with what from her own bent she divined to be the wishes of her fair friends than with the king's words; wherefore, being minded rather to afford them some diversion than, save as in duty bound, to satisfy the king, she made choice of a story which, without deviating from the prescribed theme, should move a laugh, and thus began: ’Tis a proverb current among the vulgar, that – 'Whoso being wicked, is righteous reputed, May sin as he will, and 'twill ne'er be imputed.' Which proverb furnishes me with abundant matter of discourse, germane to our theme, besides occasion to exhibit the quality and degree of the hypocrisy of the religious, who flaunt it in ample flowing robes, and, with faces made pallid by art, with voices low and gentle to beg alms, most loud and haughty to reprove in others their own sins, would make believe that their way of salvation lies in taking from us and ours in giving to them; nay, more, as if they had not like us Paradise to win, but were already its lords and masters, assign therein to each that dies a place more or less exalted according to the amount of the money that he has bequeathed to them; which if they believe, 'tis by dint of self-delusion, and to the effect of deluding all that put faith in their words. Of whose guile were it lawful for me to make as full exposure as were fitting, not a few simple folk should soon be enlightened as to what they cloak within the folds of their voluminous habits. But would to God all might have the like reward of their lies as a certain friar minor, no novice, but one that was reputed among their greatest* at Venice; whose story, rather than aught else, I am minded to tell you, if so I may, perchance, by laughter and jollity relieve in some degree your souls that are heavy laden with pity for the death of Ghismonda –

Know then, noble ladies, that there was in Imola a man of evil and corrupt life, Berto della Massa by name, whose pestilent practices came at length to be so well known to the good folk of Imola that 'twas all one whether he lied or spoke the truth, for there was not a soul in Imola that believed a word he said: wherefore, seeing that his tricks would pass no longer there, he removed, as in despair, to Venice, that common sink of all abominations, thinking there to find other means than he had found elsewhere to the prosecution of his nefarious designs. And, as if conscience-stricken for his past misdeeds, he assumed an air of the deepest humility, turned the best Catholic of them all, and went and made himself a friar minor, taking the name of Fra Alberto da Imola. With his habit he put on a show of austerity, highly commending penitence and abstinence, and eating or drinking no sort of meat or wine but such as was to his taste. And scarce a soul was there that wist that the thief, the pimp, the cheat, the assassin, had not been suddenly converted into a great preacher without continuing

* *de' maggior cassesi*. No such word as *cassesi* is known to the lexicographers or commentators; and no plausible emendation has yet been suggested.

in the practice of the said iniquities, whensoever the same was privily possible. And withal, having got himself made priest, as often as he celebrated at the altar, he would weep over the passion of our Lord, so there were folk in plenty to see, for tears cost him little enough, when he had a mind to shed them. In short, what with his sermons and his tears, he duped the folk of Venice to such a tune that scarce a will was there made but he was its executor and depositary; nay, not a few made him trustee of their moneys, and most, or well-nigh most, men and women alike, their confessor and counsellor: in short, he had put off the wolf and put on the shepherd, and the fame of his holiness was such in those parts that St Francis himself had never the like at Assisi.

Now it so befell that among the ladies that came to confess to this holy friar was one Monna Lisetta of Ca' Quirino, the young, silly, empty-headed wife of a great merchant, who was gone with the galleys to Flanders. Like a Venetian – for unstable are they all – though she placed herself at his feet, she told him but a part of her sins, and when Fra Alberto asked her whether she had a lover, she replied with black looks – 'How now, master friar? have you not eyes in your head? See you no difference between my charms and those of other women? Lovers in plenty might I have, so I would: but charms such as mine must not be cheapened: 'tis not every man that might presume to love me. How many ladies have you seen whose beauty is comparable to mine? I should adorn Paradise itself.' Whereto she added so much more in praise of her beauty that the friar could scarce hear her with patience. Howbeit, discerning at a glance that she was none too well furnished with sense, he deemed the soil meet for his plough, and fell forthwith inordinately in love with her, though he deferred his blandishments to a more convenient season, and by way of supporting his character for holiness began instead to chide her, telling her (among other novelties) that this was vainglory: whereto the lady retorted that he was a blockhead, and could not distinguish one degree of beauty from another. Wherefore Fra Alberto, lest he should occasion her too much chagrin, cut short the confession, and suffered her to depart with the other ladies. Some days after, accompanied by a single trusty friend, he hied him to Monna Lisetta's house, and having withdrawn with her alone into a saloon, where they were safe from observation, he fell on his knees at her feet, and said – 'Madam, for the love of God I crave your pardon of that which I said to you on Sunday, when you spoke to me of your beauty, for so grievously was I chastised therefore that very night, that 'tis but today that I have been able to quit my bed.' 'And by whom,' quoth my Lady Battledore, 'were you so chastised?' 'I will tell you,' returned Fra Alberto. 'That night I was, as is ever my wont, at my prayers when suddenly a great light shone in my cell, and before I could turn me to see what it was, I saw standing over me a right goodly youth with a stout cudgel in his hand, who seized me by the habit and threw me at his feet and belaboured me till I was bruised from head to foot. And when I asked him why he used me thus, he answered – " 'Tis because thou didst today presume to speak slightingly of the celestial charms of Monna Lisetta, whom I love next to God Himself." Whereupon I asked – "And who are you?" And he made answer that he was the Angel Gabriel. Then said I – "O my lord. I pray you pardon me." Whereto he answered – "I pardon thee on condition that thou go to her, with what speed thou mayst, and obtain her pardon, which if she accord thee not, I shall come back hither and give thee belabourings enough with my cudgel to make thee a sad man for the rest of thy days." What more he said, I dare not tell you, unless you first pardon me.' Whereat our flimsy pumpkin-pated Lady Lackbrain was overjoyed, taking all the friar's words for gospel. So after a while she said – 'And did I not tell you, Fra Alberto, that my charms were celestial? But, so help me God, I am moved to pity of you, and forthwith I pardon you, lest worse should befall you, so only you tell me what more the Angel said.' 'So will I gladly, Madam,' returned Fra Alberto, 'now that I have your pardon; this only I bid you bear in mind, that you have a care that never a soul in the world hear from you a single word of what I shall say to you, if you would not spoil your good fortune, wherein there is not today in the whole world a lady that may compare with you. Know then that the Angel Gabriel bade me tell you that you stand so high in his favour that again and again he would have come to pass the night with you, but that he doubted he should affright you. So now he sends you word through me that he would fain come one night, and stay a while with you; and seeing that, being an angel, if he should visit you in his angelic shape, he might not be touched by you, he would, to pleasure you, present himself in human shape; and so he bids you send him word, when you would have him come, and in whose shape, and he will come; for which cause you may deem yourself more blessed than any other lady that lives.' My Lady Vanity then said that she was highly flattered to be beloved of the Angel Gabriel; whom she herself loved so well that she had never grudged four soldi to burn a candle before his picture, wherever she saw it, and that he was welcome to visit her as often as he liked, and would always find her alone in her room; on the understanding, however, that he should not desert her for the Virgin Mary, whom she had heard he did mightily affect, and indeed 'twould so appear, for, wherever she saw him, he was always on his knees at her feet: for the rest he might even come in what shape he pleased, so that it was not such as to terrify her. Then said Fra Alberto – 'Madam, 'tis wisely spoken; and I will arrange it all with him just as you say. But 'tis in your power to do me a great favour, which will cost you nothing; and this favour is that you be consenting that he visit you in my shape. Now hear wherein you will confer this favour: thus will it be: he will disembody my soul, and set it in Paradise, entering himself into my body; and, as long as he shall be with you, my soul will be in Paradise.' Whereto my Lady Slenderwit – 'So be it,' she said; 'I am well pleased that you have this solace to salve the bruises that he gives you on my account.' 'Good,' said Fra Alberto; 'then you will see to it that tonight he find, when he comes, your outer door unlatched, that he may have ingress; for, coming, as he will, in human shape, he will not be able to enter save by the door.' 'It shall be done,' replied the lady. Whereupon Fra Alberto took his leave, and the lady remained in such a state of exaltation that her nether end knew not her chemise, and it seemed to her a thousand years until the Angel Gabriel should come to visit her. Fra Alberto, bethinking him that 'twas not as an angel, but as a cavalier that he must acquit himself that night, fell to fortifying himself with comfits and other dainties, that he might not lose his saddle for slight cause. Then, leave of absence gotten, he betook him at nightfall, with a single companion, to the house of a woman that was his friend, which house had served on former occasions as his base when he went a-chasing the fillies; and having there disguised himself, he hied him, when he deemed 'twas time, to the house of the lady, where, donning the gewgaws he had brought with him, he transformed himself into an angel, and going up, entered the lady's chamber. No sooner saw she this dazzling apparition than she fell on her knees before the Angel, who gave her his blessing, raised her to her feet, and motioned her to go to bed. She, nothing loath, obeyed forthwith, and the Angel lay down beside his devotee. Now Fra Alberto was a stout, handsome fellow, whose legs bore themselves right bravely; and being bedded with Monna Lisetta, who was lusty and delicate, he covered her after another fashion than her husband had been wont, and took many a flight that night without wings, so that she heartily cried him content; and not a little therewithal did he tell her of the glory celestial. Then towards daybreak, all being ready for his return, he hied him forth, and repaired, caparisoned as he was, to his friend, whom, lest he should be affrighted, sleeping alone, the good woman of the house had solaced with her company. The lady, so soon as she had breakfasted, betook her to Fra

Alberto, and reported the Angel Gabriel's visit, and what he had told her of the glory of the life eternal, describing his appearance, not without some added marvels of her own invention. Whereto Fra Alberto replied – 'Madam, I know not how you fared with him; but this I know, that last night he came to me, and for that I had done his errand with you, he suddenly transported my soul among such a multitude of flowers and roses as was never seen here below, and my soul – what became of my body I know not – tarried in one of the most delightful places that ever was from that hour until matins.' 'As for your body,' said the lady, 'do I not tell you whose it was? It lay all night long with the Angel Gabriel in my arms; and if you believe me not, you have but to look under your left pap, where I gave the Angel a mighty kiss, of which the mark will last for some days.' 'Why then,' said Fra Alberto, 'I will even do today what 'tis long since I did, to wit, undress, that I may see if you say sooth.' So they fooled it a long while, and then the lady went home, where Fra Alberto afterwards paid her many a visit without any let. However, one day it so befell that while Monna Lisetta was with one of her friends canvassing beauties, she, being minded to exalt her own charms above all others, and having, as we know, none too much wit in her pumpkin-pate, observed – 'Did you but know by whom my charms are prized, then, for sure, you would have nought to say of the rest.' Her friend, all agog to hear, for well she knew her foible, answered – 'Madam, it may be as you say, but still, while one knows not who he may be, one cannot alter one's mind so rapidly.' Whereupon my Lady Featherbrain – 'Friend,' said she, ' 'tis not for common talk, but he that I wot of is the Angel Gabriel, who loves me more dearly than himself for that I am, so he tells me, the fairest lady in all the world, ay, and in the Maremma to boot.'* Whereat her friend would fain have laughed, but held herself in, being minded to hear more from her. Wherefore she said – 'God's faith, Madam, if 'tis the Angel Gabriel, and he tells you so, why, so of course it must needs be; but I wist not the angels meddled with such matters.' 'There you erred,' said the lady: 'zounds, he does it better than my husband, and he tells me they do it above there too, but, as he rates my charms above any that are in heaven, he is enamoured of me, and not seldom visits me: so now dost see?' So away went the friend so agog to tell the story, that it seemed to her a thousand years till she was where it might be done; and being met for recreation with a great company of ladies, she narrated it all in detail: whereby it passed to the ladies' husbands, and to other ladies, and

* With this ineptitude cf. the friar's 'flowers and roses' above.

from them to yet other ladies, so that in less than two days all Venice was full of it. But among others, whose ears it reached, were Monna Lisetta's brothers-in-law, who, keeping their own counsel, resolved to find this angel and make out whether he knew how to fly; to which end they kept watch for some nights. Whereof no hint, as it happened, reached Fra Alberto's ears; and so, one night when he was come to enjoy the lady once more, he was scarce undressed when her brothers-in-law, who had seen him come, were at the door of the room and already opening it, when Fra Alberto, hearing the noise and apprehending the danger, started up, and having no other resource, threw open a window that looked on to the Grand Canal, and plunged into the water. The depth was great, and he was an expert swimmer; so that he took no hurt, but, having reached the other bank, found a house open, and forthwith entered it praying the good man that was within, for God's sake to save his life, and trumping up a story to account for his being there at so late an hour, and stripped to the skin. The good man took pity on him, and having occasion to go out, he put him in his own bed, bidding him stay there until his return; and so, having locked him in, he went about his business.

Now when the lady's brothers-in-law entered the room, and found that the Angel Gabriel had taken flight, leaving his wings behind him, being baulked of their prey, they roundly rated the lady, and then, leaving her disconsolate, betook themselves home with the Angel's spoils. Whereby it befell, that, when 'twas broad day, the good man, being on the Rialto, heard tell how the Angel Gabriel had come to pass the night with Monna Lisetta, and, being surprised by her brothers-in-law, had taken fright, and thrown himself into the Canal, and none knew what was become of him. The good man guessed in a trice that the said Angel was no other than the man he had at home, whom on his return he recognised, and, after much chaffering, brought him to promise him fifty ducats that he might not be given up to the lady's brothers-in-law. The bargain struck, Fra Alberto signified a desire to be going. Whereupon – 'There is no way,' said the good man, 'but one, if you are minded to take it. Today we hold a revel, wherein folk lead others about in various disguises; as, one man will present a bear, another a wild man, and so forth; and then in the piazza of San Marco there is a hunt, which done, the revel is ended; and then away they hie them, whither they will, each with the man he has led about. If you are willing to be led by me in one or another of these disguises, before it can get wind that you are here, I can bring you whither you would go; otherwise I see not how you are to quit this place without being known;

and the lady's brothers-in-law, reckoning that you must be lurking somewhere in this quarter, have set guards all about to take you.' Loath indeed was Fra Alberto to go in such a guise, but such was his fear of the lady's relations that he consented, and told the good man whither he desired to be taken, and that he was content to leave the choice of the disguise to him. The good man then smeared him all over with honey, and covered him with down, set a chain on his neck and a vizard on his face, gave him a stout cudgel to carry in one hand and two huge dogs, which he had brought from the shambles, to lead with the other, and sent a man to the Rialto to announce that whoso would see the Angel Gabriel should hie him to the piazza of San Marco; in all which he acted as a loyal Venetian. And so, after a while, he led him forth, and then, making him go before, held him by the chain behind, and through a great throng that clamoured – 'What manner of thing is this? what manner of thing is this?' he brought him to the piazza, where, what with those that followed them, and those that had come from the Rialto on hearing the announcement, there were folk without end. Arrived at the piazza, he fastened his wild man to a column in a high and exposed place, making as if he were minded to wait till the hunt should begin; whereby the flies and gadflies, attracted by the honey with which he was smeared, caused him most grievous distress. However, the good man waited only until the piazza was thronged, and then, making as if he would unchain his wild man, he tore the vizard from Fra Alberto's face, saying – 'Gentlemen, as the boar comes not to the hunt, and the hunt does not take place, that it be not for nothing that you are come hither, I am minded to give you a view of the Angel Gabriel, who comes down from heaven to earth by night to solace the ladies of Venice.' The vizard was no sooner withdrawn than all recognised Fra Alberto, and greeted him with hootings, rating him in language as offensive and opprobrious as ever rogue was abused withal, and pelting him in the face with every sort of filth that came to hand: in which plight they kept him an exceeding great while, until by chance the bruit thereof reached his brethren, of whom some six thereupon put themselves in motion, and, arrived at the piazza, clapped a habit on his back, and unchained him, and amid an immense uproar led him off to their convent, where, after languishing a while in prison, 'tis believed that he died.

So this man, by reason that, being reputed righteous, he did evil, and 'twas not imputed to him, presumed to counterfeit the Angel Gabriel, and, being transformed into a wild man, was in the end put to shame, as he deserved, and vainly bewailed his misdeeds. God grant that so it may betide all his likes.

19

The tenth story of the fourth day, in which the wife of a leech, deeming her lover, who has taken an opiate, to be dead, puts him in a chest, which, with him therein, two usurers carry off to their house. He comes to himself, and is taken for a thief; but, the lady's maid giving the Signory to understand that she had put him in the chest which the usurers stole, he escapes the gallows, and the usurers are mulcted in moneys for the theft of the chest.

Now it only remained for Dioneo to do his part, which he witting, and being thereto bidden by the king, thus began: Sore have I – to say nought of you, my ladies – been of eyes and heart to hear the woeful histories of ill-starred love, insomuch that I have desired of all things that they might have an end. Wherefore now that, thank God, ended they are, unless indeed I were minded, which God forbid, to add to such pernicious stuff a supplement of the like evil quality, no such dolorous theme do I purpose to ensue but to make a fresh start with somewhat of a better and more cheerful sort, which perchance may serve to suggest tomorrow's argument –

You are to know, then, fairest my damsels, that 'tis not long since there dwelt at Salerno a leech most eminent in surgery, his name, Master Mazzeo della Montagna, who in his extreme old age took to wife a fair damsel of the same city, whom he kept in nobler and richer array of dresses and jewels, and all other finery that the sex affects, than any other lady in Salerno. Howbeit, she was none too warm most of her time, being ill covered abed by the doctor; who gave her to understand – even as Messer Ricciardo di Chinzica, of whom we spoke a while since, taught his lady the feasts – that for once that a man lay with a woman he needed I know not how many days to recover, and the like nonsense: whereby she lived as ill content as might be; and, lacking neither sense nor spirit, she determined to economise at home, and taking to the street, to live at others' expense. So, having passed in review divers young men, she at last found one that was to her mind, on whom she set all her heart and hopes of happiness. Which the gallant perceiving was mightily flattered, and in like manner gave her all his love. Ruggieri da Jeroli – such was the gallant's name – was of noble birth, but of life and conversation so evil and reprehensible that kinsman or friend he had none left that wished him well, or cared to see him; and all Salerno knew him for a common thief and rogue of the vilest character. Whereof the lady took little heed, having a mind to him for another reason; and so with the help of her maid she arranged a meeting with him. But after they had solaced themselves a while, the lady began to censure his past life, and to implore him for love of her to depart from such evil ways; and to afford him the means thereto, she from time to time furnished him with money. While thus with all discretion they continued their intercourse, it chanced that a man halt of one of his legs was placed under the leech's care. The leech saw what was amiss with him, and told his kinsfolk, that unless a gangrened bone that he had in his leg were taken out, he must die, or have the whole leg amputated; that if the bone were removed he might recover; but that otherwise he would not answer for his life: whereupon the relatives assented that the bone should be removed, and left the patient in the hands of the leech; who, deeming that by reason of the pain 'twas not possible for him to endure the treatment without an opiate, caused to be distilled in the morning a certain water of his own concoction, whereby the patient, drinking it, might be ensured sleep during such time as he deemed the operation, which he meant to perform about vespers, would occupy. In the meantime he had the water brought into his house, and set it in the window of his room, telling no one what it was. But when the vesper hour was come, and the leech was about to visit his patient, a messenger arrived from some very great friends of his at Amalfi, bearing tidings of a great riot there had been there, in which not a few had been wounded, and bidding him on no account omit to hie him thither forthwith. Wherefore the leech put off the treatment of the leg to the morrow, and took boat to Amalfi; and the lady, knowing that he would not return home that night, did as she was wont in such a case, to wit, brought Ruggieri in privily, and locked him in her chamber until certain other folk that were in the house were gone to sleep. Ruggieri, then, being thus in the chamber, awaiting the lady, and having – whether it were that he had had a fatiguing day, or eaten something salt, or, perchance, that 'twas his habit of body – a mighty thirst, glancing at the window, caught sight of the bottle containing the water which the leech had prepared for the patient, and taking it to be drinking water, set it to his lips and drank it all, and in no long time fell into a deep sleep.

So soon as she was able the lady hied her to the room, and there finding Ruggieri asleep, touched him and softly told him to get up: to no purpose, however; he neither answered nor stirred a limb. Wherefore the lady, rather losing patience, applied somewhat more force, and gave him a push, saying – 'Get up, sleepy-head; if thou hadst a mind to sleep, thou shouldst have gone home, and not have come hither.' Thus pushed Ruggieri fell down from a box on which he lay, and, falling, showed no more sign of animation than if he had been a corpse. The lady, now somewhat alarmed, essayed to lift him, and shook him roughly, and took him by the nose, and pulled him by the beard; again to no purpose: he had tethered his ass to a stout pin. So the lady began to fear he must be dead: however, she went on to pinch him shrewdly, and singe him with the flame of a candle; but when these methods also failed she, being, for all she was a leech's wife, no leech herself, believed for sure that he was dead; and as there was nought in the world that she loved so much, it boots not to ask if she was sore distressed; wherefore silently, for she dared not lament aloud, she began to weep over him and bewail such a misadventure. But, after a while, fearing lest her loss should not be without a sequel of shame, she bethought her that she must contrive without delay to get the body out of the house; and standing in need of another's advice, she quietly summoned her maid, showed her the mishap that had befallen her, and craved her counsel. Whereat the maid marvelled not a little; and she too fell to pulling Ruggieri this way and that, and pinching him, and, as she found no sign of life in him, concurred with her mistress that he was verily dead, and advised her to remove him from the house. 'And where,' said the lady, 'shall we put him, that tomorrow, when he is discovered, it be not suspected that 'twas hence he was carried?' 'Madam,' answered the maid, 'late last evening I marked in front of our neighbour the carpenter's shop a chest, not too large, which, if he have not put it back in the house, will come in very handy for our purpose, for we will put him inside, and give him two or three cuts with a knife, and so leave him. When he is found, I know not why it should be thought that 'twas from this house rather than from any other that he was put there; nay, as he was an evil-liver, 'twill more likely be supposed, that, as he hied him on some evil errand, some enemy slew him, and then put him in the chest.' The lady said there was nought in the world she might so ill brook as that Ruggieri should receive any wound; but with that exception she approved her maid's proposal, and sent her to see if the chest were still where she had seen it. The maid, returning, reported that there it was, and, being young and strong, got Ruggieri, with the lady's help, upon her shoulders; and so the lady, going before to espy if any folk came that way, and the maid following, they came to the chest, and having laid Ruggieri therein, closed it and left him there.

Now a few days before, two young men, that were usurers, had taken up their quarters in a house a little further on: they had seen the chest during the day, and being short of furniture, and having a mind to make great gain with little expenditure, they had resolved that, if it were still there at night, they would take it home with them. So at midnight forth they hied them, and finding the chest, were at no pains to examine it closely, but forthwith, though it seemed somewhat heavy, bore it off to their house, and set it down beside a room in which their women slept; and without being at pains to adjust it too securely they left it there for the time, and went to bed.

Towards matins Ruggieri, having had a long sleep and digested the draught and exhausted its efficacy, awoke, but albeit his slumber was broken, and his senses had recovered their powers, yet his brain remained in a sort of torpor which kept him bemused for some days; and when he opened his eyes and saw nothing, and stretched his hands hither and thither and found himself in the chest, it was with difficulty that he collected his thoughts. 'How is this?' he said to himself. 'Where am I? Do I sleep or wake? I remember coming this evening to my lady's chamber; and now it seems I am in a chest. What means it? Can the leech have returned, or somewhat else have happened that caused the lady, while I slept, to hide me here? That was it, I suppose. Without a doubt it must have been so.' And having come to this conclusion, he composed himself to listen, if haply he might hear something, and being somewhat ill at ease in the chest, which was none too large, and the side on which he lay paining him, he must needs turn over to the other, and did so with such adroitness that, bringing his loins smartly against one of the sides of the chest, which was set on an uneven floor, he caused it to tilt and then fall; and such was the noise that it made as it fell that the women that slept there awoke, albeit for fear they kept silence. Ruggieri was not a little disconcerted by the fall, but, finding that thereby the chest was come open, he judged that, happen what might, he would be better out of it than in it; and not knowing where he was, and being otherwise at his wits' end, he began to grope about the house, if haply he might find a stair or door whereby he might take himself off. Hearing him thus groping his way, the alarmed women gave tongue with – 'Who is there?' Ruggieri, not knowing the voice, made no answer: wherefore the women fell to calling the two young men, who, having had a long day, were fast asleep, and heard nought of what went on. Which served to increase the fright of the women, who rose and got them to divers windows, and raised the cry – 'Take thief, take thief!' At which summons there came running from divers quarters not a few of the neighbours, who got into the house by the roof or otherwise as each best might: likewise the young men, aroused by the din, got up; and, Ruggieri being now all but beside himself for sheer amazement, and knowing not whither to turn him to escape them, they took him and delivered him to the officers of the Governor of the city, who, hearing the uproar, had hasted to the spot. And so he was brought before the Governor, who, knowing him to be held of all a most arrant evil-doer, put him forthwith to the torture, and, upon his confessing that he had entered the house of the usurers with intent to rob, was minded to make short work of it, and have him hanged by the neck.

In the morning 'twas bruited throughout all Salerno that Ruggieri had been taken a-thieving in the house of the usurers. Whereat the lady and her maid were all amazement and bewilderment, insomuch that they were within an ace of persuading themselves that what they had done the night before they had not done, but had only dreamed it; besides which, the peril in which Ruggieri stood caused the lady such anxiety as brought her to the verge of madness. Shortly after half tierce the leech, being returned from Amalfi, and minded now to treat his patient, called for his water, and finding the bottle empty made a great commotion, protesting that nought in his house could be let alone. The lady, having other cause of annoy, lost temper, and said – 'What would you say, Master, of an important matter, when you raise such a din because a bottle of water has been upset? Is there never another to be found in the world?' 'Madam,' replied the leech, 'thou takest this to have been mere water: 'twas no such thing, but an artificial water of a soporiferous virtue;' and he told her for what purpose he had made it. Which the lady no sooner heard, than, guessing that Ruggieri had drunk it, and so had seemed to them to be dead, she said – 'Master, we knew it not; wherefore make you another.' And so the leech, seeing that there was no help for it, had another made. Not long after, the maid who by the lady's command had gone to find out what folk said of Ruggieri, returned, saying – 'Madam, of Ruggieri they say nought but evil, nor, by what I have been able to discover, has he friend or kinsman that has or will come to his aid; and 'tis held for certain that tomorrow the Stadic* will have him hanged. Besides which, I have that to tell you which will surprise you; for, methinks, I have found out how he came into the usurers' house. List, then, how it was: you know the carpenter in front of whose shop stood the chest we put Ruggieri into: he had today the most violent altercation in the world with one to whom it would seem the chest belongs, by whom he was required to make good the value of the chest, to which he made answer that he had not sold it, but that it had been stolen from him in the night. "Not so," said the other; "thou soldst it to the two young usurers, as they themselves told me last night, when I saw it in their house at the time Ruggieri was taken." "They lie," replied the carpenter. "I never sold it them, but they must have stolen it from me last night; go we to them." So with one accord off they went to the usurers' house, and I came back here. And so, you see, I make out that 'twas on such wise that Ruggieri was brought where he was found; but how he came to life again, I am at a loss to conjecture.' The lady now understood exactly how things were, and accordingly told the maid what she had learned from the leech, and besought her to aid her to get Ruggieri off, for so she might, if she would, and at the same time preserve her honour. 'Madam,' said the maid, 'do but show me how; and glad shall I be to do just as you wish.' Whereupon the lady, to whom necessity taught invention, formed her plan on the spur of the moment, and expounded it in detail to the maid; who (as the first step) hied her to the leech, and, weeping, thus addressed him – 'Sir, it behoves me to ask your pardon of a great wrong that I have done you.' 'And what may that be?' enquired the leech. 'Sir,' said the maid, who ceased not to weep, 'you know what manner of man is Ruggieri da Jeroli. Now he took a fancy to me, and partly for fear, partly for love, I this year agreed to be his mistress; and knowing yestereve that you were from home, he coaxed me into bringing him into your house to sleep with me in my room. Now he was athirst, and I, having no mind to be seen by your lady, who was in the hall, and knowing not whither I might sooner betake me for wine or water, bethought me that I had seen a bottle of water in your room, and ran and fetched it, and gave it him to drink, and then put the bottle back in the place whence I had taken it; touching which I find that you have

* The Neapolitan term for the chief of police.

made a great stir in the house. Verily I confess that I did wrong; but who is there that does not wrong sometimes? Sorry indeed am I to have so done, but 'tis not for such a cause and that which ensued thereon that Ruggieri should lose his life. Wherefore, I do most earnestly beseech you, pardon me, and suffer me to go help him as best I may be able.' Wroth though he was at what he heard, the leech replied in a bantering tone – 'Thy pardon thou hast by thine own deed; for, whereas thou didst last night think to have with thee a gallant that would thoroughly dust thy pelisse for thee, he was but a sleepy-head; wherefore get thee gone, and do what thou mayst for the deliverance of thy lover, and for the future look thou bring him not into the house; else I will pay thee for that turn and this to boot.' The maid, deeming that she had come off well in the first brush, hied her with all speed to the prison where Ruggieri lay, and by her cajoleries prevailed upon the warders to let her speak with him; and having told him how he must answer the Stadic if he would get off, she succeeded in obtaining preaudience of the Stadic; who, seeing that the baggage was lusty and mettlesome, was minded before he heard her to grapple her with the hook, to which she was by no means averse, knowing that such a preliminary would secure her a better hearing. When she had undergone the operation and was risen – 'Sir,' said she, 'you have here Ruggieri da Jeroli, apprehended on a charge of theft; which charge is false.' Whereupon she told him the whole story from beginning to end, how she, being Ruggieri's mistress, had brought him into the leech's house and had given him the opiate, not knowing it for such, and taking him to be dead, had put him in the chest; and then recounting what she had heard pass between the carpenter and the owner of the chest, she showed him how Ruggieri came into the house of the usurers. Seeing that 'twas easy enough to find out whether the story were true, the Stadic began by questioning the leech as to the water, and found that 'twas as she had said: he then summoned the carpenter, the owner of the chest and the usurers, and after much further parley ascertained that the usurers had stolen the chest during the night, and brought it into their house: finally he sent for Ruggieri, and asked him where he had lodged that night, to which Ruggieri answered that where he had lodged he knew not, but he well remembered going to pass the night with Master Mazzeo's maid, in whose room he had drunk some water by reason of a great thirst that he had; but what happened to him afterwards, except that, when he awoke, he found himself in a chest in the house of the usurers, he knew not. All which matters the Stadic heard with great interest, and caused the maid and

Ruggieri and the carpenter and the usurers to rehearse them several times. In the end, seeing that Ruggieri was innocent, he released him, and mulcted the usurers in fifteen ounces for the theft of the chest. How glad Ruggieri was thus to escape, it boots not to ask; and glad beyond measure was his lady. And so, many a time did they laugh and make merry together over the affair, she and he and the dear maid that had proposed to give him a taste of the knife; and remaining constant in their love, they had ever better and better solace thereof. The like whereof befall me, sans the being put in the chest.

Heartsore as the gentle ladies had been made by the preceding stories, this last of Dioneo provoked them to such merriment, more especially the passage about the Stadic and the hook, that they lacked not relief of the piteous mood engendered by the others. But the king observing that the sun was now taking a yellowish tinge, and that the end of his sovereignty was come, in terms most courtly made his excuse to the fair ladies, that he had made so direful a theme as lovers' infelicity the topic of their discourse; after which he rose, took the laurel wreath from his head, and, while the ladies watched to see to whom he would give it, set it graciously upon the blonde head of Fiammetta, saying – 'Herewith I crown thee, as deeming that thou, better than any other, wilt know how to make tomorrow console our fair companions for the rude trials of today.' Fiammetta, whose wavy tresses fell in a flood of gold over her white and delicate shoulders, whose softly rounded face was all radiant with the very tints of the white lily blended with the red of the rose, who carried two eyes in her head that matched those of a peregrine falcon, while her tiny sweet mouth showed a pair of lips that shone as rubies, replied with a smile – 'And gladly take I the wreath, Filostrato, and that thou mayst more truly understand what thou hast done, 'tis my present will and pleasure that each make ready to discourse tomorrow of good fortune befalling lovers after divers direful or disastrous adventures.' The theme propounded was approved by all; whereupon the queen called the seneschal and having made with him all meet arrangements, rose and gaily dismissed all the company until the supper hour; wherefore, some straying about the garden, the beauties of which were not such as soon to pall, others bending their steps towards the mills that were grinding without, each, as and where it seemed best, they took meanwhile their several pleasures. The supper hour come, they all gathered in their wonted order by the fair fountain, and in the gayest of spirits and well served they supped. Then rising they addressed them, as was their wont, to dance and song, and while Filomena led the dance –

'Filostrato,' said the queen, 'being minded to follow in the footsteps of our predecessors and that, as by their, so by our command a song be sung; and well witting that thy songs are even as thy stories, to the end that no day but this be vexed with thy misfortunes, we ordain that thou give us one of them, whichever thou mayst prefer.' Filostrato answered that he would gladly do so; and without delay began to sing on this wise –

Full well my tears attest,
O traitor Love, with what just cause the heart,
With which thou once hast broken faith, doth smart.

Love, when thou first didst in my heart enshrine
Her for whom still I sigh, alas! in vain,
Nor any hope do know,
A damsel so complete thou didst me show,
That light as air I counted every pain,
Wherewith behest of thine
Condemned my soul to pine.
Ah! but I gravely erred, the which to know
Too late, alas! doth but enhance my woe.

The cheat I knew not ere she did me leave,
She, she, in whom alone my hopes were placed:
For 'twas when I did most
Flatter myself with hope, and proudly boast
Myself her vassal lowliest and most graced,
Nor thought Love might bereave,
Nor dreamed he e'er might grieve,
'Twas then I found that she another's worth
Into her heart had ta'en, and me cast forth.

A plant of pain, alas! my heart did bear,
What time my hapless self cast forth I knew;
And there it doth remain;
And day and hour I curse and curse again,
When first that front of love shone on my view,
That front so queenly fair,
And bright beyond compare!
Wherefore at once my faith, my hope, my fire,
My soul doth imprecate, ere she expire.

My lord, thou knowest how comfortless my woe,
Thou, Love, my lord, whom thus I supplicate
With many a piteous moan,
Telling thee how in anguish sore I groan,
Yearning for death my pain to mitigate.
Come death, and with one blow
Cut short my span, and so
With my curst life me of my frenzy ease;
For wheresoe'er I go, 'twill sure decrease.

Save death no way of comfort doth remain:
No anodyne beside for this sore smart.
The boon, then, Love bestow;
And presently by death annul my woe,
And from this abject life release my heart.
Since from me joy is ta'en,
And every solace, deign
My prayer to grant, and let my death the cheer
Complete, that she now hath of her new fere.

Song, it may be that no one shall thee learn:
Nor do I care; for none I wot, so well
As I may chant thee, so
This one behest I lay upon thee, go
Hie thee to Love, and him in secret tell,
How I my life do spurn,
My bitter life, and yearn,
That to a better harbourage he bring
Me, of all might and grace that own him king.

Full well my tears attest, etc.

Filostrato's mood and its cause were made abundantly manifest by the words of this song; and perchance they had been made still more so by the looks of a lady that was among the dancers, had not the shades of night, which had now overtaken them, concealed the blush that suffused her face. Other songs followed until the hour for slumber arrived: whereupon at the behest of the queen all the ladies sought their several chambers.

20

The fourth story of the fifth day, in which Ricciardo Manardi is found by Messer Lizio da Valbona with his daughter, whom he marries, and remains at peace with her father.

Now the queen called for a story from Filostrato, who with a laugh began on this wise: Chidden have I been so often and by so many of you for the sore burden which I laid upon you of discourse harsh and meet for tears that, as some compensation for such annoy, I deem myself bound to tell you somewhat that may cause you to laugh a little: wherefore my story, which will be of the briefest, shall be of a love the course whereof save for sighs and a brief passage of fear mingled with shame ran smooth to a happy consummation –

Know then, noble ladies, that 'tis no long time since there dwelt in Romagna a right worthy and courteous knight, Messer Lizio da Valbona by name, who was already verging upon old age, when, as it happened, there was born to him of his wife, Madonna Giacomina, a daughter who, as she grew up, became the fairest and most debonair of all the girls of those parts and, for that she was the only daughter left to them, was most dearly loved and cherished by her father and mother, who guarded her with most jealous care, thinking to arrange some great match for her. Now there was frequently in Messer Lizio's house, and much in his company, a fine, lusty young man, one Ricciardo de' Manardi da Brettinoro, whom Messer Lizio and his wife would as little have thought of mistrusting as if he had been their own son: who now and again taking note of the damsel, that she was very fair and graceful, and in bearing and behaviour most commendable, and of marriageable age, fell vehemently in love with her, which love he was very careful to conceal. The damsel detected it, however, and in like manner plunged headlong into love with him, to Ricciardo's no small satisfaction. Again and again he was on the point of speaking to her, but refrained for fear; at length, however, he summoned up his courage and seizing his opportunity thus addressed her – 'Caterina, I implore thee, suffer me not to die for love of thee.' Whereto the damsel forthwith responded – 'Nay, God grant that it be not rather that I die for love of thee.' Greatly exhilarated and encouraged, Ricciardo made answer – ' 'Twill never be by default of mine that thou lackest aught that may pleasure thee; but it rests with thee to find the means to save thy life and mine.' Then said the damsel – 'Thou seest, Ricciardo, how closely watched I am, insomuch that I see not how 'twere possible for thee to come to me; but if thou seest aught that I may do without dishonour, speak the word, and I will do it.' Ricciardo was silent a while, pondering many matters: then of a sudden he said – 'Sweet my Caterina, there is but one way that I can see, to wit, that thou shouldst sleep either on or where thou mightst have access to the terrace by thy father's garden where, so I but knew that thou wouldst be there at night, I would without fail contrive to meet thee, albeit 'tis very high.' 'As for my sleeping there,' replied Caterina, 'I doubt not that it may be managed, if thou art sure that thou canst join me.' Ricciardo answered in the affirmative. Whereupon they exchanged a furtive kiss and parted.

On the morrow, it being now towards the close of May, the damsel began complaining to her mother that by reason of the excessive heat she had not been able to get any sleep during the night. 'Daughter,' said the lady, 'what heat was there? Nay, there was no heat at all.' 'Had you said, "to my thinking," mother,' rejoined Caterina, 'you would perhaps have said sooth; but you should bethink you how much more heat girls have in them than ladies that are advanced in years.' 'True, my daughter,' returned the lady, 'but I cannot order that it shall be hot and cold, as thou perchance wouldst like; we must take the weather as we find it and as the seasons provide it: perchance tonight it will be cooler and thou wilt sleep better.' 'God grant it be so,' said Caterina, 'but 'tis not wonted for the nights to grow cooler as the summer comes on.' 'What then,' said the lady, 'wouldst thou have me do?' 'With your leave and my father's,' answered Caterina, 'I should like to have a little bed made up on the terrace by his room and over his garden where, hearing the nightingales sing, and being in a much cooler place, I should sleep much better than in your room.' Whereupon – 'Daughter, be of good cheer,' said the mother; 'I will speak to thy father and we will do as he shall decide.' So the lady told Messer Lizio what had passed between her and the damsel; but he, being old and perhaps for that reason a little morose, said – 'What nightingale is this, to whose chant she would fain sleep? I will see to it that the cicalas shall yet lull her to sleep.' Which speech, coming to Caterina's ears, gave her such offence, that for anger, rather than by reason of the heat, she not only slept not herself that night, but suffered not her mother to sleep, keeping up a perpetual complaint of the great heat. Wherefore her mother hied her in the morning to Messer Lizio, and said to him – 'Sir, you hold your daughter none too dear; what difference can it make to you that she lie on the terrace? She has tossed about all night long by reason of the heat; and besides, can you wonder that she, girl that she is, loves to hear the nightingale sing? Young folk naturally affect their likes.' Whereto Messer Lizio made answer – 'Go, make her a bed there to your liking, and set a curtain round it, and let her sleep there, and hear the nightingale sing to her heart's content.' Which the damsel no sooner learned, than she had a bed made there with intent to sleep there that same night; wherefore she watched until she saw Ricciardo, whom by a concerted sign she gave to understand what he was to do. Messer Lizio, as soon as he had heard the damsel go to bed, locked a door that led from his room to the terrace, and went to sleep himself. When all was quiet, Ricciardo with the help of a ladder got upon a wall, and standing thereon laid hold of certain toothings of another wall, and not without great exertion and risk, had he fallen, clambered up on to the terrace, where the damsel received him quietly with the heartiest of cheer. Many a kiss they exchanged; and then got them to bed, where well-nigh all night long they had solace and joy of one another, and made the nightingale sing not a few times. But, brief being the night and great their pleasure, towards dawn, albeit they wist it not, they fell asleep, Caterina's right arm encircling Ricciardo's neck, while with her left hand she held him by that part of his person which your modesty, my ladies, is most averse to name in the company of men. So, peacefully they slept, and were still asleep when day broke and Messer Lizio rose; and calling to mind that his daughter slept on the terrace, softly opened the door, saying to himself – Let me see what sort of night's rest the nightingale has afforded our Caterina? And having entered, he gently raised the curtain that screened the bed, and saw Ricciardo asleep with her and in her embrace as described, both being quite naked and uncovered; and having taken note of Ricciardo, he went away, and hied him to his lady's room, and called her, saying – 'Up, up, wife, come and see; for thy daughter has fancied the nightingale to such purpose that she has caught him, and holds him in her hand.' 'How can this be?' said the lady. 'Come quickly, and thou shalt see,' replied Messer Lizio. So the lady huddled on her clothes, and silently followed Messer Lizio, and when they were come to the bed, and had raised the curtain, Madonna Giacomina saw plainly enough how her daughter had caught, and did hold the nightingale, whose song she had so longed to hear. Whereat the lady, deeming that Ricciardo had played her a cruel trick, would have cried out and upbraided him; but Messer Lizio said to her – 'Wife, as thou valuest my love, say not a word; for in good sooth, seeing that she has caught him, he shall be hers. Ricciardo is a gentleman and wealthy; an alliance with him cannot but be to our advantage: if he would part from me on good terms, he must first marry her, so that the nightingale shall prove to have been put in his own cage and not in that of another.' Whereby the lady was reassured, seeing that her husband took the affair so quietly, and that her daughter had had a good night, and was rested, and had caught the nightingale. So she kept silence; nor had they long to wait before Ricciardo awoke; and, seeing that 'twas broad day, deemed that 'twas as much as his life was worth, and aroused Caterina, saying – 'Alas! my soul, what shall we do, now that day has come and surprised me here?' Which question Messer Lizio answered by coming forward, and saying – 'We shall do well.' At sight of him Ricciardo felt as if his heart were torn out of his body, and sat up in the bed, and said – 'My lord, I cry you mercy for God's sake. I wot that my disloyalty and delinquency have merited death; wherefore deal with me even as it may seem best to you: however, I pray you, if so it may be, to spare my life, that I die not.' 'Ricciardo,' replied Messer Lizio, 'the love I bore thee, and the faith I reposed in thee, merited a better return; but still, as so it is, and youth has seduced thee into such a transgression, redeem thy life, and preserve my honour, by making Caterina thy lawful spouse, that thine, as she has been for this past night, she may remain for the rest of her life. In this way thou mayst secure my peace and thy safety; otherwise commend thy soul to God.' Pending this colloquy, Caterina let go the nightingale, and having covered herself, began with many a tear to implore her father to forgive Ricciardo, and Ricciardo to do as Messer Lizio required, that thereby they might securely count upon a long continuance of such nights of delight. But there needed not much supplication; for, what with remorse for the wrong done, and the wish to make amends, and the fear of death, and the desire to escape it, and above all ardent love, and the craving to possess the beloved one, Ricciardo lost no time in making frank avowal of his readiness to do as Messer Lizio would have him. Wherefore Messer Lizio, having borrowed a ring from Madonna Giacomina, Ricciardo did there and then in their presence wed Caterina. Which done, Messer Lizio and the lady took their leave, saying – 'Now rest ye a while; for so perchance 'twere better for you than if ye rose.' And so they left the young folks, who forthwith embraced, and not having travelled more than six miles during the night, went two miles further before they rose, and so concluded their first day. When they were risen, Ricciardo and Messer Lizio discussed the matter with more formality; and some days afterwards Ricciardo, as was meet, married the damsel anew in presence of their friends and kinsfolk, and brought her home with great pomp, and celebrated his nuptials with due dignity and splendour. And so for many a year thereafter he lived with her in peace and happiness, and snared the nightingales day and night to his heart's content.

21

The sixth story of the fifth day, in which Gianni di Procida, being found with a damsel that he loves, and who had been given to King Frederic, is bound with her to a stake, so to be burned. He is recognised by Ruggieri dell' Oria, is delivered, and marries her.

The fifth story, with which the ladies were greatly delighted, being ended, the queen called for one from Pampinea; who forthwith raised her noble countenance, and thus began: Mighty indeed, gracious ladies, are the forces of Love and great are the labours and excessive and unthought-of the perils which they induce lovers to brave; as is manifest enough by what we have heard today and on other occasions: howbeit I mean to show you the same once more by a story of an enamoured youth –

Hard by Naples is the island of Ischia, in which there dwelt aforetime with other young damsels one, Restituta by name, daughter of one Marin Bolgaro, a gentleman of the island. Very fair was she, and blithe of heart, and by a young gallant, Gianni by name, of the neighbouring islet of Procida, was beloved more dearly than life, and in like measure returned his love. Now, not to mention his daily resort to Ischia to see her, there were times not a few when Gianni, not being able to come by a boat, would swim across from Procida by night. that he might have sight, if of nought else, at least of the walls of her house. And while their love burned thus fervently, it so befell that one summer's day, as the damsel was all alone on the seashore, picking her way from rock to rock, detaching, as she went, shells from their beds with a knife, she came to a recess among the rocks, where for the sake, as well of the shade as of the comfort afforded by a spring of most cool water that was there, some Sicilian gallants, that were come from Naples, had put in with their felucca. Who, having taken note of the damsel, that she was very fair, and that she was not yet ware of them, and was alone, resolved to capture her, and carry her away; nor did they fail to give effect to their resolve; but, albeit she shrieked amain, they laid hands on her, and set her aboard their boat, and put to sea. Arrived at Calabria, they fell awrangling as to whose the damsel should be, and in brief each claimed her for his own: wherefore, finding no means of coming to an agreement, and fearing that worse might befall them, and she bring misfortune upon them, they resolved with one accord to give her to Frederic, King of Sicily, who was then a young man, and took no small delight in commodities of that quality; and so, being come to Palermo, they did.

Marking her beauty, the King set great store by her; but as she was somewhat indisposed, he commanded that, till she was stronger, she should be lodged and tended in a very pretty villa that was in one of his gardens, which he called Cuba; and so 'twas done. The purloining of the damsel caused no small stir in Ischia, more especially because 'twas impossible to discover by whom she had been carried off. But Gianni, more concerned than any other, despairing of finding her in Ischia, and being apprised of the course the felucca had taken, equipped one himself, and put to sea, and in hot haste scoured the whole coast from Minerva to Scalea in Calabria, making everywhere diligent search for the damsel, and in Scalea learned that she had been taken by Sicilian mariners to Palermo. Whither, accordingly, he hied him with all speed; and there after long search discovering that she had been given to the King, who kept her at Cuba, he was sore troubled, insomuch that he now scarce ventured to hope that he should ever set eyes on her, not to speak of having her for his own, again. But still, holden by Love, and seeing that none there knew him, he sent the felucca away, and tarried there, and frequently passing by Cuba, he chanced one day to catch sight of her at a window, and was seen of her, to their great mutual satisfaction. And Gianni, taking note that the place was lonely, made up to her, and had such speech of her as he might, and being taught by her after what fashion he must proceed, if he would have further speech of her, he departed, but not till he had made himself thoroughly acquainted with the configuration of the place; and having waited until night was come and indeed far spent, he returned thither, and though the ascent was such that 'twould scarce have afforded lodgment to a woodpecker, won his way up and entered the garden, where, finding a pole, he set it against the window which the damsel had pointed out as hers, and thereby swarmed up easily enough.

The damsel had aforetime shown herself somewhat distant towards him, being careful of her honour, but now deeming it already lost, she had bethought her that there was none to whom she might more worthily give herself than to him; and reckoning upon inducing him to carry her off, she had made up her mind to gratify his every desire; and to that end had left the window open that his ingress might be unimpeded. So, finding it open, Gianni softly entered, lay down beside the damsel, who was awake, and before they went further, opened to him all her mind, beseeching him most earnestly to take her thence, and carry her off. Gianni replied that there was nought that would give him so much pleasure, and that without fail, upon leaving her, he would make all needful arrangements for bringing her away when he next came. Whereupon with exceeding great delight they embraced one another, and plucked that boon than which Love has no greater to bestow; and having so done divers times, they unwittingly fell asleep in one another's arms.

Now towards daybreak the King, who had been greatly charmed with the damsel at first sight, happened to call her to mind, and feeling himself fit, resolved, notwithstanding the hour, to go lie with her a while; and so, attended by a few of his servants, he hied him privily to Cuba. Having entered the house, he passed (the door being softly opened) into the room in which he knew the damsel slept. A great blazing torch was borne before him, and so, as he bent his glance on the bed, he espied the damsel and Gianni lying asleep, naked and in one another's arms. Whereat he was seized with a sudden and vehement passion of wrath, insomuch that, albeit he said never a word, he could scarce refrain from slaying both of them there and then with a dagger that he had with him. Then, bethinking him that 'twere the depth of baseness in any man – not to say a king – to slay two naked sleepers, he mastered himself, and determined to do them to death in public and by fire. Wherefore, turning to a single companion that he had with him, he said – 'What thinkest thou of this base woman, in whom I had placed my hope?' And then he asked whether he knew the gallant, that had presumed to enter his house to do him such outrage and despite. Whereto the other replied that he minded not ever to have seen him. Thereupon the King hied him out of the room in a rage, and bade take the two lovers, naked as they were, and bind them, and, as soon as 'twas broad day, bring them to Palermo, and bind them back to back to a stake in the piazza, there to remain until tierce, that all might see them, after which they were to be burned, as they had deserved.

And having so ordered, he went back to Palermo, and shut himself up in his room, very wroth.

No sooner was he gone than there came unto the two lovers folk not a few, who, having awakened them, did forthwith ruthlessly take and bind them: whereat, how they did grieve and tremble for their lives, and weep and bitterly bewail their fate, may readily be understood.

Pursuant to the King's commandment they were brought to Palermo, and bound to a stake in the piazza; and before their eyes faggots and fire were made ready to burn them at the hour appointed by the King. Great was the concourse of the folk of Palermo, both men and women, that came to see the two lovers, the men all agog to feast their eyes on the damsel, whom they lauded for shapeliness and loveliness, and no less did the women commend the gallant, whom in like manner they crowded to see, for the same qualities. Meanwhile the two hapless lovers, both exceeding shamefast, stood with bent heads bitterly bewailing their evil fortune, and momently expecting their death by the cruel fire. So they awaited the time appointed by the King; but their offence being bruited abroad, the tidings reached the ears of Ruggieri dell' Oria, a man of peerless worth, and at that time the King's admiral, who, being likewise minded to see them, came to the place where they were bound, and after gazing on the damsel and finding her very fair, turned to look at the gallant, whom with little trouble he recognised, and drawing nearer to him, he asked him if he were Gianni di Procida. Gianni raised his head, and recognising the admiral, made answer – 'My lord, he, of whom you speak, I was; but I am now as good as no more.' The admiral then asked him what it was that had brought him to such a pass. Whereupon – 'Love and the King's wrath,' quoth Gianni. The admiral induced him to be more explicit, and having learned from him exactly how it had come about, was turning away, when Gianni called him back, saying: – 'Oh! my lord, if so it may be, procure me one favour of him by whose behest I thus stand here.' 'What favour?' demanded Ruggieri. 'I see,' returned Gianni, 'that die I must, and that right soon. I crave, then, as a favour, that, whereas this damsel and I, that have loved one another more dearly than life, are here set back to back, we may be set face to face, that I may have the consolation of gazing on her face as I depart.' Ruggieri laughed as he replied – 'With all my heart. I will so order it that thou shalt see enough of her to tire of her.' He then left him and charged the executioners to do nothing more without further order of the King; and being assured of their obedience, he hied him forthwith to the King, to whom, albeit he found him in a wrathful mood, he spared not to speak his mind, saying – 'Sire, wherein have they wronged thee, those two young folk, whom thou hast ordered to be burned down there in the piazza?' The King told him. Whereupon Ruggieri continued – 'Their offence does indeed merit such punishment, but not at thy hands, and if misdeeds should not go unpunished, services should not go unrewarded; nay, may warrant indulgence and mercy. Knowest thou who they are whom thou wouldst have burned?' The King signified that he did not. Whereupon Ruggieri – 'But I,' quoth he, 'am minded that thou shouldst know them, to the end that thou mayst know with what discretion thou surrenderest thyself to a transport of rage. The young man is the son of Landolfo di Procida, brother of Messer Gianni di Procida, to whom thou owest it that thou art lord and king of this island. The damsel is a daughter of Marin Bolgaro, whose might alone today prevents Ischia from throwing off thy yoke. Moreover, these young folk have long been lovers, and 'tis for that the might of Love constrained them, and not that they would do despite to thy lordship, that they have committed this offence, if indeed 'tis meet to call that an offence which young folk do for Love's sake. Wherefore, then, wouldst thou do them to death, when thou shouldst rather do them all cheer, and honour them with lordly gifts?' The King gave ear to Ruggieri's words, and being satisfied that he spoke sooth, repented him, not only of his evil purpose, but of what he had already done, and forthwith gave order to loose the two young folk from the stake, and bring them before him; and so 'twas done. And having fully apprised himself of their case, he saw fit to make them amends of the wrong he had done them with honours and largess. Wherefore he caused them to be splendidly arrayed, and being assured that they were both minded to wed, he himself gave Gianni his bride, and loading them with rich presents, sent them well content back to Ischia, where they were welcomed with all festal cheer, and lived long time thereafter to their mutual solace and delight.

22

The seventh story of the fifth day, in which Teodoro, being enamoured of Violante, daughter of Messer Amerigo, his lord, gets her with child, and is sentenced to the gallows; but while he is being scourged thither, he is recognised by his father, and being set at large, takes Violante to wife.

While they doubted whether the two lovers would be burned, the ladies were all fear and suspense; but when they heard of their deliverance, they all with one accord put on a cheerful countenance, praising God. The story ended, the queen ordained that the next should be told by Lauretta, who blithely thus began:

Fairest ladies, what time good King Guglielmo ruled Sicily there dwelt on the island a gentleman, Messer Amerigo Abate da Trapani by name, who was well provided, as with other temporal goods, so also with children. For which cause being in need of servants, he took occasion of the appearance in Trapani waters of certain Genoese corsairs from the Levant who, scouring the coast of Armenia, had captured not a few boys, to purchase of them some of these youngsters, supposing them to be Turks; among whom, albeit most showed as mere shepherd boys, there was one, Teodoro by name, whose less rustic mien seemed to betoken gentle blood. Who, though still treated as a slave, was suffered to grow up in the house with Messer Amerigo's children, and, nature getting the better of circumstance, bore himself with such grace and dignity that Messer Amerigo gladly gave him his freedom, and still deeming him to be a Turk, had him baptised and named Pietro, and made him his majordomo, and placed much trust in him. Now among the other children that grew up in Messer Amerigo's house was his fair and dainty daughter, Violante; and, as her father was in no hurry to give her in marriage, it so befell that she became enamoured of Pietro; but, for all her love and the great conceit she had of his qualities and conduct, she nevertheless was too shamefast to discover her passion to him. However, Love spared her the pains, for Pietro had cast many a furtive glance in her direction, and had grown so enamoured of her that 'twas never well with him except he saw her; but great was his fear lest any should detect his passion, for he deemed 'twould be the worse for him. The damsel, who was fain indeed of the sight of him, understood his case; and to encourage him dissembled not her exceeding great satisfaction. On which footing they remained a great while, neither venturing to say aught to the other, much as both longed to do so. But, while they both burned with a mutual flame, Fortune, as if their entanglement were of her preordaining, found means to banish the fear and hesitation that kept them tongue-tied.

Messer Amerigo possessed, a mile or so from Trapani, a goodly estate, to which he was wont not seldom to resort with his daughter and other ladies by way of recreation; and on one of these days, while there they tarried with Pietro, whom they had brought with them, suddenly, as will sometimes happen in summer, the sky became overcast with black clouds, insomuch that the lady and her companions, lest the storm should surprise them there, set out on their return to Trapani, making all the haste they might. But Pietro and the girl being young, and sped perchance by Love no less than by fear of the storm, completely outstripped her mother and the other ladies; and when they were gotten so far ahead as to be well-nigh out of sight of the lady and all the rest, the thunder burst upon them peal upon peal, hard upon which came a fall of hail very thick and close, from which the lady sought shelter in the house of a husbandman. Pietro and the damsel, finding no more convenient refuge, betook them to an old, and all but ruinous, and now deserted, cottage, which, however, still had a bit of roof left, whereunder they both took their stand in such close quarters, owing to the exiguity of the shelter, that they perforce touched one another. Which contact was the occasion that they gathered somewhat more courage to disclose their love; and so it was that Pietro began on this wise – 'Now would to God that this hail might never cease, that so I might stay here for ever!' 'And well content were I,' returned the damsel. And by and by their hands met, not without a tender pressure, and then they fell to embracing and so to kissing one another, while the hail continued. And not to dwell on every detail, the sky was not clear before they had known the last degree of love's felicity, and had taken thought how they might secretly enjoy one another in the future. The cottage being close to the city gate, they hied them thither, as soon as the storm was overpast, and having there awaited the lady, returned home with her. Nor, using all discretion, did they fail thereafter to meet from time to time in secret, to their no small solace; and the affair went so far that the damsel conceived, whereby they were both not a little disconcerted; insomuch that the damsel employed many artifices to arrest the course of nature, but to no effect. Wherefore Pietro, being in fear of his life, saw nothing for it but flight, and told her so. Whereupon – 'If thou leave me,' quoth she, 'I shall certainly kill myself.' Much as he loved her, Pietro answered – 'Nay but, my lady, wherefore wouldst thou have me tarry here? Thy pregnancy will discover our offence: thou wilt be readily forgiven; but 'twill be my woeful lot to bear the penalty of thy sin and mine.' 'Pietro,' returned the damsel, 'too well will they wot of my offence, but be sure that, if thou confess not, none will ever wot of thine.' Then quoth he – 'Since thou givest me this promise, I will stay; but mind thou keep it.'

The damsel, who had done her best to keep her condition secret, saw at length by the increase of her bulk that 'twas impossible: wherefore one day most piteously bewailing herself, she made her avowal to her mother, and besought her to shield her from the consequences. Distressed beyond measure, the lady chid her severely, and then asked her how it had come to pass. The damsel, to screen Pietro, invented a story by which she put another complexion on the affair. The lady believed her, and, that her fall might not be discovered, took her off to one of their estates; where, the time of her delivery being come, and she, as women do in such a case, crying out for pain, it so befell that Messer Amerigo, whom the lady expected not, as indeed he was scarce ever wont, to come there, did so, having been out a-hawking, and passing by the chamber where the damsel lay, marvelled to hear her cries, and forthwith entered, and asked what it meant. On sight of whom the lady rose and sorrowfully gave him her daughter's version of what had befallen her. But he, less credulous than his wife, averred that it could not be true that she knew not by whom she was pregnant, and was minded to know the whole truth: let the damsel confess and she might regain his favour; otherwise she must expect no mercy and prepare for death.

The lady did all she could to induce her husband to rest satisfied with what she had told him; but all to no purpose. Mad with rage, he rushed, drawn sword in hand, to his daughter's bedside (she, pending the parley, having given birth to a boy) and cried out – 'Declare whose this infant is, or forthwith thou diest.' Overcome by fear of death, the damsel broke her promise to Pietro, and made a clean breast of all that had passed between him and her. Whereat the knight, grown fell with rage, could scarce refrain from slaying her. However, having given vent to his wrath in such words as it dictated, he remounted his horse and rode to Trapani, and there before one Messer Currado, the King's lieutenant, laid information of the wrong done him by Pietro, in consequence whereof Pietro, who suspected nothing, was forthwith taken, and being put to the torture, confessed all. Some days later the lieutenant sentenced him to be scourged through the city, and then hanged by the neck; and Messer Amerigo, being minded that one and the same hour should rid the earth of the two lovers and their son (for to have compassed Pietro's death was not enough to appease his wrath), mingled poison and wine in a goblet, and gave it to one of his servants with a drawn sword, saying – 'Get thee with this gear to Violante, and tell her from me to make instant choice of one of these two deaths, either the poison or the steel; else, I will have her burned, as she deserves, in view of all the citizens; which done, thou wilt take the boy that she bore a few days ago, and beat his brains out against the wall, and cast his body for a prey to the dogs.'

Hearing the remorseless doom thus passed by the angry father upon both his daughter and his grandson, the servant, prompt to do evil rather than good, hied him thence.

Now, as Pietro in execution of his sentence was being scourged to the gallows by the sergeants, 'twas so ordered by the leaders of the band that he passed by an inn, where were three noblemen of Armenia, sent by the king of that country as ambassadors to Rome, to treat with the Pope of matters of the highest importance, touching a crusade that was to be; who, having there alighted to rest and recreate them for some days, had received not a few tokens of honour from the nobles of Trapani, and most of all from Messer Amerigo. Hearing the tramp of Pietro's escort, they came to a window to see what was toward; and one of them, an aged man, and of great authority, Fineo by name, looking hard at Pietro, who was stripped from the waist up, and had his hands bound behind his back, espied on his breast a great spot of scarlet, not laid on by art, but wrought in the skin by operation of Nature, being such as the ladies here call a rose. Which he no sooner saw, than he was reminded of a son that had been stolen from him by corsairs on the coast of Lazistan some fifteen years before, nor had he since been able to hear tidings of him; and guessing the age of the poor wretch that was being scourged, he set it down as about what his son's would be, were he living, and, what with the mark and the age, he began to suspect that 'twas even his son, and bethought him that, if so, he would scarce as yet have forgotten his name or the speech of Armenia. Wherefore, as he was within earshot he called to him – 'Teodoro!' At the word Pietro raised his head: whereupon Fineo, speaking in Armenian, asked him – 'Whence and whose son art thou?' The serjeants, that were leading him, paused in deference to the great man, and so Pietro answered – 'Of Armenia was I, son of one Fineo, brought hither by folk I wot not of, when I was but a little child.' Then Fineo, witting that in very truth 'twas the boy that he had lost, came down with his companions, weeping; and, all the serjeants making way, he ran to him, and embraced him, and doffing a mantle of richest texture that he wore, he prayed the captain of the band to be pleased to tarry there until he should receive orders to go forward, and was answered by the captain that he would willingly so wait.

Fineo already knew, for 'twas bruited everywhere, the cause for which Pietro was being led to the gallows; wherefore he straightway hied him with his companions and their retinue to Messer Currado, and said to him – 'Sir, this lad, whom you are sending to the gallows like a slave, is freeborn, and my son, and is ready to take to wife her whom, as 'tis said, he has deflowered; so please you, therefore, delay the execution until such time as it may be understood whether she be minded to have him for husband, lest, should she be so minded, you be found to have broken the law.' Messer Currado marvelled to hear that Pietro was Fineo's son, and not without shame, albeit 'twas not his but Fortune's fault, confessed that 'twas even as Fineo said: and having caused Pietro to be taken home with all speed, and Messer Amerigo to be brought before him, told him the whole matter. Messer Amerigo, who supposed that by this time his daughter and grandson must be dead, was the saddest man in the world to think that 'twas by his deed, witting that, were the damsel still alive, all might very easily be set right: however, he sent post haste to his daughter's abode, revoking his orders, if they were not yet carried out. The servant, whom he had earlier despatched, had laid the sword and poison before the damsel, and, for that she was in no hurry to make her choice, was giving her foul words, and endeavouring to constrain her thereto, when the messenger arrived; but on hearing the injunction laid upon him by his lord, he desisted, and went back, and told him how things stood. Whereupon Messer Amerigo, much relieved, hied him to Fineo, and well-nigh weeping, and excusing himself for what had befallen, as best he knew how, craved his pardon, and professed himself well content to give Teodoro, so he were minded to have her, his daughter to wife. Fineo readily accepted his excuses, and made answer – ''Tis my will that my son espouse your daughter, and, so he will not, let thy sentence passed upon him be carried out.'

So Fineo and Messer Amerigo being agreed, while Teodoro still languished in fear of death, albeit he was glad at heart to have found his father, they questioned him of his will in regard of this matter.

When he heard that, if he would, he might have Violante to wife, Teodoro's delight was such that he seemed to leap from hell to paradise, and said that, if 'twas agreeable to them all, he should deem it the greatest of favours. So they sent to the damsel to learn her pleasure: who, having heard how it had fared, and was now like to fare, with Teodoro, albeit, saddest of women, she looked for nought but death, began at length to give some credence to their words, and to recover heart a little, and answered that, were she to follow the bent of her desire, nought that could happen would delight her more than to be Teodoro's wife; but nevertheless she would do as her father bade her.

So, all agreeing, the damsel was espoused with all pomp and festal cheer, to the boundless delight of all the citizens, and was comforted, and nurtured her little boy, and in no long time waxed more beautiful than ever before; and, her confinement being ended, she presented herself before Fineo, who was then about to quit Rome on his homeward journey, and did him such reverence as is due to a father. Fineo, mighty well pleased to have so fair a daughter-in-law, caused celebrate her nuptials most bravely and gaily, and received, and did ever thereafter entreat, her as his daughter.

And so he took her, not many days after the festivities were ended, with his son and little grandson, aboard a galley, and brought them to Lazistan, and there thenceforth the two lovers dwelt with him in easeful and lifelong peace.

❧ 23 ❧

The tenth story of the fifth day, in which Pietro di Vinciolo goes from home to sup; his wife brings a boy into the house to bear her company; Pietro returns, and she hides her gallant under a hen-coop; Pietro explains that in the house of Ercolano, with whom he was to have supped, there was discovered a young man bestowed there by Ercolano's wife; the lady thereupon censures Ercolano's wife; but unluckily an ass treads on the fingers of the boy that is hidden under the hen-coop, so that he cries for pain; Pietro runs to the place, sees him, and apprehends the trick played on him by his wife, which nevertheless he finally condones, for that he is not himself free from blame.

When the last speaker had done and all had praised God for the outcome of his story, Dioneo, who never waited to be bidden, thus began: ❧ I know not whether I am to term it a vice accidental and superinduced by bad habits in us mortals or whether it be a fault seated in nature that we are more prone to laugh at things dishonourable than at good deeds, and that more especially when they concern not ourselves. However, as the sole scope of all my efforts has been and still shall be to dispel your melancholy, and in lieu thereof to minister to you laughter and jollity; therefore, enamoured my damsels, albeit the ensuing story is not altogether free from matter that is scarce seemly, yet, as it may afford you pleasure, I shall not fail to relate it; premonishing you my hearers, that you take it with the like discretion as when, going into your gardens, you stretch forth your delicate hands and cull the roses, leaving the thorns alone: which, being interpreted, means that you will leave the caitiff husband to abide in sorry plight with his dishonour, and will gaily laugh at the amorous wiles of his wife, and commiserate her unfortunate gallant, when occasion requires –

'Tis no great while since there dwelt at Perugia a rich man named Pietro di Vinciolo, who rather, perchance, to blind others and mitigate the evil repute in which he was held by the citizens of Perugia, than for any desire to wed, took a wife: and such being his motive, Fortune provided him with just such a spouse as he merited. For the wife of his choice was a stout, red-haired young woman, and so hot-blooded that two husbands would have been more to her mind than one, whereas one fell to her lot that gave her only a subordinate place in his regard. Which she perceiving, while she knew herself to be fair and lusty, and felt herself to be gamesome and fit, waxed very wroth, and now and again had high words with her husband, and led but a sorry life with him at most times. Then, seeing that thereby she was more like to fret herself than to dispose her husband to conduct less base, she said to herself: – This poor creature deserts me to go walk in pattens in the dry; wherefore it shall go hard but I will bring another aboard the ship for the wet weather. I married him, and brought him a great and goodly dowry, knowing that he was a man, and supposing him to have the desires which men have and ought to have; and had I not deemed him to be a man, I should never have married him. He knew me to be a woman: why then took he me to wife, if women were not to his mind? 'Tis not to be endured. Had I not been minded to live in the world, I had become a nun; and being minded there to live, as I am, if I am to wait until I have pleasure or solace of him, I shall wait perchance until I am old; and then, too late, I shall bethink me to my sorrow that I have wasted my youth; and as to the way in which I should seek its proper solace I need no better teacher and guide than him, who finds his delight where I should find mine, and finds it to his own condemnation, whereas in me 'twere commendable. 'Tis but the laws that I shall set at nought, whereas he sets both them and Nature herself at nought.

So the good lady reasoned, and peradventure more than once; and then, casting about how she might privily compass her end, she made friends with an old beldam, that showed as a veritable Santa Verdiana, foster-mother of vipers, who was ever to be seen going to pardonings with a parcel of paternosters in her hand, and talked of nothing but the lives of the holy Fathers, and the wounds of St Francis, and was generally reputed a saint; to whom in due time she opened her whole mind. 'My daughter,' replied the beldam, 'God, who knows all things, knows that thou wilt do very rightly indeed: were it for no other reason, 'twould be meet for thee and every other young woman so to do, that the heyday of youth be not wasted; for there is no grief like that of knowing that it has been wasted. And what the devil are we women fit for when we are old – except to pore over the cinders on the hearth? The which if any know, and may attest it, 'tis I, who, now that I am old, call to mind the time that I let slip from me, not without most sore and bitter and fruitless regret: and albeit 'twas not all wasted, for I would not have thee think that I was entirely without sense, yet I did not make the best use of it: whereof when I bethink me, and that I am now, even as thou seest me, such a hag that never a spark of fire may I hope to get from any, God knows how I rue it. Now with men 'tis otherwise: they are born meet for a thousand uses, not for this alone; and the more part of them are of much greater consequence in old age than in youth: but women are fit for nought but this, and 'tis but for that they bear children that they are cherished. Whereof, if not otherwise, thou mayst assure thyself, if thou do but consider that we are ever ready for it; which is not the case with men; besides which, one woman will tire out many men without being herself tired out. Seeing then that 'tis for this we are born, I tell thee again that thou wilt do very rightly to give thy husband thy loaf for his cake, that in thy old age thy soul may have no cause of complaint against thy flesh. Everyone has just as much of this life as he appropriates: and this is especially true of women, whom therefore it behoves, much more than men, to seize the moment as it flies: indeed, as thou mayst see for thyself, when we grow old neither husband, nor any other man will spare us a glance; but, on the contrary, they banish us to the kitchen, there to tell stories to the cat, and to count the pots and pans; or, worse, they make rhymes about us – "To the damsel dainty bits; to the beldam ague-fits;" and suchlike catches. But to make no more words about it, I tell thee at once that there is no person in the world to whom thou couldst open thy mind with more advantage than to me; for there is no gentleman so fine but I dare speak my mind to him, nor any so harsh and forbidding but I know well how to soften him and fashion him to my will. Tell me only what thou wouldst have, and leave the rest to me: but one word more: I pray thee to have me in kindly remembrance, for that I am poor; and thou shalt henceforth go shares with me in all my indulgences and every paternoster that I say, that God may make thereof light and tapers for thy dead:' wherewith she ended.

So the lady came to an understanding with the beldam, that, as soon as she set eyes on a boy that often came along that street, and of whom the lady gave her a particular description, she would know what she was to do: and thereupon the lady gave her a chunk of salt meat, and bade her God-speed. The beldam before long smuggled into the lady's chamber the boy of whom she had spoken, and not long after another, such being the humour of the lady, who, standing in perpetual dread of her husband, was disposed, in this particular, to make the most of her opportunities. And one of these days, her husband being to sup in the evening with a friend named Ercolano, the lady bade the beldam bring her a boy as pretty and dainty as was to be found in Perugia; and so the beldam forthwith did. But the lady and the boy being set at table to sup, lo, Pietro's voice was heard at the door, bidding open to him. Whereupon the lady gave herself up for dead; but being fain, if she might, to screen the boy, and knowing not where else to convey or conceal him, bestowed him under a hen-coop that stood in a veranda hard by the chamber in which they were supping, and threw over it a sorry mattress that she had that day emptied of its straw; which done she hastened to open the door to her husband; saying to him as he entered – 'You have gulped your supper mighty quickly tonight.' Whereto Pietro replied – 'We have not so much as tasted it.' 'How so?' enquired the lady. 'I will tell thee,' said Pietro. 'No sooner were we set at table, Ercolano, his wife, and I, than we heard a sneeze close to us, to which, though 'twas repeated, we paid no heed; but as the sneezer continued to sneeze a third, a fourth, a fifth, and many another time to boot, we all began to wonder, and Ercolano, who was somewhat out of humour with his wife, because she had kept us a long time at the door before she opened it, burst out in a sort of rage with – "What means this? Who is't that thus sneezes?" and made off to a stair hard by, beneath which and close to its foot was a wooden closet, of the sort which, when folk are furnishing their houses, they commonly cause to be placed there, to stow things in upon occasion. And as it seemed to him that the sneezing proceeded thence, he undid the wicket, and no sooner had he opened it than out flew never so strong a stench of brimstone; albeit we had already been saluted by a whiff of it, and complained thereof, but had been put off by the lady with – " 'Tis but that a while ago I bleached my veils with brimstone, having sprinkled it on a dish, that they might catch its fumes, which dish I then placed under the stair, so that it still smells a little."

'However the door being now, as I have said, open, and the smoke somewhat less dense, Ercolano, peering in, espied the fellow that had sneezed, and who still kept sneezing, being thereto constrained by the pungency of the brimstone. And for all he sneezed, yet was he by this time so well-nigh choked with the brimstone that he was like neither to sneeze nor to do aught else again. As soon as he caught sight of him, Ercolano bawled out – "Now see I, Madam, why it was that a while ago, when we came here, we were kept waiting so long at the gate before 'twas opened; but woe betide me for the rest of my days, if I pay you not out." Whereupon the lady, perceiving that her offence was discovered, ventured no excuse, but fled from the table, whither I know not. Ercolano, ignoring his wife's flight, bade the sneezer again and again to come forth; but he, being by this time fairly spent, budged not an inch for aught that Ercolano said. Wherefore Ercolano caught him by one of his feet, and dragged him forth, and ran off for a knife with intent to kill him; but I, standing in fear of the Signory on my own account, got up and would not suffer him to kill the fellow or do him any hurt, and for his better protection raised the alarm, whereby some of the neighbours came up and took the lad, more dead than alive, and bore him off, I know not whither. However, our supper being thus rudely interrupted, not only have not gulped it, but I have not so much as tasted it, as I said before.'

Her husband's story showed his wife that there were other ladies as knowing as she, albeit misfortune might sometimes overtake them; and gladly would she have spoken out in defence of Ercolano's wife, but, thinking that, by censuring another's sin, she would secure more scope for her own, she launched out on this wise – 'Fine doings indeed, a right virtuous and saintly lady she must be: here is the loyalty of an honest woman, and one to whom I had lief have confessed, so spiritual I deemed her; and the worst of it is that, being no longer young, she sets a rare example to those that are so. Curses on the hour that she came into the world: curses upon her that she make not away with herself, basest, most faithless of women that she must needs be, the reproach of her sex, the opprobrium of all the ladies of this city, to cast aside all regard for her honour, her marriage vow, her reputation before the world, and, lost to all sense of shame, to scruple not to bring disgrace upon a man so worthy, a citizen so honourable, a husband by whom she was so well treated, ay, and upon herself to boot! By my hope of salvation no mercy should be shown to such women; they should pay the penalty with their lives; to the fire with them while they yet live, and let them be burned to ashes.' Then, calling to mind the lover that she had close at hand in the hen-coop, she fell to coaxing Pietro to get him to bed, for the hour grew late. Pietro, who was more set on eating than sleeping, only asked whether there was aught he might have by way of supper. 'Supper, forsooth!' replied the lady. 'Ay, of course 'tis our way to make much of supper when thou art not at home. As if I were Ercolano's wife! Now, wherefore tarry longer? Go, get thy night's rest: 'twere far better for thee.'

Now so it was that some of Pietro's husbandmen had come to the house that evening with divers things from the farm, and had put up their asses in a stable that adjoined the veranda, but had neglected to water them; and one of the asses being exceeding thirsty, got his head out of the halter and broke loose from the stable, and went about nosing everything, if haply he might come by water: whereby he came upon the hen-coop, beneath which was the boy; who, being constrained to stand on all fours, had the fingers of one hand somewhat protruding from under the hen-coop; and so as luck or rather ill-luck would have it, the ass trod on them; whereat, being sorely hurt, he set up a great howling, much to the surprise of Pietro, who perceived that 'twas within his house. So forth he came, and hearing the boy still moaning and groaning, for the ass still kept his hoof hard down on the fingers, called out – 'Who is there?' and ran to the hen-coop and raised it, and espied the fellow, who, besides the pain that the crushing of his fingers by the ass's hoof occasioned him, trembled in every limb for fear that Pietro should do him a mischief. He was one that Pietro had long been after for his foul purposes: so Pietro, recognising him, asked him – 'What dost thou here?' The boy making no answer, save to beseech him for the love of God to do him no hurt Pietro continued – 'Get up, have no fear that I shall hurt thee; but tell me – How, and for what cause comest thou to be here?' The boy then confessed everything. Whereupon Pietro, as elated by the discovery as his wife was distressed, took him by the hand; and led him into the room where the lady in the extremity of terror awaited him; and, having seated himself directly in front of her, said – ' 'Twas but a moment ago that thou didst curse Ercolano's wife, and averred that she ought to be burned, and that she was the reproach of your sex: why saidst thou not that of thyself? Or, if thou wast not minded to accuse thyself, how hadst thou the effrontery to censure her, knowing that thou hadst done even as she? Verily 'twas for no other reason than that ye are all fashioned thus, and study to cover your own misdeeds with the delinquencies of others: would that fire might fall from heaven and burn you all, brood of iniquity that ye are!'

The lady, marking that in the first flush of his wrath he had given her nothing worse than hard words, and discerning, as she thought, that he was secretly overjoyed to hold so beautiful a boy by the hand, took heart of grace and said – 'I doubt not indeed that thou wouldst be well pleased that fire should fall from heaven and devour us all, seeing that thou art as fond of us as a dog is of the stick, though by the Holy Rood thou wilt be disappointed; but I would fain have a little argument with thee, to know whereof thou complainest. Well indeed were it with me, didst thou but place me on an equality with Ercolano's wife, who is an old sanctimonious hypocrite, and has of him all that she wants, and is cherished by him as a wife should be: but that is not my case. For, granted that thou givest me garments and shoes to my mind, thou knowest how otherwise ill bested I am, and how long it is since last thou didst lie with me; and far liefer had I go barefoot and in rags, and have thy benevolence abed, than have all that I have, and be treated as thou dost treat me. Understand me, Pietro, be reasonable; consider that I am a woman like other women, with the like craving; whereof if thou deny me the gratification, 'tis no blame to me that I seek it elsewhere; and at least I do thee so much honour as not forgather with stable-boys or scurvy knaves.'

Pietro perceived that she was like to continue in this vein the whole night: wherefore, indifferent as he was to her, he said: – 'Now, Madam, no more of this; in the matter of which thou speakest I will content thee; but of thy great courtesy let us have something to eat by way of supper; for, methinks, the boy, as well as I, has not yet supped.' 'Ay, true enough,' said the lady, 'he has not supped; for we were but just sitting down to table to sup, when, beshrew thee, thou madest thy appearance.' 'Go then,' said Pietro, 'get us some supper; and by and by I will arrange this affair in such a way that thou shalt have no more cause of complaint.' The lady, perceiving that her husband was now tranquil, rose, and soon had the table laid again and spread with the supper which she had ready; and so they made a jolly meal of it, the caitiff husband, the lady and the boy. What after supper Pietro devised for their mutual satisfaction has slipped from my memory. But so much as this I know, that on the morrow as he wended his way to the piazza, the boy would have been puzzled to say, whether of the twain, the wife or the husband, had had the most of his company during the night. But this I would say to you, dear my ladies, that whoso gives you tit, why, just give him tat; and if you cannot do it at once, why, bear it in mind until you can, that even as the ass gives, so he may receive.

Dioneo's story, whereat the ladies laughed the less for shamefastness rather than for disrelish, being ended, the queen, taking note that the term of her sovereignty was come, rose to her feet, and took off the laurel wreath and set it graciously upon Elisa's head, saying – 'Madam, 'tis now your turn to bear sway.' The dignity accepted, Elisa followed in all respects the example of her predecessors: she first conferred with the seneschal, and directed him how meetly to order all things during the time of her sovereignty; which done to the satisfaction of the company: – 'Ofttimes,' quoth she, 'have we heard how with bright sallies, and ready retorts, and sudden devices, not a few have known how to repugn with apt checks the bites of others, or to avert imminent perils; and because 'tis an excellent argument, and may be profitable, I ordain that tomorrow, God helping us, the following be the rule of our discourse; to wit, that it be of such as by some sprightly sally have repulsed an attack, or by some ready retort or device have avoided loss, peril or scorn.' The rule being heartily approved by all, the queen rose and dismissed them till supper-time. So the honourable company, seeing the queen risen, rose all likewise, and as their wont was, betook them to their diversions as to each seemed best. But when the cicalas had hushed their chirping, all were mustered again for supper; and having blithely feasted, they all addressed them to song and dance. And the queen, while Emilia led a dance, called for a song from Dioneo, who at once came out with – 'Monna Aldruda, come perk up thy mood, a piece of glad tidings I bring thee.' Whereat all the ladies fell a-laughing, and most of all the queen, who bade him give them no more of that, but sing another. Quoth Dioneo – 'Madam, had I a tabret, I would sing – "Up with your smock, Monna Lapa!" or – "Oh! the greensward under the olive!" Or perchance you had liefer I should give you – "Woe is me, the wave of the sea!" But no tabret have I: wherefore choose which of these others you will have. Perchance you would like – "Now hie thee to us forth, that so it may be cut, as May the fields about." ' 'No,' returned the queen, 'give us another.' 'Then,' said Dioneo, 'I will sing – "Monna Simona, embarrel, embarrel. Why, 'tis not the month of October." '* 'Now a plague upon thee,' said the queen, with a laugh; 'give us a proper song, wilt thou? for we will have none of these.' 'Never fear, Madam,' replied Dioneo; 'only say which you prefer. I have more than a thousand songs by heart. Perhaps you would like – "This my little covert, make I ne'er it overt"; or – "Gently, gently, husband mine"; or – "A hundred pounds were none too high a price for me a cock to buy." ' The queen now showed some offence, though the other ladies laughed, and – 'A truce to thy jesting, Dioneo,' said she, 'and give us a proper song: else thou mayst prove the quality of my ire.' Whereupon Dioneo forthwith ceased his fooling, and sang on this wise –

* The song is evidently amoebean.

So ravishing a light
Doth from the fair eyes of my mistress move
As keeps me slave to her and thee, O Love.

A beam from those bright orbs did radiate
That flame that through mine own eyes to my breast
Did whilom entrance gain.
Thy majesty, O Love, thy might, how great
They be, 'twas her fair face did manifest:
Whereon to brood still fain,
I felt thee take and chain
Each sense, my soul enthralling on such wise
That she alone henceforth evokes my sighs.

Wherefore, O dear my Lord, myself I own
Thy slave, and, all obedience, wait and yearn,
Till thy might me console.
Yet wot I not if it be throughly known
How noble is the flame wherewith I burn,
My loyalty how whole
To her that doth control
Ev'n in such sort my mind that shall I none,
Nor would I, peace receive, save hers alone.

And so I pray thee, sweet my Lord, that thou
Give her to feel thy fire, and show her plain
How grievous my disease.
This service deign to render; for that now
Thou seest me waste for love, and in the pain
Dissolve me by degrees:
And then the apt moment seize
My cause to plead with her, as is but due
From thee to me, who fain with thee would sue.

When Dioneo's silence showed that his song was ended, the queen accorded it no stinted meed of praise; after which she caused not a few other songs to be sung. Thus passed some part of the night; and then the queen, taking note that its freshness had vanquished the heat of the day, bade all go rest them, if they would, till the morning.

☙ 24 ❧

The first story of the sixth day, in which a knight offers to carry Madonna Oretta a-horseback with a story, but tells it so ill that she prays him to dismount her.

As stars are set for an ornament in the serene expanse of heaven, and likewise in springtime flowers and leafy shrubs in the green meadows, so, damsels, in the hour of rare and excellent discourse, is wit with its bright sallies. Which, being brief, are much more proper for ladies than for men, seeing that prolixity of speech, where brevity is possible, is much less allowable to them. But for whatever cause, be it the sorry quality of our understanding or some especial enmity that heaven bears to our generation, few ladies or none are left today that, when occasion prompts, are able to meet it with apt speech, ay, or if aught of the kind they hear, can understand it aright: to our common shame be it spoken! But as, touching this matter, enough has already been said, I purpose not to enlarge thereon; but that you may know what excellence resides in speech apt for the occasion, I am minded to tell you after how courteous a fashion a lady imposed silence upon a gentleman:

❧ 'Tis no long time since there dwelt in our city a lady, noble, debonair and of excellent discourse, whom not a few of you may have seen or heard of, whose name – for such high qualities merit not oblivion – was Madonna Oretta, her husband being Messer Geri Spina. Now this lady happening to be, as we are, in the country, moving from place to place for pleasure with a company of ladies and gentlemen whom she had entertained the day before at breakfast at her house, and the place of their next sojourn, whither they were to go afoot, being some considerable distance off, one of the gentlemen of the company said to her – 'Madonna Oretta, so please you, I will carry you great part of the way a-horseback with one of the finest stories in the world.' 'Indeed, Sir,' replied the lady, 'I pray you do so; and I shall deem it the greatest of favours.' Whereupon the gentleman, who perhaps was no better master of his weapon than of his story, began a tale, which in itself was indeed excellent, but which, by repeating the same word three, four or six times, and now and again harking back, and saying – 'I said not well'; and erring not seldom in the names, setting one in place of another, he utterly spoiled; besides which, his mode of delivery accorded very ill with the character of the persons and incidents: insomuch that Madonna Oretta, as she listened, did oft sweat, and was like to faint, as if she were ill and at the point of death. And being at length able to bear no more of it, witting that the gentleman had got into a mess and was not like to get out of it, she said pleasantly to him – 'Sir, this horse of yours trots too hard; I pray you be pleased to set me down.' The gentleman, being perchance more quick of apprehension than he was skilful in narration, missed not the meaning of her sally, and took it in all good and gay humour. So, leaving unfinished the tale which he had begun, and so mishandled, he addressed himself to tell her other stories.

25

The seventh story of the sixth day, in which Madonna Filippa, being found by her husband with her lover, is cited before the court, and by a ready and jocund answer acquits herself, and brings about an alteration of the statute.

The last speaker had been silent some time, but all were still laughing when the queen called for a story from Filostrato, who thus began: Noble ladies, an excellent thing is apt speech on all occasions, but to be proficient therein I deem then most excellent when the occasion does most imperatively demand it. As was the case with a gentlewoman of whom I purpose to speak to you, who not only ministered gaiety and merriment to her hearers but extricated herself, as you shall hear, from the toils of an ignominious death –

There was aforetime in the city of Prato a statute no less censurable than harsh, which, making no distinction between the wife whom her husband took in adultery with her lover, and the woman found pleasuring a stranger for money, condemned both alike to be burned. While this statute was in force, it befell that a gentlewoman, fair and beyond measure enamoured, Madonna Filippa by name, was by her husband, Rinaldo de' Pugliesi, found in her own chamber one night in the arms of Lazzarino de' Guazzagliotri, a handsome young noble of the same city, whom she loved even as herself. Whereat Rinaldo, very wroth, scarce refrained from falling upon them and killing them on the spot; and indeed, but that he doubted how he should afterwards fare himself, he had given way to the vehemence of his anger, and so done. Nor, though he so far mastered himself, could he forbear recourse to the statute, thereby to compass that which he might not otherwise lawfully compass, to wit, the death of his lady. Wherefore, having all the evidence needful to prove her guilt, he took no further counsel; but, as soon as 'twas day, he charged the lady and had her summoned. Like most ladies that are veritably enamoured, the lady was of a high courage; and, though not a few of her friends and kinsfolk sought to dissuade her, she resolved to appear to the summons, having liefer die bravely confessing the truth than basely flee and for defiance of the law live in exile, and show herself unworthy of such a lover as had had her in his arms that night. And so, attended by many ladies and gentlemen, who all exhorted her to deny the charge, she came before the Podestà, and with a composed air and unfaltering voice asked whereof he would interrogate her. The Podestà, surveying her, and taking note of her extraordinary beauty, and exquisite manners, and the high courage that her words evinced, was touched with compassion for her, fearing she might make some admission, by reason whereof, to save his honour, he must needs do her to death. But still, as he could not refrain from examining her of that which was laid to her charge, he said – 'Madam, here, as you see, is your husband, Rinaldo, who prefers a charge against you, alleging that he has taken you in adultery, and so he demands that, pursuant to a statute which is in force here, I punish you with death: but this I may not do, except you confess; wherefore be very careful what you answer, and tell me if what your husband alleges against you be true.' The lady, no wise dismayed, and in a tone not a little jocund, thus made answer – 'True it is, Sir, that Rinaldo is my husband, and that last night he found me in the arms of Lazzarino, in whose arms for the whole-hearted love that I bear him I have ofttimes lain; nor shall I ever deny it; but, as well I wot you know, the laws ought to be common and enacted with the common consent of all that they affect; which conditions are wanting to this law, inasmuch as it binds only us poor women, in whom to be liberal is much less reprehensible than it were in men; and furthermore the consent of no woman was – I say not had, but – so much as asked before 'twas made; for which reasons it justly deserves to be called a bad law. However, if in scathe of my body and your own soul, you are minded to put it in force, 'tis your affair; but, I pray you, go not on to try this matter in any wise, until you have granted me this trifling grace, to wit, to ask my husband if I ever gainsaid him, but did not rather accord him, when and so often as he craved it, complete enjoyment of myself.' Whereto Rinaldo, without awaiting the Podestà's question, forthwith answered, that assuredly the lady had ever granted him all that he had asked of her for his gratification. 'Then,' promptly continued the lady, 'if he has ever had of me as much as sufficed for his solace, what was I or am I to do with the surplus? Am I to cast it to the dogs? Is it not much better to bestow it on a gentleman that loves me more dearly than himself, than to suffer it to come to nought or worse?' Which jocund question being heard by well-nigh all the folk of Prato, who had flocked thither all agog to see a dame so fair and of such quality on her trial for such an offence, they laughed loud and long, and then all with one accord, and as with one voice, exclaimed that the lady was in the right and said well; nor left they the court until in concert with the Podestà they had so altered the harsh statute as that thenceforth only such women as should wrong their husbands for money should be within its purview.

Wherefore Rinaldo left the court, discomfited of his foolish enterprise; and the lady blithe and free, as if rendered back to life from the burning, went home triumphant.

26

The first story of the seventh day, in which Gianni Lotteringhi hears a knocking at his door at night: he awakens his wife, who persuades him that 'tis the bogey, which they fall to exorcising with a prayer; whereupon the knocking ceases.

My lord, glad indeed had I been that, saving your good pleasure, some other than I had had precedence of discourse upon so goodly a theme as this of which we are to speak: I doubt I am but chosen to teach others confidence; but, such being your will, I will gladly obey it. And my endeavour shall be, dearest ladies, to tell you somewhat that may be serviceable to you in the future: for if you are, as I am, timorous, and that most especially of the bogey which, God wot, I know not what manner of thing it may be, nor yet have found any that knew albeit we are all alike afraid of it, you may learn from this my story how to put it to flight, should it intrude upon you, with a holy, salutary and most efficacious prayer:

There dwelt of yore at Florence, in the quarter of San Pancrazio, a master-spinner, Gianni Lotteringhi by name, one that had prospered in his business, but had little understanding of aught else; insomuch that being somewhat of a simpleton, he had many a time been chosen leader of the band of laud-singers of Santa Maria Novella, and had charge of their school; and not a few like offices had he often served, upon which he greatly plumed himself. Howbeit, 'twas all for no other reason than that, being a man of substance, he gave liberal doles to the friars; who, for that they got thereof, this one hose, another a cloak, and a third a hood, would teach him good prayers, or give him the paternoster in the vernacular, or the chant of St Alexis, or the lament of

St Bernard, or the laud of Lady Matilda, or the like sorry stuff, which he greatly prized, and guarded with jealous care, deeming them all most conducive to the salvation of his soul.

Now our simple master-spinner had a most beautiful wife, and amorous withal, her name Monna Tessa. Daughter she was of Mannuccio dalla Cuculla, and not a little knowing and keen-witted; and being enamoured of Federigo di Neri Pegolotti, a handsome and lusty gallant, as he also of her, she, knowing her husband's simplicity, took counsel with her maid, and arranged that Federigo should come to chat with her at a right goodly pleasure-house that the said Gianni had at Camerata, where she was wont to pass the summer, Gianni coming now and again to sup and sleep, and going back in the morning to his shop, or, maybe, to his laud-singers. Federigo, who desired nothing better, went up there punctually on the appointed day about vespers, and as the evening passed without Gianni making his appearance, did most comfortably, and to his no small satisfaction, sup and sleep with the lady, who lying in his arms taught him that night some six of her husband's lauds. But, as neither she nor Federigo was minded that this beginning should also be the end of their intercourse, and that it might not be needful for the maid to go each time to make the assignation with him, they came to the following understanding; to wit, that as often as he came and went between the house and an estate that he had a little higher up, he should keep an eye on a vineyard that was beside the house, where he would see an ass's head stuck on one of the poles of the vineyard, and as often as he observed the muzzle turned towards Florence, he might visit her without any sort of misgiving; and if he found not the door open, he was to tap it thrice, and she would open it; and when he saw the muzzle of the ass's head turned towards Fiesole, he was to keep away, for then Gianni would be there. Following which plan, they forgathered not seldom: but on one of these evenings, when Federigo was to sup with Monna Tessa on two fat capons that she had boiled, it so chanced that Gianni arrived there unexpectedly and very late, much to the lady's chagrin: so she had a little salt meat boiled apart, on which she supped with her husband; and the maid by her orders carried the two boiled capons laid in a spotless napkin with plenty of fresh eggs and a bottle of good wine into the garden, to which there was access otherwise than from the house, and where she was wont at times to sup with Federigo; and there the maid set them down at the foot of a peach tree, that grew beside a lawn. But in her vexation she forgot to tell the maid to wait till Federigo should come, and let him know that Gianni was there, and he must take his supper in the garden: and she and Gianni and the maid were scarce gone to bed, when Federigo came and tapped once at the door, which being hard by the bedroom, Gianni heard the tap, as did also the lady, albeit, that Gianni might have no reason to suspect her, she feigned to be asleep. Federigo waited a little, and then gave a second tap; whereupon, wondering what it might mean, Gianni nudged his wife, saying – 'Tessa, dost hear what I hear? Methinks someone has tapped at our door.' The lady, who had heard the noise much better than he, feigned to wake up, and – 'How? what sayst thou?' quoth she. 'I say,' replied Gianni, 'that, meseems, someone has tapped at our door.' 'Tapped at it?' quoth the lady. 'Alas, my Gianni, wottest thou not what that is? 'Tis the bogey, which for some nights past has so terrified me as never was, insomuch that I never hear it but I pop my head under the clothes and venture not to put it out again until 'tis broad day.' 'Come, come, wife,' quoth Gianni, 'if such it is, be not alarmed; for before we got into bed I repeated the *Te lucis*, the *Intemerata*, and divers other good prayers, besides which I made the sign of the cross in the name of the Father, Son and Holy Spirit at each corner of the bed; wherefore we need have no fear that it may avail to hurt us, whatever be its power.' The lady, lest Federigo, perchance suspecting a rival, should take offence, resolved to get up, and let him understand that Gianni was there: so she said to her husband – 'Well, well; so sayst thou; but I for my part shall never deem myself safe and secure, unless we exorcise it, seeing that thou art here.' 'Oh!' said Gianni, 'and how does one exorcise it?' 'That,' quoth the lady, 'I know right well; for t'other day, when I went to Fiesole for the pardoning, one of those anchoresses, the saintliest creature, my Gianni, God be my witness, knowing how much afraid I am of the bogey, taught me a holy and salutary prayer, which she said she had tried many a time before she was turned anchoress, and always with success. God wot, I should never have had courage to try it alone; but as thou art here, I propose that we go exorcise it together.' Gianni made answer that he was quite of the same mind; so up they got, and stole to the door, on the outside of which Federigo, now suspicious, was still waiting. And as soon as they were there – 'Now,' quoth the lady to Gianni, 'thou wilt spit, when I tell thee.' 'Good,' said Gianni. Whereupon the lady began her prayer, saying –

'Bogey, bogey that goest by night,
Tail erect, thou cam'st, tail erect, take thy flight:
Hie thee to the garden, and the great peach before,
Grease upon grease, and droppings five score

Of my hen shalt thou find:
Set the flask thy lips to,
Then away like the wind,
And no scathe unto me or my Gianni do.'

And when she had done – 'Now Gianni,' quoth she, 'spit': and Gianni spat.

There was no more room for jealousy in Federigo's mind as he heard all this from without; nay, for all his disappointment, he was like to burst with suppressed laughter, and when Gianni spat, he muttered under his breath – 'Now out with thy teeth.' The lady, having after this fashion thrice exorcised the bogey, went back to bed with her husband. Federigo, disappointed of the supper that he was to have had with her, and apprehending the words of the prayer aright, hied him to the garden, and having found the two capons and the wine and the eggs at the foot of the peach tree, took them home with him, and supped very comfortably. And many a hearty laugh had he and the lady over the exorcism during their subsequent intercourse.

Now, true it is that some say that the lady had in fact turned the ass's head towards Fiesole, but that a husbandman, passing through the vineyard, had given it a blow with his stick, whereby it had swung round, and remained fronting Florence, and so it was that Federigo thought that he was invited, and came to the house, and that the lady's prayer was on this wise –

'Bogey, a God's name, away thee hie,
For whoe'er turned the ass's head, 'twas not I:
Another it was, foul fall his eyne;
And here am I with Gianni mine.'

Wherefore Federigo was fain to take himself off, having neither slept nor supped.

But a neighbour of mine, a lady well advanced in years, tells me that, by what she heard when she was a girl, both stories are true; but that the latter concerned not Gianni Lotteringhi but one Gianni di Nello, that lived at Porta San Piero, and was no less a numskull than Gianni Lotteringhi. Wherefore, dear my ladies, you are at liberty to choose which exorcism you prefer, or take both if you like. They are both of extraordinary and approved virtue in such cases, as you have heard: get them by heart, therefore, and they may yet stand you in good stead.

☙ 27 ❧

The second story of the seventh day, in which her husband returning home, Peronella bestows her lover in a tun; which, being sold by her husband, she avers to have been already sold by herself to one that is inside examining it to see if it be sound. Whereupon the lover jumps out, and causes the husband to scour the tun for him, and afterwards to carry it to his house.

Great indeed was the laughter with which Emilia's story was received; which being ended, and her prayer commended by all as good and salutary, the king bade Filostrato follow suit; and thus Filostrato began: ❧ Dearest my ladies, so many are the tricks that men play you, and most of all your husbands, that, when from time to time it so befalls that some lady plays her husband a trick, the circumstance, whether it come within your own cognisance or be told you by another, should not only give you joy but should incite you to publish it on all hands, that men may be ware, that, knowing as they are, their ladies also, on their part, know somewhat: which cannot but be serviceable to you, for that one does not rashly essay to take another with guile whom one wots not to lack that quality. Can we doubt, then, that, should but the converse that we shall hold today touching this matter come to be bruited among men, 'twould serve to put a most notable check upon the tricks they play you, by causing them to wit of the tricks, which you, in like manner, when you are so minded, may play them? Wherefore 'tis my intention to tell you in what manner a young girl, albeit she was but of low rank, did, on the spur of the moment, beguile her husband to her own deliverance –

'Tis no long time since at Naples a poor man, a mason by craft, took to wife a fair and amorous maiden – Peronella was her name – who eked out by spinning what her husband made by his craft; and so the pair managed as best they might on very slender means. And as chance would have it, one of the gallants of the city, taking note of this Peronella one day, and being mightily pleased with her, fell in love with her, and by this means and that so prevailed that he won her to accord him her intimacy. Their times of forgathering they concerted as follows – to wit, that, her husband being wont to rise betimes of a morning to go to work or seek for work, the gallant was to be where he might see him go forth, and, the street where she dwelt, which is called Avorio, being scarce inhabited, was to come into the house as soon as her husband was well out of it; and so times not a few they did. But on one of these occasions it befell that, the good man being gone forth, and Giannello Sirignario – such was the gallant's name – being come into the house, and being with Peronella, after a while, back came the good man, though 'twas not his wont to return until the day was done; and finding the door locked, he knocked, and after knocking, he fell a-saying to himself – O God, praised be Thy name forever; for that, albeit Thou hast ordained that I be poor, at least Thou hast accorded me the consolation of a good and honest girl for wife. Mark what haste she made to shut the door when I was gone forth, that none else might enter to give her trouble.

Now Peronella knew by his knock that 'twas her husband; wherefore – 'Alas, Giannello mine,' quoth she, 'I am a dead woman, for lo, here is my husband, foul fall him, come back! What it may import, I know not, for he is never wont to come back at this hour; perchance he caught sight of thee as thou camest in. However, for the love of God, be it as it may, get thee into this tun that thou seest here, and I will go open to him, and we shall see what is the occasion of this sudden return this morning.' So Giannello forthwith got into the tun, and Peronella went to the door, and let in her husband, and gave him black looks, saying – 'This is indeed a surprise that thou art back so soon this morning! By what I see thou hast a mind to make this a holiday, that thou returnest tools in hand; if so, what are we to live on? whence shall we get bread to eat? Thinkest thou I will let thee pawn my gown and other bits of clothes? Day and night I do nought else but spin, insomuch that the flesh is fallen away from my nails, that at least I may have oil enough to keep our lamp alight. Husband, husband, there is never a woman in the neighbourhood but marvels and mocks at me, that I am at such labour and pains; and thou comest home to me with thy hands hanging idle, when thou shouldst be at work.' Which said, she fell a-weeping and repeating – 'Alas, alas, woe's me, in what evil hour was I born? in what luckless moment came I hither, I, that might have had so goodly a young man, and I would not, to take up with one that bestows never a thought on her whom he has made his wife? Other women have a good time with their lovers, and never a one have we here but has two or three; they take their pleasure, and make their husbands believe that the moon is the sun; and I, alas! for that I am an honest woman, and have no such casual amours, I suffer, and am hard bested: I know not why I provide not myself with one of these lovers, as others do. Give good heed, husband, to what I say: were I disposed to dishonour thee, I were at no loss to find the man: for here are gallants enough, that love me, and court me, and have sent me many an offer of money – no stint – or dresses or jewels, should I prefer them; but my pride would never suffer it, because I was not born of a woman of that sort: and now thou comest home to me when thou oughtest to be at work.'

Whereto the husband – 'Wife, wife, for God's sake distress not thyself: thou shouldst give me credit for knowing what manner of woman thou art, as indeed I have partly seen this morning. True it is that I went out to work; but 'tis plain that thou knowest not, as indeed I knew not, that today 'tis the feast of San Galeone, and a holiday, and that is why I am come home at this hour; but nevertheless I have found means to provide us with bread for more than a month; for I have sold to this gentleman, whom thou seest with me, the tun, thou wottest of, seeing that it has encumbered the house so long, and he will give me five gigliats for it.' Quoth then Peronella – 'And all this but adds to my trouble: thou, that art a man, and goest abroad, and shouldst know affairs, hast sold for five gigliats a tun, which I, that am but a woman, and was scarce ever out of doors, have, for that it took up so much room in the house, sold for seven gigliats to a good man, that but now, as thou cam'st back, got therein, to see if 'twere sound.' So hearing, the husband was overjoyed, and said to the man that was come to take it away; 'Good man, I wish thee Godspeed; for, as thou hearest, my wife has sold the tun for seven gigliats, whereas thou gavest me only five.' Whereupon – 'So be it,' said the good man, and took himself off. Then said Peronella to her husband – 'Now, as thou art here, come up, and arrange the matter with the good man.

Now Giannello, who, meanwhile, had been all on the alert to discover if there were aught he had to fear or be on his guard against, no sooner heard Peronella's last words, than he sprang out of the tun, and feigning to know nought of her husband's return, began thus –

'Where art thou, good dame?' Whereto the husband, coming up, answered – 'Here am I: what wouldst thou of me?' Quoth Giannello – 'And who art thou? I would speak with the lady with whom I struck the bargain for this tun.' Then said the good man – 'Have no fear, you can deal with me; for I am her husband.' Quoth then Giannello – 'The tun seems to me sound enough; but I think you must have let the lees remain in it; for 'tis all encrusted with I know not what that is so dry, that I cannot raise it with the nail; wherefore I am not minded to take it unless I first see it scoured.' Whereupon Peronella – 'To be sure: that shall not hinder the bargain; my husband will scour it clean.' And – 'Well and good,' said the husband.

So he laid down his tools, stripped himself to his vest, sent for a light and a rasp, and was in the tun, and scraping away, in a trice. Whereupon Peronella, as if she were curious to see what he did, thrust her head into the vent of the tun, which was of no great size, and therewithal one of her arms up to the shoulder, and fell a-saying – 'Scrape here, and here, and there too, and look, there is a bit left here.' So, she being in this posture, directing and admonishing her husband, Giannello, who had not, that morning fully satisfied his desire, when the husband arrived, now seeing that as he would, he might not, brought his mind to his circumstances, and resolved to take his pleasure as he might: wherefore he made up to the lady, who completely blocked the vent of the tun; and even on such wise as on the open plain the wild and lusty horses do amorously assail the mares of Parthia, he sated his youthful appetite; and so it was that almost at the same moment that he did so, and was off, the tun was scoured, the husband came forth of it, and Peronella withdrew her head from the vent, and turning to Giannello, said – 'Take this light, good man, and see if 'tis scoured to thy mind.' Whereupon Giannello, looking into the tun, said that 'twas in good trim, and that he was well content, and paid the husband the seven gigliats, and caused him carry the tun to his house.

28

The third story of the seventh day, in which Fra Rinaldo lies with his gossip: her husband finds him in the room with her; and they make him believe that he was curing his godson of worms by a charm.

Filostrato knew not how so to veil what he said touching the mares of Parthia, but that the keen-witted ladies laughed thereat, making as if 'twas at somewhat else. However, his story being ended, the king called for one from Elisa who, all obedience, thus began: Debonair my ladies, we heard from Emilia how the bogey is exorcised, and it brought to my mind a story of another incantation: 'tis not indeed so good a story as hers; but as no other germane to our theme occurs to me at present, I will relate it –

You are to know, then, that there dwelt aforetime at Sienna a young man, right gallant and of honourable family, his name Rinaldo; who, being in the last degree enamoured of one of his neighbours, a most beautiful gentlewoman and the wife of a rich man, was not without hopes that, if he could but find means to speak with her privately, he might have of her all that he desired; but seeing no way, and the lady being pregnant, he cast about how he might become her child's godfather. Wherefore, having ingratiated himself with her husband, he broached the matter to him in as graceful a manner as he might; and 'twas arranged. So Rinaldo, being now godfather to Madonna Agnesa's child, and having a more colourable pretext for speaking to her, took courage, and told her in words that message of his heart which she had long before read in his eyes; but though 'twas not displeasing to the lady to hear, it availed him but little.

Now not long afterwards it so befell that, whatever may have been his reason, Rinaldo betook him to friarage; and whether it was that he found good pasture therein, or what not, he persevered in that way of life. And though for a while after he was turned friar, he laid aside the love he bore his gossip, and certain other vanities, yet in course of time, without putting off the habit, he resumed them, and began to take a pride in his appearance, and to go dressed in fine clothes, and to be quite the trim gallant, and to compose songs and sonnets and ballades, and to sing them, and to make a brave show in all else that pertained to his new character. But why enlarge upon our Fra Rinaldo, of whom we speak? what friars are there that do not the like? Ah! opprobrium of a corrupt world? Sleek-faced and sanguine, daintily clad, dainty in all their accessories, they ruffle it shamelessly before the eyes of all, showing not as doves but as insolent cocks with raised crest and swelling bosom, and, what is worse (to say nought of the vases full of potions and unguents, the boxes packed with divers comfits, the pitchers and phials of artificial waters, and oils, the flagons brimming with Malmsey and Greek and other wines of finest quality, with which their cells are so packed that they show not as the cells of friars, but rather as apothecaries' or perfumers' shops), they blush not to be known to be gouty, flattering themselves that other folk wot not that long fasts and many of them, and coarse fare and little of it, and sober living, make men lean and thin and for the most part healthy; or if any malady come thereof, at any rate 'tis not the gout, the wonted remedy for which is chastity and all beside that belongs to the regimen of a humble friar. They flatter themselves, too, that others wot not that over and above the meagre diet, long vigils and prayers and strict discipline ought to mortify men and make them pale, and that neither St Dominic nor St Francis went clad in stuff dyed in grain or any other goodly garb, but in coarse woollen habits innocent of the dyer's art, made to keep out the cold, and not for show. To which matters 'twere well God had a care, no less than to the souls of the simple folk by whom our friars are nourished.

Fra Rinaldo, then, being come back to his first affections, took to visiting his gossip very frequently; and gaining confidence, began with more insistence than before to solicit her to that which he craved of her. So, being much urged, the good lady, to whom Fra Rinaldo, perhaps, seemed now more handsome than of yore, had recourse one day, when she felt herself unusually hard pressed by him, to the common expedient of all that would fain concede what is asked of them, and said: – 'Oh! but Fra Rinaldo, do friars then do this sort of thing?' 'Madam,' replied Fra Rinaldo, 'when I divest myself of this habit, which I shall do easily enough, you will see that I am a man furnished as other men, and no friar.' Whereto with a truly comical air the lady made answer – 'Alas! woe's me! you are my child's godfather: how might it be? nay, but 'twere a very great mischief; and many a time I have heard that 'tis a most heinous sin; and without a doubt, were it not so, I would do as you wish.' 'If,' said Fra Rinaldo, 'you forego it for such a scruple as this, you are a fool for your pains. I say not that 'tis no sin; but there is no sin so great but God pardons it, if one repent. Now tell me: whether is more truly father to your son, I that held him at the font, or your husband that begot him?' 'My husband,' replied the lady. 'Sooth say you,' returned the friar, 'and does not your husband lie with you?' 'Why, yes,' said the lady. 'Then,' rejoined the friar, 'I that am less truly your son's father than your husband, ought also to lie with you, as does your husband.' The lady was no logician, and needed little to sway her: she therefore believed or feigned to believe that what the friar said was true. So – 'Who might avail to answer your words of wisdom?' quoth she; and presently forgot the godfather in the lover, and complied with his desires. Nor had they begun their course to end it forthwith: but under cover of the friar's sponsorship, which set them more at ease, as it rendered them less open to suspicion, they forgathered again and again.

But on one of these occasions it so befell that Fra Rinaldo, being come to the lady's house, where he espied none else save a very pretty and dainty little maid that waited on the lady, sent his companion away with her into the pigeon-house, there to teach her the paternoster, while he and the lady, holding her little boy by the hand, went into the bedroom, locked themselves in, got them on to a divan that was there, and began to disport them. And while thus they sped the time, it chanced that the father returned, and, before any was ware of him, was at the bedroom door, and knocked, and called the lady by her name. Whereupon – ' 'Tis as much as my life is worth,' quoth Madonna Agnesa; 'lo, here is my husband; and, the occasion of our intimacy cannot but be now apparent to him.' 'Sooth say you,' returned Fra Rinaldo, who was undressed, that is to say, had thrown off his habit and hood, and was in his tunic; 'if I had but my habit and hood on me in any sort, 'twould be another matter; but if you let him in, and he find me thus, 'twill not be possible to put any face on it.' But with an inspiration as happy as sudden – 'Now get them on you,' quoth the lady; 'and when you have them on, take your godson in your arms, and give good heed to what I shall say to him, that your words may accord with mine; and leave the rest to me.'

The good man was still knocking, when his wife made answer: – 'Coming, coming.' And so up she got, and put on a cheerful countenance and hied her to the door, and opened it and said: – 'Husband mine: well indeed was it for us that in came Fra Rinaldo, our sponsor; 'twas God that sent him to us; for in sooth, but for that, we had today lost our boy.' Which the poor simpleton almost swooned to hear; and – 'How so?' quoth he. 'O husband mine,' replied the lady, 'he was taken but now, all of a sudden, with a fainting fit, so that I thought he was dead: and what to do or say I knew not, had not Fra Rinaldo, our sponsor, come just in the nick of time, and set him on his shoulder, and said – "Gossip, 'tis that he has worms in his body, and getting, as they do, about the heart, they might only too readily be the death of him; but fear not; I will say a charm that will kill them all; and before I take my leave, you will see your boy as whole as you ever saw him." And because to say certain of the prayers thou shouldst have been with us, and the maid knew not where to find thee, he caused his companion to say them at the top of the house, and he and I came in here. And for that 'tis not meet for any but the boy's mother to assist at such a service, that we might not be troubled with anyone else, we locked the door; and he yet has him in his arms; and I doubt not that he only waits till his companion have said his prayers, and then the charm will be complete; for the boy is already quite himself again.'

The good simple soul, taking all this for sooth, and overwrought by the love he bore his son, was entirely without suspicion of the trick his wife was playing him, and heaving a great sigh, said – 'I will go look for him.' 'Nay,' replied the wife, 'go not: thou wouldst spoil the efficacy of the charm: wait here; I will go see if thou mayst safely go; and will call thee.'

Whereupon Fra Rinaldo, who had heard all that passed, and was in his canonicals, and quite at his ease, and had the boy in his arms, having made sure that all was as it should be, cried out – 'Gossip, do I not hear the father's voice out there?' 'Ay indeed, Sir,' replied the simpleton. 'Come in then,' said Fra Rinaldo. So in came the simpleton. Whereupon quoth Fra Rinaldo – 'I restore to you your boy made whole by the grace of God, whom but now I scarce thought you would see alive at vespers. You will do well to have his image fashioned in wax, not less than life-size, and set it for a thanksgiving to God, before the statue of Master St Ambrose, by whose merits you have this favour of God.'

The boy, catching sight of his father, ran to him with joyous greetings, as little children are wont; and the father, taking him in his arms, and weeping as if he were restored to him from the grave, fell by turns a-kissing him and thanking his godfather, that he had cured him. Fra Rinaldo's companion, who had taught the maid not one paternoster only, but peradventure four or more, and by giving her a little purse of white thread that a nun had given him, had made her his devotee, no sooner heard Fra Rinaldo call the simpleton into his wife's room, than he stealthily got him to a place whence he might see and hear what was going on. Observing that the affair was now excellently arranged, he came down, and entered the chamber, saying – 'Fra Rinaldo, those four prayers that you bade me say, I have said them all.' 'Then well done, my brother,' quoth Fra Rinaldo, 'well-breathed must thou be. For my part, I had but said two, when my gossip came in; but what with thy travail and mine, God of His grace has vouchsafed us the healing of the boy.' The simpleton then had good wine and comfits brought in, and did the honours to the godfather and his companion in such sort as their occasions did most demand. He then ushered them forth of the house, commending them to God; and without delay had the waxen image made, and directed it to be set up with the others in front of the statue of St Ambrose, not, be it understood, St Ambrose of Milan.*

* The statue would doubtless be that of St Ambrose of Sienna, of the Dominican Order.

29

The fourth story of the seventh day, in which Tofano one night locks his wife out of the house; she, finding that by no entreaties may she prevail upon him to let her in, feigns to throw herself into a well, throwing therein a great stone. Tofano hies him forth of the house, and runs to the spot; she goes into the house, and locks him out, and hurls abuse at him from within.

The king no sooner wist that Elisa's story was ended than, turning to Lauretta, he signified his will that she should tell somewhat: wherefore without delay she began: O Love, how great and signal is thy potency! how notable thy stratagems, thy devices! Was there ever, shall there ever be, philosopher or adept competent to inspire, counsel and teach in such sort as thou by thine unpremeditated art dost tutor those that follow thy lead? Verily laggard teachers are they all in comparison of thee, as by the matters heretofore set forth may very well be understood. To which store I will add, loving ladies, a stratagem used by a woman of quite ordinary understanding and of such a sort that I know not by whom she could have been taught it save by Love –

Know then that there dwelt aforetime at Arezzo a rich man, Tofano by name, who took to wife Monna Ghita, a lady exceeding fair, of whom, for what cause he knew not, he presently grew jealous. Whereof the lady being ware, waxed resentful, and having on divers occasions demanded of him the reason of his jealousy, and gotten from him nought precise, but only generalities and trivialities, resolved at last to give him cause enough to die of that evil which without cause he so much dreaded. And being ware that a gallant, whom she deemed well worthy of her, was enamoured of her, she, using due discretion, came to an understanding with him; which being brought to the point that it only remained to give effect to their words in act, the lady cast about to devise how this might be. And witting that, among other bad habits that her husband had, he was too fond of his cups, she would not only commend indulgence, but cunningly and not seldom incite him thereto; insomuch that, well-nigh as often as she was so minded, she led him to drink to excess; and when she saw that he was well drunken, she would put him to bed; and so not once only but divers times without any manner of risk she forgathered with her lover; nay, presuming upon her husband's intoxication, she grew so bold that, not content with bringing her lover into her house, she would at times go spend a great part of the night with him at his house, which was not far off.

Now such being the enamoured lady's constant practice, it so befell that the dishonoured husband took note that, while she egged him on to drink, she herself drank never a drop; whereby he came to suspect the truth, to wit, that the lady was making him drunk, that afterwards she might take her pleasure while he slept. And being minded to put his surmise to the proof, one evening, having drunken nought all day, he mimicked never so drunken a sot both in speech and in carriage. The lady, deeming him to be really as he appeared, and that 'twas needless to ply him with liquor, presently put him to bed. Which done, she, as she at times was wont, hied her forth to her lover's house, where she tarried until midnight. Tofano no sooner perceived that his wife was gone, than up he got, hied him to the door, locked it, and then posted himself at the window to observe her return, and let her know that he was ware of her misconduct. So there he stood until the lady returned, and finding herself locked out, was annoyed beyond measure, and sought to force the door open. Tofano let her try her strength upon it a while, and then – 'Madam,' quoth he, ' 'tis all to no purpose: thou canst not get in. Go get thee back thither where thou hast tarried all this while, and rest assured that thou shalt never recross this threshold, until I have done thee such honour as is meet for thee in the presence of thy kinsfolk and neighbours.' Thereupon the lady fell entreating him to be pleased to open to her for the love of God, for that she was not come whence he supposed, but had only been passing the time with one of her gossips, because the nights were long, and she could not spend the whole time either in sleep or in solitary watching. But her supplications availed her nothing, for the fool was determined that all Arezzo should know their shame, whereof as yet none wist aught. So as 'twas idle to entreat, the lady assumed a menacing tone, saying – 'So thou open not to me, I will make thee the saddest man alive.' Whereto Tofano made answer – 'And what then canst thou do?' The lady, her wits sharpened by Love, rejoined – 'Rather than endure the indignity to which thou wouldst unjustly subject me, I will cast myself into the well hard by here, and when I am found dead there, all the world will believe that 'twas thou that didst it in thy cups and so thou wilt either have to flee and lose all that thou hast and be outlawed, or forfeit thy head as guilty of my death, as indeed thou wilt be.' But, for all she said, Tofano wavered not a jot in his foolish purpose. So at last – 'Lo, now,' quoth the lady, 'I can no more abide thy surly humour: God forgive thee: I leave thee my distaff here, which be careful to bestow in a safe place.' So saying, away she hied her to the well, and, the night being so dark that wayfarers could scarce see one another as they passed, she took up a huge stone that was by the well, and ejaculating, 'God forgive me!' dropped it therein. Tofano, hearing the mighty splash that the stone made as it struck the water, never doubted that she had cast herself in: so, bucket and rope in hand, he flung himself out of the house, and came running to the well to her rescue. The lady had meanwhile hidden herself hard by the door, and seeing him make for the well, was in the house in a trice, and having locked the door, hied her to the window, and greeted him with – ' 'Tis while thou art drinking, not now, when the night is far spent, that thou shouldst temper thy wine with water.' Thus derided, Tofano came back to the door, and finding his ingress barred, began adjuring her to let him in. Whereupon, changing the low tone she had hitherto used for one so shrill that 'twas well-nigh a shriek, she broke out with: – 'By the Holy Rood, tedious drunken sot that thou art, thou gettest no admittance here tonight; thy ways are more than I can endure: 'tis time I let all the world know what manner of man thou art, and at what hour of the night thou comest home.' Tofano, on his part, now grew angry, and began loudly to upbraid her; insomuch that the neighbours, aroused by the noise, got up, men and women alike, and looked out of the windows, and asked what was the matter. Whereupon the lady fell a-weeping and saying – ' 'Tis this wicked man, who comes home drunk at even, or falls asleep in some tavern, and then returns at this hour. Long and to no purpose have I borne with him; but 'tis now past endurance, and I have done him this indignity of locking him out of the house in the hope that perchance it may cause him to mend his ways.'

Tofano, on his part, told, dolt that he was, just what had happened, and was mighty menacing. Whereupon – 'Now mark,' quoth the lady to the neighbours, 'the sort of man he is! What would you say if I were, as he is, in the street, and he were in the house, as I am? God's faith, I doubt you would believe what he said. Hereby you may gauge his sense. He tells you that I have done just what, I doubt not, he has done himself. He thought to terrify me by throwing I know not what into the well, wherein would to God he had thrown himself indeed, and drowned himself, whereby the wine of which he has taken more than enough, had been watered to some purpose!' The neighbours, men and women alike, now with one accord gave tongue, censuring Tofano, throwing all the blame upon him, and answering what he alleged against the lady with loud recrimination; and in short the bruit, passing from neighbour to neighbour, reached at last the ears of the lady's kinsfolk; who hied them to the spot, and being apprised of the affair from this, that and the other of the neighbours, laid hands on Tofano, and beat him till he was black and blue from head to foot. Which done, they entered his house, stripped it of all that belonged to the lady, and took her home with them, bidding Tofano look for worse to come. Thus hard bested, and ruing the plight in which his jealousy had landed him, Tofano, who loved his wife with all his heart, set some friends to work to patch matters up, whereby he did in fact induce his lady to forgive him and live with him again; albeit he was fain to promise her never again to be jealous, and to give her leave to amuse herself to her heart's content, provided she used such discretion that he should not be ware of it. On such wise, like the churl and booby that he was, being despoiled, he made terms. Now long live Love, and perish war, and all that wage it!

30

The fifth story of the seventh day, in which a jealous husband disguises himself as a priest, and hears his own wife's confession: she tells him that she loves a priest, who comes to her every night. The husband posts himself at the door to watch for the priest, and meanwhile the lady brings her lover in by the roof, and tarries with him.

When Lauretta had done speaking and all had commended the lady, for that she had done well and treated her caitiff husband as he had deserved, the king, not to lose time, turned to Fiammetta and graciously bade her take up her parable; which she did on this wise: Most noble ladies, the foregoing story prompts me likewise to discourse of one of these jealous husbands, deeming that they are justly requited by their wives, more especially when they grow jealous without due cause. And had our legislators taken account of everything, I am of opinion that they would have visited ladies in such a case with no other penalty than such as they provide for those that offend in self-defence, seeing that a jealous husband does cunningly practise against the life of his lady, and most assiduously machinate her death. All the week the wife stays at home, occupied with her domestic duties; after which, on the day that is sacred to joy, she, like everyone else, craves some solace, some peace, some recreation, not unreasonably, for she craves but what the husbandmen take in the fields, the craftsmen in the city, the magistrates in the courts, nay what God Himself took, when He rested from all His labours on the seventh day, and which laws human and Divine, mindful alike to the honour of God and the common well-being, have ordained, appropriating certain days to work, and others to repose. To which ordinance these jealous

> husbands will in no wise conform; on the contrary by then most sedulously secluding their wives, they make those days which to all other women are gladsome, to them most grievous and dolorous. And what an affliction it is to the poor creatures, they alone know, who have proved it; for which reason, to sum up, I say that a wife is rather to be commended than censured, if she take her revenge upon a husband that is jealous without cause –

Know then that at Rimini there dwelt a merchant, a man of great substance in lands and goods and money, who, having a most beautiful woman to wife, waxed inordinately jealous of her, and that for no better reason than that, loving her greatly, and esteeming her exceeding fair, and knowing that she did her utmost endeavour to pleasure him, he must needs suppose that every man loved her, and esteemed her fair, and that she, moreover, was as zealous to stand well with every other man as with himself; whereby you may see that he was a poor creature, and of little sense. Being thus so deeply infected with jealousy, he kept so strict and close watch over her, that some, maybe, have lain under sentence of death and been less rigorously confined by their warders. 'Twas not merely that the lady might not go to a wedding, or a festal gathering, or even to church, or indeed set foot out of doors in any sort; but she dared not so much as show herself at a window, or cast a glance outside the house, no matter for what purpose. Wherefore she led a most woeful life of it, and found it all the harder to bear because she knew herself to be innocent. Accordingly, seeing herself evilly entreated by her husband without good cause, she cast about how for her own consolation she might devise means to justify his usage of her. And for that, as she might not show herself at the window, there could be no interchange of amorous glances between her and any man that passed along the street, but she wist that in the next house there was a goodly and debonair gallant, she bethought her, that, if there were but a hole in the wall that divided the two houses, she might watch thereat, until she should have sight of the gallant on such wise that she might speak to him, and give him her love, if he cared to have it, and, if so it might be contrived, forgather with him now and again, and after this fashion relieve the burden of her woeful life, until such time as the evil spirit should depart from her husband. So peering about, now here, now there, when her husband was away, she found in a very remote part of the house a place, where, by chance, the wall had a little chink in it. Peering through which, she made out, though not without great difficulty, that on the other side was a room, and said to herself: – If this were Filippo's room – Filippo was the name of the gallant, her neighbour – I should be already halfway to my goal. So cautiously, through her maid, who was grieved to see her thus languish, she made quest, and discovered that it was indeed the gallant's room, where he slept quite alone. Wherefore she now betook her frequently to the aperture, and whenever she was ware that the gallant was in the room, she would let fall a pebble or the like trifle; whereby at length she brought the gallant to the other side of the aperture to see what the matter was. Whereupon she softly called him, and he knowing her voice, answered; and so, having now the opportunity she had sought, she in few words opened to him all her mind. The gallant, being overjoyed, wrought at the aperture on such wise that albeit none might be ware thereof, he enlarged it; and there many a time they held converse together, and touched hands, though further they might not go by reason of the assiduous watch that the jealous husband kept.

Now towards Christmas the lady told her husband that, if he approved, she would fain go on Christmas morning to church, and confess and communicate, like other Christians. 'And what sins,' quoth he, 'hast thou committed, that wouldst be shriven?' 'How?' returned the lady; 'dost thou take me for a saint? For all thou keepest me so close, thou must know very well that I am like all other mortals. However, I am not minded to confess to thee, for that thou art no priest.' Her husband, whose suspicions were excited by what she had said, cast about how he might discover these sins of hers, and having bethought him of what seemed an apt expedient, made answer that she had his consent, but he would not have her go to any church but their own chapel, where she might hie her betimes in the morning, and confess either to their own chaplain or some other priest that the chaplain might assign her, but to none other, and presently return to the house. The lady thought she half understood him, but she answered only that she would do as he required. Christmas morning came, and with the dawn the lady rose, dressed herself, and hied her to the church appointed by her husband, who also rose, and hied him to the same church, where he arrived before her; and having already concerted matters with the priest that was in charge, he forthwith put on one of the priest's robes with a great hood, overshadowing the face, such as we see priests wear, and which he pulled somewhat forward; and so disguised he seated himself in the choir.

On entering the church the lady asked for the priest, who came, and learning that she was minded to confess, said that he could not hear her himself, but would send her one of his brethren; so away he hied him and sent her, in an evil hour for him, her husband. For though he wore an air of great solemnity, and 'twas not yet broad day, and he had pulled the hood well over his eyes, yet all did not avail, but that his lady forthwith recognised him, and said to herself – God be praised! why, the jealous rogue is turned priest: but leave it to me to give him that whereof he is in quest. So she feigned not to know him, and seated herself at his feet. (I should tell you that he had put some pebbles in his mouth, that his speech, being impeded, might not betray him to his wife, and in all other respects he deemed himself so thoroughly disguised that there was nought whereby she might recognise him.) Now, to come to the confession, the lady, after informing him that she was married, told him among other matters that she was enamoured of a priest, who came every night to lie with her. Which to hear was to her husband as if he were stricken through the heart with a knife; and had it not been that he was bent on knowing more, he would have forthwith given over the confession, and taken himself off. However he kept his place, and – 'How?' said he to the lady, 'does not your husband lie with you?' The lady replied in the affirmative. 'How, then,' quoth the husband, 'can the priest also lie with you?' 'Sir,' replied she, 'what art the priest employs I know not; but door there is none, however well locked, in the house, that comes not open at his touch; and he tells me that, being come to the door of my room, before he opens it, he says certain words, whereby my husband forthwith falls asleep; whereupon he opens the door, and enters the room, and lies with me; and so 'tis always, without fail.' 'Then 'tis very wrong, Madam, and you must give it up altogether,' said the husband. 'That, Sir,' returned the lady, 'I doubt I can never do; for I love him too much.' 'In that case,' quoth the husband, 'I cannot give you absolution.' 'The pity of it!' ejaculated the lady; 'I came not hither to tell you falsehoods: if I could give it up, I would.' 'Madam,' replied the husband, 'indeed I am sorry for you; for I see that you are in a fair way to lose your soul. However, this I will do for you; I will make special supplication to God on your behalf; and perchance you may be profited thereby. And from time to time I will send you one of my young clerks; and you will tell him whether my prayers have been of any help to you, or no, and if they have been so, I shall know what to do next.' 'Nay, Sir,' quoth the lady, 'do not so; send no man to me at home; for, should my husband come to know it, he is so jealous that nothing in the world would ever disabuse him of the idea that he came but for an evil purpose, and so I should have no peace with him all the year long.' 'Madam,' returned the husband, 'have no fear; rest assured that I will so order matters that you shall never hear a word about it from him.' 'If you can make sure of that,' quoth the lady, 'I have no more to say.' And so, her confession ended, and her penance enjoined, she rose, and went to mass, while the luckless husband, fuming and fretting, hasted to divest himself of his priest's trappings, and then went home bent upon devising some means to bring the priest and his wife together, and take his revenge upon them both.

When the lady came home from church she read in her husband's face that she had spoiled his Christmas for him, albeit he dissembled to the uttermost, lest she should discover what he had done, and supposed himself to have learned. His mind was made up to keep watch for the priest that very night by his own front door. So to the lady he said – 'I have to go out tonight to sup and sleep; so thou wilt take care that the front door, and the mid-stair door, and the bedroom door are well locked; and for the rest thou mayst go to bed, at thine own time.' 'Well and good,' replied the lady: and as soon as she was able, off she hied her to the aperture, and gave the wonted signal, which Filippo no sooner heard, than he was at the spot. The lady then told him what she had done in the morning, and what her husband had said to her after breakfast, adding – 'Sure I am that he will not stir out of the house, but will keep watch beside the door; wherefore contrive to come in tonight by the roof, that we may be together.' 'Madam,' replied the gallant, nothing loath, 'trust me for that.'

Night came, the husband armed, and noiselessly hid himself in a room on the ground floor: the lady locked all the doors, being especially careful to secure the mid-stair door, to bar her husband's ascent; and in due time the gallant, having found his way cautiously enough over the roof, they got them to bed, and there had solace of one another and a good time; and at daybreak the gallant hied him back to his house. Meanwhile the husband, rueful and supperless, half-dead with cold, kept his armed watch beside his door, momently expecting the priest, for the best part of the night; but towards daybreak, his powers failing him, he lay down and slept in the ground-floor room. 'Twas hard upon tierce when he awoke, and the front door was then open; so, making as if he had just come in, he went upstairs and breakfasted. Not long afterwards he sent to his wife a young fellow, disguised as the priest's underling, who asked her if he of whom she wist had been with her again. The lady, who quite understood what that meant, made answer that he had not come that night, and that, if he continued to neglect her so, 'twas possible he might be forgotten, though she had no mind to forget him.

Now, to make a long story short, the husband passed many a night in the same way, hoping to catch the priest as he came in, the lady and her gallant meanwhile having a good time. But at last the husband, being able to stand it no longer, sternly demanded of his wife what she had said to the priest the morning when she was confessed. The lady answered that she was not minded to tell him, for that 'twas not seemly or proper so to do. Whereupon – 'Sinful woman,' quoth the husband, 'in thy despite I know what thou saidst to him, and know I must and will who this priest is of whom thou art enamoured, and who by dint of his incantations lies with thee a-nights, or I will sluice thy veins for thee.' ' 'Tis not true,' replied the lady, 'that I am enamoured of a priest.' 'How?' quoth the husband, 'saidst thou not as much to the priest that confessed thee?' 'Thou canst not have had it from him,' rejoined the lady. 'Wast thou then present thyself? For sure I never told him so.' 'Then tell me,' quoth the husband, 'who this priest is; and lose no time about it.' Whereat the lady began to smile and – 'I find it not a little diverting,' quoth she, 'that a wise man should suffer himself to be led by a simple woman as a ram is led by the horns to the shambles; albeit no wise man art thou: not since that fatal hour when thou gavest harbourage in thy breast, thou wist not why, to the evil spirit of jealousy; and the more foolish and insensate thou art, the less glory have I. Deemest thou, my husband, that I am as blind of the bodily eye as thou art of the mind's eye? Nay, but for sure I am not so. I knew at a glance the priest that confessed me, and that 'twas even thyself. But I was minded to give thee that of which thou wast in quest, and I gave it thee. Howbeit, if thou hadst been the wise man thou takest thyself to be, thou wouldst not have chosen such a way as that to worm out thy good lady's secrets, nor wouldst thou have fallen a prey to a baseless suspicion, but wouldst have understood that what she confessed was true, and she all the while guiltless. I told thee that I loved a priest; and wast not thou, whom I love, though ill enough dost thou deserve it, turned priest? I told thee that there was no door in my house but would open when he was minded to lie with me: and when thou wouldst fain have access to me, what door was ever closed against thee? I told thee that the priest lay nightly with me: and what night was there that thou didst not lie with me? Thou sentest thy young clerk to me: and thou knowest that, as often as thou hadst not been with me, I sent word that the priest had not been with me. Who but thou, that hast suffered jealousy to blind thee, would have been so witless as not to read such a riddle? But thou must needs mount guard at night beside the door, and think to make me believe that thou hadst gone out to sup and sleep. Consider thy ways, and court not the mockery of those that know them as I do, but turn a man again as thou wast wont to be: and let there be no more of this strict restraint in which thou keepest me; for I swear to thee by God that, if I were minded to set horns on thy brow, I should not fail so to take my pastime that thou wouldst never find it out, though thou hadst a hundred eyes, as thou hast but two.'

Thus admonished, the jealous caitiff, who had flattered himself that he had very cunningly discovered his wife's secret, was ashamed and made no answer save to commend his wife's wit and honour; and thus, having cause for jealousy, he discarded it, as he had erstwhile been jealous without cause. And so the adroit lady had, as it were, a charter of indulgence and needed no more to contrive for her lover to come to her over the roof like a cat, but admitted him by the door, and using due discretion had many a good time with him and sped her life gaily.

31

The sixth story of the seventh day, in which Madonna Isabella has with her Leonetto, her accepted lover, when she is surprised by one Messer Lambertuccio, by whom she is beloved; her husband coming home about the same time, she sends Messer Lambertuccio forth of the house drawn sword in hand, and the husband afterwards escorts Leonetto home.

Wondrous was the delight that all the company had of Fiammetta's story, nor was there any but affirmed that the lady had done excellent well, and dealt with her insensate husband as he deserved. However, it being ended, the king bade Pampinea follow suit; which she did on this wise: Not a few there are that in their simplicity aver that Love deranges the mind, insomuch that whoso loves becomes as it were witless: the folly of which opinion, albeit I doubt it not and deem it abundantly proven by what has been already said, I purpose once again to demonstrate –

In our city, rich in all manner of good things, there dwelt a young gentlewoman, fair exceedingly, and wedded to a most worthy and excellent gentleman. And as it not seldom happens that one cannot keep ever to the same diet, but would fain at times vary it, so this lady, finding her husband not altogether to her mind, became enamoured of a gallant, Leonetto by name, who, though of no high rank, was not a little debonair and courteous, and he in like manner fell in love with her; and (as you know that 'tis seldom that what is mutually desired fails to come about) 'twas not long before they had fruition of their love. Now the lady being, as I said, fair and winsome, it so befell that a gentleman, Messer Lambertuccio by name, grew mightily enamoured of her, but so tiresome and odious did she find him, that for the world she could not bring herself to love him. So, growing tired of fruitlessly soliciting her favour by courtship, Messer Lambertuccio, who was a powerful signior, sent her at last another sort of message in which he threatened to defame her if she complied not with his wishes. Wherefore the lady, knowing her man, was terrified, and disposed herself to pleasure him.

Now it so chanced that Madonna Isabella, for such was the lady's name, being gone, as is our Florentine custom in the summer, to spend some time on a very goodly estate that she had in the contado, one morning finding herself alone, for her husband had ridden off to tarry some days elsewhere, she sent for Leonetto to come and keep her company; and Leonetto came forthwith in high glee. But while they were together, Messer Lambertuccio, who, having got wind that the husband was away, had mounted his horse and ridden thither quite alone, knocked at the door. Whereupon the lady's maid hied her forthwith to her mistress, who was alone with Leonetto, and called her, saying – 'Madam, Messer Lambertuccio is here below, quite alone.' Whereat the lady was vexed beyond measure; and being also not a little dismayed, she said to Leonetto – 'Prithee, let it not irk thee to withdraw behind the curtain, and there keep close until Messer Lambertuccio be gone.' Leonetto, who stood in no less fear of Messer Lambertuccio than did the lady, got into his hiding-place; and the lady bade the maid go open to Messer Lambertuccio: she did so; and having dismounted and fastened his palfrey to a pin, he ascended the stairs; at the head of which the lady received him with a smile and as gladsome a greeting as she could find words for, and asked him on what errand he was come. The gentleman embraced and kissed her, saying – 'My soul, I am informed that your husband is not here, and therefore I am come to stay a while with you.' Which said, they went into the room, and locked them in, and Messer Lambertuccio fell a-toying with her.

Now, while thus he sped the time with her, it befell that the lady's husband, albeit she nowise expected him, came home, and, as he drew nigh the palace, was observed by the maid, who forthwith ran to the lady's chamber, and said – 'Madam, the master will be here anon; I doubt he is already in the courtyard.' Whereupon, for that she had two men in the house, and the knight's palfrey, that was in the courtyard, made it impossible to hide him, the lady gave herself up for dead. Nevertheless she made up her mind on the spur of the moment, and springing out of bed – 'Sir,' quoth she to Messer Lambertuccio, 'if you have any regard for me, and would save my life, you will do as I bid you: that is to say, you will draw your blade, and put on a fell and wrathful countenance, and hie you downstairs, saying – "By God, he shall not escape me elsewhere." And if my husband would stop you, or ask you aught, say nought but what I have told you, and get you on horseback and tarry with him on no account.' 'To hear is to obey,' quoth Messer Lambertuccio, who, with the flush of his recent exertion and the rage that he felt at the husband's return still on his face, and drawn sword in hand, did as she bade him. The lady's husband, being now dismounted in the courtyard, and not a little surprised to see the palfrey there, was about to go up the stairs, when he saw Messer Lambertuccio coming down them, and marvelling both at his words and at his mien – 'What means this, Sir?' quoth he. But Messer Lambertuccio clapped foot in stirrup, and mounted, saying nought but – 'Zounds, but I will meet him elsewhere;' and so he rode off.

The gentleman then ascended the stairs, at the head of which he found his lady distraught with terror, to whom he said – 'What manner of thing is this? After whom goes Messer Lambertuccio, so wrathful and menacing?' Whereto the lady, drawing nigher the room, that Leonetto might hear her, made answer – 'Never, Sir, had I such a fright as this. There came running in here a young man, who to me is quite a stranger, and at his heels Messer Lambertuccio with a drawn sword in his hand; and as it happened the young man found the door of this room open, and trembling in every limb, cried out – "Madam, your succour, for God's sake, that I die not in your arms." So up I got, and would have asked him who he was, and how bested, when up came Messer Lambertuccio, exclaiming – "Where art thou, traitor?" I planted myself in the doorway, and kept him from entering, and seeing that I was not minded to give him admittance, he was courteous enough, after not a little parley, to take himself off, as you saw.' Whereupon – 'Wife,' quoth the husband, 'thou didst very right. Great indeed had been the scandal, had someone been slain here, and 'twas a gross affront on Messer Lambertuccio's part to pursue a fugitive within the house.' He then asked where the young man was. Whereto the lady answered – 'Nay, where he may be hiding, Sir, I wot not.' So – 'Where art thou?' quoth the knight. 'Fear not to show thyself.' Then forth of his hiding-place, all of a tremble, for in truth he had been thoroughly terrified, crept Leonetto, who had heard all that had passed. To whom – 'What hast thou to do with Messer Lambertuccio?' quoth the knight. 'Nothing in the world,' replied the young man: 'wherefore, I doubt he must either be out of his mind, or have mistaken me for another: for no sooner had he sight of me in the street hard by the palace, than he laid his hand on his sword, and exclaimed – "Traitor, thou art a dead man." Whereupon I sought not to know why, but fled with all speed, and got me here, and so, thanks to God and this gentlewoman, I escaped his hands.' 'Now away with thy fears,' quoth the knight; 'I will see thee home safe and sound; and then 'twill be for thee to determine how thou shalt deal with him.' And so, when they had supped, he set him on horseback, and escorted him to Florence, and left him not until he was safe in his own house. And the very same evening, following the lady's instructions, Leonetto spoke privily with Messer Lambertuccio, and so composed the affair with him, that, though it occasioned not a little talk, the knight never wist how he had been tricked by his wife.

32

The seventh story of the seventh day, in which Lodovico discovers to Madonna Beatrice the love that he bears her; she sends Egano, her husband, into a garden disguised as herself, and lies with Lodovico; who thereafter, being risen, hies him to the garden and cudgels Egano.

This device of Madonna Isabella thus recounted by Pampinea was held nothing short of marvellous by all the company. But being bidden by the king to tell the next story, thus spoke Filomena: Loving ladies, if I mistake not, the device of which you shall presently hear from me will prove to be no less excellent than the last –

You are to know, then, that there dwelt aforetime at Paris a Florentine gentleman who being by reason of poverty turned merchant, had prospered so well in his affairs that he was become very wealthy; and having by his lady an only son, Lodovico by name, whose nobility disrelished trade, he would not put him in any shop; but that he might be with other gentlemen, he caused him to enter the service of the King of France, whereby he acquired very fine manners and other accomplishments. Being in this service, Lodovico was one day with some other young gallants that talked of the fair ladies of France, and England, and other parts of the world, when they were joined by certain knights that were returned from the Holy Sepulchre; and hearing their discourse, one of the knights fell a-saying, that of a surety in the whole world, so far as he had explored it, there was not any lady, of all that he had ever seen, that might compare for beauty with Madonna Beatrice, the wife of Egano de' Galluzzi, of Bologna: wherein all his companions, who in common with him had seen the lady at Bologna, concurred. Which report Lodovico, who was as yet fancy-free, no sooner heard, than he burned with such a yearning to see the lady that he was able to think of nought else: insomuch that he made up his mind to betake him to Bologna to see her, and if she pleased him, to remain there; to which end he gave his father to understand that he would fain visit the Holy Sepulchre, whereto his father after no little demur consented.

So to Bologna Anichino – for so he now called himself – came; and, as Fortune would have it, the very next day, he saw the lady at a festal gathering, and deemed her vastly more beautiful than he had expected: wherefore he waxed most ardently enamoured of her, and resolved never to quit Bologna, until he had gained her love. So, casting about how he should proceed, he could devise no other way but to enter her husband's service, which was the more easy that he kept not a few retainers: on this wise Lodovico surmised that, peradventure, he might compass his end. He therefore sold his horses and meetly bestowed his servants, bidding them make as if they knew him not; and being pretty familiar with his host, he told him that he was minded to take service with some worthy lord, if any such he might find. 'Thou wouldst make,' quoth the host, 'the very sort of retainer to suit a gentleman of this city, Egano by name, who keeps not a few of them, and will have all of them presentable like thee: I will mention the matter to him.' And so he accordingly did, and before he took leave of Egano had placed Anichino with him, to Egano's complete satisfaction.

Being thus resident with Egano, and having abundant opportunities of seeing the fair lady, Anichino set himself to serve Egano with no little zeal; wherein he succeeded so well, that Egano was more than satisfied, insomuch that by and by there was nought he could do without his advice, and he entrusted to him the guidance not only of himself, but of all his affairs. Now it so befell that one day when Egano was gone a-hawking, having left Anichino at home, Madonna Beatrice, who as yet wist not of his love, albeit she had from time to time taken note of him and his manners, and had not a little approved and commended them, sat herself down with him to a game of chess, which, to please her, Anichino most dexterously contrived to lose, to the lady's prodigious delight. After a while, the lady's women, one and all, gave over watching their play, and left them to it; whereupon Anichino heaved a mighty sigh. The lady, looking hard at him, said – 'What ails thee, Anichino? Is it, then, such a mortification to thee to be conquered by me?' 'Nay, Madam,' replied Anichino, 'my sigh was prompted by a much graver matter.' 'Then, if thou hast any regard for me,' quoth the lady, 'tell me what it is.' Hearing himself thus adjured by 'any regard' he had for her whom he loved more than aught else, Anichino heaved a yet mightier sigh, which caused the lady to renew her request that he would be pleased to tell her the occasion of his sighs. Whereupon – 'Madam,' said Anichino, 'I greatly fear me, that, were I to tell it you, 'twould but vex you; and, moreover, I doubt you might repeat it to someone else.' 'Rest assured,' returned the lady, 'that I shall neither be annoyed, nor, without thy leave, ever repeat to any other soul aught that thou mayst say.' 'Then,' said Anichino, 'having this pledge from you, I will tell it you.' And, while the tears all but stood in his eyes, he told her, who he was, the report he had heard of her, and where and how he had become enamoured of her, and with what intent he had taken service with her husband: after which, he humbly besought her, that, if it might be, she would have pity on him, and gratify this his secret and ardent desire; and that, if she were not minded so to do, she would suffer him to retain his place there, and love her. Ah! Bologna! how sweetly mixed are the elements in thy women! How commendable in such a case are they all! No delight have they in sighs and tears, but are ever inclinable to prayers, and ready to yield to the solicitations of Love. Had I but words apt to praise them as they deserve, my eloquence were inexhaustible.

The gentlewoman's gaze was fixed on Anichino as he spoke; she made no doubt that all he said was true, and yielding to his appeal, she entertained his love within her heart in such measure that she too began to sigh, and after a sigh or two made answer: – 'Sweet my Anichino, be of good cheer; neither presents nor promises, nor any courting by gentleman, or lord, or whoso else (for I have been and am still courted by not a few) was ever able to sway my soul to love any of them: but thou, by the few words that thou hast said, hast so wrought with me that, brief though the time has been, I am already in far greater measure thine than mine. My love I deem thee to have won right worthily; and so I give it thee, and vow to give thee proof thereof before the coming night be past. To which end thou wilt come to my room about midnight; I will leave the door open; thou knowest the side of the bed on which I sleep; thou wilt come there; should I be asleep, thou hast but to touch me, and I shall awake, and give thee solace of thy long-pent desire. In earnest whereof I will even give thee a kiss.' So saying, she threw her arms about his neck, and lovingly kissed him, as Anichino her.

Their colloquy thus ended, Anichino betook him elsewhere about some matters which he had to attend to, looking forward to midnight with boundless exultation. Egano came in from his hawking; and after supper, being weary, went straight to bed, whither the lady soon followed him, leaving, as she had promised, the door of the chamber open. Thither accordingly, at the appointed hour, came Anichino, and having softly entered the chamber, and closed the door behind him, stole up to where the lady lay, and laying his hand upon her breast, found that she was awake. Now, as soon as she wist that Anichino was come, she took his hand in both her own; and keeping fast hold of him, she turned about in the bed, until she awoke Egano; whereupon – 'Husband,' quoth she, 'I would not say aught of this to thee, yestereve, because I judged thou wast weary; but tell me, upon thy hope of salvation, Egano, whom deemest thou thy best and most loyal retainer, and the most attached to thee, of all that thou hast in the house?' 'What a question is this, wife?' returned Egano. 'Dost not know him? Retainer I have none, nor ever had, so trusted, or loved, as Anichino. But wherefore put such a question?'

Now, when Anichino wist that Egano was awake, and heard them talk of himself, he more than once tried to withdraw his hand, being mightily afraid lest the lady meant to play him false; but she held it so tightly that he might not get free, while thus she made answer to Egano – 'I will tell thee what he is. I thought that he was all thou sayst, and that none was so loyal to thee as he, but he has undeceived me, for that yesterday, when thou wast out a-hawking, he, being here, chose his time, and had the shamelessness to crave of me compliance with his wanton desires: and I, that I might not need other evidence than that of thine own senses to prove his guilt to thee, I made answer, that I was well content, and that tonight, after midnight, I would get me into the garden, and await him there at the foot of the pine. Now go thither I shall certainly not; but, if thou wouldst prove the loyalty of thy retainer, thou canst readily do so, if thou but slip on one of my loose robes, and cover thy face with a veil, and go down and attend his coming, for come, I doubt not, he will.' Whereto Egano – 'Meet indeed it is,' quoth he, 'that I should go see;' and straightway up he got, and, as best he might in the dark, he put on one of the lady's loose robes and veiled his face, and then hied him to the garden, and sat down at the foot of the pine to await Anichino. The lady no sooner wist that he was out of the room, than she rose, and locked the door. Anichino, who had never been so terrified in all his life, and had struggled with all his might to disengage his hand from the lady's clasp, and had inwardly cursed her and his love, and himself for trusting her, a hundred thousand times, was overjoyed beyond measure at this last turn that she had given the affair. And so, the lady having got her to bed again, and he, at her bidding, having stripped and laid him down beside her, they had solace and enjoyment of one another for a good while. Then, the lady, deeming it unmeet for Anichino to tarry longer with her, caused him to get up and resume his clothes, saying to him – 'Sweet my mouth, thou wilt take a stout cudgel, and get thee to the garden, and making as if I were there, and thy suit to me had been but to try me, thou wilt give Egano a sound rating with thy tongue and a sound belabouring with thy cudgel, the sequel whereof will be wondrously gladsome and delightful.' Whereupon Anichino hied him off to the garden, armed with a staff of wild willow; and as he drew nigh the pinc, Egano saw him, and rose and came forward to meet him as if he would receive him with the heartiest of cheer. But. – 'Ah! wicked woman!' quoth Anichino; 'so thou art come! Thou didst verily believe, then, that I was, that I am, minded thus to wrong my lord? Foul fall thee a thousand times!' And therewith he raised his cudgel, and began to lay about him. Egano, however, had heard and seen enough, and without a word took to flight, while Anichino pursued him, crying out – 'Away with thee! God send thee a bad year, lewd woman that thou art; nor doubt that Egano shall hear of this tomorrow.' Egano, having received sundry round knocks, got him back to his chamber with what speed he might; and being asked by the lady, whether Anichino had come into the garden – 'Would to God he had not!' quoth he, 'for that, taking me for thee, he has beaten me black and blue with his cudgel, and rated me like the vilest woman that ever was: passing strange, indeed, it had seemed to me that he should have said those words to thee with intent to dishonour me; and now 'tis plain that 'twas but that, seeing thee so blithe and frolicsome, he was minded to prove thee.' Whereto – 'God be praised' returned the lady, 'that he proved me by words, as thee by acts: and I doubt not he may say that I bear his words with more patience than thou his acts. But since he is so loyal to thee, we must make much of him and do him honour.' 'Ay, indeed,' quoth Egano, 'thou sayst sooth.'

Thus was Egano fortified in the belief that never had any gentleman wife so true, or retainer so loyal, as he; and many a hearty laugh had he with Anichino and his lady over this affair, which to them was the occasion that, with far less let than might else have been, they were able to have solace and enjoyment of one another, so long as it pleased Anichino to tarry at Bologna.

33

The eighth story of the seventh day, in which a husband grows jealous of his wife, and discovers that she has warning of her lover's approach by a piece of pack-thread, which she ties to her great toe at night. While he is pursuing her lover, she puts another woman in bed in her place. The husband, finding her there, beats her, and cuts off her hair. He then goes and calls his wife's brothers, who, holding his accusation to be false, give him a rating.

Rare indeed was deemed by common consent the subtlety shown by Madonna Beatrice in the beguilement of her husband, and all affirmed that the terror of Anichino must have been prodigious when, the lady still keeping fast hold of him, he had heard her say that he had made suit of love to her. However, Filomena being silent, the king turned to Neifile saying – ' 'Tis now for you to tell.' Whereupon Neifile, while a slight smile died away upon her lips, thus began: Fair ladies, to entertain you with a goodly story such as those which my predecessors have delighted you withal is indeed a heavy burden but, God helping me, I trust fairly well to acquit myself thereof –

You are to know, then, that there dwelt aforetime in our city a most wealthy merchant, Arriguccio Berlinghieri by name, who foolishly, as we wot by daily experience is the way of merchants, thinking to compass gentility by matrimony, took to wife a young gentlewoman, by no means suited to him, whose name was Monna Sismonda. Now Monna Sismonda, seeing that her husband was much abroad, and gave her little of his company, became enamoured of a young gallant, Ruberto by name, who had long courted her: and she being grown pretty familiar with him, and using, perchance, too little discretion, for she affected him extremely, it so befell that Arriguccio, whether it was that he detected somewhat, or howsoever, waxed of all men the most jealous, and gave up going abroad, and changed his way of life altogether, and made it his sole care to watch over his wife, insomuch that he never allowed himself a wink of sleep until he had seen her to bed: which occasioned the lady the most grievous dumps, because 'twas on no wise possible for her to be with her Ruberto. So, casting about in many ways how she might contrive to meet him, and being thereto not a little plied by Ruberto himself, she bethought her at last of the following expedient: to wit, her room fronting the street, and Arriguccio, as she had often observed, being very hard put to it to get him to sleep, but thereafter sleeping very soundly, she resolved to arrange with Ruberto that he should come to the front door about midnight, whereupon she would get her down, and open the door, and stay some time with him while her husband was in his deep sleep. And that she might have tidings of his arrival, yet so as that none else might wot aught thereof, she adopted the device of lowering a pack-thread from the bedroom window on such wise that, while with one end it should all but touch the ground, it should traverse the floor of the room, until it reached the bed, and then be brought under the clothes, so that, when she was abed, she might attach it to her great toe. Having so done, she sent word to Ruberto, that when he came, he must be sure to jerk the pack-thread, and, if her husband were asleep, she would loose it, and go open to him; but, if he were awake, she would hold it taut and draw it to herself, to let him know that he must not expect her. Ruberto fell in with the idea, came there many times, and now forgathered with her and again did not. But at last, they still using this cunning practice, it so befell that one night, while the lady slept, Arriguccio, letting his foot stray more than he was wont about the bed, came upon the pack-thread, and laying his hand upon it, found that it was attached to his lady's great toe, and said to himself – This must be some trick: and afterwards discovering that the thread passed out of the window, was confirmed in his surmise. Wherefore, he softly severed it from the lady's toe, and affixed it to his own; and waited, all attention, to learn the result of his experiment. Nor had he long to wait before Ruberto came, and Arriguccio felt him jerk the thread according to his wont: and as Arriguccio had not known how to attach the thread securely, and Ruberto jerked it with some force, it gave way, whereby he understood that he was to wait, and did so. Arriguccio straightway arose, caught up his arms, and hasted to the door to see who might be there, intent to do him a mischief. Now Arriguccio, for all he was a merchant, was a man of spirit, and of thews and sinews; and being come to the door, he opened it by no means gingerly, as the lady was wont; whereby Ruberto, who was in waiting, surmised the truth, to wit, that 'twas Arriguccio by whom the door was opened. Wherefore he forthwith took to flight, followed by Arriguccio. But at length, when he had run a long way, as Arriguccio gave not up the pursuit, he being also armed, drew his sword, and faced about; and so they fell to, Arriguccio attacking, and Ruberto defending himself.

Now when Arriguccio undid the bedroom door, the lady awoke, and finding the pack-thread cut loose from her toe, saw at a glance that her trick was discovered; and hearing Arriguccio running after Ruberto, she forthwith got up, foreboding what the result was like to be, and called her maid, who was entirely in her confidence: whom she so plied with her obsecrations that at last she got her into bed in her room, beseeching her not to say who she was, but to bear patiently all the blows that Arriguccio might give her; and she would so reward her that she should have no reason to complain. Then, extinguishing the light that was in the room, forth she hied her, and having found a convenient hiding-place in the house, awaited the turn of events. Now Arriguccio and Ruberto being hotly engaged in the street, the neighbours, roused by the din of the combat, got up and launched their curses upon them. Wherefore Arriguccio, fearing lest he should be recognised, drew off before he had so much as discovered who the young gallant was or done him any scathe, and in a fell and wrathful mood betook him home. Stumbling into the bedroom, he cried out angrily: – 'Where art thou, lewd woman? Thou hast put out the light, that I may not be able to find thee; but thou hast miscalculated.' And going to the bedside, he laid hold of the maid. taking her to be his wife, and fell a-pummelling and kicking her with all the strength he had in his hands and feet, insomuch that he pounded her face well-nigh to pulp, rating her the while like the vilest woman that ever was; and last of all he cut off her hair. The maid wept bitterly, as indeed she well might; and though from time to time she ejaculated an 'Alas! Mercy, for God's sake!' or 'Spare me, spare me;' yet her voice was so broken by her sobs, and Arriguccio's hearing so dulled by his wrath, that he was not able to discern that 'twas not his wife's voice but that of another woman. So, having soundly thrashed her, and cut off her hair, as we said – 'Wicked woman,' quoth he, 'I touch thee no more; but I go to find thy brothers, and shall do them to wit of thy good works; and then they may come here, and deal with thee as they may deem their honour demands, and take thee hence, for be sure thou shalt no more abide in this house.' With this he was gone, locking the door of the room behind him, and quitted the house alone.

Now no sooner did Monna Sismonda, who had heard all that passed, perceive that her husband was gone, than she opened the door of the bedroom, rekindled the light, and finding her maid all bruises and tears, did what she could to comfort her, and carried her back to her own room, where, causing her to be privily waited on and tended, she helped her so liberally from Arriguccio's own store, that she confessed herself content. The maid thus bestowed in her room, the lady presently hied her back to her own, which she set all in neat and trim order, remaking the bed, so that it might appear as if it had not been slept in, relighting the lamp, and dressing and tiring herself, until she looked as if she had not been abed that night; then, taking with her a lighted lamp and some work, she sat her down at the head of the stairs, and began sewing, while she waited to see how the affair would end.

Arriguccio meanwhile had hied him with all speed straight from the house to that of his wife's brothers, where by dint of much knocking he made himself heard, and was admitted. The lady's three brothers, and her mother, being informed that 'twas Arriguccio, got up, and having set lights a-burning, came to him and asked him on what errand he was come there at that hour, and alone. Whereupon Arriguccio, beginning with the discovery of the pack-thread attached to his lady's great toe, gave them the whole narrative of his discoveries and doings down to the very end; and to clinch the whole matter, he put in their hands the locks which he had cut, as he believed, from his wife's head, adding that 'twas now for them to come for her and deal with her on such wise as they might deem their honour required, seeing that he would nevermore have her in his house. Firmly believing what he told them, the lady's brothers were very wroth with her, and having provided themselves with lighted torches, set out with Arriguccio, and hied them to his house with intent to scorn her, while their mother followed, weeping and beseeching now one, now another, not to credit these matters so hastily, until they had seen or heard somewhat more thereof; for that the husband might have some other reason to be wroth with her, and having ill-treated her, might have trumped up this charge by way of exculpation, adding that, if true, 'twas passing strange, for well she knew her daughter, whom she had brought up from her tenderest years, and much more to the like effect.

However, being come to Arriguccio's house, they entered, and were mounting the stairs, when Monna Sismonda, hearing them, called out – 'Who is there?' Whereto one of the brothers responded – 'Lewd woman, thou shalt soon have cause enough to know who it is.' 'Now Lord love us!' quoth Monna Sismonda, 'what would he be at?' Then, rising, she greeted them with – 'Welcome, my brothers; but what seek ye abroad at this hour, all three of you?' They had seen her sitting and sewing with never a sign of a blow on her face, whereas Arriguccio had averred that he had pummelled her all over: wherefore their first impression was one of wonder, and refraining the vehemence of their wrath, they asked her what might be the truth of the matter which Arriguccio laid to her charge, and threatened her with direful consequences, if she should conceal aught. Whereto the lady – 'What you would have me tell you,' quoth she, 'or what Arriguccio may have laid to my charge, that know not I.' Arriguccio could but gaze upon her, as one that had taken leave of his wits, calling to mind how he had pummelled her about the face times without number, and scratched it for her, and mishandled her in all manner of ways, and there he now saw her with no trace of aught of it all upon her. However, to make a long story short, the lady's brothers told her what Arriguccio had told them touching the pack-thread and the beating and all the rest of it. Whereupon the lady turned to him with – 'Alas, my husband, what is this that I hear? Why givest thou me, to thy own great shame, the reputation of a lewd woman, when such I am not, and thyself the reputation of a wicked and cruel man, which thou art not? Wast thou ever tonight, I say not in my company, but so much as in the house until now? Or when didst thou beat me? For my part I mind me not of it.' Arriguccio began – 'How sayst thou, lewd woman? Did we not go to bed together? Did I not come back, after chasing thy lover? Did I not give thee bruises not a few, and cut thy hair for thee?' But the lady interrupted him, saying – 'Nay, thou didst not lie here tonight. But leave we this, of which my true words are my sole witness, and pass we to this of the beating thou sayst thou gavest me, and how thou didst cut my hair. Never a beating had I from thee, and I bid all that are here, and thee among them, look at me, and say if I have any trace of a beating on my person; nor should I advise thee to dare lay hand upon me; for, by the Holy Rood, I would spoil thy beauty for thee. Nor didst thou cut my hair, for aught that I saw or felt: however, thou didst it, perchance, on such wise that I was not ware thereof: so let me see whether 'tis cut or no.' Then, unveiling herself, she showed that her hair was uncut and entire. Wherefore her brothers and mother now turned to Arriguccio with – 'What means this, Arriguccio? This accords not with what thou gavest us to understand thou hadst done;

nor know we how thou wilt prove the residue.'

Arriguccio was lost, as it were, in a dream, and yet he would fain have spoken; but, seeing that what he had thought to prove was otherwise, he essayed no reply. So the lady turning to her brothers – 'I see,' quoth she, 'what he would have: he will not be satisfied unless I do what I never would otherwise have done, to wit, give you to know what a pitiful caitiff he is; as now I shall not fail to do. I make no manner of doubt that, as he has said, even so it befell, and so he did. How, you shall hear. This worthy man, to whom, worse luck! you gave me to wife, a merchant, as he calls himself, and as such would fain have credit, and who ought to be more temperate than a religious, and more continent than a girl, lets scarce an evening pass but he goes a-boozing in the taverns, and consorting with this or the other woman of the town; and 'tis for me to await his return until midnight or sometimes until matins, even as you now find me. I doubt not that, being thoroughly well drunk, he got him to bed with one of these wantons, and, awaking, found the pack-thread on her foot, and afterwards did actually perform all these brave exploits of which he speaks, and in the end came back to her, and beat her, and cut her hair off, and being not yet quite recovered from his debauch, believed, and, I doubt not, still believes, that 'twas I that he thus treated; and if you will but scan his face closely, you will see that he is still half drunk. But, whatever he may have said about me, I would have you account it as nothing more than the disordered speech of a tipsy man; and forgive him as I do.' Whereupon the lady's mother raised no small outcry, saying – 'By the Holy Rood, my daughter, this may not be! A daughter, such as thou, to be mated with one so unworthy of thee! The pestilent, insensate cur should be slain on the spot! A pretty state of things, indeed! Why, he might have picked thee up from the gutter! Now foul fall him! but thou shalt no more be vexed with the tedious drivel of a petty dealer in ass's dung, some blackguard, belike, that came hither from the country because he was dismissed the service of some petty squire, clad in romagnole, with belfry-breeches, and a pen in his arse, and, for that he has a few pence, must needs have a gentleman's daughter, and a fine lady to wife, and set up a coat of arms, and say – "I am of the such and such," and "my ancestors did thus and thus." Ah! had my sons but followed my advice! Thy honour were safe in the house of the Counts Guidi, where they might have bestowed thee, though thou hadst but a morsel of bread to thy dowry: but they must needs give thee to this rare treasure, who, though better daughter and more chaste there is none than thou in Florence, has not blushed this very midnight and in our presence to call thee a strumpet, as if we knew thee not. God's faith! so I were hearkened to, he should shrewdly smart for it.' Then, turning to her sons, she said – 'My sons, I told you plainly enough that this ought not to be. Now, have you heard how your worthy brother-in-law treats your sister? Petty twopenny trader that he is: were it for me to act, as it is for you, after what he has said of her and done to her, nought would satisfy or appease me, till I had rid the earth of him. And were I a man, who am but a woman, none other but myself should meddle with the affair. God's curse upon him, the woeful, shameless sot!' Whereupon the young men, incensed by what they had seen and heard, turned to Arriguccio, and after giving him the soundest rating that ever was bestowed upon caitiff, concluded as follows – 'This once we pardon thee, witting thee to be a drunken knave; but as thou holdest thy life dear, have a care that henceforth we hear no such tales of thee; for rest assured that if aught of the kind do reach our ears, we will requite thee for both turns.' Which said, they departed. Arriguccio, standing there like one dazed, not witting whether his late doings were actual fact or but a dream, made no more words about the matter, but left his wife in peace. Thus did she by her address not only escape imminent peril, but open a way whereby in time to come she was able to gratify her passion to the full without any farther fear of her husband.

34

The ninth story of the seventh day, in which Lydia, wife of Nicostratus, loves Pyrrhus, who to assure himself thereof, asks three things of her, all of which she does, and therewithal enjoys him in presence of Nicostratus, and makes Nicostratus believe that what he saw was not real.

So diverting did the ladies find Neifile's story that it kept them still laughing and talking though the king, having bidden Pamfilo tell his story, had several times enjoined silence upon them. However, as soon as they had done, Pamfilo thus began: Methinks, worshipful ladies, there is no venture, though fraught with gravest peril, that whoso loves ardently will not make: of which truth, exemplified though it has been in stories not a few, I purpose to afford you yet more signal proof in one which I shall tell you; wherein you will hear of a lady who in her enterprises owed far more to the favour of Fortune than to the guidance of reason: wherefore I should not advise any of you rashly to follow in her footsteps, seeing that Fortune is not always in a kindly mood, nor are the eyes of all men equally holden –

In Argos, that most ancient city of Achaia, the fame of whose kings of old time is out of all proportion to its size, there dwelt of yore Nicostratus, a nobleman, to whom, when he was already verging on old age, Fortune gave to wife a great lady, Lydia by name, whose courage matched her charms. Nicostratus, as suited with his rank and wealth, kept not a few retainers and hounds and hawks, and was mightily addicted to the chase. Among his dependants was a young man named Pyrrhus, a gallant of no mean accomplishment, and goodly of person and beloved and trusted by Nicostratus above all other. Of whom Lydia grew mighty enamoured, insomuch that neither by day nor by night might her thoughts stray from him: but, whether it was that Pyrrhus wist not her love, or would have none of it, he gave no sign of recognition; whereby the lady's suffering waxing more than she could bear, she made up her mind to declare her love to him; and having a chambermaid, Lusca by name, in whom she placed great trust, she called her, and said – 'Lusca, tokens thou hast had from me of my regard that should ensure thy obedience and loyalty; wherefore have a care that what I shall now tell thee reach the ears of none but him to whom I shall bid thee impart it. Thou seest, Lusca, that I am in the prime of my youth and lustihead, and have neither lack nor stint of all such things as folk desire, save only, to be brief, that I have one cause to repine, to wit, that my husband's years so far outnumber my own. Wherefore with that wherein young ladies take most pleasure I am but ill provided, and, as my desire is no less than theirs, 'tis now some while since I determined that, if Fortune has shown herself so little friendly to me by giving me a husband so advanced in years, at least I will not be mine own enemy by sparing to devise the means whereby my happiness and health may be assured; and that herein, as in all other matters, my joy may be complete, I have chosen, thereto to minister by his embraces, our Pyrrhus, deeming him more worthy than any other man, and have so set my heart upon him that I am ever ill at ease save when he is present either to my sight or to my mind, insomuch that, unless I forgather with him without delay, I doubt not that 'twill be the death of me. And so, if thou holdest my life dear, thou wilt show him my love on such wise as thou mayst deem best, and make my suit to him that he be pleased to come to me, when thou shalt go to fetch him.' 'That gladly will I,' replied the chambermaid; and as soon as she found convenient time and place, she drew Pyrrhus apart, and, as best she knew how, conveyed her lady's message to him. Which Pyrrhus found passing strange to hear, for 'twas in truth a complete surprise to him, and he doubted the lady did but mean to try him. Wherefore he presently, and with some asperity, answered thus – 'Lusca, believe I cannot that this message comes from my lady: have a care, therefore, what thou sayst, and if, perchance, it does come from her, I doubt she does not mean it; and if, perchance, she does mean it, why, then I am honoured by my lord above what I deserve, and I would not for my life do him such a wrong: so have a care never to speak of such matters to me again.' Lusca, nowise disconcerted by his uncompliant tone, rejoined – 'I shall speak to thee, Pyrrhus, of these and all other matters, wherewith I may be commissioned by my lady, as often as she shall bid me, whether it pleases or irks thee; but thou art a blockhead.'

So, somewhat chafed, Lusca bore Pyrrhus' answer back to her lady, who would fain have died, when she heard it, and some days afterwards resumed the topic, saying – 'Thou knowest, Lusca, that 'tis not the first stroke that fells the oak; wherefore, methinks, thou wert best go back to this strange man, who is minded to evince his loyalty at my expense, and choosing a convenient time, declare to him all my passion, and do thy best endeavour that the affair be carried through; for if it should thus lapse, 'twould be the death of me; besides which, he would think we had but trifled with him, and, whereas 'tis his love we would have, we should earn his hatred.' So, after comforting the lady, the maid hied her in quest of Pyrrhus, whom she found in a gladsome and propitious mood, and thus addressed – ' 'Tis not many days, Pyrrhus, since I declared to thee how ardent is the flame with which thy lady and mine is consumed for love of thee, and now again I do thee to wit thereof, and that, if thou shalt not relent of the harshness that thou didst manifest the other day, thou mayst rest assured that her life will be short: wherefore I pray thee to be pleased to give her solace of her desire, and shouldst thou persist in thy obduracy, I, that gave thee credit for not a little sense, shall deem thee a great fool. How flattered thou shouldst be to know thyself beloved above all else by a lady so beauteous and high-born! And how indebted shouldst thou feel thyself to Fortune, seeing that she has in store for thee a boon so great and so suited to the cravings of thy youth, ay, and so like to be of service to thee upon occasion of need! Bethink thee, if there be any of thine equals whose life is ordered more agreeably than thine will be if thou but be wise. Which of them wilt thou find so well furnished with arms and horses, clothes and money as thou shalt be, if thou but give my lady thy love? Receive, then, my words with open mind; be thyself again; bethink thee that 'tis Fortune's way to confront a man but once with smiling mien and open lap, and, if he then accept not her bounty, he has but himself to blame, if afterward he find himself in want, in beggary. Besides which, no such loyalty is demanded between servants and their masters as between friends and kinsfolk; rather 'tis for servants, so far as they may, to behave towards their masters as their masters behave towards them. Thinkest thou, that, if thou hadst a fair wife or mother or daughter or sister that found favour in Nicostratus' eyes, he would be so scrupulous on the point of loyalty as thou art disposed to be in regard of his lady? Thou art a fool, if so thou dost believe. Hold it for certain, that, if blandishments and supplications did not suffice, he would, whatever thou mightest think of it, have recourse to force. Observe we, then, towards them and theirs the same rule which they observe towards us and ours. Take the boon that Fortune offers thee; repulse her not; rather go thou to meet her, and hail her advance; for be sure that, if thou do not so, to say nought of thy lady's health, which will certainly ensue, thou thyself wilt repent thee thereof so often that thou wilt be fain of death.'

Since he had last seen Lusca, Pyrrhus had repeatedly pondered what she had said to him, and had made his mind up that, should she come again, he would answer her in another sort, and comply in all respects with the lady's desires, provided he might be assured that she was not merely putting him to the proof; wherefore he now made answer – 'Lo, now, Lusca, I acknowledge the truth of all that thou sayst; but, on the other hand, I know that my lord is not a little wise and wary, and, as he has committed all his affairs to my charge, I sorely misdoubt me that 'tis with his approbation, and by his advice, and but to prove me, that Lydia does this: wherefore let her do three things which I shall demand of her for my assurance, and then there is nought that she shall crave of me, but I will certainly render her prompt obedience. Which three things are these – first, let her in Nicostratus' presence kill his fine sparrow-hawk: then she must send me a lock of Nicostratus' beard, and lastly one of his best teeth.' Hard seemed these terms to Lusca, and hard beyond measure to the lady, but Love, that great fecilitator of enterprise, and master of stratagem, gave her resolution to address herself to their performance: wherefore through the chambermaid she sent him word that what he required of her she would do, and that without either reservation or delay; and therewithal she told him, that, as he deemed Nicostratus so wise, she would contrive that they should enjoy one another in Nicostratus' presence, and that Nicostratus should believe that 'twas a mere show. Pyrrhus, therefore, anxiously expected what the lady would do. Some days thus passed, and then Nicostratus gave a great breakfast, as was his frequent wont, to certain gentlemen, and when the tables were removed, the lady, robed in green samite, and richly adorned, came forth of her chamber into the hall wherein they sat, and before the eyes of Pyrrhus and all the rest of the company hied her to the perch, on which stood the sparrow-hawk that Nicostratus so much prized, and loosed him, and, as if she were minded to carry him on her hand, took him by the jesses and dashed him against the wall so that he died. Whereupon – 'Alas! my lady, what hast thou done?' exclaimed Nicostratus: but she vouchsafed no answer, save that, turning to the gentlemen that had sat at meat with him, she said – 'My lords, ill fitted were I to take vengeance on a king that had done me despite, if I lacked the courage to be avenged on a sparrow-hawk. You are to know that by this bird I have long been cheated of all the time that ought to be devoted by gentlemen to pleasuring their ladies; for with the first streaks of dawn Nicostratus has been up and got him to horse, and hawk on hand hied him to the champaign to see him fly, leaving me, such as you see me, alone and ill content abed. For which cause I have oftentimes been minded to do that which I have now done, and have only refrained therefrom, that, biding my time, I might do it in the presence of men that should judge my cause justly, as I trust you will do.' Which hearing, the gentlemen, who deemed her affections no less fixed on Nicostratus than her words imported, broke with one accord into a laugh, and turning to Nicostratus, who was sore displeased, fell a-saying – 'Now well done of the lady to avenge her wrongs by the death of the sparrow-hawk!' and so, the lady being withdrawn to her chamber, they passed the affair off with divers pleasantries, turning the wrath of Nicostratus to laughter.

Pyrrhus, who had witnessed what had passed, said to himself – Nobly indeed has my lady begun, and on such wise as promises well for the felicity of my love. God grant that she so continue. And even so Lydia did: for not many days after she had killed the sparrow-hawk, she, being with Nicostratus in her chamber, from caressing passed to toying and trifling with him, and he, sportively pulling her by the hair, gave her occasion to fulfil the second of Pyrrhus' demands; which she did by nimbly laying hold of one of the lesser tufts of his beard, and, laughing the while, plucking it so hard that she tore it out of his chin. Which Nicostratus somewhat resenting – 'Now what cause hast thou,' quoth she, 'to make such a wry face? 'Tis but that I have plucked some half-dozen hairs from thy beard. Thou didst not feel it as much as did I but now thy tugging of my hair.' And so they continued jesting and sporting with one another, the lady jealously guarding the tuft that she had torn from the beard, which the very same day she sent to her cherished lover. The third demand caused the lady more thought; but, being amply endowed with wit, and powerfully seconded by Love, she failed not to hit upon an apt expedient.

Nicostratus had in his service two lads, who, being of gentle birth, had been placed with him by their kinsfolk, that they might learn manners, one of whom, when Nicostratus sat at meat, carved before him, while the other gave him to drink. Both lads Lydia called to her, and gave them to understand that their breath smelt, and admonished them that, when they waited on Nicostratus, they should hold their heads as far back as possible, saying never a word of the matter to any.

The lads believing her, did as she bade them. Whereupon she took occasion to say to Nicostratus – 'Hast thou marked what these lads do when they wait upon thee?' 'Troth, that have I,' replied Nicostratus; 'indeed I have often had it in mind to ask them why they do so.' 'Nay,' rejoined the lady, 'spare thyself the pains; for I can tell thee the reason, which I have for some time kept close, lest it should vex thee; but as I now see that others begin to be ware of it, it need no longer be withheld from thee. 'Tis for that thy breath stinks shrewdly that they thus avert their heads from thee: 'twas not wont to be so, nor know I why it should be so; and 'tis most offensive when thou art in converse with gentlemen; and therefore 'twould be well to find some way of curing it.' 'I wonder what it could be,' returned Nicostratus; 'is it perchance that I have a decayed tooth in my jaw?' 'That may well be,' quoth Lydia: and taking him to a window, she caused him open his mouth, and after regarding it on this side and that – 'Oh! Nicostratus,' quoth she, 'how couldst thou have endured it so long? Thou hast a tooth here, which, by what I see, is not only decayed, but actually rotten throughout; and beyond all manner of doubt, if thou let it remain long in thy head, 'twill infect its neighbours; so 'tis my advice that thou out with it before the matter grows worse.' 'My judgement jumps with thine,' quoth Nicostratus; 'wherefore send without delay for a surgeon to draw it.' 'God forbid,' returned the lady, 'that a surgeon come hither for such a purpose; methinks, the case is such that I can very well dispense with him, and draw the tooth myself. Besides which, these surgeons do these things in such a cruel way, that I could never endure to see thee or know thee under the hands of any of them: wherefore my mind is quite made up to do it myself, that, at least, if thou shalt suffer too much, I may give it over at once, as a surgeon would not do.' And so she caused the instruments that are used on such occasions to be brought her, and having dismissed all other attendants save Lusca from the chamber, and locked the door, made Nicostratus lie down on a table, set the pincers in his mouth, and clapped them on one of his teeth, which, while Lusca held him, so that, albeit he roared for pain, he might not move, she wrenched by main force from his jaw, and keeping it close, took from Lusca's hand another and horribly decayed tooth, which she showed him, suffering and half-dead as he was, saying – 'See what thou hadst in thy jaw; mark how far gone it is.' Believing what she said, and deeming that, now the tooth was out, his breath would no more be offensive, and being somewhat eased of the pain, which had been extreme, and still remained, so that he murmured not little, by divers comforting applications, he quitted the chamber:

whereupon the lady forthwith sent the tooth to her lover, who, having now full assurance of her love, placed himself entirely at her service. But the lady being minded to make his assurance yet more sure, and deeming each hour a thousand till she might be with him, now saw fit, for the more ready performance of the promise she had given him, to feign sickness; and Nicostratus, coming to see her one day after breakfast, attended only by Pyrrhus, she besought him for her better solacement, to help her down to the garden. Wherefore Nicostratus on one side, and Pyrrhus on the other, took her and bore her down to the garden, and set her on a lawn at the foot of a beautiful pear tree: and after they had sat there a while, the lady, who had already given Pyrrhus to understand what he must do, said to him – 'Pyrrhus, I should greatly like to have some of those pears; get thee up the tree, and shake some of them down.' Pyrrhus climbed the tree in a trice, and began to shake down the pears, and while he did so – 'Fie! Sir,' quoth he, 'what is this you do? And you, Madam, have you no shame, that you suffer him to do so in my presence? Think you that I am blind? 'Twas but now that you were gravely indisposed. Your cure has been speedy indeed to permit of your so behaving: and as for such a purpose you have so many goodly chambers, why betake you not yourselves to one of them, if you must needs so disport yourselves? 'Twould be much more decent than to do so in my presence.' Whereupon the lady, turning to her husband – 'Now what can Pyrrhus mean?' said she. 'Is he mad?' 'Nay, Madam,' quoth Pyrrhus; 'mad am not I. Think you I see you not?' Whereat Nicostratus marvelled not a little; and: – 'Pyrrhus,' quoth he, 'I verily believe thou dreamest.' 'Nay, my lord,' replied Pyrrhus, 'not a whit do I dream; neither do you; rather you wag it with such vigour, that, if this pear tree did the like, there would be never a pear left on it.' Then the lady – 'What can this mean?' quoth she: 'can it be that it really seems to him to be as he says? Upon my hope of salvation, were I but in my former health, I would get me up there to judge for myself what these wonders are which he professes to see.' Whereupon, as Pyrrhus in the pear tree continued talking in the same strange strain – 'Come down,' quoth Nicostratus; and when he was down – 'Now what,' said Nicostratus, 'is it thou sayst thou seest up there?' 'I suppose,' replied Pyrrhus, 'that you take me to be deluded or dreaming: but as I must needs tell you the truth, I saw you lying upon your wife, and then, when I came down, I saw you get up and sit you down here where you now are.' 'Therein,' said Nicostratus, 'thou wast certainly deluded, for, since thou climbest the pear tree, we have not budged a jot, save as thou seest.' Then said Pyrrhus – 'Why make more words about the matter? See you I certainly did; and, seeing you, I saw you lying upon your own.' Nicostratus' wonder now waxed momently, insomuch that he said – 'I am minded to see if this pear tree be enchanted, so that whoso is in it sees marvels;' and so he got him up into it. Whereupon the lady and Pyrrhus fell to disporting them, and Nicostratus, seeing what they were about, exclaimed – 'Ah! lewd woman, what is this thou doest? And thou, Pyrrhus, in whom I so much trusted!' And so saying, he began to climb down. Meanwhile the lady and Pyrrhus had made answer – 'We are sitting here:' and seeing him descending, they placed themselves as they had been when he had left them, whom Nicostratus, being come down, no sooner saw, than he fell a-rating them. Then quoth Pyrrhus – 'Verily, Nicostratus, I now acknowledge, that, as you said a while ago, what I saw when I was in the pear tree was but a false show, albeit I had never understood that so it was but that I now see and know that thou hast also seen a false show. And that I speak truth, you may sufficiently assure yourself, if you but reflect whether 'tis likely that your wife, who for virtue and discretion has not her peer among women, would, if she were minded so to dishonour you, see fit to do so before your very eyes. Of myself I say nought, albeit I had liefer be hewn in pieces than that I should so much as think of such a thing, much less do it in your presence. Wherefore 'tis evident that 'tis some illusion of sight that is propagated from the pear tree; for nought in the world would have made me believe that I saw not you lying there in carnal intercourse with your wife, had I not heard you say that you saw me doing that which most assuredly, so far from doing, I never so much as thought of.' The lady then started up with a most resentful mien, and burst out with – 'Foul fall thee, if thou knowest so little of me as to suppose that, if I were minded to do thee such foul dishonour as thou sayst thou didst see me do, I would come hither to do it before thine eyes! Rest assured that for such a purpose, were it ever mine, I should deem one of our chambers more meet, and it should go hard but I would so order the matter that thou shouldst never know aught of it.' Nicostratus, having heard both, and deeming that what they both averred must be true, to wit, that they would never have ventured upon such an act in his presence, passed from chiding to talk of the singularity of the thing, and how marvellous it was that the vision should reshape itself for everyone that climbed the tree. The lady, however, made a show of being distressed that Nicostratus should so have thought of her, and – 'Verily,' quoth she, 'no woman, neither I nor another, shall again suffer loss of honour by this pear tree: run, Pyrrhus, and bring hither an axe, and at one and the same time vindicate thy honour and mine by felling it, albeit 'twere better far Nicostratus' skull should feel the weight of the axe, seeing that in utter heedlessness he so readily suffered the eyes of his mind to be blinded; for, albeit this vision was seen by the bodily eye, yet ought the understanding by no means to have entertained and affirmed it as real.'

So Pyrrhus presently hied him to fetch the axe, and returning therewith felled the pear; whereupon the lady, turning towards Nicostratus – 'Now that this foe of my honour is fallen,' quoth she, 'my wrath is gone from me.' Nicostratus then craving her pardon, she graciously granted it him, bidding him never again to suffer himself to be betrayed into thinking such a thing of her who loved him more dearly than herself. So the poor duped husband went back with her and her lover to the palace, where not seldom in time to come Pyrrhus and Lydia took their pastime together more at ease. God grant us the like.

35

The first story of the eighth day in which Gulfardo borrows moneys of Guasparruolo, which he has agreed to give Guasparruolo's wife, that he may lie with her. He gives them to her, and in her presence tells Guasparruolo that he has done so, and she acknowledges that 'tis true.

When the sun was past the meridian the queen mustered them again for the wonted pastime; and all being seated by the fair fountain thus, at her command, Neifile began: Since God has ordained that 'tis for me to take the lead today with my story, well pleased am I. And for that, loving ladies, much has been said touching the tricks that women play men, I am minded to tell you of one that a man played a woman, not because I would censure what the man did or say that 'twas not merited by the woman, but rather to commend the man and censure the woman and to show that men may beguile those that think to beguile them, as well as be beguiled by those they think to beguile; for peradventure what I am about to relate should in strictness of speech not be termed beguilement but rather retaliation; for as it behoves woman to be most strictly virtuous and to guard her chastity as her very life nor on any account to allow herself to sully it, which notwithstanding, 'tis not possible by reason of our frailty that there should be as perfect an observance of this law as were meet, I affirm that she that allows herself to infringe it for money merits the fire; whereas she that so offends under the prepotent stress of Love will receive pardon from any judge that knows how to temper justice with mercy: witness what but the other day [see page 205] we heard from Filostrato touching Madonna Filippa at Prato –

Know, then, that there was once at Milan a German mercenary, Gulfardo by name, a doughty man, and very loyal to those with whom he took service; a quality most uncommon in Germans. And as he was wont to be most faithful in repaying whatever moneys he borrowed, he would have had no difficulty in finding a merchant to advance him any amount of money at a low rate of interest. Now, tarrying thus at Milan, Gulfardo fixed his affection on a very fine woman, named Madonna Ambruogia, the wife of a wealthy merchant, one Guasparruolo Cagastraccio, with whom he was well acquainted and on friendly terms: which amour he managed with such discretion that neither the husband nor anyone else wist aught of it. So one day he sent her a message, beseeching her of her courtesy to gratify his passion, and assuring her that he on his part was ready to obey her every behest.

The lady made a great many words about the affair, the upshot of which was that she would do as Gulfardo desired upon the following terms: to wit, that, in the first place, he should never discover the matter to a soul, and, secondly, that, as for some purpose or another she required two hundred florins of gold, he out of his abundance should supply her necessity; these conditions being satisfied she would be ever at his service. Offended by such base sordidness in one whom he had supposed to be an honourable woman, Gulfardo passed from ardent love to something very like hatred, and cast about how he might flout her. So he sent her word that he would right gladly pleasure her in this and in any other matter that might be in his power; let her but say when he was to come to see her, and he would bring the moneys with him, and none should know of the matter except a comrade of his, in whom he placed much trust, and who was privy to all that he did. The lady, if she should not rather be called the punk, gleefully made answer that in the course of a few days her husband, Guasparruolo, was to go to Genoa on business, and that, when he was gone, she would let Gulfardo know, and appoint a time for him to visit her. Gulfardo thereupon chose a convenient time, and hied him to Guasparruolo, to whom – 'I am come,' quoth he, 'about a little matter of business which I have on hand, for which I require two hundred florins of gold, and I should be glad if thou wouldst lend them me at the rate of interest which thou art wont to charge me.' 'That gladly will I,' replied Guasparruolo, and told out the money at once. A few days later Guasparruolo being gone to Genoa, as the lady had said, she sent word to Gulfardo that he should bring her the two hundred florins of gold. So Gulfardo hied him with his comrade to the lady's house, where he found her expecting him, and lost no time in handing her the two hundred florins of gold in his comrade's presence, saying – 'You will keep the money, Madam, and give it to your husband when he returns.' Witting not why Gulfardo so said, but thinking that 'twas but to conceal from his comrade that it was given by way of price, the lady made answer – 'That will I gladly; but I must first see whether the amount is right;' whereupon she told the florins out upon a table, and when she found that the two hundred were there, she put them away in high glee, and turning to Gulfardo, took him into her chamber, where, not on that night only but on many another night, while her husband was away, he had of her all that he craved. On Guasparruolo's return Gulfardo presently paid him a visit, having first made sure that the lady would be with him, and so in her presence – 'Guasparruolo,' quoth he, 'I had after all no occasion for the money, to wit, the two hundred florins of gold that thou didst lend me the other day, being unable to carry through the transaction for which I borrowed them, and so I took an early opportunity of bringing them to thy wife, and gave them to her: thou wilt therefore cancel the account.' Whereupon Guasparruolo turned to the lady, and asked her if she had had them. She, not daring to deny the fact in presence of the witness, answered – 'Why, yes, I had them, and quite forgot to tell thee.' 'Good,' quoth then Guasparruolo, 'we are quits, Gulfardo; make thy mind easy; I will see that thy account is set right.' Gulfardo then withdrew, leaving the flouted lady to hand over her ill-gotten gains to her husband; and so the astute lover had his pleasure of his greedy mistress for nothing.

ꙮ 36 ꙮ

The second story of the eighth day, in which the priest of Varlungo lies with Monna Belcolore; he leaves with her his cloak by way of pledge, and receives from her a mortar. He returns the mortar, and demands of her the cloak that he had left in pledge, which the good lady returns him with a gibe.

Ladies and men alike commended Gulfardo for the check that he gave to the greed of the Milanese lady; but before they had done, the queen turned to Pamfilo and with a smile bade him follow suit: wherefore thus Pamfilo began: Fair my ladies, it occurs to me to tell you a short story which reflects no credit on those by whom we are continually wronged without being able to retaliate, to wit the priests, who have instituted a crusade against our wives, and deem that when they have made conquest of one of them they have done a work every whit as worthy of recompense by remission of sin and punishment as if they had brought the Soldan in chains to Avignon: in which respect 'tis not possible for the hapless laity to be even with them: howbeit they are as hot to make reprisals on the priests' mothers, sisters, mistresses, and daughters as the priests to attack their wives. Wherefore I am minded to give you, as I may do in few words, the history of a rustic amour, the conclusion whereof was not a little laughable nor barren of moral, for you may also gather therefrom that 'tis not always well to believe everything that a priest says –

I say then that at Varlungo, a village hard by here as all of you, my ladies, should wot either of your own knowledge or by report, there dwelt a worthy priest, and doughty of body in the service of the ladies: who, albeit he was none too quick at his book, had no lack of precious and blessed solecisms to edify his flock withal of a Sunday under the elm. And when the men were out of doors he would visit their wives as never a priest had done before him, bringing them feast-day gowns and holy water and now and again a bit of candle, and giving them his blessing. Now it so befell that among those of his fair parishioners whom he most affected the first place was at length taken by one Monna Belcolore, the wife of a husbandman that called himself Bentivegna del Mazzo. And in good sooth she was a winsome and lusty country lass, brown as a berry and buxom enough, and fitter than e'er another for his mill. Moreover she had not her match in playing the tabret and singing – The borage is full sappy,* and in leading a brawl or a breakdown, no matter who might be next her, with a fair and dainty kerchief in her hand. Which spells so wrought upon Master Priest that for love of her he grew distracted and did nought all day long but loiter about the village on the chance of catching sight of her. And if of a Sunday morning he espied her in church, he strove might and main to acquit himself of his Kyrie and Sanctus in the style of a great singer, albeit his performance was liker to the braying of an ass: whereas, if he saw her not, he scarce exerted himself at all. However, he managed with such discretion that neither Bentivegna del Mazzo nor any of the neighbours wist aught of his love. And hoping thereby to ingratiate himself with Monna Belcolore, he from time to time would send her presents, now a clove of fresh garlic, the best in all the countryside, from his own garden which he tilled with his own hands, and anon a basket of beans or a bunch of chives or shallots; and, when he thought it might serve his turn he would give her a sly glance and follow it up with a little amorous mocking and mowing, which she, with rustic awkwardness, feigned not to understand, and ever maintained her reserve so that Master Priest made no headway.

* For this folk-song see *Cantilene e Ballate*, *Strambotti e Madrigali*, ed. Carducci (1871), p. 60. The fragment there printed may be freely rendered as follows:

The borage is full sappy,
   And clusters red we see,
And my love would make me happy;
   So that maiden gave to me.

Ill set I find this dance,
   And better might it be:
So, comrade mine, advance,
   And, changing place with me,
Stand thou thy love beside.

Now it so befell that one day, when the priest at high noon was aimlessly gadding about the village, he encountered Bentivegna del Mazzo at the tail of a well laden ass, and greeted him, asking him whither he was going. 'I'faith, Sir,' quoth Bentivegna, 'for sure 'tis to town I go, having an affair or two to attend to there; and I am taking these things to Ser Buonaccorri da Ginestreto, to get him to stand by me in I wot not what matter, whereof the justice o' th' coram has by his provoker served me with a pertrumpery summons to appear before him.' Whereupon – ' 'Tis well, my son,' quoth the priest, overjoyed, 'my blessing go with thee: good luck to thee and a speedy return; and hark ye, shouldst thou see Lapuccio or Naldino, do not forget to tell them to send me those thongs for my flails.' 'It shall be done,' quoth Bentivegna, and jogged on towards Florence, while the priest, thinking that now was his time to hie him to Belcolore and try his fortune, put his best leg forward, and stayed not till he was at the house, which entering, he said – 'God be gracious to us! Who is within?' Belcolore, who was up in the loft, made answer – 'Welcome, Sir; but what dost thou, gadding about in the heat?' 'Why, as I hope for God's blessing,' quoth he, 'I am just come to stay with thee a while, having met thy husband on his way to town.' Whereupon down came Belcolore, took a seat, and began sifting cabbage-seed that her husband had lately threshed. By and by the priest began – 'So, Belcolore, wilt thou keep me ever a-dying thus?' Whereat Belcolore tittered, and said – 'Why, what is't I do to you?' 'Truly nothing at all,' replied the priest: 'but thou sufferest me not to do to thee that which I had lief, and which God commands.' 'Now away with you!' returned Belcolore, 'do priests do that sort of thing?' 'Indeed we do,' quoth the priest, 'and to better purpose than others: why not? I tell you our grinding is far better; and wouldst thou know why? 'tis because 'tis intermittent. And in truth 'twill be well worth thy while to keep thine own counsel, and let me do it.' 'Worth my while!' ejaculated Belcolore. 'How may that be? There is never a one of you but would overreach the very Devil.' ' 'Tis not for me to say,' returned the priest; 'say but what thou wouldst have: shall it be a pair of dainty shoes? Or wouldst thou prefer a fillet? Or perchance a gay riband? What's thy will?' 'Marry, no lack have I,' quoth Belcolore, 'of such things as these. But, if you wish me so well, why do me not a service? and I would then be at your command.' 'Name but the service,' returned the priest, 'and gladly will I do it.' Quoth then Belcolore – 'On Saturday I have to go to Florence to deliver some wool that I have spun, and to get my spinning-wheel put in order: lend me but five pounds – I know you have them – and I will redeem my perse petticoat from the pawnshop, and also the girdle that I wear on saints' days, and that I had when I was married – you see that without them I cannot go to church or anywhere else, and then I will do just as you wish thenceforth and forever.' Whereupon – 'So God give me a good year,' quoth he, 'as I have not the money with me: but never fear that I will see that thou hast it before Saturday with all the pleasure in life.' 'Ay, ay,' rejoined Belcolore, 'you all make great promises, but then you never keep them. Think you to serve me as you served Biliuzza, whom you left in the lurch at last? God's faith, you do not so. To think that she turned woman of the world just for that! If you have not the money with you, why, go and get it.' 'Prithee,' returned the priest, 'send me not home just now. For, seest thou, 'tis the very nick of time with me, and the coast is clear, and perchance it might not be so on my return, and in short I know not when it would be likely to go so well as now.' Whereto she did but rejoin – 'Good; if you are minded to go, get you gone; if not, stay where you are.' The priest, therefore, seeing that she was not disposed to give him what he wanted, as he was fain, to wit, on his own terms, but was bent upon having a *quid pro quo*, changed his tone; and – 'Lo, now,' quoth he, 'thou doubtest I will not bring thee the money; so to set thy mind at rest, I will leave thee this cloak – thou seest 'tis good sky-blue silk – in pledge.' So raising her head and glancing at the cloak – 'And what may the cloak be worth?' quoth Belcolore. 'Worth!' ejaculated the priest: 'I would have thee know that 'tis all Douai, not to say Trouai, make: nay, there are some of our folk here that say 'tis Quadrouai; and 'tis not a fortnight since I bought it of Lotto, the second-hand dealer, for seven good pounds, and then had it five good soldi under value, by what I hear from Buglietto, who, thou knowest, is an excellent judge of these articles.' 'Oh! say you so?' exclaimed Belcolore. 'So help me God, I should not have thought it; however, let me look at it.' So Master Priest, being ready for action, doffed the cloak and handed it to her. And she, having put it in a safe place, said to him – 'Now, Sir, we will away to the hut; there is never a soul goes there;' and so they did. And there Master Priest, giving her many a mighty buss and straining her to his sacred person, solaced himself with her no little while.

Which done, he hied him away in his cassock, as if he were come from officiating at a wedding; but, when he was back in his holy quarters, he bethought him that not all the candles that he received by way of offering in the course of an entire year would amount to the half of five pounds, and saw that he had made a bad bargain, and repented him that he had left the cloak in pledge, and cast about how he might recover it without paying anything. And as he did not lack cunning, he hit upon an excellent expedient, by which he compassed his end. So on the morrow, being a saint's day, he sent a neighbour's lad to Monna Belcolore with a request that she would be so good as to lend him her stone mortar, for that Binguccio dal Poggio and Nuto Buglietti were to breakfast with him that morning, and he therefore wished to make a sauce. Belcolore having sent the mortar, the priest, about breakfast time, reckoning that Bentivegna del Mazzo and Belcolore would be at their meal, called his clerk, and said to him – 'Take the mortar back to Belcolore, and say – "My master thanks you very kindly, and bids you return the cloak that the lad left with you in pledge." ' The clerk took the mortar to Belcolore's house, where, finding her at table with Bentivegna, he set the mortar down and delivered the priest's message. Whereto Belcolore would fain have demurred; but Bentivegna gave her a threatening glance, saying – 'So, then, thou takest a pledge from Master Priest? By Christ, I vow, I have half a mind to give thee a great clout o' the chin. Go, give it back at once, a murrain on thee! And look to it that whatever he may have a mind to, were it our very ass, he be never denied.' So, with a very bad grace, Belcolore got up, and went to the wardrobe, and took out the cloak, and gave it to the clerk, saying – 'Tell thy master from me – Would to God he may never ply pestle in my mortar again, such honour has he done me for this turn!' So the clerk returned with the cloak, and delivered the message to Master Priest; who, laughing, made answer: – 'Tell her, when thou next seest her, that, so she lend us not the mortar, I will not lend her the pestle: be it tit for tat.'

Bentivegna made no account of his wife's words, deeming that 'twas but his chiding that had provoked them. But Belcolore was not a little displeased with Master Priest, and had never a word to say to him till the vintage; after which, what with the salutary fear in which she stood of the mouth of Lucifer the Great, to which he threatened to consign her, and the must and roast chestnuts that he sent her, she made it up with him, and many a jolly time they had together. And though she got not the five pounds from him, he put a new skin on her tabret, and fitted it with a little bell, wherewith she was satisfied.

37

The fourth story of the eighth day, in which the Rector of Fiesole loves a widow lady, by whom he is not loved, and thinking to lie with her, lies with her maid, with whom the lady's brothers cause him to be found by his Bishop.

The speaker having come to the end of the third story, which in the telling had yielded no small delight to all the company, the queen turning to Emilia signified her will that her story should ensue at once. And thus with alacrity Emilia began: Noble ladies, how we are teased and tormented by these priests and friars, and indeed by clergy of all sorts, I mind me to have been set forth in more than one of the stories that have been told; but as 'twere not possible to say so much thereof but that more would yet remain to say, I purpose to supplement them with the story of a rector who, in defiance of all the world, was bent upon having the favour of a gentlewoman, whether she would or no. Which gentlewoman, being discreet above a little, treated him as he deserved –

Fiesole, whose hill is here within sight, is, as each of you knows, a city of immense antiquity, and was aforetime great, though now 'tis fallen into complete decay; which notwithstanding, it always was, and still is the see of a bishop. Now there was once a gentlewoman, Monna Piccarda by name, a widow, that had an estate at Fiesole, hard by the cathedral, on which, for that she was not in the easiest circumstances, she lived most part of the year, and with her her two brothers, very worthy and courteous young men, both of them. And the lady being wont frequently to resort to the cathedral, and being still quite young and fair and debonair withal, it so befell that the rector grew in the last degree enamoured of her, and waxed at length so bold, that he himself avowed his passion to the lady, praying her to entertain his love, and requite it in like measure. The rector was advanced in years, but otherwise the veriest youngster, being bold and of a high spirit, of a boundless conceit of himself, and of mien and manners most affected and in the worst taste, and withal so tiresome and insufferable that he was on bad terms with everybody, and, if with one person more than another, with this lady, who not only cared not a jot for him, but had liefer have had a headache than his company. Wherefore the lady discreetly made answer – 'I may well prize your love, Sir, and love you I should and will right gladly; but such love as yours and mine may never admit of aught that is not honourable. You are my spiritual father and a priest, and now verging towards old age, circumstances which should ensure your honour and chastity; and I, on my part, am no longer a girl, such as these love affairs might beseem, but a widow, and well you wot how it behoves widows to be chaste. Wherefore I pray you to have me excused; for, after the sort you crave, you shall never have my love, nor would I in such sort be loved by you.' With this answer the rector was for the nonce fain to be content; but he was not the man to be dismayed and routed by a first repulse; and with his wonted temerity and effrontery he plied her again and again with letters and messages, and also by word of mouth, when he espied her entering the church. Wherefore the lady finding this persecution more grievous and harassing than she could well bear, cast about how she might be quit thereof in such fashion as he deserved, seeing that he left her no choice; howbeit she would do nought in the matter until she had conferred with her brothers. She therefore told them how the rector pursued her, and how she meant to foil him; and, with their full concurrence, some few days afterwards she went, as she was wont, to church. The rector no sooner saw her, than he approached and accosted her, as he was wont, in a tone of easy familiarity. The lady greeted him, as he came up, with a glance of gladsome recognition; and when he had treated her to not a little of his wonted eloquence, she drew him aside, and heaving a great sigh, said – 'I have oftentimes heard it said, Sir, that there is no castle so strong, but that, if the siege be continued day by day, it will sooner or later be taken; which I now plainly perceive is my own case. For so fairly have you hemmed me in with this, that, and the other pretty speech or the like blandishments, that you have constrained me to make nought of my former resolve, and, seeing that I find such favour with you, to surrender myself unto you.' Whereto, overjoyed, the rector made answer – 'Madam, I am greatly honoured; and, sooth to say, I marvelled not a little how you should hold out so long, seeing that I have never had the like experience with any other woman, insomuch that I have at times said – "Were women of silver, they would not be worth a denier, for there is none but would give under the hammer." But no more of this: when and where may we come together?' 'Sweet my lord,' replied the lady, 'for the when, 'tis just as we may think best, for I have no husband to whom to render account of my nights, but the where passes my wit to conjecture.' 'How so?' quoth the rector. 'Why not in your own house?' 'Sir,' replied the lady, 'you know that I have two brothers, both young men, who day and night bring their comrades into the house, which is none too large: for which reason it might not be done there, unless we were minded to make ourselves, as it were, dumb and blind, uttering never a word, not so much as a monosyllable, and abiding in the dark: in such sort indeed it might be, because they do not intrude upon my chamber; but theirs is so near to mine that the very least whisper could not but be heard.' 'Nay but, Madam,' returned the rector, 'let not this stand in our way for a night or two, until I may bethink me where else we might be more at our ease.' 'Be that as you will, Sir,' quoth the lady, 'I do but entreat that the affair be kept close, so that never a word of it get wind.' 'Have no fear on that score, Madam,' replied the priest; 'and if so it may be, let us forgather tonight.' 'With pleasure,' returned the lady; and having appointed him how and when to come, she left him and went home.

Now the lady had a maid that was none too young and had a countenance the ugliest and most misshapen that ever was seen; for indeed she was flat-nosed, wry-mouthed, and thick-lipped, with huge, ill-set teeth, eyes that squinted and were ever bleared, and a complexion betwixt green and yellow, that showed as if she had spent the summer not at Fiesole but at Sinigaglia: besides which she was hipshot and somewhat halting on the right side. Her name was Ciuta, but, for that she was such a scurvy bitch to look upon, she was called by all folk Ciutazza.* And being thus misshapen of body, she was also not without her share of guile. So the lady called her and said – 'Ciutazza, if thou wilt do me a service tonight, I will give thee a fine new shift.' At the mention of the shift Ciutazza made answer – 'If you give me a shift, Madam, I will throw myself into the very fire.' 'Good,' said the lady; 'then I would have thee lie tonight in my bed with a man, whom thou wilt caress; but look thou say never a word, that my brothers, who, as thou knowest, sleep in the next room, hear thee not; and afterwards I will give thee the shift.' 'Sleep with a man!' quoth Ciutazza: 'why, if

* An augmentative form, with a suggestion of *cagnazza*, bitch-like.

need be, I will sleep with six.' So in the evening Master Rector came, as he had been bidden; and the two young men, as the lady had arranged, being in their room, and making themselves very audible, he stole noiselessly, and in the dark, into the lady's room, and got him on to the bed, which Ciutazza, well advised by the lady how to behave, mounted from the other side. Whereupon Master Rector, thinking to have the lady by his side, took Ciutazza in his arms, and fell a-kissing her, saying never a word the while, and Ciutazza did the like; and so he enjoyed her, plucking the boon which he had so long desired.

The rector and Ciutazza thus closeted, the lady charged her brothers to execute the rest of her plan. They accordingly stole quietly out of their room, and hied them to the piazza, where Fortune proved propitious beyond what they had craved of her; for, it being a very hot night, the bishop had been seeking them, purposing to go home with them, and solace himself with their society, and quench his thirst. With which desire he acquainted them, as soon as he espied them coming into the piazza; and so they escorted him to their house, and there in the cool of their little courtyard, which was bright with many a lamp, he took, to his no small comfort, a draught of their good wine. Which done – 'Sir,' said the young men, 'since of your great courtesy you have deigned to visit our poor house, to which we were but now about to invite you, we should be gratified if you would be pleased to give a look at somewhat, a mere trifle though it be, which we have here to show you.' The bishop replied that he would do so with pleasure. Whereupon one of the young men took a lighted torch and led the way, the bishop and the rest following, to the chamber where Master Rector lay with Ciutazza.

Now the rector, being in hot haste, had ridden hard, insomuch that he was already gotten above three miles on his way when they arrived; and so, being somewhat tired, he was resting, but, hot though the night was, he still held Ciutazza in his arms. In which posture he was shown to the bishop, when, preceded by the young man bearing the light, and followed by the others, he entered the chamber. And being roused, and observing the light and the folk that stood about him, Master Rector was mighty ashamed and affrighted, and popped his head under the clothes. But the bishop, reprimanding him severely, constrained him to thrust his head out again, and take a view of his bed-fellow. Thus made aware of the trick which the lady had played him, the rector was now, both on that score and by reason of his signal disgrace, the saddest man that ever was; and his discomfiture was complete, when, having donned his clothes, he was committed by the bishop's command to close custody and sent to prison, there to expiate his offence by a rigorous penance.

The bishop was then fain to know how it had come about that he had forgathered there with Ciutazza. Whereupon the young men related the whole story; which ended, the bishop commended both the lady and the young men not a little, for that they had taken condign vengeance upon him without imbruing their hands in the blood of a priest. The bishop caused him to bewail his transgression forty days; but what with his love, and the scornful requital which it had received, he bewailed it more than forty and nine days, not to mention that for a great while he could not show himself in the street but the boys would point the finger at him and say – 'There goes he that lay with Ciutazza.' Which was such an affliction to him that he was like to go mad. On this wise the worthy lady rid herself of the rector's vexatious importunity, and Ciutazza had a jolly night and earned her shift.

38

The seventh story of the eighth day, in which scholar loves a widow lady, who, being enamoured of another, causes him to spend a winter's night awaiting her in the snow. He afterwards by a stratagem causes her to stand for a whole day in July, naked upon a tower, exposed to the flies, the gadflies, and the sun.

The sixth story being ended, the queen bade Pampinea give them hers: and thus forthwith Pampinea began: Dearest ladies, it happens oftentimes that the artful scorner meets his match; wherefore 'tis only little wits that delight to scorn. In a series of stories we have heard tell of tricks played without aught in the way of reprisals following: by mine I purpose in some degree to excite your compassion for a gentlewoman of our city (albeit the retribution that came upon her was but just) whose flout was returned in the like sort, and to such effect that she well-nigh died thereof. The which to hear will not be unprofitable to you, for thereby you will learn to be more careful how you flout others and therein you will do very wisely –

'Tis not many years since there dwelt at Florence a lady young and fair, and of a high spirit, as also of right gentle lineage, and tolerably well endowed with temporal goods. Now Elena – such was the lady's name – being left a widow, was minded never to marry again, being enamoured of a handsome young gallant of her own choosing, with whom she, recking nought of any other lover, did, by the help of a maid in whom she placed much trust, not seldom speed the time gaily and with marvellous delight. Meanwhile it so befell that a young nobleman of our city, Rinieri by name, who had spent much time in study at Paris, not that he might thereafter sell his knowledge by retail, but that he might learn the reasons and causes of things, which accomplishment shows to most excellent advantage in a gentleman, returned to Florence, and there lived as a citizen in no small honour with his fellows, both by reason of his rank and of his learning. But as it is often the case that those who are most versed in deep matters are the soonest mastered by Love, so was it with Rinieri. For at a festal gathering, to which one day he went, there appeared before his eyes this Elena, of whom we spoke, clad in black, as is the wont of our Florentine widows, and showing to his mind so much fairer and more debonair than any other woman that he had ever seen, that happy indeed he deemed the man might call himself, to whom God in His goodness should grant the right to hold her naked in his arms. So now and again he eyed her stealthily, and knowing that boons goodly and precious are not to be gotten without trouble, he made up his mind to study and labour with all assiduity how best to please her, that so he might win her love, and thereby the enjoyment of her.

The young gentlewoman was not used to keep her eyes bent ever towards the infernal regions; but, rating herself at no less, if not more, than her deserts, she was dexterous to move them to and fro, and thus busily scanning her company, soon detected the men who regarded her with pleasure. By which means having discovered Rinieri's passion, she inwardly laughed, and said: – 'Twill turn out that 'twas not for nothing that I came here today, for, if I mistake not, I have caught a gander by the bill. So she gave him an occasional sidelong glance, and sought as best she might to make him believe that she was not indifferent to him, deeming that the more men she might captivate by her charms, the higher those charms would be rated, and most especially by him whom she had made lord of them and her love. The erudite scholar bade adieu to philosophical meditation, for the lady entirely engrossed his mind; and, having discovered her house, he, thinking to please her, found divers pretexts for frequently passing by it. Whereon the lady, her vanity flattered for the reason aforesaid, plumed herself not a little, and showed herself pleased to see him. Thus encouraged, the scholar found means to make friends with her maid, to whom he discovered his love, praying her to do her endeavour with her mistress, that he might have her favour. The maid was profuse of promises, and gave her mistress his message, which she no sooner heard, than she was convulsed with laughter, and replied – 'He brought sense enough hither from Paris: knowest thou where he has since been to lose it? Go to, now; let us give him that which he seeks. Tell him, when he next speaks to you of the matter, that I love him vastly more than he loves me, but that I must have regard to my reputation, so that I may be able to hold my head up among other ladies; which, if he is really the wise man they say, will cause him to affect me much more.' Ah! poor woman! poor woman! she little knew, my ladies, how rash it is to try conclusions with scholars.

The maid found the scholar, and did her mistress's errand. The scholar, overjoyed, proceeded to urge his suit with more ardour, to indite letters, and send presents. The lady received all that he sent her, but vouchsafed no answers save such as were couched in general terms: and on this wise she kept him dangling a long while. At last, having disclosed the whole affair to her lover, who evinced some resentment and jealousy, she, to convince him that his suspicions were groundless, and for that she was much importuned by the scholar, sent word to him by her maid, that never since he had assured her of his love, had occasion served her to do him pleasure, but that next Christmastide she hoped to be with him; wherefore, if he were minded to await her in the courtyard of her house on the night of the day next following the feast, she would meet him there as soon as she could. Elated as ne'er another, the scholar hied him at the appointed time to the lady's house, and being ushered into a courtyard by the maid, who forthwith turned the key upon him, addressed himself there to await the lady's coming.

Now the lady's lover, by her appointment, was with her that evening; and, when they had gaily supped, she told him what she had in hand that night, adding – 'And so thou wilt be able to gauge the love which I have borne and bear this scholar, whom thou hast foolishly regarded as a rival.' The lover heard the lady's words with no small delight, and waited in eager expectancy to see her make them good. The scholar, hanging about there in the courtyard, began to find it somewhat chillier than he would have liked, for it had snowed hard all day long, so that the snow lay everywhere thick on the ground; however, he bore it patiently, expecting to be recompensed by and by. After a while the lady said to her lover – 'Go we to the chamber and take a peep through a lattice at him of whom thou art turned jealous, and mark what he does, and how he will answer the maid, whom I have bidden go speak with him.' So the pair hied them to a lattice, wherethrough they could see without being seen, and heard the maid call from another lattice to the scholar, saying – 'Rinieri, my lady is distressed as never woman was, for that one of her brothers is come here tonight, and after talking a long while with her, must needs sup with her, and is not yet gone, but, I think, he will soon be off; and that is the reason why she has not been able to come to thee, but she will come soon now. She trusts it does not irk thee to wait so long.' Whereto the scholar, supposing that 'twas true, made answer – 'Tell my lady to give herself no anxiety on my account, until she can conveniently come to me, but to do so as soon as she may.' Whereupon the maid withdrew from the window, and went to bed; while the lady said to her lover – 'Now, what sayst thou? Thinkst thou that, if I had that regard for him, which thou fearest, I would suffer him to tarry below there to get frozen?' Which said, the lady and her now partly reassured lover got them to bed, where for a great while they disported them right gamesomely, laughing together and making merry over the luckless scholar.

The scholar, meanwhile, paced up and down the courtyard to keep himself warm, nor indeed had he where to sit, or take shelter: in this plight he bestowed many a curse upon the lady's brother for his long tarrying, and never a sound did he hear but he thought that 'twas the lady opening the door. But vain indeed were his hopes: the lady, having solaced herself with her lover until hard upon midnight, then said to him – 'How ratest thou our scholar, my soul? whether is the greater his wit, or the love I bear him, thinkst thou? Will the cold, that, of my ordaining, he now suffers, banish from thy breast the suspicion which my light words the other day implanted there?' 'Ay, indeed, heart of my body!' replied the lover, 'well wot I now that even as thou art to me, my weal, my consolation, my bliss, so am I to thee.' 'So:' quoth the lady, 'then I must have full a thousand kisses from thee, to prove that thou sayst sooth.' The lover's answer was to strain her to his heart, and give her not merely a thousand but a hundred thousand kisses. In such converse they dallied a while longer, and then: – 'Get we up, now,' quoth the lady, 'that we may go see if 'tis quite spent, that fire, with which, as he wrote to me daily, this new lover of mine used to burn.' So up they got and hied them to the lattice which they had used before, and peering out into the courtyard, saw the scholar dancing a hornpipe to the music that his own teeth made, a-chattering for extremity of cold; nor had they ever seen it footed so nimbly and at such a pace. Whereupon – 'How sayst thou, sweet my hope?' quoth the lady. 'Know I not how to make men dance without the aid of either trumpet or cornemuse?' 'Indeed thou dost, my heart's delight,' replied the lover. Quoth then the lady – 'I have a mind that we go down to the door. Thou wilt keep quiet, and I will speak to him, and we shall hear what he says, which, peradventure, we shall find no less diverting than the sight of him.'

So they stole softly out of the chamber and down to the door, which leaving fast closed, the lady set her lips to a little hole that was there, and with a low voice called the scholar, who, hearing her call him, praised God, making too sure that he was to be admitted, and being come to the door, said – 'Here am I, Madam; open for God's sake; let me in, for I die of cold.' 'Oh! ay,' replied the lady, 'I know thou hast a chill, and of course, there being a little snow about, 'tis mighty cold; but well I wot the nights are colder far at Paris. I cannot let thee in as yet, because my accursed brother, that came to sup here this evening, is still with me; but he will soon take himself off, and then I will let thee in without a moment's delay. I have but now with no small difficulty given him the slip, to come and give thee heart that the waiting irk thee not.' 'Nay but, Madam,' replied the scholar, 'for the love of God, I entreat you, let me in, that I may have a roof over my head, because for some time past there has been never so thick a fall of snow, and 'tis yet snowing; and then I will wait as long as you please.' 'Alas! sweet my love,' quoth the lady, 'that I may not, for this door makes such a din, when one opens it, that my brother would be sure to hear, were I to let thee in; but I will go tell him to get him gone, and so come back and admit thee.' 'Go at once, then,' returned the scholar, 'and prithee, see that a good fire be kindled, that, when I get in, I may warm myself, for I am now so chilled through and through that I have scarce any feeling left.' 'That can scarce be,' rejoined the lady, 'if it be true, what thou hast so protested in thy letters, that thou art all afire for love of me: 'tis plain to me now that thou didst but mock me. I now take my leave of thee: wait and be of good cheer.'

So the lady and her lover, who, to his immense delight, had heard all that passed, betook them to bed; however, little sleep had they that night, but spent the best part of it in disporting themselves and making merry over the unfortunate scholar, who, his teeth now chattering to such a tune that he seemed to have been metamorphosed into a stork, perceived that he had been befooled, and after making divers fruitless attempts to open the door and seeking means of egress to no better purpose, paced to and fro like a lion, cursing the villainous weather, the long night, his simplicity, and the perversity of the lady, against whom (the vehemence of his wrath suddenly converting the love he had so long borne her to bitter and remorseless enmity) he now plotted within himself divers and grand schemes of revenge, on which he was far more bent than ever he had been on forgathering with her.

Slowly the night wore away, and with the first streaks of dawn the maid, by her mistress's direction, came down, opened the door of the courtyard, and putting on a compassionate air, greeted Rinieri with –

'Foul fall him that came here yestereve; he has afflicted us with his presence all night long, and has kept thee a-freezing out here: but hark ye, take it not amiss; that which might not be tonight shall be another time: well wot I that nought could have befallen that my lady could so ill brook.' For all his wrath, the scholar, witting, like the wise man he was, that menaces serve but to put the menaced on his guard, kept pent within his breast that which unbridled resentment would have uttered, and said quietly, and without betraying the least trace of anger – 'In truth 'twas the worst night I ever spent, but I understood quite well that the lady was in no wise to blame, for that she herself, being moved to pity of me, came down here to make her excuses, and to comfort me; and, as thou sayst, what has not been tonight will be another time: wherefore commend me to her, and so, adieu!' Then, well-nigh paralysed for cold, he got him, as best he might, home, where, weary and fit to die for drowsiness, he threw himself on his bed, and fell into a deep sleep, from which he awoke to find that he had all but lost the use of his arms and legs. He therefore sent for some physicians, and having told them what a chill he had gotten, caused them have a care to his health. But, though they treated him with active and most drastic remedies, it cost them some time and no little trouble to restore to the cramped muscles their wonted pliancy, and, indeed, but for his youth and the milder weather that was at hand, 'twould have gone very hard with him.

However, recover he did his health and lustihood, and nursing his enmity, feigned to be vastly more enamoured of his widow than ever before. And so it was that after a while Fortune furnished him with an opportunity of satisfying his resentment, for the gallant of whom the widow was enamoured, utterly regardless of the love she bore him, grew enamoured of another lady, and was minded no more to pleasure the widow in aught either by word or by deed; wherefore she now pined in tears and bitterness of spirit. However, her maid, who commiserated her not a little, and knew not how to dispel the dumps that the loss of her lover had caused her, espying the scholar pass along the street, as he had been wont, conceived the silly idea that the lady's lover might be induced to return to his old love by some practice of a necromantic order, wherein she doubted not that the scholar must be a thorough adept; which idea she imparted to her mistress. The lady, being none too well furnished with sense, never thinking that, if the scholar had been an adept in necromancy, he would have made use of it in his own behoof, gave heed to what her maid said, and forthwith bade her learn of the scholar whether he would place his skill at her service, and assure him that, if he so did, she, in reward thereof, would do his pleasure. The maid did her mistress's errand well and faithfully. The scholar no sooner heard the message, than he said to himself – Praised be Thy name, O God, that the time is now come, when with Thy help I may be avenged upon this wicked woman of the wrong she did me in requital of the great love I bore her. Then, turning to the maid, he said – 'Tell my lady to set her mind at ease touching this matter; for that, were her lover in India, I would forthwith bring him hither to crave her pardon of that wherein he has offended her. As to the course she should take in the matter, I tarry but her pleasure to make it known to her, when and where she may think fit: tell her so, and bid her from me to be of good cheer.' The maid carried his answer to her mistress, and arranged that they should meet in the church of Santa Lucia of Prato. Thither accordingly they came, the lady and the scholar, and conversed apart, and the lady, quite oblivious of the ill-usage by which she had well-nigh done him to death, opened all her mind to him, and besought him, if he had any regard to her welfare, to aid her to the attainment of her desire. 'Madam,' replied the scholar, 'true it is that among other lore that I acquired at Paris was this of necromancy, whereof, indeed, I know all that may be known; but, as 'tis in the last degree displeasing to God, I had sworn never to practise it either for my own or for any other's behoof. 'Tis also true that the love I bear you is such that I know not how to refuse you aught that you would have me do for you; and so, were this single essay enough to consign me to hell, I would adventure it to pleasure you. But I mind me that 'tis a matter scarce so easy of performance as, perchance, you suppose, most especially when a woman would fain recover the love of a man, or a man that of a woman, for then it must be done by the postulant in proper person, and at night, and in lonely places, and unattended, so that it needs a stout heart; nor know I whether you are disposed to comply with these conditions.' The lady, too enamoured to be discreet, made answer – 'So shrewdly does Love goad me, that there is nought I would not do to bring him back to me who wrongfully has deserted me; but tell me, prithee, wherein it is that I have need of this stout heart.' 'Madam,' returned the despiteful scholar, ' 'twill be my part to fashion in tin an image of him you would fain lure back to you: and when I have sent you the image, 'twill be for you, when the moon is well on the wane, to dip yourself, being stark naked, and the image, seven times in a flowing stream, and this you must do quite alone about the hour of first sleep, and afterwards, still naked, you must get you upon some tree or some deserted house, and facing the North, with the image in your hand, say certain words that I shall give you in writing seven times; which, when you have done, there will come to you two damsels, the fairest you ever saw, who will greet you graciously, and ask of you what you would fain have; to whom you will disclose frankly and fully all that you crave; and see to it that you make no mistake in the name; and when you have said all, they will depart, and you may then descend and return to the spot where you left your clothes, and resume them, and go home. And rest assured, that before the ensuing midnight your lover will come to you in tears, and crave your pardon and mercy, and that thenceforth he will never again desert you for any other woman.'

The lady gave entire credence to the scholar's words, and deeming her lover as good as in her arms again, recovered half her wonted spirits: wherefore – 'Make no doubt,' quoth she 'that I shall do as thou biddest; and indeed I am most favoured by circumstance; for in upper Val d'Arno I have an estate adjoining the river, and 'tis now July, so that to bathe will be delightful. Ay, and now I mind me that at no great distance from the river there is a little tower, which is deserted, save that now and again the shepherds will get them up by the chestnut-wood ladder to the roof, thence to look out for their strayed sheep; 'tis a place lonely indeed, and quite out of ken; and when I have climbed it, as climb it I will, I doubt not 'twill be the best place in all the world to give effect to your instructions.'

Well pleased to be certified of the lady's intention, the scholar, to whom her estate and the tower were very well known, made answer – 'I was never in those parts, Madam, and therefore know neither your estate nor the tower, but, if 'tis as you say, 'twill certainly be the best place in the world for your purpose. So, when time shall serve, I will send you the image and the prayer. But I pray you, when you shall have your heart's desire, and know that I have done you good service, do not forget me, but keep your promise to me.' 'That will I without fail,' quoth the lady; and so she bade him farewell, and went home. The scholar, gleefully anticipating the success of his enterprise, fashioned an image, and inscribed it with certain magical signs, and wrote some gibberish by way of prayer, which in due time he sent to the lady, bidding her the very next night do as he had prescribed: and thereupon he hied him privily with one of his servants to the house of a friend hard by the tower, there to carry his purpose into effect. The lady, on her part, set out with her maid, and betook her to her estate, and, night being come, sent the maid to bed, as if she were minded to go to rest herself; and about the hour of first sleep stole out of the house and down to the tower, beside the Arno; and when, having carefully looked about her, she was satisfied that never a soul was to be seen or heard, she took off her clothes and hid them under a bush; then, with the image in her hand, she dipped herself seven times in the river; which done, she hied her with the image to the tower. The scholar, having at nightfall couched himself with his servant among the willows and other trees that fringed the bank, marked all that she did, and how, as she passed by him, the whiteness of her flesh dispelled the shades of night, and scanning attentively her bosom and every other part of her body, and finding them very fair, felt, as he bethought him what would shortly befall them, some pity of her; while, on the other hand, he was suddenly assailed by the solicitations of the flesh which caused that to stand which had been inert, and prompted him to sally forth of his ambush and take her by force, and have his pleasure of her. And, what with his compassion and passion, he was like to be worsted; but then, as he bethought him who he was, and what a grievous wrong had been done him, and for what cause, and by whom, his wrath, thus rekindled, got the better of the other affections, so that he swerved not from his resolve, but suffered her to go her way.

The lady ascended the tower, and standing with her face to the North, began to recite the scholar's prayer, while he, having stolen into the tower but a little behind her, cautiously shifted the ladder that led up to the roof on which the lady stood, and waited to observe what she would say and do. Seven times the lady said the prayer, and then awaited the appearance of the two damsels; and so long had she to wait – not to mention that the night was a good deal cooler than she would have liked – that she saw day break; whereupon, disconcerted that it had not fallen out as the scholar had promised, she said to herself – I misdoubt me he was minded to give me such a night as I gave him; but if such was his intent, he is but maladroit in his revenge, for this night is not as long by a third as his was, besides which, the cold is of another quality. And that day might not overtake her there, she began to think of descending, but, finding that the ladder was removed, she felt as if the world had come to nought beneath her feet, her senses reeled, and she fell in a swoon upon the floor of the roof. When she came to herself, she burst into tears and piteous lamentations, and witting now very well that 'twas the doing of the scholar, she began to repent her that she had first offended him, and then trusted him unduly, having such good cause to reckon upon his enmity; in which frame she abode long time. Then, searching if haply she might find some means of descent, and finding none, she fell a-weeping again, and bitterly to herself she said – Alas for thee, wretched woman! what will thy brothers, thy kinsmen, thy neighbours, nay, what will all Florence say of thee, when 'tis known that thou hast been found here naked? Thy honour, hitherto unsuspect, will be known to have been but a show, and shouldst thou seek thy defence in lying excuses, if any such may be fashioned, the accursed scholar, who knows all thy doings, will not suffer it. Ah! poor wretch! that at one and the same time hast lost thy too dearly cherished gallant and thine own honour! And therewith she was taken with such a transport of grief, that she was like to cast herself from the tower to the ground. Then, bethinking her that if she might espy some lad making towards the tower with his sheep, she might send him for her maid, for the sun was now risen, she approached one of the parapets of the tower, and looked out, and so it befell that the scholar, awakening from a slumber, in which he had lain a while at the foot of a bush, espied her, and she him. Whereupon – 'Good-day, Madam,' quoth he: 'are the damsels yet come?' The lady saw and heard him not without bursting afresh into a flood of tears, and besought him to come into the tower, that she might speak with him: a request which the scholar very courteously granted. The lady then threw herself prone on the floor of the roof; and, only her head being visible through the aperture, thus through her sobs she spoke – 'Verily, Rinieri, if I gave thee a bad night, thou art well avenged on me, for, though it be July, meseemed I was sore a-cold last night, standing here with never a thread upon me, and, besides, I have so bitterly bewept both the trick I played thee and my own folly in trusting thee, that I marvel that I have still eyes in my head. Wherefore I implore thee, not for love of me, whom thou hast no cause to love, but for the respect thou hast for thyself as a gentleman, that thou let that which thou hast already done suffice thee to avenge the wrong I did thee, and bring me my clothes, that I may be able to get me down from here, and spare to take from me that which, however thou mightst hereafter wish, thou couldst not restore to me, to wit, my honour; whereas, if I deprived thee of that one night with me, 'tis in my power to give thee many another night in recompense thereof, and thou hast but to choose thine own times. Let this, then, suffice, and like a worthy gentleman be satisfied to have taken thy revenge, and to have let me know it: put not forth thy might against a woman: 'tis no glory to the eagle to have vanquished a dove; wherefore for God's and thine own honour's sake have mercy on me.'

The scholar, albeit his haughty spirit still brooded on her evil entreatment of him, yet saw her not weep and supplicate without a certain compunction mingling with his exultation; but vengeance he had desired above all things, to have wreaked it was indeed sweet, and albeit his humanity prompted him to have compassion on the hapless woman, yet it availed not to subdue the fierceness of his resentment; wherefore thus he made answer – 'Madam Elena, had my prayers (albeit art I had none to mingle with them tears and honeyed words as thou dost with thine) inclined thee that night, when I stood perishing with cold amid the snow that filled thy courtyard, to accord me the very least shelter, 'twere but a light matter for me to hearken now to thine; but, if thou art now so much more careful of thy honour than thou wast wont to be, and it irks thee to tarry there naked, address thy prayers to him in whose arms it irked thee not naked to pass that night thou mindest thee of, albeit thou wist that I with hasty foot was beating time upon the snow in thy courtyard to the accompaniment of chattering teeth: 'tis he that thou shouldst call to succour thee, to fetch thy clothes, to adjust the ladder for thy descent; 'tis he in whom thou shouldst labour to inspire this tenderness thou now showest for thy honour, that honour which for his sake thou hast not scrupled to jeopardise both now and on a thousand other occasions. Why, then, call'st thou not him to come to thy succour? To whom pertains it rather than to him? Thou art his. And of whom will he have a care, whom will he succour, if not thee? Thou askedst him that night, when thou wast wantoning with him, whether seemed to him the greater, my folly or the love thou didst bear him: call him now, foolish woman, and see if the love thou bearest him, and thy wit and his, may avail to deliver thee from my folly. 'Tis now no longer in thy power to show me courtesy of that which I no more desire, nor yet to refuse it, did I desire it. Reserve thy nights for thy lover, if so be thou go hence alive. Be they all thine and his. One of them was more than I cared for; 'tis enough for me to have been flouted once. Ay, and by thy cunning of speech thou strivest might and main to conciliate my goodwill, calling me worthy gentleman, by which insinuation thou wouldst fain induce me magnanimously to desist from further chastisement of thy baseness. But thy cajoleries shall not now cloud the eyes of my mind, as did once thy false promises. I know myself, and better now for thy one night's instruction than for all the time I spent at Paris. But, granted that I were disposed to be magnanimous, thou art not of those to whom 'tis meet to show magnanimity. A wild beast such as thou, having merited vengeance, can claim no relief from suffering save death, though in the case of a human being 'twould suffice to temper vengeance with mercy, as thou saidst. Wherefore I, albeit no eagle, witting thee to be no dove, but a venomous serpent, mankind's most ancient enemy, am minded, bating no jot of malice or of might, to harry thee to the bitter end: nevertheless this which I do is not properly to be called vengeance but rather just retribution; seeing that vengeance should be in excess of the offence, and this my chastisement of thee will fall short of it; for, were I minded to be avenged on thee, considering what account thou madest of my heart and soul, 'twould not suffice me to take thy life, no, nor the lives of a hundred others such as thee; for I should but slay a vile and base and wicked woman. And what the Devil art thou more than any other pitiful baggage, that I should spare thy little store of beauty, which a few years will ruin, covering thy face with wrinkles? And yet 'twas not for want of will that thou didst fail to do to death a worthy gentleman, as thou but now didst call me, of whom in a single day of his life the world may well have more profit than of a hundred thousand like thee while the world shall last. Wherefore by this rude discipline I will teach thee what it is to flout men of spirit, and more especially what it is to flout scholars, that if thou escape with thy life thou mayst have good cause ever hereafter to shun such folly. But if thou art so fain to make the descent, why cast not thyself down, whereby, God helping, thou wouldst at once break thy neck, be quit of the torment thou endurest, and make me the happiest man alive? I have no more to say to thee. 'Twas my art and craft thus caused thee climb; be it thine to find the way down: thou hadst cunning enough, when thou wast minded to flout me.'

While the scholar thus spoke, the hapless lady wept incessantly, and before he had done, to aggravate her misery, the sun was high in the heaven. However, when he was silent, thus she made answer – 'Ah! ruthless man, if that accursed night has so rankled with thee, and thou deemest my fault so grave that neither my youth and beauty, nor my bitter tears, nor yet my humble supplications may move thee to pity, let this at least move thee, and abate somewhat of thy remorseless severity, that 'twas my act alone, in that of late I trusted thee, and discovered to thee all my secret, that did open the way to compass thy end, and make me cognisant of my guilt, seeing that, had I not confided in thee, on no wise mightst thou have been avenged on me; which thou wouldst seem so ardently to have desired. Turn thee, then, turn thee, I pray thee, from thy wrath, and pardon me. So thou wilt pardon me, and get me down hence, right gladly will I give up for ever my faithless gallant, and thou shalt be my sole lover and lord, albeit thou sayst hard things of my beauty, slight and short-lived as thou wouldst have it to be, which, however it may compare with others, is, I wot, to be prized, if for no other reason, yet for this, that 'tis the admiration and solace and delight of young men, and thou art not yet old. And albeit I have been harshly treated by thee, yet believe I cannot that thou wouldst have me do myself so shamefully to death as to cast me down, like some abandoned wretch, before thine eyes, in which, unless thou wast then, as thou hast since shown thyself, a liar, I found such favour. Ah! have pity on me for God's and mercy's sake! The sun waxes exceeding hot, and having suffered not a little by the cold of last night, I now begin to be sorely afflicted by the heat.'

'Madam,' rejoined the scholar, who held her in parley with no small delight, ' 'twas not for any love that thou didst bear me that thou trustedst me, but that thou mightst recover that which thou hadst lost, for which cause thou meritest but the greater punishment; and foolish indeed art thou if thou supposest that such was the sole means available for my revenge. I had a thousand others, and, while I feigned to love thee, I had laid a thousand gins for thy feet, into one or other of which in no long time, though this had not occurred, thou must needs have fallen, and that too to thy more grievous suffering and shame; nor was it to spare thee, but that I might be the sooner rejoiced by thy discomfiture that I took my present course. And though all other means had failed me, I had still the pen, with which I would have written of thee such matters and in such a sort, that when thou wist them, as thou shouldst have done, thou wouldst have regretted a thousand times that thou hadst ever been born. The might of the pen is greater far than they suppose, who have not proved it by experience. By God I swear, so may He, who has prospered me thus far in this my revenge, prosper me to the end! that I would have written of thee things that would have so shamed thee in thine own – not to speak of others' – sight that thou hadst put out thine eyes that thou mightst no more see thyself; wherefore chide not the sea, for that it has sent forth a tiny rivulet. For thy love, or whether thou be mine or no, nought care I. Be thou still his, whose thou hast been, if thou canst. Hate him as I once did, I now love him, by reason of his present entreatment of thee. Ye go getting you enamoured, ye women, and nought will satisfy you but young gallants, because ye mark that their flesh is ruddier, and their beards are blacker, than other folk's, and that they carry themselves well, and foot it featly in the dance, and joust; but those that are now more mature were even as they, and possess a knowledge which they have yet to acquire. And therewithal ye deem that they ride better, and cover more miles in a day, than men of riper age. Now that they dust the pelisse with more vigour I certainly allow, but their seniors, being more experienced, know better the places where the fleas lurk; and spare and dainty diet is preferable to abundance without savour: moreover hard trotting will gall and jade even the youngest, whereas an easy pace, though it bring one somewhat later to the inn, at any rate brings one thither fresh. Ye discern not, witless creatures that ye are, how much of evil this little show of bravery serves to hide. Your young gallant is never content with one woman, but lusts after as many as he sets eyes on; nor is there any but he deems himself worthy of her: wherefore 'tis not possible that their love should be lasting, as thou hast but now proved and mayst only too truly witness. Moreover to be worshipped, to be caressed by their ladies they deem but their due; nor is there aught whereon they plume and boast them so proudly as their conquests: which impertinence has caused not a few women to surrender to the friars, who keep their own counsel. Peradventure thou wilt say that never a soul save thy maid and I wist aught of thy loves; but, if so, thou hast been misinformed, and if thou so believest, thou dost misbelieve. Scarce aught else is talked of either in his quarter or in thine; but most often 'tis those most concerned whose ears such matters reach last. Moreover, they rob you, these young gallants, whereas the others make you presents. So, then, having made a bad choice, be thou still his to whom thou hast given thyself, and leave me, whom thou didst flout, to another, for I have found a lady of much greater charms than thine, and that has understood me better than thou didst. And that thou mayst get thee to the other world better certified of the desire of my eyes than thou wouldst seem to be here by my words, delay no more, but cast thyself down, whereby thy soul, taken forthwith, as I doubt not she will be, into the embrace of the Devil, may see whether thy headlong fall afflicts mine eyes, or no. But, for that I doubt thou meanest not thus to gladden me, I bid thee, if thou findest the sun begin to scorch thee, remember the cold thou didst cause me to endure, wherewith, by admixture, thou mayst readily temper the sun's heat.'

The hapless lady, seeing that the scholar's words were ever to the same ruthless effect, burst afresh into tears, and said – 'Lo, now, since nought that pertains to me may move thee, be thou at least moved by the love thou bearest this lady of whom thou speakest, who, thou sayst, is wiser than I, and loves thee, and for love of her pardon me, and fetch me my clothes, that I may resume them, and get me down hence.' Whereat the scholar fell a-laughing, and seeing that 'twas not a little past tierce, made answer – 'Lo, now, I know not how to deny thee, adjuring me as thou dost by such a lady: tell me, then, where thy clothes are, and I will go fetch them, and bring thee down.' The lady, believing him, was somewhat comforted, and told him where she had laid her clothes. The scholar then quitted the tower, bidding his servant on no account to stir from his post, but to keep close by, and, as best he might, bar the tower against all comers until his return: which said, he betook him to the house of his friend, where he breakfasted much at his ease, and thereafter went to sleep. Left alone upon the tower, the lady, somewhat cheered by her fond hope, but still exceeding sorrowful, drew nigh to a part of the wall where there was a little shade, and there sat down to wait. And now lost in most melancholy brooding, now dissolved in tears, now plunged in despair of ever seeing the scholar return with her clothes, but never more than a brief while in any one mood, spent with grief and the night's vigil, she by and by fell asleep. The sun was now in the zenith, and smote with extreme fervour full and unmitigated upon her tender and delicate frame, and upon her bare head, insomuch that his rays did not only scorch but bit by bit excoriate every part of her flesh that was exposed to them, and so shrewdly burn her that, albeit she was in a deep sleep, the pain awoke her. And as by reason thereof she writhed a little, she felt the scorched skin part in sunder and shed itself, as will happen when one tugs at a parchment that has been singed by the fire, while her head ached so sore that it seemed like to split, and no wonder. Nor might she find place either to lie or to stand on the floor of the roof, but ever went to and fro, weeping. Besides which there stirred not the least breath of wind, and flies and gadflies did swarm in prodigious quantity, which, settling upon her excoriate flesh, stung her so shrewdly that 'twas as if she received so many stabs with a javelin, and she was ever restlessly feeling her sores with her hands, and cursing herself, her life, her lover, and the scholar.

Thus by the exorbitant heat of the sun, by the flies and gadflies, harassed, goaded, and lacerated, tormented also by hunger, and yet more by thirst, and thereto by a thousand distressful thoughts, she planted herself erect on her feet, and looked about her, if haply she might see or hear anyone, with intent, come what might, to call to him and crave his succour. But even this hostile Fortune had disallowed her. The husbandmen were all gone from the fields by reason of the heat, and indeed there had come none to work that day in the neighbourhood of the tower, for that all were employed in threshing their corn beside their cottages: wherefore she heard but the cicalas, while Arno, tantalising her with the sight of his waters, increased rather than diminished her thirst. Ay, and in like manner, wherever she espied a copse, or a patch of shade, or a house, 'twas a torment to her, for the longing she had for it. What more is to be said of this hapless woman? Only this: that what with the heat of the sun above and the floor beneath her, and the scarification of her flesh in every part by the flies and gadflies, that flesh, which in the night had dispelled the gloom by its whiteness, was now become red as madder, and so besprent with clots of blood, that whoso had seen her would have deemed her the most hideous object in the world.

Thus resourceless and hopeless, she passed the long hours, expecting death rather than aught else, until half noon was come and gone; when, his siesta ended, the scholar bethought him of his lady, and being minded to see how she fared, hied him back to the tower, and sent his servant away to break his fast. As soon as the lady espied him, she came, spent and crushed by her sore affliction, to the aperture, and thus addressed him – 'Rinieri, the cup of thy vengeance is full to overflowing: for if I gave thee a night of freezing in my courtyard, thou hast given me upon this tower a day of scorching, nay, of burning, and therewithal of perishing of hunger and thirst: wherefore, by God I entreat thee to come up hither, and as my heart fails me to take my life, take it thou, for 'tis death I desire of all things, such and so grievous is my suffering. But if this grace thou wilt not grant, at least bring me a cup of water wherewith to lave my mouth, for which my tears do not suffice, so parched and torrid is it within.' Well wist the scholar by her voice how spent she was; he also saw a part of her body burned through and through by the sun; whereby, and by reason of the lowliness of her entreaties, he felt some little pity for her; but all the same he made answer – 'Nay, wicked woman, 'tis not by my hands thou shalt die; thou canst die by thine own whenever thou art so minded; and to temper thy heat thou shalt have just as much water from me as I had fire from thee to mitigate my cold. I only regret that for the cure of my chill the physicians were fain to use foul-smelling muck, whereas thy burns can be treated with fragrant rose-water; and that, whereas I was like to lose my muscles and the use of my limbs, thou, for all thy excoriation by the heat, wilt yet be fair again, like a snake that has sloughed off the old skin.' 'Alas! woe's me!' replied the lady, 'for charms acquired at such a cost, God grant them to those that hate me. But thou, most fell of all wild beasts, how hast thou borne thus to torture me? What more had I to expect of thee or any other, had I done all thy kith and kin to death with direst torments? Verily, I know not what more cruel suffering thou couldst have inflicted on a traitor that had put a whole city to the slaughter than this which thou hast allotted to me, to be thus roasted, and devoured of the flies, and therewithal to refuse me even a cup of water, though the very murderers condemned to death by the law, as they go to execution, not seldom are allowed wine to drink, so they but ask it. Lo now, I see that thou art inexorable in thy ruthlessness, and on no wise to be moved by my suffering: wherefore with resignation I will compose me to await death, that God may have mercy on my soul. And may this that thou doest escape not the searching glance of His just eyes.' Which said, she dragged herself, sore suffering, toward the middle of the floor, despairing of ever escaping from her fiery torment, besides which, not once only, but a thousand times she thought to choke for thirst, and ever she wept bitterly and bewailed her evil fate. But at length the day wore to vespers, and the scholar, being sated with his revenge, caused his servant to take her clothes and wrap them in his cloak, and hied them with the servant to the hapless lady's house, where, finding her maid sitting disconsolate and woebegone and resourceless at the door – 'Good woman,' quoth he, 'what has befallen thy mistress?' Whereto – 'Sir, I know not,' replied the maid. 'I looked to find her this morning abed, for methought she went to bed last night, but neither there nor anywhere else could I find her, nor know I what is become of here; wherefore exceeding great is my distress; but have you, Sir, nought to say of the matter?' 'Only this,' returned the scholar, 'that I would I had had thee with her there where I have had her, that I might have requited thee of thy offence, even as I have requited her of hers. But be assured that thou shalt not escape my hands, until thou hast from me such a wage of thy labour that thou shalt never flout man more, but thou shalt mind thee of me.' Then, turning to his servant, he said – 'Give her these clothes, and tell her she may go bring her mistress away, if she will.' The servant did his bidding; and the maid, what with the message and her recognition of the clothes, was mighty afraid, lest they had slain the lady, and scarce suppressing a shriek, took the clothes, and bursting into tears, set off, as soon as the scholar was gone, at a run for the tower.

Now one of the lady's husbandmen had had the misfortune to lose two of his hogs that day and, seeking them, came to the tower not long after the scholar had gone thence, and peering about all quarters, if haply he might have sight of his hogs, heard the woeful lamentation that the hapless lady made, and got him up into the tower, and called out as loud as he might – 'Who wails up there?' The lady recognised her husbandman's voice, and called him by name saying – 'Prithee, go fetch my maid, and cause her come hither to me.' The husbandman, knowing her by voice, replied – 'Alas! Madam, who set you there? Your maid has been seeking you all day long: but who would ever have supposed that you were there?' Whereupon he took the props of the ladder, and set them in position, and proceeded to secure the rounds to them with withies. Thus engaged he was found by the maid, who, as she entered the tower, beat her face and breast, and unable longer to keep silence, cried out – 'Alas, sweet my lady, where are you?' Whereto the lady made answer as loud as she might – 'O my sister, here above am I, weep not, but fetch me my clothes forthwith,' Wellnigh restored to heart, to hear her mistress's voice, the maid, assisted by the husbandman, ascended the ladder, which he had now all but set in order, and gaining the roof, and seeing her lady lie there naked, spent and fordone, and liker to a half-burned stump than to a human being, she planted her nails in her face and fell a-weeping over her, as if she were a corpse. However, the lady bade her for God's sake be silent, and help her to dress, and having learned from her that none knew where she had been, save those that had brought her her clothes and the husbandman that was there present, was somewhat consoled, and besought her for God's sake to say nought of the matter to any. Thus long time they conversed, and then the husbandman took the lady on his shoulders, for walk she could not, and bore her safely out of the tower. The unfortunate maid, following after with somewhat less caution, slipped, and falling from the ladder to the ground, broke her thigh, and roared for pain like any lion. So the husbandman set the lady down upon a grassy mead, while he went to see what had befallen the maid, whom, finding her thigh broken, he brought, and laid beside the lady: who, seeing her woes completed by this last misfortune, and that she of whom, most of all, she had expected succour, was lamed of a thigh, was distressed beyond measure, and wept again so piteously that not only was the husbandman powerless to comfort her, but was himself fain to weep. However, as the sun was now low, that they might not be there surprised by night, he, with the disconsolate lady's approval, hied him home, and called to his aid two of his brothers and his wife, who returned with him, bearing a plank, whereon they laid the maid, and so they carried her to the lady's house. There, by dint of cold water and words of cheer, they restored some heart to the lady, whom the husbandman then took upon his shoulders, and bore to her chamber. The husbandman's wife fed her with sops of bread, and then undressed her, and put her to bed. They also provided the means to carry her and the maid to Florence; and so 'twas done. There the lady, who was very fertile in artifices, invented an entirely fictitious story of what had happened as well in regard of her maid as of herself, whereby she persuaded both her brothers and her sisters and everyone else, that 'twas all due to the enchantments of evil spirits. The physicians lost no time, and, albeit the lady's suffering and mortification were extreme, for she left more than one skin sticking to the sheets, they cured her of a high fever, and certain attendant maladies; as also the maid of her fractured thigh. The end of all which was that the lady forgot her lover, and having learned discretion, was thenceforth careful neither to love nor to flout; and the scholar, learning that the maid had broken her thigh, deemed his vengeance complete, and was satisfied to say never a word more of the affair. Such then were the consequences of her flouts to this foolish young woman, who deemed that she might trifle with a scholar with the like impunity as with others, not duly understanding that they – I say not all, but the more part – know where the Devil keeps his tail.* Wherefore, my ladies, have a care how you flout men, and more especially scholars.

* i.e. are a match for the Devil himself in cunning.

39

The eighth story of the eighth day, in which two men keep with one another; the one lies with the other's wife; the other, being ware thereof, manages with the aid of his wife to have the one locked in a chest, upon which he then lies with the wife of him that is locked therein.

Grievous and distressful was it to the ladies to hear how it fared with Elena; but as they accounted the retribution in a measure righteous, they were satisfied to expend upon her but a moderate degree of compassion, albeit they censured the scholar as severe, intemperately relentless, and indeed ruthless, in his vengeance. However, Pampinea having brought the story to a close, the queen bade Fiammetta follow suit; and prompt to obey, Fiammetta thus spoke: Debonair my ladies, as, methinks, your feelings must have been somewhat harrowed by the severity of the resentful scholar, I deem it meet to soothe your vexed spirits with something of a more cheerful order. Wherefore I am minded to tell you a little story of a young man who bore an affront in a milder temper, and avenged himself with more moderation. Whereby you may understand that one should be satisfied if the ass and the wall are quits, nor by indulging a vindictive spirit to excess turn the requital of a wrong into an occasion of wrong-doing –

You are to know then that at Sienna, as I have heard tell, there dwelt two young men of good substance, and, for plebeians, of good family, the one Spinelloccio Tanena, the other Zeppa di Mino by name; who, their houses being contiguous in the Camollia,* kept ever together

* A suburb of Sienna.

and, by what appeared, loved each other as brothers, or even more so, and had each a very fine woman to wife. Now it so befell that Spinelloccio, being much in Zeppa's house, as well when Zeppa was not, as when he was there, grew so familiar with Zeppa's wife that he sometimes lay with her; and on this wise they continued to forgather a great while before anyone was ware of it. However, one of these days Zeppa being at home, though the lady wist it not, Spinelloccio came in quest of him; and, the lady sending word that he was not at home, he forthwith went upstairs and found the lady in the saloon, and seeing none else there, kissed her, as did she him.

Zeppa saw all that passed, but said nothing and kept close, being minded to see how the game would end, and soon saw his wife and Spinelloccio, still in one another's arms, hie them to her chamber and lock themselves in: whereat he was mightily incensed. But, witting that to make a noise, or do aught else overt, would not lessen but rather increase his dishonour, he cast about how he might be avenged on such wise that, without the affair getting wind, he might content his soul; and, having after long pondering, hit, as he thought, upon the expedient, he budged not from his retreat, until Spinelloccio had parted from the lady. Whereupon he hied him into the chamber, and there finding the lady with her head-gear, which Spinelloccio in toying with her had disarranged, scarce yet readjusted – 'Madam, what dost thou?' quoth he. Whereto – 'Why, dost not see?' returned the lady. 'Troth do I,' rejoined he, 'and somewhat else have I seen that I would I had not.' And so he questioned her of what had passed, and she, being mightily afraid, did after long parley confess that which she might not plausibly deny, to wit, her intimacy with Spinelloccio, and fell a-beseeching him with tears to pardon her. 'Lo, now, wife,' quoth Zeppa, 'thou hast done wrong, and, so thou wouldst have me pardon thee, have a care to do exactly as I shall bid thee; to wit, on this wise: thou must tell Spinelloccio to find some occasion to part from me tomorrow morning about tierce, and come hither to thee; and while he is here I will come back, and when thou hearest me coming, thou wilt get him into this chest, and lock him in there; which when thou hast done, I will tell thee what else thou hast to do, which thou mayst do without the least misgiving, for I promise thee I will do him no harm.' The lady, to content him, promised to do as he bade, and she kept her word.

The morrow came, and Zeppa and Spinelloccio being together about tierce, Spinelloccio, having promised the lady to come to see her at that hour, said to Zeppa – 'I must breakfast with a friend, whom I had lief not keep in waiting; therefore, adieu!' 'Nay, but,' quoth Zeppa, ' 'tis not yet breakfast-time.' 'No matter,' returned Spinelloccio, 'I have business on which I must speak with him; so I must be in good time.' Whereupon Spinelloccio took his leave of Zeppa, and having reached Zeppa's house by a slightly circuitous route, and finding his wife there was taken by her into the chamber, where they had not been long together when Zeppa returned. Hearing him come, the lady, feigning no small alarm, bundled Spinelloccio into the chest, as her husband had bidden her, and having locked him in, left him there. As Zeppa came upstairs – 'Wife,' quoth he, 'is it breakfast time?' 'Ay, husband, 'tis so,' replied the lady. Whereupon – 'Spinelloccio is gone to breakfast with a friend today,' quoth Zeppa, 'leaving his wife at home: get thee to the window, and call her, and bid her come and breakfast with us.' The lady, whose fear for herself made her mighty obedient, did as her husband bade her; and after much pressing Spinelloccio's wife came to breakfast with them, though she was given to understand that her husband would not be of the company. So, she being come, Zeppa received her most affectionately, and taking her familiarly by the hand, bade his wife, in an undertone, get her to the kitchen; he then led Spinelloccio's wife into the chamber, and locked the door. Hearing the key turn in the lock – 'Alas!' quoth the lady, 'what means this, Zeppa? Is't for this you have brought me here? Is this the love you bear Spinelloccio? Is this your loyalty to him as your friend and comrade?' By the time she had done speaking, Zeppa, still keeping fast hold of her, was beside the chest, in which her husband was locked. Wherefore – 'Madam,' quoth he, 'spare me thy reproaches, until thou hast heard what I have to say to thee. I have loved, I yet love, Spinelloccio as a brother; and yesterday, though he knew it not, I discovered that the trust I reposed in him has for its reward that he lies with my wife, as with thee. Now, for that I love him, I purpose not to be avenged upon him save in the sort in which he offended. He has had my wife, and I intend to have thee. So thou wilt not grant me what I crave of thee, be sure I shall not fail to take it; and having no mind to let this affront pass unavenged, will make such play with him that neither thou nor he shall ever be happy again.' The lady hearkening, and by dint of his repeated asseverations coming at length to believe him – 'Zeppa mine,' quoth she, 'as this thy vengeance is to light upon me, well content am I; so only thou let not this which we are to do embroil me with thy wife, with whom, notwithstanding the evil turn she has done me, I am minded to remain at peace.' 'Have no fear on that score,' replied Zeppa; 'nay, I will give thee into the bargain a jewel so rare and fair that thou hast not the like.' Which said, he took her in his arms and fell a-kissing her, and having laid her on the chest, in which her husband was safe under lock and key, did there disport himself with her to his heart's content, as she with him.

Spinelloccio in the chest heard all that Zeppa had said, and how he was answered by the lady, and the Trevisan dance that afterwards went on over his head; whereat his mortification was such that for a great while he scarce hoped to live through it; and, but for the fear he had of Zeppa, he would have given his wife a sound rating, close prisoner though he was. But, as he bethought him that 'twas he that had given the first affront, and that Zeppa had good cause for acting as he did, and that he had dealt with him considerately and as a good fellow should, he resolved that if it were agreeable to Zeppa, they should be faster friends than ever before. However, Zeppa, having had his pleasure with the lady, got down from the chest, and being reminded by the lady of his promise of the jewel, opened the door of the chamber and brought his wife in. Quoth she with a laugh – 'Madam, you have given me tit for tat,' and never a word more. Whereupon – 'Open the chest,' quoth Zeppa; and she obeying, he showed the lady her Spinelloccio lying therein. 'Twould be hard to say whether of the twain was the more shame-stricken, Spinelloccio to be confronted with Zeppa, knowing that Zeppa wist what he had done, or the lady to meet her husband's eyes, knowing that he had heard what went on above his head. 'Lo, here is the jewel I give thee,' quoth Zeppa to her, pointing to Spinelloccio, who, as he came forth of the chest, blurted out – 'Zeppa, we are quits, and so 'twere best, as thou saidst a while ago to my wife, that we still be friends as we were wont, and as we had nought separate, save our wives, that henceforth we have them also in common.' 'Content,' quoth Zeppa; and so in perfect peace and accord they all four breakfasted together. And thenceforth each of the ladies had two husbands, and each of the husbands two wives; nor was there ever the least dispute or contention between them on that score.

◆ 40 ◆

The second story of the ninth day, in which an abbess rises in haste and in the dark, with intent to surprise an accused nun abed with her lover; thinking to put on her veil, she puts on instead the breeches of a priest that she has with her; the nun, espying her headgear, and doing her to wit thereof, is acquitted, and thenceforth finds it easier to forgather with her lover.

The first story being ended the queen turned to Elisa and with a charming air – 'Now, Elisa, follow,' quoth she: whereupon Elisa began on this wise: ◆ Dearest ladies, 'twas cleverly done of Madonna Francesca to disembarrass herself in the way we have heard: but I have to tell of a young nun who by a happy retort and the favour of Fortune delivered herself from imminent peril. And as you know that there are not a few most foolish folk who, notwithstanding their folly, take upon themselves the governance and correction of others; so you may learn from my story that Fortune at times justly puts them to shame; which befell the abbess, who was the superior of the nun of whom I am about to speak –

You are to know then that in a convent in Lombardy of very great repute for strict and holy living there was, among other ladies that there wore the veil, a young woman of noble family and extraordinary beauty. Now Isabetta – for such was her name – having speech one day of one of her kinsmen at the grate, became enamoured of a fine young gallant that was with him; who, seeing her to be very fair and reading her passion in her eyes, was kindled with a like flame for her: which mutual and unsolaced love they bore a great while not without great suffering to both. But at length, both being intent thereon, the gallant discovered a way by which he might with all secrecy visit his nun; and she approving, he paid her not one visit only, but many, to their no small mutual solace. But, while thus they continued their intercourse, it so befell that one night one of the sisters observed him take his leave of Isabetta and depart, albeit neither he nor she was ware that they had thus been discovered. The sister imparted what she had seen to several others. At first they were minded to denounce her to the abbess, one Madonna Usimbalda, who was reputed by the nuns, and indeed by all that knew her, to be a good and holy woman; but on second thoughts they deemed it expedient, that there might be no room for denial, to cause the abbess to take her and the gallant in the act. So they held their peace, and arranged between them to keep her in watch and close espial, that they might catch her unawares. Of which practice Isabetta recking, witting nought, it so befell that one night, when she had her lover to see her, the sisters that were on the watch were soon ware of it, and at what they deemed the nick of time parted into two companies, of which one mounted guard at the threshold of Isabetta's cell, while the other hasted to the abbess's chamber, and knocking at the door, roused her, and as soon as they heard her voice, said – 'Up, Madam, without delay: we have discovered that Isabetta has a young man with her in her cell.'

Now that night the abbess had with her a priest whom she used not seldom to have conveyed to her in a chest; and the report of the sisters making her apprehensive lest for excess of zeal and hurry they should force the door open, she rose in a trice; and huddling on her clothes as best she might in the dark, instead of the veil that they wear, which they call the psalter, she caught up the priest's breeches, and having clapped them on her head, hied her forth, and locked the door behind her, saying – 'Where is this woman accursed of God?' And so, guided by the sisters, all so agog to catch Isabetta a-sinning that they perceived not what manner of headgear the abbess wore, she made her way to the cell, and with their aid broke open the door; and entering they found the two lovers abed in one another's arms; who, as it were, thunder-struck to be thus surprised, lay there, witting not what to do. The sisters took the young nun forthwith, and by command of the abbess brought her to the chapter-house. The gallant, left behind in the cell, put on his clothes and waited to see how the affair would end, being minded to make as many nuns as he might come at pay dearly for any despite that might be done his mistress, and to bring her off with him. The abbess, seated in the chapter-house with all her nuns about her, and all eyes bent upon the culprit, began giving her the severest reprimand that ever woman got, for that by her disgraceful and abominable conduct should it get wind, she had sullied the fair fame of the convent; whereto she added menaces most dire. Shamefast and timorous, the culprit essayed no defence, and her silence begat pity of her in the rest; but, while the abbess waxed more and more voluble, it chanced that the girl raised her head and espied the abbess's headgear, and the points that hung down on this side and that. The significance whereof being by no means lost upon her, she quite plucked up heart, and – 'Madam,' quoth she, 'so help you God, tie up your coif, and then you may say what you will to me.' Whereto the abbess, not understanding her, replied: – 'What coif, lewd woman? So thou hast the effrontery to jest! Think'st thou that what thou hast done is a matter meet for jests?' Whereupon – 'Madam,' quoth the girl again, 'I pray you, tie up your coif, and then you may say to me whatever you please.' Which occasioned not a few of the nuns to look up at the abbess's head, and the abbess herself to raise her hands thereto, and so she and they at one and the same time apprehended Isabetta's meaning. Wherefore the abbess, finding herself detected by all in the same sin, and that no disguise was possible, changed her tone, and held quite another sort of language than before, the upshot of which was that 'twas impossible to withstand the assaults of the flesh, and that, accordingly, observing due secrecy as theretofore, all might give themselves a good time, as they had opportunity. So, having dismissed Isabetta to rejoin her lover in her cell, she herself returned to lie with her priest. And many a time thereafter, in spite of the envious, Isabetta had her gallant to see her, the others, that lacked lovers, doing in secret the best they might to push their fortunes.

41

The third story of the ninth day, in which Master Simone, at the instance of Bruno and Buffalmacco and Nello, makes Calandrino believe that he is with child. Calandrino, accordingly, gives them capons and money for medicines, and is cured without being delivered.

When Elisa had ended her story and all had given thanks to God that He had vouchsafed the young nun a happy escape from the fangs of her envious companions, the queen bade Filostrato follow suit; and without expecting a second command, thus Filostrato began: Fairest my ladies, the uncouth judge from the Marches, of whom I told you yesterday, took from the tip of my tongue a story of Calandrino which I was on the point of narrating: and as nought can be said of him without mightily enhancing our jollity, albeit not a little has already been said touching him and his comrades, I will now give you the story which I had meant yesterday to give you –

Who they were, this Calandrino and the others that I am to tell of in this story, has already been sufficiently explained; wherefore, without more ado, I say that one of Calandrino's aunts having died, leaving him two hundred pounds in petty cash, Calandrino gave out that he was minded to purchase an estate, and, as if he had had ten thousand florins of gold to invest, engaged every broker in Florence to treat for him, the negotiation always falling through, as soon as the price was named. Bruno and Buffalmacco, knowing what was afoot, told him again and again that he had better give himself a jolly time with them than go about buying earth as if he must needs make pellets;* but so far were

* i.e. bolts of clay for the crossbow.

they from effecting their purpose, that they could not even prevail upon him to give them a single meal. Whereat as one day they grumbled, being joined by a comrade of theirs, one Nello, also a painter, they all three took counsel how they might wet their whistle at Calandrino's expense; and, their plan being soon concerted, the next morning Calandrino was scarce gone out, when Nello met him, saying: – 'Good-day, Calandrino:' whereto Calandrino replied – 'God give thee a good-day and a good year.' Nello then drew back a little, and looked him steadily in the face, until – 'What seest thou to stare at?' quoth Calandrino. 'Hadst thou no pain in the night?' returned Nello; 'thou seemest not thyself to me.' Which Calandrino no sooner heard, than he began to be disquieted, and – 'Alas! How sayst thou?' quoth he. 'What tak'st thou to be the matter with me?' 'Why, as to that I have nothing to say,' returned Nello; 'but thou seemest to be quite changed: perchance 'tis not what I suppose;' and with that he left him.

Calandrino, anxious, though he could not in the least have said why, went on; and soon Buffalmacco, who was not far off, and had observed him part from Nello, made up to him, and greeted him, asking him if he was not in pain. 'I cannot say,' replied Calandrino; ' 'twas but now that Nello told me that I looked quite changed: can it be that there is aught the matter with me?' 'Aught?' quoth Buffalmacco, 'ay, indeed, there might be a trifle the matter with thee. Thou look'st to be half-dead, man.' Calandrino now began to think he must have a fever. And then up came Bruno; and the first thing he said was – 'Why, Calandrino, how ill thou look'st! thy appearance is that of a corpse. How dost thou feel?' To be thus accosted by all three left no doubt in Calandrino's mind that he was ill, and so – 'What shall I do?' quoth he, in a great fright. 'My advice,' replied Bruno, 'is that thou go home and get thee to bed and cover thee well up, and send thy water to Master Simone, who, as thou knowest, is such a friend of ours. He will tell thee at once what thou must do; and we will come to see thee, and will do aught that may be needful.' And Nello then joining them, they all three went home with Calandrino, who, now quite spent, went straight to his room, and said to his wife – 'Come now, wrap me well up; I feel very ill.' And so he laid himself on the bed, and sent a maid with his water to Master Simone, who had then his shop in the Mercato Vecchio, at the sign of the pumpkin. Whereupon quoth Bruno to his comrades – 'You will stay here with him, and I will go hear what the doctor has to say, and if need be, will bring him hither.' 'Prithee, do so, my friend,' quoth Calandrino, 'and bring me word how it is with me, for I feel as how I cannot say in my inside.' So Bruno hied him to Master Simone, and before the maid arrived with the water, told him what was afoot. The Master, thus primed inspected the water, and then said to the maid – 'Go tell Calandrino to keep himself very warm, and I will come at once, and let him know what is the matter with him and what he must do.' With which message the maid was scarce returned when the Master and Bruno arrived, and the Master, having seated himself beside Calandrino, felt his pulse, and by and by, in the presence of his wife, said – 'Hark ye, Calandrino, I speak to thee as a friend, and I tell thee that what is amiss with thee is just that thou art with child.' Whereupon Calandrino cried out querulously – 'Woe's me! 'Tis thy doing, Tessa, for that thou must needs be uppermost: I told thee plainly what would come of it.' Whereat the lady, being not a little modest, coloured from brow to neck, and with downcast eyes, withdrew from the room, saying never a word by way of answer. Calandrino ran on in the same plaintive strain – 'Alas! woe's me! What shall I do? How shall I be delivered of this child? What passage can it find? Ah! I see only too plainly that the lasciviousness of this wife of mine has been the death of me: God make her as wretched as I would fain be happy! Were I as well as I am not, I would get me up and thrash her, till I left not a whole bone in her body, albeit it does but serve me right for letting her get the upper place; but if I do win through this, she shall never have it again; verily she might pine to death for it, but she should not have it.'

Which to hear, Bruno and Buffalmacco and Nello were like to burst with suppressed laughter and Master Scimmione* laughed so frantically, that all his teeth were ready to start from his jaws. However, at length, in answer to Calandrino's appeals and entreaties for counsel and succour – 'Calandrino,' quoth the Master, 'thou mayst dismiss thy fears, for, God be praised, we were apprised of thy state in such good time that with but little trouble, in the course of a few days, I shall set thee right; but 'twill cost a little.' 'Woe's me,' returned Calandrino, 'be it so, Master, for the love of God: I have here two hundred pounds, with which I had thoughts of buying an estate: take them all, all, if you must have all, so only I may escape being delivered, for I know not how I should manage it, seeing that women, albeit 'tis much easier for them, do make such a noise in the hour of their labour, that I misdoubt me, if I suffered so, I should die before I was delivered.' 'Disquiet not thyself,' said the doctor: 'I will have a potion distilled for thee; of rare virtue it is, and not a little palatable, and in the course of three days 'twill purge thee of all, and leave thee in better fettle than a fish; but thou wilt do

* i.e. great ape: with a play on Simone.

well to be careful thereafter, and commit no such indiscretions again. Now to make this potion we must have three pair of good fat capons, and, for divers other ingredients, thou wilt give one of thy friends here five pounds in small change to purchase them, and thou wilt have everything sent to my shop, and so, please God, I will send thee this distilled potion tomorrow morning, and thou wilt take a good beakerful each time.' Whereupon – 'Be it as you bid, Master mine,' quoth Calandrino, and handing Bruno five pounds, and money enough to purchase three pair of capons, he begged him, if it were not too much trouble, to do him the service to buy these things for him. So away went the doctor, and made a little decoction by way of draught, and sent it him. Bruno bought the capons and all else that was needed to furnish forth the feast, with which he and his comrades and the doctor regaled them. Calandrino drank of the decoction for three mornings, after which he had a visit from his friends and the doctor, who felt his pulse, and then – 'Beyond a doubt, Calandrino,' quoth he, 'thou art cured, and so thou hast no more occasion to keep indoors, but needst have no fear to do whatever thou hast a mind to.' Much relieved, Calandrino got up, and resumed his accustomed way of life, and, wherever he found anyone to talk to, was loud in praise of Master Simone for the excellent manner in which he had cured him, causing him in three days without the least suffering to be quit of his pregnancy. And Bruno and Buffalmacco and Nello were not a little pleased with themselves that they had so cleverly got the better of Calandrino's niggardliness, albeit Monna Tessa, who was not deceived, murmured not a little against her husband.

☙ 42 ❧

The fifth story of the ninth day, in which Calandrino, being enamoured of a damsel, Bruno gives him a scroll, averring that, if he but touch her therewith, she will go with him: he is found with her by his wife, who subjects him to a most severe and vexatious examination.

Upon the close of the fourth story, the queen, turning to Fiammetta, bade her follow with another. Fiammetta with mien most gladsome made answer that she willingly obeyed, and thus began: ❧ As I doubt not ye know, ladies most debonair, be the topic of discourse never so well worn it will still continue to please if the speaker knows how to make due choice of time and occasion meet. Wherefore, considering the reason for which we are here (how that 'tis to make merry and speed the time gaily, and that merely) I deem that there is nought that may afford us mirth and solace but here may find time and occasion meet and, after serving a thousand turns of discourse, should still prove not unpleasing for another thousand. Wherefore, notwithstanding that of Calandrino and his doings not a little has from time to time been said among us, yet considering that, as a while ago Filostrato observed, there is nought that concerns him that is not entertaining, I will make bold to add to the preceding stories another which I might well, had I been minded to deviate from the truth, have disguised, and so recounted it to you under other names; but as whoso in telling a story diverges from the truth does thereby in no small measure diminish the delight of his hearers, I purpose for the reason aforesaid to give you the narrative in proper form –

Niccolò Cornacchini, one of our citizens, and a man of wealth, had among other estates a fine one at Camerata, on which he had a grand house built, and engaged Bruno and Buffalmacco to paint it throughout; in which task, for that 'twas by no means light, they associated with them Nello and Calandrino, and so set to work. There were a few rooms in the house provided with beds and other furniture, and an old female servant lived there as caretaker, but otherwise the house was unoccupied, for which cause Niccolò's son, Filippo, being a young man and a bachelor, was wont sometimes to bring thither a woman for his pleasure, and after keeping her there for a few days to escort her thence again. Now on one of these occasions it befell that he brought thither one Niccolosa, whom a vile fellow, named Mangione, kept in a house at Camaldoli as a common prostitute. And a fine piece of flesh she was, and wore fine clothes, and, for one of her sort, knew how to comport herself becomingly and talk agreeably.

Now one day at high noon forth tripped the damsel from her chamber in a white gown, her locks braided about her head, to wash her hands and face at a well that was in the courtyard of the house, and, while she was so engaged, it befell that Calandrino came there for water, and greeted her familiarly. Having returned his salutation, she, rather because Calandrino struck her as something out of the common, than for any other interest she felt in him, regarded him attentively. Calandrino did the like by her, and being smitten by her beauty, found reasons enough why he should not go back to his comrades with the water; but, as he knew not who she was, he made not bold to address her. She, upon whom his gaze was not lost, being minded to amuse herself at his expense, let her glance from time to time rest upon him, while she heaved a slight sigh or two. Whereby Calandrino was forthwith captivated, and tarried in the courtyard, until Filippo called her back into the chamber. Returned to his work, Calandrino sighed like a furnace: which Bruno, who was ever regardful of his doings for the diversion they afforded him, failed not to mark, and by and by – 'What the Devil is amiss with thee, comrade Calandrino?' quoth he. 'Thou dost nought but puff and blow.' 'Comrade,' replied Calandrino, 'I should be in luck, had I but one to help me.' 'How so?' quoth Bruno. 'Why,' returned Calandrino, ' 'tis not to go farther, but there is a damsel below, fairer than a lamia, and so mightily in love with me that 'twould astonish thee. I observed it but now, when I went to fetch the water.' 'Nay, but, Calandrino, make sure she be not Filippo's wife,' quoth Bruno. 'I doubt 'tis even so,' replied Calandrino, 'for he called her and she joined him in the chamber; but what signifies it? I would circumvent Christ Himself in such case, not to say Filippo. Of a truth, comrade, I tell thee she pleases me I could not say how.' 'Comrade,' returned Bruno, 'I will find out for thee who she is, and if she be Filippo's wife, two words from me will make it all straight for thee, for she is much my friend. But how shall we prevent Buffalmacco knowing it? I can never have a word with her, but he is with me.' 'As to Buffalmacco,' replied Calandrino, 'I care not if he do know it; but let us make sure that it come not to Nello's ears, for he is of kin to Monna Tessa, and would spoil it all.' Whereto – 'Thou art in the right,' returned Bruno.

Now Bruno knew what the damsel was, for he had seen Her arrive, and moreover Filippo had told him. So, Calandrino having given over working for a while, and betaken him to her, Bruno acquainted Nello and Buffalmacco with the whole story; and thereupon they privily concerted how to entreat him in regard of this love affair. Wherefore, upon his return, quoth Bruno softly – 'Didst see her?' 'Ay, woe's me!' replied Calandrino: 'she has stricken me to the death.' Quoth Bruno – 'I will go see if she be the lady I take her to be, and if I find that 'tis so, leave the rest to me.' Whereupon down went Bruno, and found Filippo and the damsel, and fully apprised them what sort of fellow Calandrino was, and what he had told them, and concerted with them what each should do and say, that they might have a merry time together over Calandrino's love affair. He then rejoined Calandrino, saying: – ' 'Tis the very same; and therefore the affair needs very delicate handling, for, if Filippo were but ware thereof, not all Arno's waters would suffice to cleanse us. However, what should I say to her from thee, if by chance I should get speech of her?' 'I'faith,' replied Calandrino, 'why, first, first of all, thou wilt tell her that I wish her a thousand bushels of the good seed of generation, and then that I am her servant, and if she is fain of – aught – thou tak'st me?' 'Ay,' quoth Bruno, 'leave it to me.'

Supper-time came; and, the day's work done, they went down into the courtyard, Filippo and Niccolosa being there, and there they tarried a while to advance Calandrino's suit. Calandrino's gaze was soon riveted on Niccolosa, and such and so strange and startling were the gestures that he made that they would have given sight to the blind. She on her part used all her arts to inflame his passion, primed as she had been by Bruno, and diverted beyond measure as she was by Calandrino's antics, while Filippo, Buffalmacco and the rest feigned to be occupied in converse, and to see nought of what passed. However, after a while, to Calandrino's extreme disgust, they took their leave; and as they bent their steps towards Florence: – 'I warrant thee,' quoth Bruno to Calandrino, 'she wastes away for thee like ice in the sunlight;

by the body o' God if thou wert to bring thy rebeck, and sing her one or two of thy love-songs, she'd throw herself out of window to be with thee.' Quoth Calandrino – 'Think'st thou, comrade, think'st thou, 'twere well I brought it?' 'Ay, indeed,' returned Bruno. Whereupon – 'Ah! comrade,' quoth Calandrino, 'so thou wouldst not believe me when I told thee today? Of a truth I perceive there's ne'er another knows so well what he would be at as I. Who but I would have known how so soon to win the love of a lady like that? Lucky indeed might they deem themselves, if they did it, those young gallants that go about, day and night, up and down, a-strumming on the one-stringed viol, and would not know how to gather a handful of nuts once in a millennium. Mayst thou be by to see when I bring her the rebeck! thou wilt see fine sport. List well what I say: I am not so old as I look; and she knows it right well: ay, and anyhow I will soon let her know it, when I come to grapple her. By the very body of Christ I will have such sport with her, that she will follow me as any love-sick maid follows her swain.' 'Oh!' quoth Bruno, 'I doubt not thou wilt make her thy prey: and I seem to see thee bite her dainty vermeil mouth and her cheeks, that show as twin roses, with thy teeth, that are as so many lute-pegs, and afterwards devour her bodily.' So encouraged, Calandrino fancied himself already in action, and went about singing and capering in such high glee that 'twas as if he would burst his skin. And so next day he brought the rebeck, and to the no small amusement of all the company sang several songs to her. And, in short, by frequently seeing her, he waxed so mad with passion that he gave over working; and a thousand times a day he would run now to the window, now to the door, and anon to the courtyard on the chance of catching sight of her; nor did she, astutely following Bruno's instructions, fail to afford him abundance of opportunity. Bruno played the go-between, bearing him her answers to all his messages, and sometimes bringing him messages from her. When she was not at home, which was most frequently the case, he would send him letters from her, in which she gave great encouragement to his hopes, at the same time giving him to understand that she was at the house of her kinsfolk, where as yet he might not visit her.

On this wise Bruno and Buffalmacco so managed the affair as to divert themselves inordinately, causing him to send her, as at her request, now an ivory comb, now a purse, now a little knife, and other such dainty trifles; in return for which they brought him, now and again, a counterfeit ring of no value, with which Calandrino was marvellously pleased. And Calandrino, to stimulate their zeal in his interest, would entertain them hospitably at table, and otherwise flatter them. Now, when they had thus kept him in play for two good months, and the affair was just where it had been, Calandrino, seeing that the work was coming to an end, and bethinking him that, if it did so before he had brought his love affair to a successful issue, he must give up all hopes of ever so doing, began to be very instant and importunate with Bruno. So, in the presence of the damsel, and by preconcert with her and Filippo, quoth Bruno to Calandrino – 'Hark ye, comrade, this lady has vowed to me a thousand times that she will do as thou wouldst have her, and as, for all that, she does nought to pleasure thee, I am of opinion that she leads thee by the nose: wherefore, as she keeps not her promises, we will make her do so, willy-nilly, if thou art so minded.' 'Nay, but, for the love of God, so be it,' replied Calandrino, 'and that speedily.' 'Darest thou touch her, then, with a scroll that I shall give thee?' quoth Bruno. 'I dare,' replied Calandrino. 'Fetch me, then,' quoth Bruno, 'a bit of the skin of an unborn lamb, a live bat, three grains of incense, and a blessed candle; and leave the rest to me.' To catch the bat taxed all Calandrino's art and craft for the whole of the evening; but having at length taken him, he brought him with the other matters to Bruno: who, having withdrawn into a room by himself, wrote on the skin some cabalistic jargon, and handed it to him, saying – 'Know, Calandrino, that, if thou touch her with this scroll, she will follow thee forthwith, and do whatever thou shalt wish. Wherefore, should Filippo go abroad today, get thee somehow up to her, and touch her; and then go into the barn that is hereby – 'tis the best place we have, for never a soul goes there – and thou wilt see that she will come there too. When she is there, thou wottest well what to do.' Calandrino, overjoyed as ne'er another, took the scroll, saying only – 'Comrade, leave that to me.'

Now Nello, whom Calandrino mistrusted, entered with no less zest than the others into the affair, and was their confederate for Calandrino's discomfiture; accordingly by Bruno's direction he hied to Florence, and finding Monna Tessa – 'Thou hast scarce forgotten, Tessa,' quoth he, 'what a beating Calandrino gave thee, without the least cause, that day when he same home with the stones from Mugnone; for which I would have thee be avenged, and, so thou wilt not, call me no more kinsman or friend. He is fallen in love with a lady up there, who is abandoned enough to go closeting herself not seldom with him, and 'tis but a short while since they made assignation to forgather forthwith: so I would have thee go there, and surprise him in the act, and give him a sound trouncing.' Which when the lady heard, she deemed it no laughing matter; but started up and broke out with – 'Alas, the arrant knave! is't thus he treats me? By the Holy Rood, never fear but I will pay him out!' And wrapping herself in her cloak, and taking a young woman with her for companion, she sped more at a run than at a walk, escorted by Nello, up to Camerata. Bruno, espying her from afar, said to Filippo – 'Lo, here comes our friend.' Whereupon Filippo went to the place where Calandrino and the others were at work, and said – 'My masters, I must needs go at once to Florence; slacken not on that account.' And so off he went, and hid himself where, unobserved, he might see what Calandrino would do. Calandrino waited only until he saw that Filippo was at some distance, and then he went down into the courtyard, where he found Niccolosa alone, and fell a-talking with her. She, knowing well what she had to do, drew close to him, and showed him a little more familiarity than she was wont: whereupon Calandrino touched her with the scroll, and having so done, saying never a word, bent his steps towards the barn, whither Niccolosa followed him, and being entered, shut the door, and forthwith embraced him, threw him down on the straw that lay there, and got astride of him, and holding him fast by the arms about the shoulders, suffered him not to approach his face to hers, but gazing upon him, as if he were the delight of her heart – 'O Calandrino, sweet my Calandrino,' quoth she, 'heart of my body, my very soul, my bliss, my consolation, ah! how long have I yearned to hold thee in my arms and have thee all my own! Thy endearing ways have utterly disarmed me; thou hast made prize of my heart with thy rebeck. Do I indeed hold thee in mine embrace?' Calandrino, scarce able to move, murmured –'Ah! sweet my soul, suffer me to kiss thee.' Whereto – 'Nay, but thou art too hasty,' replied Niccolosa. 'Let me first feast mine eyes on thee; let me but sate them with this sweet face of thine.'

Meanwhile Bruno and Buffalmacco had joined Filippo, so that what passed was seen and heard by all three. And while Calandrino was thus intent to kiss Niccolosa, lo, up came Nello with Monna Tessa. 'By God, I swear they are both there,' ejaculated Nello, as they entered the doorway; but the lady, now fairly furious, laid hold of him and thrust him aside, and rushing in, espied Niccolosa astride of Calandrino. Niccolosa no sooner caught sight of the lady, than up she jumped, and in a trice was beside Filippo. Monna Tessa fell upon Calandrino, who was still on the floor, planted her nails in his face, and scratched it all over: she then seized him by the hair and haling him to and fro about the barn – 'Foul, pestilent cur,' quoth she, 'is this the way thou treatest me? Thou old fool! A murrain on the love I have borne thee! Hast thou not enough to do at home, that thou must needs go falling in love with strange women? And a fine lover thou wouldst make! Dost not know thyself, knave? Dost not know thyself, wretch? Thou, from whose whole body 'twere not possible to wring enough sap for a sauce! God's faith, 'twas not Tessa that got thee with child: God's curse on her, whoever she was: verily she must be a poor creature to be enamoured of a jewel of thy rare quality.' At sight of his wife, Calandrino, suspended, as it were, between life and death, ventured no defence; but, his face torn to shreds, his hair and clothes all disordered, fumbled about for his capuche, which having found, up he got, and humbly besought his wife not to publish the matter, unless she were minded that he should be cut to pieces, for that she that was with him was the wife of the master of the house. 'Then God give her a bad year,' replied the lady. Whereupon Bruno and Buffalmacco, who by this time had laughed their fill with Filippo and Niccolosa, came up as if attracted by the noise; and after not a little ado pacified the lady, and counselled Calandrino to go back to Florence, and stay there, lest Filippo should get wind of the affair, and do him a mischief. So Calandrino, crestfallen and woebegone, got him back to Florence with his face torn to shreds; where, daring not to show himself at Camerata again, he endured day and night the grievous torment of his wife's vituperation. Such was the issue, to which, after ministering not a little mirth to his comrades, as also to Niccolosa and Filippo, this ardent lover brought his amour.

43

The sixth story of the ninth day, in which two young men lodge at an inn, of whom the one lies with the host's daughter, his wife by inadvertence lying with the other. He that lay with the daughter afterwards gets into her father's bed and tells him all, taking him to be his comrade. They bandy words; whereupon the good woman, apprehending the circumstances, gets her to bed with her daughter, and by divers apt words re-establishes perfect accord.

Calandrino as on former occasions, so also on this, moved the company to laughter. However, when the ladies had done talking of his doings, the queen called for a story from Pamfilo, who thus spoke: Worshipful ladies, this Niccolosa that Calandrino loved has brought to my mind a story of another Niccolosa; which I am minded to tell you because 'twill show you how a good woman by her quick apprehension avoided a great scandal –

In the plain of Mugnone there was not long ago a good man that furnished travellers with meat and drink for money, and, for that he was in poor circumstances, and had but a little house, gave not lodging to every comer, but only to a few that he knew, and if they were hard bested. Now the good man had to wife a very fine woman, and by her had two children, to wit, a pretty and winsome girl of some fifteen or sixteen summers, as yet unmarried, and a little boy, not yet one year old, whom the mother suckled at her own breast. The girl had found favour in the eyes of a goodly and mannerly young gentleman of our city, who was not seldom in those parts, and loved her to the point of passion. And she, being mightily flattered to be loved by such a gallant, studied how to comport herself so debonairly as to retain his regard, and while she did so, grew likewise enamoured of him; and divers times, by consent of both, their love had had its fruition, but that Pinuccio – such was the gallant's name – shrank from the disgrace that 'twould bring upon the girl and himself alike. But, as his passion daily waxed apace, Pinuccio, yearning to find himself abed with her, bethought him that he were best contrive to lodge with her father, deeming, from what he knew of her father's economy, that, if he did so, he might effect his purpose, and never a soul be the wiser: which idea no sooner struck him, than he set about carrying it into effect.

So, late one evening Pinuccio and a trusty comrade, Adriano by name, to whom he had confided his love, hired two nags, and having set upon them two valises, filled with straw or suchlike stuff, sallied forth of Florence, and rode by a circuitous route to the plain of Mugnone, which they reached after nightfall; and having fetched a compass, so that it might seem as if they were coming from Romagna, they rode up to the good man's house, and knocked at the door. The good man, knowing them both very well, opened to them forthwith: whereupon – 'Thou must even put us up tonight,' quoth Pinuccio; 'we thought to get into Florence, but, for all the speed we could make, we are but arrived here, as thou seest, at this hour.' 'Pinuccio,' replied the host, 'thou well knowest that I can but make a sorry shift to lodge gentlemen like you; but yet, as night has overtaken you here, and time serves not to betake you elsewhere, I will gladly give you such accommodation as I may.' The two gallants then dismounted and entered the inn, and having first looked to their horses, brought out some supper that they had carried with them, and supped with the host.

Now the host had but one little bedroom, in which were three beds, set, as conveniently as he could contrive, two on one side of the room, and the third on the opposite side, but, for all that, there was scarce room enough to pass through. The host had the least discomfortable of the three beds made up for the two friends; and having quartered them there, some little while afterwards, both being awake, but feigning to be asleep, he caused his daughter to get into one of the other two beds, while he and his wife took their places in the third, the good woman setting the cradle, in which was her little boy, beside the bed. Such, then, being the partition made of the beds, Pinuccio, who had taken exact note thereof, waited only until he deemed all but himself to be asleep, and then got softly up and stole to the bed in which lay his beloved, and laid himself beside her; and she according him albeit a timorous yet a gladsome welcome, he stayed there, taking with her that solace of which both were most fain.

Pinuccio being thus with the girl, it chanced that certain things, being overset by a cat, fell with a noise that aroused the good woman, who, fearing that it might be a matter of more consequence, got up as best she might in the dark, and betook her to the place whence the noise seemed to proceed. At the same time Adriano, not by reason of the noise, which he heeded not, but perchance to answer the call of nature, also got up, and questing about for a convenient place, came upon the cradle beside the good woman's bed; and not being able otherwise to go by, took it up, and set it beside his own bed, and when he had accomplished his purpose, went back, and giving never a thought to the cradle got him to bed. The good woman searched until she found that the accident was no such matter as she had supposed; so without troubling to strike a light to investigate it further, she reproved the cat, and returned to the room, and groped her way straight to the bed in which her husband lay asleep; but not finding the cradle there, quoth she to herself – Alas! blunderer that I am, what was I about? God's faith! I was going straight to the guest's bed; and proceeding a little further, she found the cradle, and laid herself down by Adriano in the bed that was beside it, taking Adriano for her husband; and Adriano, who was still awake, received her with all due benignity, and tackled her more than once to her no small delight.

Meanwhile Pinuccio fearing lest sleep should overtake him while he was yet with his mistress, and having satisfied his desire, got up and left her, to return to his bed; but when he got there, coming upon the cradle, he supposed that 'twas the host's bed; and so going a little further, he laid him down beside the host, who thereupon awoke. Supposing that he had Adriano beside him – 'I warrant thee,' quoth Pinuccio to the host, 'there was never so sweet a piece of flesh as Niccolosa: by the body of God, such delight have I had of her as never had man of woman; and, mark me, since I left thee, I have gotten me up to the farm some six times.' Which tidings the host being none too well pleased to learn, said first of all to himself – What the Devil does this fellow here? Then, his resentment getting the better of his prudence – ' 'Tis a gross affront thou hast put upon me, Pinuccio,' quoth he; 'nor know I what occasion thou hast to do me such a wrong; but by the body of God I will pay thee out.' Pinuccio, who was not the most discreet of gallants, albeit he was now apprised of his error, instead of doing his best to repair it, retorted – 'And how wilt thou pay me out? What canst thou do?' 'Hark what high words our guests are at together!' quoth meanwhile the host's wife to Adriano, deeming that she spoke to her husband. 'Let them be,' replied Adriano with a laugh: 'God give them a bad year: they drank too much yestereve.' The good woman had already half recognised her husband's angry tones, and now that she heard Adriano's voice, she at once knew where she was and with whom. Accordingly, being a discreet woman, she started up, and saying never a word, took her child's cradle, and, though there was not a ray of light in the room, bore it, divining rather than feeling her way, to the side of the bed in which her daughter slept; and then, as if aroused by the noise made by her husband, she called him, and asked what he and Pinuccio were bandying words about. 'Hearest thou not,' replied the husband, 'what he says he has this very night done to Niccolosa?' 'Tush! he lies in the throat,' returned the good woman: 'he has not lain with Niccolosa; for what time he might have done so, I laid me beside her myself, and I have been wide awake ever since; and thou art a fool to believe him. You men take so many cups before going to bed that then you dream, and walk in your sleep, and imagine wonders. 'Tis a great pity you do not break your necks. What does Pinuccio there? Why keeps he not in his own bed?'

Whereupon Adriano, in his turn, seeing how adroitly the good woman cloaked her own and her daughter's shame – 'Pinuccio,' quoth he, 'I have told thee a hundred times, that thou shouldst not walk about at night; for this thy bad habit of getting up in thy dreams and relating thy dreams for truth will get thee into a scrape sometime or another: come back, and God send thee a bad night.' Hearing Adriano thus confirm what his wife had said, the host began to think that Pinuccio must be really dreaming; so he took him by the shoulder, and fell a-shaking him, and calling him by his name, saying – 'Pinuccio, wake up, and go back to thy bed.' Pinuccio, taking his cue from what he had heard, began as a dreamer would be like to do, to talk wanderingly; whereat the host laughed amain. Then, feigning to be aroused by the shaking, Pinuccio uttered Adriano's name, saying – 'Is't already day, that thou callest me?' 'Ay, 'tis so,' quoth Adriano – 'come hither.' Whereupon Pinuccio, making as if he were mighty drowsy, got him up from beside the host, and back to bed with Adriano. On the morrow, when they were risen, the host fell a-laughing and making merry touching Pinuccio and his dreams. And so the jest passed from mouth to mouth, while the gallants' horses were groomed and saddled, and their valises adjusted: which done, they drank with the host, mounted and rode to Florence, no less pleased with the manner than with the matter of the night's adventure. Nor, afterwards, did Pinuccio fail to find other means of meeting Niccolosa, who assured her mother that he had unquestionably dreamed. For which cause the good woman, calling to mind Adriano's embrace, accounted herself the only one that had watched.

⊰ 44 ⊱

The tenth story of the tenth day, in which the Marquis of Saluzzo, overborne by the entreaties of his vassals, consents to take a wife, but, being minded to please himself in the choice of her, takes a husbandman's daughter. He has two children by her, both of whom he makes her believe that he has put to death. Afterward, feigning to be tired of her, and to have taken another wife, he turns her out of doors in her shift, and brings his daughter into the house in guise of his bride; but, finding her patient under it all, he brings her home again, and shows her her children, now grown up, and honours her, and causes her to be honoured, as Marchioness.

Dioneo, with a laugh, witting that it now only remained for him to tell, thus began: ⊱ Gentle my ladies, this day meseems is dedicated to Kings and Soldans and folk of the like quality; wherefore, that I stray not too far from you, I am minded to tell you somewhat of a Marquis; certes, nought magnificent, but a piece of mad folly, albeit there came good thereof to him in the end. The which I counsel none to copy, for that great pity 'twas that it turned out well with him –

There was in olden days a certain Marquis of Saluzzo, Gualtieri by name, a young man but head of the house, who, having neither wife nor child, passed his time in nought else but in hawking and hunting, and of taking a wife and begetting children had no thought; wherein he should have been accounted very wise: but his vassals, brooking it ill, did oftentimes entreat him to take a wife, that he might not die without an heir, and they be left without a lord; offering to find him one of such a pattern, and of such parentage, that he might marry with good hope, and be well content with the sequel. To whom – 'My friends,' replied

Gualtieri, 'you enforce me to that which I had resolved never to do, seeing how hard it is to find a wife, whose ways accord well with one's own, and how plentiful is the supply of such as run counter thereto, and how grievous a life he leads who chances upon a lady that matches ill with him. And to say that you think to know the daughters by the qualities of their fathers and mothers, and thereby – so you would argue – to provide me with a wife to my liking, is but folly; for I wot not how you may penetrate the secrets of their mothers so as to know their fathers; and granted that you do know them, daughters oftentimes resemble neither of their parents. However, as you are minded to rivet these fetters upon me, I am content that so it be; and that I may have no cause to reproach any but myself, should it turn out ill, I am resolved that my wife shall be of my own choosing; but of this rest assured, that, no matter whom I choose, if she receive not from you the honour due to a lady, you shall prove to your great cost, how sorely I resent being thus constrained by your importunity to take a wife against my will.'

The worthy men replied that they were well content, so only he would marry without more ado. And Gualtieri, who had long noted with approval the mien of a poor girl that dwelt on a farm hard by his house, and found her fair enough, deemed that with her he might pass a tolerably happy life. Wherefore he sought no further, but forthwith resolved to marry her; and having sent for her father, who was a very poor man, he contracted with him to take her to wife. Which done, Gualtieri assembled all the friends he had in those parts, and – 'My friends,' quoth he, 'you were and are minded that I should take a wife, and rather to comply with your wishes, than for any desire that I had to marry, I have made up my mind to do so. You remember the promise you gave me, to wit, that, whomsoever I should take, you would pay her the honour due to a lady. Which promise I now require you to keep, the time being come when I am to keep mine. I have found hard by here a maiden after mine own heart, whom I purpose to take to wife, and to bring hither to my house in the course of a few days. Wherefore bethink you, how you may make the nuptial feast splendid, and welcome her with all honour; that I may confess myself satisfied with your observance of your promise, as you will be with my observance of mine.' The worthy men, one and all, answered with alacrity that they were well content, and that, whoever she might be, they would entreat her as a lady, and pay her all due honour as such. After which, they all addressed them to make goodly and grand and gladsome celebration of the event, as did also Gualtieri. He arranged for a wedding most stately and fair, and bade thereto a goodly number of his friends and kinsfolk, and great gentlemen, and others, of the neighbourhood; and therewithal he caused many a fine and costly robe to be cut and fashioned to the figure of a girl who seemed to him of the like proportions as the girl that he purposed to wed; and laid in store, besides, of girdles and rings, with a costly and beautiful crown, and all the other paraphernalia of a bride.

The day that he had appointed for the wedding being come, about half tierce he got him to horse with as many as had come to do him honour, and having made all needful dispositions – 'Gentlemen,' quoth he, ' 'tis time to go bring home the bride.' And so away he rode with his company to the village; where, being come to the house of the girl's father, they found her returning from the spring with a bucket of water, making all the haste she could, that she might afterwards go with the other women to see Gualtieri's bride come by. Whom Gualtieri no sooner saw, than he called her by her name, to wit, Griselda, and asked her where her father was. To whom she modestly made answer – 'My lord, he is in the house.' Whereupon Gualtieri dismounted, and having bidden the rest await him without, entered the cottage alone; and meeting her father, whose name was Giannucolo – 'I am come,' quoth he, 'to wed Griselda, but first of all there are some matters I would learn from her own lips in thy presence.' He then asked her, whether, if he took her to wife, she would study to comply with his wishes, and be not wroth, no matter what he might say or do, and be obedient, with not a few other questions of a like sort: to all which she answered, ay. Whereupon Gualtieri took her by the hand, led her forth, and before the eyes of all his company, and as many other folk as were there, caused her to be stripped naked, and let bring the garments that he had had fashioned for her, and had her forthwith arrayed therein, and upon her unkempt head let set a crown; and then, while all wondered – 'Gentlemen,' quoth he, 'this is she whom I purpose to make my wife, so she be minded to have me for husband.' Then, she standing abashed and astonished, he turned to her, saying – 'Griselda, wilt thou have me for thy husband?' To whom – 'Ay, my lord,' answered she.

'And I will have thee to wife,' said he, and married her before them all. And having set her upon a palfrey, he brought her home with pomp.

The wedding was fair and stately, and had he married a daughter of the King of France, the feast could not have been more splendid. It seemed as if, with the change of her garb, the bride had acquired a new dignity of mind and mien. She was, as we have said, fair of form and feature; and therewithal she was now grown so engaging and gracious and debonair, that she showed no longer as the shepherdess, and the daughter of Giannucolo, but as the daughter of some noble lord, insomuch that she caused as many as had known her before to marvel. Moreover, she was so obedient and devoted to her husband, that he deemed himself the happiest and luckiest man in the world. And likewise so gracious and kindly was she to her husband's vassals, that there was none of them but loved her more dearly than himself, and was zealous to do her honour, and prayed for her welfare and prosperity and aggrandisement, and instead of, as erstwhile, saying that Gualtieri had done foolishly to take her to wife, now averred that he had not his like in the world for wisdom and discernment, for that, save to him, her noble qualities would ever have remained hidden under her sorry apparel and the garb of the peasant girl. And in short she so comported herself as in no long time to bring it to pass that, not only in the marquisate, but far and wide besides, her virtues and her admirable conversation were matter of common talk, and, if aught had been said to the disadvantage of her husband, when he married her, the judgement was now altogether to the contrary effect.

She had not been long with Gualtieri before she conceived; and in due time she was delivered of a girl; whereat Gualtieri made great cheer. But, soon after, a strange humour took possession of him, to wit, to put her patience to the proof by prolonged and intolerable hard usage; wherefore he began by afflicting her with his gibes, putting on a vexed air, and telling her that his vassals were most sorely dissatisfied with her by reason of her base condition, and all the more so since they saw that she was a mother, and that they did nought but most ruefully murmur at the birth of a daughter. Whereto Griselda, without the least change of countenance or sign of discomposure, made answer – 'My lord, do with me as thou mayst deem best for thine own honour and comfort, for well I wot that I am of less account than they, and unworthy of this honourable estate to which of thy courtesy thou hast advanced me.' By which answer Gualtieri was well pleased, witting that she was in no degree puffed up with pride by his, or any other's, honourable entreatment of her. A while afterwards, having in general terms given his wife to understand that the vassals could not endure her daughter, he sent her a message by a servant. So the servant came, and – 'Madam,' quoth he with a most dolorous mien, 'so I value my life, I must needs do my lord's bidding. He has bidden me take your daughter and . . . ' He said no more, but the lady by what she heard, and read in his face, and remembered of her husband's words, understood that he was bidden to put the child to death. Whereupon she presently took the child from the cradle, and having kissed and blessed her, albeit she was very sore at heart, she changed not countenance, but placed it in the servant's arms, saying – 'See that thou leave nought undone that my lord and thine has charged thee to do, but leave her not so that the beasts and the birds devour her, unless he have so bidden thee.' So the servant took the child, and told Gualtieri what the lady had said; and Gualtieri, marvelling at her constancy, sent him with the child to Bologna, to one of his kinswomen, whom he besought to rear and educate the child with all care, but never to let it be known whose child she was.

Soon after it befell that the lady again conceived, and in due time was delivered of a son, whereat Gualtieri was overjoyed. But, not content with what he had done, he now even more poignantly afflicted the lady; and one day with a ruffled mien: – 'Wife,' quoth he, 'since thou gavest birth to this boy, I may on no wise live in peace with my vassals, so bitterly do they reproach me that a grandson of Giannucolo is to succeed me as their lord; and therefore I fear that, so I be not minded to be sent a-packing hence, I must even do herein as I did before, and in the end put thee away, and take another wife.' The lady heard him patiently, and answered only – 'My lord, study how thou mayst content thee and best please thyself, and waste no thought upon me, for there is nought I desire save in so far as I know that 'tis thy pleasure.' Not many days after, Gualtieri, in like manner as he had sent for the daughter, sent for the son, and having made a show of putting him to death, provided for his, as for the girl's, nurture at Bologna. Whereat the lady showed no more discomposure of countenance or speech than at the loss of her daughter: which Gualtieri found passing strange, and inwardly affirmed that there was never another woman in the world that would have so done. And but that he had marked that she was most tenderly affectionate towards her children, while 'twas well pleasing to him, he had supposed that she was tired of them, whereas he knew that 'twas of her discretion that she so did. His vassals, who believed that he had put the children to death, held him mightily to blame for his cruelty, and felt the utmost compassion for the lady. She, however, said never aught to the ladies that condoled with her on the death of her children, but that the pleasure of him that had begotten them was her pleasure likewise.

Years not a few had passed since the girl's birth, when Gualtieri at length deemed the time come to put his wife's patience to the final proof. Accordingly, in the presence of a great company of his vassals he declared that on no wise might he longer brook to have Griselda to wife, that he confessed that in taking her he had done a sorry thing and the act of a stripling, and that he therefore meant to do what he could to procure the Pope's dispensation to put Griselda away, and take another wife: for which cause being much upbraided by many worthy men, he made no other answer but only that needs must it so be. Whereof the lady being apprised, and now deeming that she must look to go back to her father's house, and perchance tend the sheep, as she had aforetime, and see him, to whom she was utterly devoted, engrossed by another woman, did inwardly bewail herself right sorely: but still with the same composed mien with which she had borne Fortune's former buffets, she set herself to endure this last outrage. Nor was it long before Gualtieri by counterfeit letters, which he caused to be sent to him from Rome, made his vassals believe that the Pope had thereby given him a dispensation to put Griselda away, and take another wife. Wherefore, having caused her to be brought before him, he said to her in the presence of not a few – 'Wife, by license granted me by the Pope, I am now free to put thee away, and take another wife; and, for that my forbears have always been great gentlemen and lords of these parts, whereas thine have ever been husbandmen, I purpose that thou go back to Giannucolo's house with the dowry that thou broughtest me; whereupon I shall bring home a lady that I have found, and who is meet to be my wife.'

'Twas not without travail most grievous that the lady, as she heard this announcement, got the better of her woman's nature, and suppressing her tears, made answer – 'My lord, I ever knew that my low degree was on no wise congruous with your nobility, and acknowledged that the rank I had with you was of your and God's bestowal, nor did I ever make as if it were mine by gift, or so esteem it, but still accounted it as a loan. 'Tis your pleasure to recall it, and therefore it should be, and is, my pleasure to render it up to you. So, here is your ring, with which you espoused me; take it back. You bid me take with me the dowry that I brought you; which to do will require neither paymaster on your part nor purse nor pack-horse on mine; for I am not unmindful that naked was I when you first had me. And if you deem it seemly that that body in which I have borne children, by you begotten, be beheld of all, naked will I depart; but yet, I pray you, be pleased, in reward of the virginity that I brought you and take not away, to suffer me to bear hence upon my back a single shift – I crave no more – besides my dowry.' There was nought of which Gualtieri was so fain as to weep; but yet, setting his face as a flint, he made answer – 'I allow thee a shift to thy back; so get thee hence.' All that stood by besought him to give her a robe, that she, who had been his wife for thirteen years and more, might not be seen to quit his house in so sorry and shameful a plight, having nought on her but a shift. But their entreaties went for nothing: the lady in her shift, and barefoot and bareheaded, having bade them adieu, departed the house, and went back to her father amid the tears and lamentations of all that saw her. Giannucolo, who had ever deemed it a thing incredible that Gualtieri should keep his daughter to wife, and had looked for this to happen every day, and had kept the clothes that she had put off on the morning that Gualtieri had wedded her, now brought them to her; and she, having resumed them, applied herself to the petty drudgery of her father's house, as she had been wont, enduring with fortitude this cruel visitation of adverse Fortune.

Now no sooner had Gualtieri dismissed Griselda, than he gave his vassals to understand that he had taken to wife a daughter of one of the Counts of Panago. He accordingly made great preparations as for the nuptials, during which he sent for Griselda. To whom, being come, quoth he – 'I am bringing hither my new bride, and in this her first home-coming I purpose to show her honour; and thou knowest that women I have none in the house that know how to set chambers in due order, or attend to the many other matters that so joyful an event requires; wherefore do thou, that understandest these things better than another, see to all that needs be done, and bid hither such ladies as thou mayst see fit, and receive them, as if thou wert the lady of the house, and then, when the nuptials are ended, thou mayst go back to thy cottage.' Albeit each of these words pierced Griselda's heart like a knife, for that, in resigning her good fortune, she had not been able to renounce the love she bore Gualtieri, nevertheless – 'My lord,' she made answer, 'I am ready and prompt to do your pleasure.' And so, clad in her sorry garments of coarse romagnole, she entered the house, which, but a little before, she had quitted in her shift, and addressed her to sweep the chambers, and arrange arras and cushions in the halls, and make ready the kitchen, and set her hand to everything, as if she had been a paltry serving-wench: nor did she rest until she had brought all into such meet and seemly trim as the occasion demanded. This done, she invited in Gualtieri's name all the ladies of those parts to be present at his nuptials, and awaited the event. The day being come, still wearing her sorry weeds, but in heart and soul and mien the lady, she received the ladies as they came, and gave each a gladsome greeting.

Now Gualtieri, as we said, had caused his children to be carefully nurtured and brought up by a kinswoman of his at Bologna, which kinswoman was married into the family of the Counts of Panago; and, the girl being now twelve years old, and the loveliest creature that ever was seen, and the boy being about six years old, he had sent word to his kinswoman's husband at Bologna, praying him to be pleased to come with this girl and boy of his to Saluzzo, and to see that he brought a goodly and honourable company with him, and to give all to understand that he brought the girl to him to wife, and on no wise to disclose to any, who she really was. The gentleman did as the Marquis bade him, and within a few days of his setting forth arrived at Saluzzo about breakfast-time with the girl, and her brother, and a noble company, and found all the folk of those parts, and much people besides, gathered there in expectation of Gualtieri's new bride. Who, being received by the ladies, was no sooner come into the hall, where the tables were set, than Griselda advanced to meet her, saying with hearty cheer – 'Welcome, my lady.' So the ladies, who had with much instance, but in vain, besought Gualtieri, either to let Griselda keep in another room, or at any rate to furnish her with one of the robes that had been hers, that she might not present herself in such a sorry guise before the strangers, sat down to table; and the service being begun, the eyes of all were set on the girl, and everyone said that Gualtieri had made a good exchange, and Griselda joined with the rest in greatly commending her, and also her little brother. And now Gualtieri, sated at last with all that he had seen of his wife's patience, marking that this new and strange turn made not the least alteration in her demeanour, and being well assured that 'twas not due to apathy, for he knew her to be of excellent understanding, deemed it time to relieve her of the suffering which he judged her to dissemble under a resolute front; and so, having called her to him in presence of them all, he said with a smile – 'And what thinkst thou of our bride?' 'My lord,' replied Griselda, 'I think mighty well of her; and if she be but as discreet as she is fair – and so I deem her – I make no doubt but you may reckon to lead with her a life of incomparable felicity; but with all earnestness I entreat you, that you spare her those tribulations which you did once inflict upon another that was yours, for I scarce think she would be able to bear them, as well because she is younger, as for that she has been delicately nurtured, whereas that other had known no respite of hardship since she was but a little child.' Marking that she made no doubt but that the girl was to be his wife, and yet spoke never a whit the less sweetly, Gualtieri caused her to sit down beside him, and – 'Griselda,' said he, ' 'tis now time that thou see the reward of thy long patience, and that those, who have deemed me cruel and unjust and insensate, should know that what I did was done of purpose aforethought, for that I was minded to give both thee and them a lesson, that thou mightst learn to be a wife, and they in like manner might learn how to take and keep a wife, and that I might beget me perpetual peace with thee for the rest of my life; whereof being in great fear, when I came to take a wife, lest I should be disappointed, I therefore, to put the matter to the proof, did, and how sorely thou knowest, harass and afflict thee. And since I never knew thee either by deed or by word to deviate from my will, I now, deeming myself to have of thee that assurance of happiness which I desired, am minded to restore to thee at once all that, step by step, I took from thee, and by extremity of joy to compensate the tribulations that I inflicted on thee. Receive, then. this girl, whom thou supposest to be my bride, and her brother with glad heart, as thy children and mine. These are they, whom by thee and many another it has long been supposed that I did ruthlessly to death, and I am thy husband, that loves thee more dearly than aught else, deeming that other there is none that has the like good cause to be well content with his wife.'

Which said, he embraced and kissed her; and then, while she wept for joy, they rose and hied them there where sat the daughter, all astonished to hear the news, whom, as also her brother, they tenderly embraced, and explained to them, and many others that stood by, the whole mystery. Whereat the ladies, transported with delight, rose from table and betook them with Griselda to a chamber, and, with better omen, divested her of her sorry garb, and arrayed her in one of her own robes of state; and so, in guise of a lady (howbeit in her rags she had showed as no less) they led her back into the hall. Wondrous was the cheer which there they made with the children; and, all overjoyed at the event, they revelled and made merry amain, and prolonged the festivities for several days; and very discreet they pronounced Gualtieri, albeit they censured as intolerably harsh the probation to which he had subjected Griselda, and most discreet beyond all compare they accounted Griselda.

Some days after, the Count of Panago returned to Bologna, and Gualtieri took Giannucolo from his husbandry, and established him in honour as his father-in-law, wherein to his great solace he lived for the rest of his days. Gualtieri himself, having mated his daughter with a husband of high degree, lived long and happily thereafter with Griselda, to whom he ever paid all honour.

Now what shall we say in this case but that even into the cots of the poor the heavens let fall at times spirits divine, as into the palaces of kings souls that are fitter to tend hogs than to exercise lordship over men? Who but Griselda had been able, with a countenance not only tearless, but cheerful, to endure the hard and unheard-of trials to which Gualtieri subjected her? Who perhaps might have deemed himself to have made no bad investment, had he chanced upon one, who, having been turned out of his house in her shift, had found means so to dust the pelisse of another as to get herself thereby a fine robe.

So ended Dioneo's story, whereof the ladies, diversely inclining, one to censure where another found matter for commendation, had discoursed not a little, when the king, having glanced at the sky, and marked that the sun was now low, insomuch that 'twas nigh the vesper hour, still keeping his seat, thus began – 'Exquisite my ladies, as, methinks, you wot, 'tis not only in minding them of the past and apprehending the present that the wit of mortals consists; but by one means or the other to be able to foresee the future is by the sages accounted the height of wisdom. Now, tomorrow, as you know, 'twill be fifteen days since, in quest of recreation and for the conservation of our health and life, we, shunning the dismal and dolorous and afflicting spectacles that have ceased not in our city since this season of pestilence began, took our departure from Florence. Wherein, to my thinking, we have done nought that was not seemly; for, if I have duly used my powers of observation, albeit some gay stories, and of a kind to stimulate concupiscence, have here been told, and we have daily known no lack of dainty dishes and good wine, nor yet of music and song, things, one and all, apt to incite weak minds to that which is not seemly, neither on your part, nor on ours, have I marked deed or word, or aught of any kind, that called for reprehension; but, by what I have seen and heard, seemliness and the sweet intimacy of brothers and sisters have ever reigned among us. Which, assuredly, for the honour and advantage which you and I have had thereof, is most grateful to me. Wherefore, lest too long continuance in this way of life might beget some occasion of weariness, and that no man may be able to misconstrue our too long abidance here, and as we have all of us had our day's share of the honour which still remains in me, I should deem it meet, so you be of like mind, that we now go back whence we came: and that rather than our company, the bruit whereof has already reached divers others that are in our neighbourhood, might be so increased that all our pleasure would be destroyed. And so, if my counsel meet with your approval, I will keep the crown I have received of you until our departure, which, I purpose, shall be tomorrow morning. Should you decide otherwise, I have already determined whom to crown for the ensuing day.'

Much debate ensued among the ladies and young men; but in the end they approved the king's proposal as expedient and seemly; and resolved to do even as he had said. The king therefore summoned the seneschal; and having conferred with him of the order he was to observe on the morrow, he dismissed the company until supper-time. So, the king being risen, the ladies and the rest likewise rose, and betook them, as they were wont, to their several diversions. Supper-time being come, they supped with exceeding great delight. Which done, they addressed them to song and music and dancing; and, while Lauretta was leading a dance, the king bade Fiammetta give them a song; whereupon Fiammetta right debonairly sang on this wise –

So came but Love and brought no jealousy,
So blithe, I wot, as I,
Dame were there none, be she whoe'er she be.

If youth's fresh, lusty pride
May lady of her lover well content,
Or valour's just renown,
Hardihood, prowess tried,
Wit, noble mien, discourse most excellent,
And of all grace the crown;
That she am I, who, fain for love to swoun,
There where my hope doth lie
These several virtues all conjoined do see.

But, for that I less wise
Than me no whit do other dames discern,
Trembling with sore dismay,
I still the worst surmise,
Deeming their hearts with the same flame to burn
That of mine maketh prey:
Wherefore of him that is my hope's one stay
Disconsolate I sigh,
Yea mightily, and daily do me dree.

If but my lord as true
As worthy to be loved I might approve,
I were not jealous then:

But, for that charmer new
Doth all too often gallant lure to love,
Forsworn I hold all men,
And sick at heart I am, of death full fain;
Nor lady doth him eye,
But I do quake, lest she him wrest from me.

'Fore God, then, let each she
List to my prayer, nor e'er in my despite
Such grievous wrong essay;
For should there any be
That by or speech or mien's allurements light
Of him to rob me may
Study or plot, I, witting, shall find way,
My beauty it aby!
To cause her sore lament such frenesie.

As soon as Fiammetta had ended her song, Dioneo, who was beside her, said with a laugh – 'Madam, 'twould be a great courtesy on your part to do all ladies to wit who he is, that he be not stolen from you in ignorance, seeing that you threaten such dire resentment.' Several other songs followed; and it being then nigh upon midnight all, as the king was pleased to order, betook them to rest. With the first light of the new day they rose and the seneschal having already conveyed thence all their chattels they, following the lead of their discreet king, hied them back to Florence; and in Santa Maria Novella whence they had set forth, the three young men took leave of the seven ladies and departed to find other diversions elsewhere, while the ladies in due time repaired to their homes.

Wordsworth Classic Erotica

ANONYMOUS

The Autobiography of a Flea

Beatrice

Eveline

'Frank' and I

First Training

A Night in a Moorish Harem

The Pearl

Randiana

The Romance of Lust

Sadopaideia

Suburban Souls

Teleny

The Way of a Man with a Maid

The Whippingham Papers

GUILLAUME APOLLINAIRE

The Amorous Exploits of a Young Rakehell

AUBREY BEARDSLEY & JOHN GLASSCO

The Story of Venus and Tannhauser

GIOVANNI BOCCACCIO

Selections from The Decameron

JOHN CLELAND

Memoirs of a Woman of Pleasure – Fanny Hill

SHEIKH NEFZAOUI

The Perfumed Garden

TRANSLATED BY SIR RICHARD BURTON

EDWARD SELLON

The New Epicurean

SMITHERS AND BURTON

Priapaia

VATSYAYANA

The Kama Sutra

TRANSLATED BY SIR RICHARD BURTON & F. F. ARBUTHNOT

'WALTER'

My Secret Life – Volume One

My Secret Life – Volume Two

LI YU

The Carnal Prayer Mat